Lightning from the West:

A Novel of Courage, Honor and Valor

Fred Melchiorre

PublishAmerica
Baltimore

First printing

Cover painting: *Sergeant Ben Crippen* by Mark Maritato
www.maritato.com

Harrison Elington rough sketches drawn by Fred Melchiorre

ISBN: 1-4137-4941-0
PUBLISHED BY PUBLISHAMERICA, LLLP
www.publishamerica.com
Baltimore

Printed in the United States of America

This book is dedicated to my wife, Peggy,
for her unending support for me in everything I do.
The love of my life.

It is also dedicated to the thousands who died in
the Civil War and to their families
both Union and Confederate.

"Let us at all times remember that all American citizens are brothers of a common country, and shall dwell together in the bonds of fraternal feeling."

Abraham Lincoln

Acknowledgments and Historical Note

Lightning from the West is a work of fiction set in a real historical time period during the American Civil War, 1861 to 1865. Many hours of historical research led me to several different and diverse primary and secondary sources. However, five works stand out from all of the research.

I would like to acknowledge the work of Rod Gragg in his book *Covered With Glory*. This book sparked many of the ideas I developed for the fictional story of Lieutenant Harrison Elington and served for much of my historical research on the 26th North Carolina Infantry of 1862 and 1863. Henry Pfanz's work, *Gettysburg—The First Day*, and David Gilbert's book, *Gettysburg July 1st*, were also used for the research of this crucial first day's battle on the ridges north and west of Gettysburg

Thanks to the volume *Philadelphia, A 300-Year History* for its candid descriptions of Philadelphia during the Civil War. This book illustrates the internal workings of the city and gave me a very concise background to city politics and city attitudes toward slavery and the sectional conflict.

The last work I want to acknowledge is *Making Arms in the Machine Age, Philadelphia's Frankford Arsenal 1816-1870*, by James Farley. This was the only volume I could find that specifically relayed information concerning the layout of the arsenal grounds in 1863. Thus, I was able to make a connection between the arsenal, the Confederacy, and the lead character in the story, Harrison Elington.

My special thanks to Mark Maritato for his front cover design and for his permission to use his painting, *Sergeant Ben Crippen,* for the cover of this book. What a joy it is to have this historic painting as part of this project.

The "what ifs" of history can lead to many fascinating discussions and re-evaluation of historical evidence. The Battle of Gettysburg was the bloodiest three days in the Civil War. General Robert E. Lee and his Confederate Army were taking enormous risks traveling into the North in June of 1863. What if

Philadelphia would have been invaded and its arsenal destroyed by a Southern army? Would the great civil conflict have turned out different? Would Northern civilian groups, especially the Peace Democrats, have pressured the Lincoln administration and Congress to halt military operations in the war and move to recognize the independence of the Southern Confederacy? I know many people interested in this time period wonder what would have become of this nation if the Confederate States of America won their independence from the Union.

This work does not attempt to tell the story of a Confederate victory in the war itself, but it does attempt to address issues relating to an alternate plan of action simultaneous with the Battle of Gettysburg; that being an attack on Philadelphia and the subsequent destruction of the Frankford Arsenal by a Confederate brigade.

– Chapter 1 –
Malvern Hill

July 1862

The smell of early morning dew penetrated the air throughout the Virginia countryside. The July morning dawned to birds singing, rays of sun bathing the trees, and uncertainty mounting in the minds of soldiers. The 26th North Carolina Infantry Regiment broke camp at about ten o'clock. A farm was ahead of the columns, covered in the ravages of internal war. Northern and Southern soldiers disseminated the once tranquil landscape with their cries of pain, their wounded spirits and their mangled companies. Blood, muskets, private letters and death were all combined into a whirlwind of destruction; and all were there in the open. The marching soldiers of the 26th North Carolina entered the battlefield faced with a baptism of literal fire.

The dead, hot lead of Minie balls hitting flesh caused men to shriek with pain and agony. The shrieks and calls for help did nothing to stop the engine of human battle as other Confederate soldiers entered the maelstrom in front of the 26th.

The familiar sounds of the engine were imbedded into the minds of Confederate and Union soldiers alike; especially Lieutenant Harrison Elington of the 26th North Carolina Infantry.

In his journal he often described the mechanics of battle through analogies, so one day he could testify to his students of the man-made fury. Opening volleys raked the fields with musket fire. Cannon rounds of solid shot and case shot softened the resistance of the enemy. The combination of rifle and artillery fire generated the great engine into a seething quagmire, where death and mayhem persisted upon every breathing moment.

The engine functioned efficiently for hours at a time. Its iron fuel, fired from the bowels of hell from hundreds of muskets and tens of cannon, made the exhaust hot and loathsome. The exhaust, the waste of the engine, the ingredients the engine no longer needed, was the dead soldier lying upon the field of battle. The dead no longer produced the spark which had produced the projectile that ultimately entered human flesh, tearing and severing the vital organs of the creator of the engine itself.

Men became killers of each other upon peaceful fields of golden wheat, oats and orchards polluted by the human exhaust of death.

He saw the hill ahead of his regiment. Lieutenant Elington, along with Corporal Lewis Fry and Private Alfred Abshire, marched directly toward the fortified position.

"I can see the flames from those cannon up there, lieutenant!"

"Just hold steady, corporal. We have to tighten our lines before we can attack. General Magruder needs our support on his flank. General Huger has ordered us to move in support of the other forward brigades!"

"Attack the position, lieutenant?" asked Private Abshire with a surprised shout. "We're all crazy today, boys."

"General McClellan has sure got himself a real good line of fire right toward us. Hey, lieutenant?"

"You're straight on about that, Lewis. Watch out, Lewis!" Shells began hissing and bursting all around the brigade lines. The heavy smoke, the solid blasts and the belching fire smashed through the air atop Malvern Hill.

General George McClellan's 5th Army Corps occupied the hill. The 5th Army Corp was part of the Army of the Potomac organized by President Lincoln and his administration to bring the rebellious seceded states back into the Union.

President Abraham Lincoln had said upon entering the White House: "This United States, masterfully crafted by such men as Jefferson, Madison, Hamilton and Washington, must endure according to the tenets of our sacred national Constitution. Our government must continue to be a perpetual Union. Secession is not an option."

Malvern Hill, a plateau located near the James River in eastern Virginia, stood 150 feet in elevation. McClellan positioned sharpshooters near the base of the slope to ravage, flank, or center attacks upon the hill. Artillery was massed on the plain. The elevation stretched a half-mile in length and about a mile and a half in width. At least 150 cannon were prepared to rip Confederate brigades apart if they attempted to charge the position. Union regiments were also stacked near the cannon to reinforce the whole nightmarish position set upon the hill.

In late June, 1862, General McClellan tried to abandon his slow and unsuccessful Peninsula Campaign. He thought he could slowly wear down and humiliate General Robert E. Lee's armies. However, McClellan was on the run. He had not made it to Richmond. Robert E. Lee's will to fight persisted throughout the campaign on the Virginia Peninsula, where it had initiated in March.

Lieutenant Elington, serving under Major General Benjamin Huger's division, Department of Northern Virginia, and attached to Brigadier General Robert Ransom's brigade, marched his men of F Company, 26th North Carolina Infantry, along the Quaker Church Road.

Elington's hazel eyes gazed upon the hundreds of men assembled for battle. He couldn't help tapping his hand on the revolver holstered on his left side. He waited for the firing to start as he reached for some water from a wooden canteen.

Harrison Elington, forty years old and a middle-class schoolteacher with grayish-black hair, was from western North Carolina, in Caldwell County. He had resigned his commission as lieutenant in the United States Army in 1856, after seventeen years of service, vowing to fight for North Carolina and its right to secede from the Union. Although troubled by the breakup of the Union and its consequences for the South, Elington debated each day that maybe his allegiance to the new Confederate government under President Jefferson Davis was treasonous. He could not escape his devotion to honor and duty as a Southern gentleman.

His wife, Abigail Sumner Elington, named after Abigail Adams, the former First Lady of the United States, was a strong supporter of the Union and of Abraham Lincoln's gradual slave emancipation plan. Born in Philadelphia, Pennsylvania, a northern city known for its pro-Southern sympathies and strong Democratic Party, Abigail was well educated and advocated the Union cause to keep the democratic heritage of the United States alive and well.

Elington had two sons: Danny, who was eighteen and a private in the 5th North Carolina Artillery Battalion, Battery D. He fought for the Confederacy. Jesse, nineteen and a member of the 83rd Pennsylvania Infantry Regiment, fought for the Union Army. Harrison Elington's grandfather had fought the British at the Battle of Cowpens some eighty years before the sectional driven Civil War tore the United States apart. Jesse and Danny always took pride in having a heritage of military honor in the family. Lieutenant Elington had an inquisitive mind regarding secession, but now struggled every day with what he thought was a wrong decision fighting for the Confederate cause.

General Lee, utilizing eighteen of his Confederate brigades, ordered a complete frontal assault on Malvern Hill to drive the Union Army off of his beloved Virginia soil.

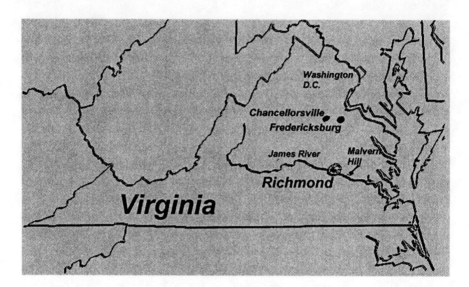

Malvern Hill Map

"Our orders, men of F Company, are to inflict as much damage as possible on the artillery batteries positioned at the crest of the hill in our front," shouted Elington, wearing his pristine gray uniform.

"Sir! Our scouts and skirmishers report about 150 cannon on top of the hill," shouted one captain, choking from the sulfuric smoke.

"Sir! Officers from the 1st and 3rd North Carolina Regiments, from General Ripley's brigade, are telling us those 150 cannon are supported by infantry on the flanks," shouted a second captain. "I can see Union infantry spreading out a defensive wall along the base of the hill, sir, near the cannon positions!"

"Colonel! There are ravines and swamplands around the flanks of the hill!" Elington said. "The lead brigade skirmishers are reporting dense foliage and wetlands that could make it hard for the boys, sir! Is it possible to land sharpshooters ahead of our lines to help our boys face less artillery fire from this God-forsaken position?"

The 26th continued their march among the turmoil.

"No, Lieutenant Elington!" said Colonel Vance. "We need to establish a more secure and efficient position first, and then we will order sharpshooters to flank their lines. Our skirmish line is enough for now, but we need to get more skirmishers into position before we attack."

"Yes, sir!" Elington responded, chewing on his cheek full of tobacco. "Corporal Fry! Go and see if other company commanders can spare more skirmishers. We need more skirmishers to guide our lines to the front. Go!"

"Yes, sir, lieutenant."

"Sir! It looks like the whole cursed Union artillery is stacked on the hill before us," reported F Company's Captain Nathaniel Rankin to Colonel Vance.

Colonel Zebulon Vance, known for his sharp speaking skills and infantry training methods, heard every report and waited for orders to take the hill. Along with the other waiting brigades, Vance and the 26th North Carolina observed the glowing Union lines on Malvern Hill. After marching a little way along the Quaker Church Road, Ransom's whole brigade halted.

The 26th North Carolina had been assigned and placed under the brigade command of Brigadier General Robert Ransom, Jr., thirty-four years old and a graduate of West Point. Ransom was an uncompromising drill master in preparing his brigade for battle.

Colonel Vance watched as the fearsome barrage of shrapnel, grape and canister shells broke wide holes in the other Confederate infantry brigades advancing in front of the heavily fortified Union lines on Malvern Hill.

"I believe this charge upon the fortified hill is contradictory to our cause of fighting a defensive strategy in our own country, and it will cause more casualties than we can tolerate in our regiments," Vance told officers in the 26th.

Elington agreed, saying, "Sometimes I don't know why I'm fighting a cause which seems impossible for my men and, sometimes, treasonous. But my men! I can't let them down! They have fought too bravely and courageously for the cause of our country."

His face cringed from the heavy fire before him.

11

"We can disagree on military strategy, lieutenant, but we are not committing treason here today," said Colonel Vance with a stern voice.

*****

He had debated and fought his own thoughts about secession and what it would mean for the great experiment of the United States of America. Since the late 1840s and into the volatile decade of the 1850s, tumultuous events forced Elington to ask provocative questions concerning his future allegiance to the Union.

Questions of states' rights versus the powers in Washington, D.C.; slavery versus free soil in the new Western lands; nullification versus secession; and the question of ever taking arms against his beloved North Carolina. The state would be the last to secede in 1861, for there were pro-Union forces in the state government. They held out at first, but then went ahead with secession over President Lincoln's failure to remove Union troops from strategic Southern garrisons; also over his call for 75,000 troops to be mustered into service for the imminent invasion of the South and its way of life.

Also, during the hot and persuasive 1850s, a compromise had been set forth by the famous Senator Henry Clay, from Kentucky, who tried to save the faltering Union one last time. Harriet Beecher Stowe wrote her book *Uncle Tom's Cabin*, inflaming passions in both North and South over the issue of slavery; Southern plantation owners accusing her of maltreatment. Southerners lashed out at the contents of the book, claiming the author had not visited the Deep South to witness firsthand the "peculiar institution" of slavery. In 1854 the Kansas-Nebraska Act provided popular sovereignty for the people in those territories, causing a gallant rush to take over as much land as possible by both Missouri ruffians and supporters of anti-slave organizations in the North.

1856 would be a year Elington never forgot. The tense situation in Kansas came to a head over the legitimacy of Stephen Douglas's popular sovereignty plan. A mini civil war broke out when ruffians—pro-slavery men—burned Lawrence, Kansas, to the ground, arguing it represented the limitations and abuses of the federal government in Washington and its determined attempts to limit the spread of slavery into the new lands. Senator Charles Sumner was violently attacked in the Senate by Preston Brooks, nephew of Congressman Andrew Butler of South Carolina, who was angry at Sumner's never-ending vexations toward Butler and the Southern aristocracy. This kind of violence had never occurred in the chambers of Congress, especially in the Senate, where the reigns of government had become almost sacred to the causes of democracy.

Elington was quite upset upon hearing about the Kansas situation and the uncertainty looming in Congress. He also became irritated with President James Buchanan's silence and inaction upon the pressing issues of the nation. Elington resigned from the U.S. Army in 1856. Then, in 1859, news of John Brown's raid at Harpers Ferry, West Virginia, seemed to solidify the position and determination of the Southern movement toward secession. Brown, a convulsive abolitionist, tried to raid the federal arsenal at the Ferry, with hopes of getting his specially ordered pikes and additional muskets from the arsenal to the slaves. He had planned to spread his rebellion into the deeper South.

South Carolina would be the first to secede back in December of 1860, resulting from the election of the Republican from Illinois, Abraham Lincoln. Elington didn't mind Lincoln's ascendancy into the White House. He reasoned the President couldn't free slaves without an act of Congress. Lincoln had vowed not to tamper with the institution where it already existed—the South—but he did take a stand on the extension of slavery into the new Western lands acquired through the Louisiana Purchase of 1803, the Mexican Cession of 1848, and the Texas Annexation of 1845.

Elington still had a lot on his mind as he prepared for the hellfire of real battle on July 1, 1862, in the surroundings of Virginia.

*****

Near dusk, at the closing of the day on July 1, the soldiers of the 26th North Carolina, along with many other regiments and brigades, journeyed into the firestorm of a larger and more complicated battle for the first time in the war. Except for their holding action at New Bern, a town in North Carolina known for the strategic importance of its railway, the men of the 26th engaged in little combat. The raw, acrid odor of gunpowder in the air and the shrieking of the artillery positions set upon Malvern Hill sent the chill of fear and anticipated destruction through the minds of the men marching toward their goal. The engine of human battle was in full motion.

Will the regiment prove itself today? Will I die, or continue for the cause set before many of us? Elington thought. *Will all of my years of military service in the U.S. Army sustain me in this political and economic struggle for freedom? Will I ever go home the same man as when I left many months ago? Are the leaders on the field capable, or should I continue to question their motives and abilities? Will I lead my men of F Company the right way, the honorable way?*

Elington debated these questions often in his mind and now they penetrated through his racing conscience like Minie balls penetrating flesh.

Margaret and Tobacco! Is there a way back to my life and my hope? Corporal Lewis Fry pondered this thought, waiting in the gloom of the day. Sucking on the corncob pipe inherited from his grandfather and thinking of the farm back home, he said to Elington, "I hope I don't wind up in the hands of the sawbones after this fight, lieutenant! Those sawbone doctors will cut me to pieces if I'm so darned unlucky to get a hornet or some other piece of wretched, hot iron in the arm, leg, or other unfortunate part of my body!"

Moving out of his state of ponderance, Elington answered jokingly, "Sawbones or not, Lewis, you better not hold back today when we get into the fight up on that hill."

Part of F Company from its beginning, Corporal Lewis Fry, Jr. was also from Caldwell County. Fry, a thirty-six-year-old farmer, owned four slaves. He grew tobacco to support his wife, Margaret, and their three children. He really enjoyed the smell of the earth and the natural toil of being a farmer. His temper would always flare; especially when embroiled in talk concerning the secession of the South and abolitionism. He was ensconced in his beliefs:

"All of the talk and hollering about abolition is nonsense!" said Fry frantically to his wife in 1860.

Fry once told his father, Lewis, Sr., that, "The abolitionists are the cause for any future war, and they will not get their way in heaven or in hell! Their beliefs about this country are wrong and their motivations self-serving! Slaves were meant to be laborers, not businessmen."

Fry was eager to join the army if war broke out against the Union of the United States of America.

"This can't be my last day on earth. Death mystifies my inner being and it is something I haven't prepared for, my Jesus in Heaven," prayed Alfred out loud.

He began to shake. The deep roar, concussions and repercussions of the artillery, continued its unrelenting aim at the Confederate brigades in the marshes of Western Run near Malvern Hill.

Alfred Abshire, a twenty-year-old upper-class college student, left his studies to fight the war and to achieve states' rights, which were, according to Abshire, "Blatantly and systematically robbed from the South." He was studying government, history and politics at Bowdoin College in Maine before the war. He decided to live away from home for his college years. He also left behind his fiancée, Krista Morris, in Maine. Despair and loneliness permeated the August day when Alfred left his comfortable and tranquil college town for the rigors of training camp at Lenoir and Camp Crabtree, North Carolina. Alfred, a devout Christian, placed his faith and life in the hands of Jesus Christ, the Savior of his soul.

"You better pray the darn sawbones don't get your limbs tonight, Alfred, my boy," joked Fry. Lewis continued his questions and comments to the men. Joking, making noises, breaking wind, talking about home and offending others in the regiment often seemed to calm the boys before battle in the unit. Some smiles would appear briefly on soldier's faces.

Lewis then became serious in his thoughts along with the other troops.

"Lieutenant Colonel Burgwyn, do you think we will make it through that artillery barrage on the hill before us?"

"Keep your head low, but watch your every step toward your position, corporal! Listen to your orders from Lieutenant Elington and Captain Rankin! We'll be fine. We will hit them hard."

"I see cannon fire straight ahead, sir," said Elington.

"Stay on line, Elington, and keep your company ready to fire on the lines up there," ordered Burgwyn.

"We will do that, sir! We will do it!"

Lieutenant Colonel Henry Burgwyn was one of the youngest officers to serve in the Confederate Army. At twenty-two years old, he was a graduate of the Virginia Military Institute. Very well educated and from a well-to-do family in North Carolina, he was well liked by his men in the regiment, even though he pushed them to their limits in physical drill. He had a young fiancée back in North Carolina waiting for him to finish his duty. At one point during training back at Camp Crabtree, though, the men were once plotting to "take care" of the young lieutenant colonel when they got a chance to assume battling duty.

"Maybe an accidental slip of a musket trigger would end the hell of marching four hours a day, for weeks on end," said one 26th private.

The sounds and repercussion from the cannon echoed more deafening toward the positions of the lead regiments and the 26th North Carolina.

Nervously, Elington continued to tap on his revolver, adjust his black slouch hat, straighten his lieutenant's frock coat, and chew his ration of tobacco. The regiment approached the right-center of the Union line. The Confederates, all along the line near the hill, were now feeling the accuracy of the cannon.

Major General John Magruder's brigades were supposed to hit the right flank of the Union line, supporting General Lewis Armistead's Virginians, but General Ransom led his brigade in a wrong direction, mistakenly deviating from Lee's original orders. Inaccurate maps and unsubstantiated reports, stating McClellan was moving off of the hill, caused some of Magruder's and Ransom's problems during the day. Ransom eventually got on line, but his position was now to the left-center of the Union fortress.

"These problematic dispositions of my troopers and the changing orders of our generals will result in catastrophes for our ranks. These failures cannot be solely laid upon my command," said Magruder during the start of the battle to his pondering staff. The brigades of Armistead, Mahone, Wright, Gordon, Anderson, Barksdale, Toombs, Ripley, Garland, Colquitt, Law, Hood and Trimble all slammed into the fury of the Union lines on the hill before Ransom's brigade and the 26th attacked.

Artillery fire, like lightning in the summer sky, consumed the elements of nature all around the Confederate brigades. Overshot shells hit trees. Branches fell to the ground, singeing the green landscape and shattering the silence of the otherwise peaceful day. Small fires from the hot shrapnel were burning on the ground, smoke coiling into the air; an ever-present spirit of danger consuming the conditions. Naval ordnance from the Union gunboats Galena and Mahaska fired on the brigades from the James River, located southwest of Malvern Hill. The ninety-six members of F Company looked on as the sky, lit-up before them. They heard the crying, the agony and the pain of the wounded veterans before them. Yells for help, shouts of panic and cries of horror echoed from the battlefield:

"Give us water! Please! Please!"

"Someone stop this hot pain … my side!"

"Water … water … anyone who can help us!"

"Tell the boys to retreat from this hell!" shouted one private.

"Tell the boys this is hell on earth. Get out of here if you want to live today! You won't be counted as cowards for this day's work!" shouted another private from the insufferable conditions on the field.

"I'm shot twice in the leg! I think I'm bleeding to death! Get me … get me out of here!"

"Plug those holes boys, or we won't be able to help the wounded at all," ordered an officer along the line.

Colonel Vance shouted, "Form your line, boys! It's only a matter of time before we fire! Dress on the colors, men!"

"Tell my wife I love her dearly," said one private, who had been shot through the stomach. The maelstrom continued with fury.

"I can't stop shivering from the pain ..."

"I'm hit in the head! I'm hit right in the bloody head!"

"Form the line! Form the line," ordered Vance. The 26th approached within yards of the massive, unfaltering line of the Union Army.

Lieutenant Colonel Burgwyn assisted Colonel Vance, bringing the men into an orderly and fixed line. The regiment could now begin to send volleys into the lead brigades of the Union forces. Some of the Union men fighting across from the 26th were from General Caldwell's and General Sickle's brigades, representing the 2nd and 3rd Corps. They were putting up stiff resistance on the right side of the Union line against the Confederates.

Assisting the Union brigades to their left were the brigades of Generals Griffin, Martindale and Butterfield from the 5th Corps, with General Sykes on the extreme left flank of the hill.

General Meagher, of Sumner's 2nd Corp, was in advance of all the other brigades, right behind Berdan's sharpshooters.

Generals' Abercrombie and Howe from the 4th Army Corps held the positions on the extreme right side of the line, with Generals Kearny, Hooker and Sumner in support also from the 2nd and 3rd Corps.

The Union gunboats from the James River rammed heavy shells into the flanks of the Confederate forces. The Union artillery and infantry continued to bombard them.

Rabbits and deer were seen by the Confederate companies from the 26th, only to bring pleasant memories of innocent days gone by into the fire and proscription of vehement war before them now. Corporal Fry saw a fox running from the scene of the battle. He earnestly thought about doing the same.

Changing from solid, to case, then to canister shot, the Union gunners tore huge and deadly holes into the Confederate brigades, resulting in high casualties and lightning destruction upon the Southerners.

Haversacks, canteens, muskets, smoking pipes, skillets, food rations, shoes, grass mixed with blood, and sword scabbards flew through the air. The volley of musket fire shattered the neatly dressed lines of Ransom's brigade.

"Watch out overhead! Watch out overhead!" shouted Elington, Rankin and Burgwyn to the men of F Company.

They stayed online to prepare to fire toward the enemy.

– Chapter 2 –
"Those Napoleons Are Too Much"

July 1st, 1862

"Elington!" shouted Corporal Fry. "The men of the 3rd North Carolina are coming off the field in desperation! It looks as if casualties are darn high and the men are worn out, sir! We have to get in there and break those lines of batteries, in our front, before they darn well break us. Capture their guns, or do something! We have to reinforce those battered regiments before us."

Fry began his habit of pushing the private soldiers forward, angrily warning them they better fight as men and not as sissies dressed in their Sunday best.

"Those Napoleons are too much on our lines!" said Elington to Colonel Vance. Elington was standing firm and in an upright position over his men. Indifferent to the hail of bullets flying around him in the small skirmishes the 26th had been involved in up to this fight, Elington focused on assisting Captain Rankin and Colonel Vance in leading and plotting a course for the men of the 26th Regiment.

"I can see the devastation all down the line. We have to get into a better position to try and flank those guns before we have both the batteries of artillery and the infantry trying to take us down for good!" replied Vance.

The regiment proceeded through the grainy fields of wheat, coated with the mangled wounded and dead from other brigades and regiments. Men, in gray and butternut, struggled desperately to get away from the constant, searing fire.

Batteries from the Rhode Island Light Artillery, the New York Light Artillery, from United States Battalions of Artillery, and from many other units consisting of the 150 guns, along with the supporting infantry units, kept up a constant fire. Napoleons, twenty-pound Parrott guns, and three-inch ordnance guns were all employed on the hill. Crackles, hisses and shrieks continued to fly in the faces of the Confederates. The surroundings near the hill became a cauldron, overflowing with human carnage. The fog of war made it appear the raking fire was coming from the western sky, like lightning convulsing from heaven, shattering the sinful souls of men. However, most of the fire was coming down from the south, atop Malvern Hill.

The 26th North Carolina tried to maneuver into a better firing position. The men of the 83rd Pennsylvania, the 57th Pennsylvania, the 2nd Maine, the 63rd, 69th, and 88th New York Regiments all pounded the left flank of the Confederate brigades.

Again and again the thunderous roars of cannon smashed forward toward the 26th. The screeching, whistling and hissing of the solid shot and case shot filled the air with radiant horror. At the same time, as men looked into the sky, they saw parallel lines of fire and smoke from the same threatening cannons; seeming to recreate beautiful painted scenery that tickled the senses in an ironic mental silence for seconds at a time. The smell and taste of gunpowder condensed the evening air. Reality came back to the soldiers as friends and comrades lost limbs, lost equipment and rations, lost their sense of honor, adventure and glory they thought they once possessed; and finally, many lost their lives on the hill.

The hill, on the green landscape of a Southern slave state where the smells of the James River flowed with the summer breeze; where animals grazed in the fields; where the sky was blue on any given day; now became a killing field thrashing with the lacerated dead and wounded. The landscape turned crimson as the blood of the many ebbed and flowed into the ravines, into the creek, and puddled in the wheat fields. The men of North Carolina never thought, pondered, or dreamt of such an awful fate as young boys playing and singing in their schoolrooms and mingling with their friends and families back in old Granite Falls.

Why would men such as these fight? Elington thought about this on many occasions since becoming a soldier and veteran. *What makes a soldier do the things he does for a cause perpetrated by faraway governments? Governments do not have a personal side,* he thought. *Governments do not know love or compassion. Governments drive the instruments of economics above everything else in society and governments will do anything to protect the political and social institutions producing economic benefit.*

Was this why my men of the 26th North Carolina were attacking? Was it for the protection of their impersonal governments, or something else? Elington continued in thought, somehow, with the heat of battle around him. *Might it simply be plain patriotism and honorable heritage that drove these individual heroes beyond their mental and physical attributes?*

Elington, all of a sudden, felt the burning pain in his stomach; a pain which plagued him at least two times a month, lasting all day when it hit. Some digestive problem he couldn't figure out. He began, again, to tap his left hand against the Colt Navy revolver resting in his holster. He cherished the gun from his days in the U.S. Army when he would pal around with Colonel James Longstreet and Colonel Winfield Hancock out in the Missouri country. He placed a new wad of tobacco into his mouth and slowly clenched his teeth.

"Got that burning in the bread basket again, Henry. It's just not the time to have pain going into battle, sir," Elington said softly to Burgwyn, who was ready to give orders to companies along the lines.

The men of the 26th, after going down a wrong bend of road—a result of bad maps—finally streamlined and dressed their battle lines. They got down on the ground and waited for a chance to fire solid volleys at the enemy on the hill. The fears and trepidations among the men intensified with every passing minute.

"Rise men! Make sure your muskets are loaded!" ordered Colonel Vance to his regiment along with his company captains.

A handsome, dressed line of Confederate gray stood impeccably facing the enemy guns.

"Ready! Aim! Fire!"

"Fire! Pour it on boys! F Company pour it on ..." ordered Elington, along with Vance, Burgwyn and all the company commanders of the 26th.

Elington analyzed the accuracy and response of the infantry from the left side of his company line. F Company was positioned to the right of the color guard and E Company was on the left. At the start of the maneuver, Vance commanded from the center of the regiment, Burgwyn commanded on the right and Major John Jones commanded on the left.

"Pour it on boys! Smash those artillery lines!" ordered Captain Rankin from the right side of F Company. "Reload ... reload!" yelled Captain Rankin. "Plug the holes, men! Plug those holes!"

The line began to slowly move forward with men reloading their muskets. Cartridge papers flew everywhere, percussion caps clicked and ramrods churned and clattered against metal barrels.

"I can see the regiment line forming a salient, sir! We're going to get hit hard, on the right, if we don't realign, and fast, sir," said Elington passionately to Captain Rankin.

"Get the officers all down the line to straighten and reform," ordered Rankin to Elington. Tell all company commanders to dress their lines on the color guard in the center. See if Colonel Vance sees the salient, lieutenant. Get one of your corporals to send the message to Vance immediately. Hurry; now hurry, Elington!" shouted Rankin above the whirlwind of battle.

Elington accomplished his orders and got back to the job of guiding F Company along the marshy ground at the foot of Malvern Hill. Burgwyn tried his best to straighten out the right side of the regimental battle line converging toward the hill.

"Corporal Fry! Tell the captains from A, E and K Companies to send out twelve sharpshooters. Tell them to send the shooters to the left side. We can try to break their flank up, or at least begin to break it apart; break it to pieces!" ordered Vance.

"Yes, sir, colonel! I'm right on it!" Fry ran off with exhilarated quickness, knowing a flanking maneuver could cause a break in an enemy line and result in victory; a victory he sure wanted to be part of this active and bloody day. Elington would gladly agree with the order after hearing it from the men of those companies. He had much confidence in the sharpshooters.

"Reload boys! Reload men! Take good aim at the batteries on the Union right," shouted Captain Rankin. Elington echoed the orders to the left of his company again and again.

"Fire! Fire! Fire!" yelled all officers.

Volley after volley of musket fire erupted from the 26th as they poured more shots into the Union barricades. Companies from the center, to the right and left of the line, fired with accuracy.

"Fire! Fire! Fire!" continued officers traversing the position. From the hill, the cannon blazed and spewed iron fragments like a dragon from the depths of hell; legions of evil confiscating the lifeblood of the innocent martyrs of freedom.

Hearing the crackling and the hissing of bullets and the men firing at will toward the enemy, Private Alfred Abshire, shaking from the sound of the cannon on Malvern Hill, helped one of his fellow soldiers bandage his head and arm wounds in the bloodstained wheat field. He tried to steady himself to accomplish his chore. He then shouted to Elington, "I'm getting afraid, sir. I'm not a coward, but I'm still afraid, sir!" His jaw shuddered as fear overtook him. His body shook, aghast and tempered by fear.

Elington responded and continued giving orders:

"Give your fear to your Savior in Heaven. Pray for strength, pray for our attack, and pray for the wounded boy you're tending to. I used to be afraid, private, when I was green. But you get over it, one way or another, unless you're a true, treasonous coward like many of the deserters and stragglers from our ranks."

The men were slowed by small trees growing near the base of the hill. The golden fields of wheat continued to turn red with blood. However, in the midst of the battle, men could smell the summer grasses. Sometimes through the odor of gunpowder they could smell the river with all of its life implanted around it. The hope of life permeated among much death and destruction.

Less than 150 yards out from the Union positions, the volleys from the 26th slammed, smashed and pulverized the regiments and batteries of the Union brigades across the hill.

"Our boys saw limbs from poor souls fly in the air as a combination of musket and artillery shells were hitting targets with pristine accuracy just a few minutes ago," Elington told Colonel Vance, who was passing by his company.

Cries of injury and shock shrieked across the battlefield. The 26th kept up a hot, steady fire from their reorganized line. The salient in the regiment's line was remedied by the regimental officers.

The Confederate artillery, ineffective during the course of most of the battle, fired deadly solid and case shot into the dreaded Union lines. Union cannon exploded into pieces and shattered the stillness of the enemy lines, giving the boys confidence in their attacks. Volleys of fire crashed into the hill in front of them. The Confederate batteries could not keep a steady and sustained fire for long, though.

The choking and blinding smoke from the constant and unrelenting fire from both sides consumed the air above the battlefield.

Suddenly, artillery batteries spotted the 26th's massive line forming on the Union right-center. The smoke cleared, exposing the 26th to the batteries. A relentless shuffle to aim, load and fire was underway on the hill. Like a quick-moving thunder and lightning storm, the artillery from atop the hill took heavy aim at the Confederates. This time, remnants of the 3rd, 25th,

35th, 26th North Carolina and the 3rd Alabama Regiments were all open targets for the cannon. Ordnance sprayed a massive fire upon the men. Elington, Fry and Abshire did everything they could to protect themselves and their fellow infantrymen. The hailstorm of lead raked the ranks time after time. One soldier cried: "The gates of hell, with its army of demons, are brought upon us this day. Pray without ceasing, men of the South!"

"I'm hit! I'm hit! It's my arm!" Abshire cried.

"Plug the holes, boys!" Elington ordered after Abshire and another private went down. Waving his thirty-six caliber Colt Navy revolver side to side along the enemy lines, Elington fired at the artillerymen on the hill. Loud concussions riveted back toward him. The rolling thunder of fire sustained through the countryside.

"Ouch ! That cursed lead ... that loathsome lead!" yelped Fry, falling with a Minie ball smacking into his left hand, then ricocheting and hitting a tree.

"Plug those holes in the center of the line!" shouted Colonel Vance. He ran along the entire line, first to the right and then to the left, lending support and direction to a chaotic situation. Crackles and whizzes of bullets were heard.

Smash!

A thud of iron crashed into the ranks.

"I'm hit in the leg!" cried Elington! "I'm hit in the leg! Burgwyn, can you get me some water?"

"No!" replied Burgwyn, who was now leading I Company because of the death of their captain, whose head was blown completely off by solid shot. "Stay right where you are. I will get help and water for you soon. I need to reform this company."

Burgwyn shouted to his regiment, "Hold on, boys ... I'm sending a message to General Ransom to see if we have to stay in this living hell any longer. We need reinforcements for our left! Only by God's grace can we survive this carnage all around us!

"Major Jones! Send this message to General Ransom through one of your couriers, with my compliments! Now hurry, major! Hurry ... get it to General Ransom!"

"Yes sir! Yes sir! I'm going. I'll take care of it."

Abshire prayed: "Savior in Heaven ... dear Jesus, help me, through the power of your Spirit, to hold on today, that I may continue to help in this hellish battle placed before me ...."

Like a direct answer from God to Abshire's prayer, artillery expanded the air with thundercracks and deep resonating bombilations. Abshire stayed

24

down on the ground and continued to pray as another private from F Company got Alfred's bleeding under control. Corporal Fry continued to complain about his hand wound. His blood poured forth in a stream toward the ground. A private from F Company wrapped his hand with a handkerchief, bringing no relief for Fry. The color guard was still intact upon the field. The 26th's battle flag waved and snapped above the explosions of gunfire. The men continued to dress on the colors.

The sulfuric smell and texture of the gunpowder smoldered through the battlefield, solidifying the dense air around the men of F Company, making it hard to breathe. Elington struggled to lift his leg to ease the petrifying pains racing through the leg and the rest of his body. No one was there to help him in the minutes after he received his wound. Loneliness and a sense of peril consumed him. Night began to fall on the field where Elington agonized.

Elington reloaded his revolver, making sure his percussion caps were secure on the cones. Quickly trying to accomplish this task, he heard a Union artillery officer say, "Swab that barrel, reload … reload … hurry."

He stood up in a brave passion of desperation and moved forward, out from the high wheat to where more wheat had been scythed by cannon shot, and fired all six bullets from his revolver, hitting and seeming to kill the crew of one of the cannons in front of him. He fell back to the ground in desperate pain to shield himself from retaliatory fire. The smoke from the continuous fire of cannon hid Elington from the musket volley ringing out from behind the unmanned, three-inch ordnance gun. He hid in a swale of wheat and small trees. The marshy soil, though, hampered his attempts to relieve his pain.

*****

Shades of evening began to spread throughout the Virginia countryside, showing its expanse with hues of blue, gray and amber. The men of the 26th, and the other regiments around them, fell back to more defensive lines and simply fell to the ground in exhaustion. They waited for further orders. Elington was detached from the main force of his regiment. For three hours the men waited, laying among the dead and wounded in a slope of ground that gave them protection. The Federal batteries still fired intermittently from Malvern Hill. Some men fell asleep from the long and tiring day and from the stress of battle. The putrid smells of excrement, body parts, perspiration and vomit oscillated through the air of the battlefield.

Cannon seemed to be firing in threes: Boom … Boom … Boom …

A pause occurred and the guns repeated the pattern. F Company was growing restless, for darkness started to traverse the evening sky, replacing the tinges of twilight with blackness from the night.

"Lieutenant Elington? Lieutenant Elington? Can you hear me?" shouted Private Abshire. He was nursing his left arm, torn near the biceps muscle by a piece of canister shot.

"Lieutenant Elington? Lieutenant Elington? Is there a way out of here, sir?" cried Corporal Fry. Blood saturated his hands and sleeve from the Minie ball wound to his left finger.

"Harrison? Harrison? Where are you? Your men need you!" whispered Lieutenant Colonel Burgwyn. He then circumambulated the bodies lying on the battlefield, searching for Elington. It was a ghastly sight for Burgwyn. *A sight the eyes of the young should be spared*, he thought.

A lament came from the wreckage upon the field.

"He can't be gone! He just can't be gone from us !" Abshire said to Burgwyn, who was still searching for a sign from Elington. "He is my strength and comforter through this whole ordeal, lieutenant colonel, showing me how to rely on my faith in the Savior of heaven."

Silence, for a moment, covered the expanse of the place called Malvern Hill. As long as the boys from North Carolina lived on the earth, they would always remember Malvern Hill; a hill considered not only landscape in their memories, but a hill considered part of a soul, part of a spirit, and part of a collective mind.

The silence continued, then out of the eerie quiet came a shout.

"I'm over here! I'm over here!" Elington shouted from a swale to the left of F Company, where he was trying to begin and lead a maneuver around one of the federal batteries. Elington had a small entry wound in the upper right thigh; it was bleeding and the pain was severe.

*****

It was now 11:30 at night and, finally, General Ransom sent couriers to order his brigade, the 26th North Carolina and the other mangled regiments from their positions. After hours of continuous fire upon the Confederates, the thundercracks of artillery ceased. The 26th and its wounded fell back from the field in good, efficient order to defensive lines in the marshes of Western Run. Elington was helped from the battlefield. Corporal Fry and Private Abshire, through an unknown strength after the terrible day, helped

Elington off the field and back to the defensive lines where camp was set for the night. Elington needed a surgeon immediately to stop his bleeding wound.

The storm, with all of its manmade thunder and lightning, was over for now. The men of the 26th rested for a little while, anticipating the physical pain, certainly, to be part of their existence in the hours ahead.

*****

General McClellan's 5th Army Corps began to buckle down for the night. Holding the defensive position they fought for all day on July 1, the men stopped to eat and to drink quantities of food and water, trying desperately to satisfy their dry mouths and empty stomachs. They also tended to their wounded comrades. The cannon from the massive artillery wall that still stood on Malvern Hill smoked and sizzled from the dense heat caused by firing repeated rounds into the Confederates. Burgwyn, later in the night, figured about fifty cannon were firing every minute against the Confederate lines. Several pieces of Union artillery were strewn along the hill. Dismembered and blown apart, Rebel artillery and infantry produced some successes.

General McClellan looked onto the field. Feeling the familiar sense of being out-manned and out-numbered in equipment, he said to some of his staff officers, "The men have performed today with valor, honor and courage never measured in such sacrifice upon a battlefield where U.S. soldiers have been engaged. The country owes a great deal to these men of valor."

Like their counterparts across the battlefield, the men of the Federal Union Army rested only for a while in the stillness and peacefulness of the night. McClellan was still in motion, always in motion, to keep his continuous, cautious distance from General Lee's smaller forces. Scout reports and surveillances usually verified to corps commanders in the Union ranks that Lee's armies were limited in all areas compared to Union forces. However, McClellan would not realize in his blind, hesitant caution that the Reb army always consisted of smaller forces when across from his immense Union contingents. He continually relied on reports from other sources, apart from his corps commanders, to convince himself of Lee's 175,000 to 200,000 troops waiting to destroy his Union Army and take Washington, D.C.

Many corps commanders in the field complained of McClellan's caution. Infantry, artillery, ammunition, uniforms, food and medicines were elements that could have made a difference in defeating Confederate Armies, only if

McClellan would have taken more chances with the 95,000 troops he was entrusted with during the Peninsula Campaign in 1862.

Cautiously, in the early morning hours of July 2, 1862, McClellan proceeded to remove his army from the peninsula and proceeded to the "more secure environs" of Northern Virginia at Harrison's Landing. By daybreak, the Confederates found only the remnants of soldiers: mangled tents, empty haversacks and knapsacks, some food rations like hardtack and beef, canteens, playing cards, and journals laying there as if a whirlwind passed through the hill; a whirlwind caused not by the Confederate brigades, as General Lee contemplated and hoped, but by an army in retreat led by their overly cautious general.

*****

July 1, 1862, brought a horrific and terrible episode in the history of the Confederate Army of Northern Virginia. Uncoordinated troop dispositions, marshy terrain, and poor communications between officers and men in the field hampered the whole attack. Colonel Zebulon Vance of the 26th North Carolina thought the attack should have never taken place under mismanaged and ill-advised conditions.

Elington, Fry and Abshire all turned their attention to the things of home. As the night wore on, the wounded troopers of the 26th North Carolina envisioned the mundane, but pleasant, pursuits of life as it once was in Granite Falls. The mountains and the rich green landscapes were now beckoning to the weak spirits of the soldiers who were trying to cope with their wounds.

For the rest of July, the men of the 26th North Carolina were involved in the recovery of wounded troopers, resupplying brigades, taking Union prisoners south, and the defense of Richmond.

The Battle of Malvern Hill caused the Confederate enlisted men to question whether or not they could win the war with their new commanding officer, General Robert E. Lee. This attitude only prevailed for a short time within the ranks, for the Confederate spirit of independence always remained daring and resolute.

*****

On July 3, Corporal Fry had his wounds tended to by the sawbones in camp.

"You're gonna have to knock me out, you crazy sawbone, to get at this finger. You guys love butchering people, don't you, now!" shouted Fry as the surgeons tried to calm him for the amputation needed on his wounded left ring finger.

"Give me some tar water, so I don't feel the pain, man! I need some strong stuff before you butcher me, you darned, cursed devils. Give me some whiskey!"

Fry wrangled with the surgeons and the attendants, causing tables to be overturned, other wounded men to be hit by flying debris, and surgical tools to be smashed into the sides of the medical tent where the brigade hospital was pitched.

General Lee ordered an advance to chase down McClellan's Army, north of their present position in Virginia. The 26th was back on the road again.

"Ouch, you rotten! Ouch! Ah! You stinking sawbone demons!" cried Fry.

The blade cut into the bone and severed the finger from his hand. Fry cursed and swore uncontrollably. He breathed heavily and saw dots and starry specks in his eyes. Fry passed out and slept, staying in the tent of Second Lieutenant John Holloway for two days.

When he woke up on July 5, his friends Elington and Abshire, who he referred to as the Possum because of all the hunting done for possum back in Caldwell County, were given furlough because of wounds incurred while attempting to do their duty at Malvern Hill. They were on their way home, transported first by an ambulance wagon crossing rugged terrain in eastern Virginia, then by train through Weldon and Raleigh, and finally by another train to Granite Falls.

Corporal Fry remained attached to F Company after his wounds were tended to. He was back to the common chores of camp life in summertime: cooking rations, cleaning muskets, filling his haversack, lightening loads for marching, bossing Thaddeus Curtis and Jackson Coffey around, hearing the cries of the wounded, and more drill and practice. This characterized camp conditions in the 26th North Carolina. Fry hated the present situation of having Elington and Abshire gone from camp. What would he do now? Who would he associate with in the company he had arrogantly treated in the last year. He wished he was homebound to Caldwell County to see his wife and three children, who he missed dearly; but he never showed his emotional side around the Possum. He missed the comradery and arguing politics with his friends. The past year was an experience for Fry.

"I sure seem to be a stranger around here," he said to Lieutenant Holloway.

"What stranger, Fry? Remember you are a corporal in this company of brave men who tried their best the other day; tried their best for the Confederacy, for Lee, General Huger, and General Ransom."

"I'm gonna go and rest in your tent, lieutenant," Fry said in a tired fashion. He began to whistle Dixie. With his dirty, bloodied uniform still on him from July 1, Fry went over to a tree in the camp, slid his skinny form against an old walnut and began to daydream as he often did back on the farm. He pulled out a flask with some strong whiskey in it, took a swig and then lit his grandfather's corncob pipe to smoke in the quiet shade of the meadow.

"Tobacco and Margaret ... some day ... some day ... I'll get out of this war and back home to the smells of the animals and plants all around, the touch of my wife, and sounds of cardinals, bluebirds and sparrows singing and flapping in the gentle breezes of home," he murmured to himself.

He continued to daydream.

His hand still throbbing with pain from the amputation, Fry retired to the tent and fell sound asleep.

Peace came for a short while.

— Chapter 3 —
Granite Falls

August-November 1862

The train steamed toward the destination of Granite Falls, Caldwell County, in the upper northwest reaches of the Tarheel state. It clattered along the tracks and images of peace and comfort bathed the mind of Harrison Elington. His leg was still throbbing from the surgeon's instruments, but his heart pumped with the excitement of seeing home, once again, after a year in the army of the Confederacy. The black smoke and white steam from the clanking ebony locomotive puffed into the blue skies.

Wearing his cleaned and perfectly fitted cadet gray army uniform with its gold sleeve lieutenant's insignia; lieutenant's bars on his collar; sword scabbard buckled around his waist; his unique, black wide-brimmed slouch hat with its CSA insignia on the front; and the cherished thirty-six caliber Colt Navy revolver; the lieutenant waited patiently for the train to reach Hickory Tavern. Part of Catawba County, Hickory Tavern had the nearest rail station to Granite Falls, where Abigail waited for her husband.

"I hope Abigail was able to get a hold of the letters I sent her. I only received a few responses from her," said Elington to Alfred Abshire. Alfred was also anticipating going home to Granite Falls to see his parents and recover from his wound.

He couldn't possibly go North to see Krista Morris, his fiancée. She was "trapped in 'Yankee Land' up there in Maine," he had said to Elington earlier on the journey back home.

31

"I'm quite sure she got those letters, lieutenant. Everything is going to be all right today, sir," said Alfred, perceiving the nervous tension starting to build in Harrison.

"You know my Abby well enough by now. If she thinks I didn't write to her to let her know what is going on in the war and my feelings concerning the war, well, it's not going to be a pleasant scene here today."

"I will have to agree with your point, lieutenant. Abigail, we both know, is strong-willed; what some would call a lady with her own mind, liberated to an extent, and very opinionated when it comes to the cause of the Confederacy and the place North Carolina should play in this whole secessionist mess."

"Thanks for a clear reflection and reminder of my own wife! You're right about everything you've said, but remember, I love her dearly, with all my heart, even if she was born in your so-called 'Yankee land' up there in the North."

The train slowed down and the beautiful reflections of light against the mountainous majesty of the Blue Ridge began to come into view. The craggy and scabrous surfaces and peaks of the mountains protruded into the sky like the hand of God calling attention to His faithful. *If Christians served Him above all else, maybe wars would never start in the world or in our own land,* Harrison thought. The memories of hunting in the hills and swimming in the cold mountain water flushed Harrison's mind, pushing out all images of the recent battle from his thoughts. The secluded times of gazing at mountain peaks and the lush greenery of the Piedmont region, which spread across the eastern edge of the Blue Ridge, stirred more memories of childhood for Harrison and Alfred. They continued to daydream their way back home on the smooth riding rails.

Harrison thought of Christmases past. Grandmother cooked-up a Christmas Eve dinner fit for a king, father went with his son to chop down the perfect Christmas tree for the parlor; a tree he had watched grow from a sapling. A fire would warm the cold house covered in white Christmas snow.

*****

Alfred, noticing the contemplation, anxiety and love of Harrison Elington toward his wife, began to consider the ambiguity of his own situation as a student and future husband. He only received three letters from Krista Morris, his fiancée, in the year since he was mustered into service for the

Confederate cause. He was anxious to see his parents back in Granite Falls. He knew he could talk to them about Krista.

Only three letters from her, not good for a future marriage, he thought.

He was very fond of Krista, even though she was from Maine. None of the political staunchness that plagued the Union and Confederate, the free and slave, or Yankee and Reb crusades aroused or constrained the couple to argue, fuss, or even threaten one another. Krista's parents welcomed the refined Alfred Abshire into their lives. They admired his copious thoughts about democratic government, his North Carolina ancestry, and even his thoughts pertaining to the "peculiar institution" of Southern slavery.

Dinner was always an academic contest between Krista's father, Thomas; her older brother, Charles; and Alfred. Alfred continually raked the conversation at the table with questions and debates concerning the impregnable and ignitable situation between the secessionist South and the solidified North.

He always pondered and put forth questions of states' rights and slavery as the motivating, destructive cause for the tearing of the political experiment of America, a nation still in its infancy at eighty-four years old in 1860.

"If John C. Calhoun was alive to see this, he would argue that the sovereign states of the South had every Constitutional right to nullify a federal law. He would not make slavery a centerpiece for the South seceding from the Union. He, like Thomas Jefferson before him, believed the states made a compact agreement at the Constitutional Convention in Philadelphia back in 1787. Under the agreement, the states could leave the Union if any of them grew dissatisfied with the political processes of the majority national government." Alfred said this at one of the many dinner engagements with the Morrises in Maine.

He also said, "The present situation is based on the idea of sovereign rule. Unionism, in the form of the national government in Washington, D.C., tries to limit and coerce the states in the South to relinquish its right to govern itself. It is like history repeated upon the days of British monarchial tyranny and Parliamentary absolutism, where the colonists labored as puppets of the mercantilistic mother country. Similarly, representation is null upon the South and the South's motivations are fragmented toward the national government. The Northern politicians want their way only and that's it!"

Fit to be tied, Thomas Morris would jump out of his seat and challenge every Southern discourse coming out of Alfred's mouth. The ladies would retire from the table and relax by the fireplace in the parlor.

"The new Republican Party is the future of this democratic experiment called the United States of America," shouted Morris at the table on one occasion during a cold Maine winter before the war. "Gradual emancipation of the slave is the way our country will eventually wipe the scourge from the land. The only reason John Calhoun and his cronies in the Southern state governments labored as staunch supporters of states' rights was to protect, preserve and benefit from the extension of slavery into the new territories in the Western frontier. Cotton and tobacco would become more profitable cash crops in areas of the west and southwestern part of the Mexican Cession lands. It all comes down to profits, Alfred."

After the hot debates the challengers composed themselves, shook hands and went to the parlor to mingle with the ladies of the house. These discourses and arguments were only academic and, actually, for a time, brought Thomas Morris, Charles Morris and Alfred together as comrades, forming a bond that invigorated friendship and admiration above the country's woes.

"Differences of opinion in a democratic society were a healthy thing," Charles would say.

Harrison Elington and Alfred Abshire neither owned slaves nor really cared about the "peculiar institution" of slavery. Raised and nurtured in the North Carolinian Blue Ridge area of Caldwell County, they had little need for slaves. The geographic nature of their environment prevented slavery. Except for a few tobacco farmers, who were not very abundant in the county, slavery existed mostly on the coasts and along the central Piedmont areas where the climate was better for growing tobacco.

*****

The clanking and clattering of the train subsided as Harrison gazed out the passenger car window, searching for more mountainous scenery and aberrations in the sky. As his focus began to come back to him, aided by the fading rhythmic rolling of the train, he saw the figure of a woman with light brown hair, smooth skin and thin build, wearing a light blue elliptical hoop skirt with layers of flounces and a matching bodice. The woman wore her best formal attire to greet her visitor. Harrison felt warmness in his being as the train pulled into Hickory Tavern.

"It's Abigail!" shouted Harrison to Alfred.

He shouted again, this time triumphantly from the rail car window, "Abby! Abby! It's me, Harrison!"

"I can hear you, Harrison! My dear Harrison," she shouted from the platform.

"I'll be right out!"

"Hurry, Harrison!"

"How are you, Mrs. Elington? It's Alfred, Alfred Abshire!"

"Yes, I can see you now, Boy Alfred!" said Abigail, referring to Alfred in her familiar refined tone of placing "Boy" in front of his name to denote a refined college lad whom she admired.

The men exited the train, standing tall and proud in their gray Confederate uniforms, but strained with melancholy faces ensuant from the cruelties of war, stained forever by the oddities of battle conditions few ever see in their lifetimes.

"Harrison!" Abigail shouted again.

"Abby? Come over here!"

"Give me a great hug, Abby; it's been too long."

"I love you and it is great to see you, my beloved husband," whispered Abigail into Harrison's ear.

"Hug me and kiss me, Abby, but watch out for my bad leg! Ouch!"

"Oh, come here you handsome man with the bad leg."

The couple continued to hold each other for a long time. Abigail began to cry. Tears fell freely from her face. She couldn't decide if they were tears of happiness and contentment, or tears of sorrow and despair. She cried silently as Harrison held her gently in the summer sun. Harrison, not wanting ever to let her go again, thought immediately of his imminent return to the front lines. There he would be brought back into the firestorm and hellfire of war and destruction; back in Virginia, where Corporal Lewis Fry was left to recover from his injuries and where that awful hill stood silent now.

"Alfred? It is good to see you, my friend!"

"It is good to see you too, Mrs. Elington." They hugged.

"You men look brave and proud ..."

"Yes, my dear, but we are also tired, injured and hungry for some home cooking from the Elington residence.

"How is your leg, dear?"

"Not good at all. This medicine for keeping it clean is a terrible solution."

"How is your arm, Boy Alfred?"

"I think, I think it's doing fine. I'll be all right soon."

"Have you heard anything new from Danny or from the 26th regiment?" asked Harrison, thinking of his two boys fighting in the war. "Any word from

Jesse, from the 83rd Pennsylvania?"

"Nothing new, dear, since I received word of your wounds and your furlough, but I know they are safe. That's what I have to believe."

"Let's get out of here and go home, sweet home," Harrison said.

"The carriage is over past the station. Let's go!" said Abigail politely, but forcefully. Harrison limped over to the carriage.

"You have taken care of the carriage like I never left, Abby."

"What do you think I am, Harrison? A wounded, old maid who can't work for herself!"

"No! Absolutely not."

"Abby! I'm going to need help into the carriage. Please, let's not call any attention to this wound. Alfred, help Abby get me into the carriage and we can get home."

"Is that how he orders you around the battlefields, Boy Alfred?"

"Yes, ma'am, and I have no complaints about the lieutenant, ma'am!"

"Well, Boy Alfred, wait until you see who the captain of the house is while you're staying with us."

"Staying with you?"

"Yes, Alfred. Your parents had to go to Raleigh to petition the state government for financial aid for the operations of your gristmill. The mill has suffered through hard times. This Godforsaken war has brought too much strain to our county. Railroad service has been cut in half. Confederate Army use of the railroads is up and transportation of wheat is lagging behind its usual promptness. Food supplies have been slowed by the war effort. I feel like a peasant in a foreign land."

"Giddyap, Bandit!" Abigail shouted.

The carriage was pulled by a muscular workhorse; a colt of the Shire breed with a fine, dark brown coat and blonde mane. They slowly pulled away from the train station. Harrison could see the boundaries of the road lined up between the poll of the colt. Trotting down the dirt road, they headed toward Granite Falls.

"Abby, my precious girl! Take it easy! My leg is still mending from the wound at Malvern Hill!"

"Malvern Hill?" Where is that?"

"Where is that?"

"It's in Virginia," said Alfred to Abigail.

"Please forgive me, dear! Please forgive my memory. I did read about Malvern Hill in the papers. What a catastrophe for the Army of Northern

Virginia, for you dear, and for General Robert E. Lee."

"I don't want to speak of it now, Abby."

"Neither do I, Mrs. Elington; ma'am."

"It must have been a bad and horrible time for all in the regiment," Abigail said, steering along the roads home.

The carriage, with its passengers, traveled northwest under a pleasantly cool afternoon sky. The smells and sights of Granite Falls embraced the two soldiers like children on a Christmas morning; children with high expectations of toys and presents stacked in the parlor. The sounds of the wheat gristmills, the sounds of the lumber mills, the smell of the fresh pine trees radiating from the eastern slopes of the great and mysterious mountains, and the touch and fragrance of Abigail singed Harrison's heart like a blessing of angels upon his soul and upon the earth.

"We'll have a lot to converse about in the days to come, Abby," said Harrison, enjoying the serenity of home.

The carriage finally pulled up to the stoned-front, two-story farmhouse on Sunset Road in the western part of Granite Falls. The house sat high off the road, with its gray stonework along the front of the structure and white clap-board siding encompassing the rest of the house. The porch had a railing around it where Abigail and Harrison would sit for hours, talking and drinking hot coffee on crisp and clear fall days now removed from their lives. The barn was built at the right rear part of the main house, and a post and rail fence that kept the farm animals from roaming too far hemmed in the whole property. The barn was white with a black-shingled roof and large doors on the front and sides. Harrison approached the porch from the carriage. He saw his dark-stained oak chair still there as if he never left for war.

"Well, Abby, I can truly say the place looks grand. Even my chair is in sitting condition!"

"I re-coated the finish all by my little, Ms. Prissy self!"

The house, the barn and the animals seem nestled, protected and unafflicted by time and by the gruesome blemishes of war, Harrison thought. Gruesome blemishes he hesitated to talk about since July 1.

Everyone went inside to a well kept home. Harrison was used to organization in all aspects of his life. The parlor was scented by candles, which lit the room in a peaceful hue. The grand living room was whitened by painted walls and accented with dark oak furniture and trimmed oak woodwork all around. In the corner sat Harrison's desk, where he prepared lessons in writing, grammar, history and math for his class of secondary level students at the local academy in Granite Falls. Harrison loved the mechanics of the learning process, but often was discouraged and agitated by the immaturity of his students and the ineptness of his administrative leaders.

Besides teaching, Harrison developed and cultivated a farm, where he grew oats, winter wheat and sweet potatoes for market sale in town and throughout the county. His summers were full with maintaining the farm and tending to chores around the house. His military pension brought in additional income, particularly needed in summer, when school was not in session.

Always seeming content with his life back in the days before the war, Harrison then formulated a conflict of mind: his own mind, with the constant contentions of Union versus state, slavery versus free soil, and nullification versus secession. With an indomitable sense and belief in historical analysis, he started to question the leaders of the Southern cause, even though he felt a powerful loyalty to the South.

"Why would any state want to secede from the heritage, from the protection, and from the ability of the United States and its people to forge a civilization beyond comprehension?" said Harrison to Abigail on a clear day in April 1861. "The United States is a country like no other and it will one day surpass other countries in its industry, agriculture and historical heritage."

Abigail had always entered the conversation brought on by Harrison, enjoying the philosophical debates and conclusions rendered from the discussions.

Abigail Sumner Elington was the daughter of Senator Robert Sumner from Pennsylvania. Well educated, through her father's efforts, she was a Union supporter. Like many of her friends and neighbors in Caldwell County, she advocated the idea of remaining in the Union when many Southerners, particularly in South Carolina, called for radical and deliberate secessionist action against the new United States and its new President, Abraham Lincoln. She did not think the Union should end, especially upon the preponderance of states' rights and for the sake of answering the slave question. She perceived this question as an issue needing gradual attention, as Lincoln believed, being the leader of the Executive Branch in Washington, D.C.

"Negroes and whites will never be able to coexist in the same country after many decades of servitude upon the slave race in the Americas," she once read in Thomas Jefferson's works out of Virginia.

Lincoln, she thought, believed the same way as Jefferson, thus bringing unity between a Southerner and a Northerner in the same fractured Union.

She believed compromise was still useful between the North and the South. Gradual emancipation offered to heal many wounds upon the nation. She harbored and stood firm in her beliefs, even when Harrison received his furlough for his wound. Abigail hated the idea of upright, educated and hardworking men going to war to kill each other in order to resolve the slave question or any other questions of disunion caused by the radical fire eaters such as Edwin Ruffin in South Carolina.

"Boy Alfred, you will stay in Jesse's room upstairs," said Abigail.

"That will be fine with me, ma'am. I really appreciate this. It would feel real lonely if I had to stay by myself in our house without mother and father there. I will have a chance to go and see the old place later."

Abigail went upstairs to freshen-up the room for Alfred.

"I'm glad you can spend time with us," said Harrison, comfortably.

"It's hard not to think about it, lieutenant. The cries for help, the blood, the killing … that hill, sir."

"Yeah … it's hard."

"The firing never seemed to stop. The wounded and dead, sir, the roaring of the cannon. The faces of the boys."

"All of it still haunts you, too?"

"You know how afraid I was on the battlefield. I told you right then and there how I couldn't stop shaking from the cannon fire. It scared me."

"I remember …"

"Do you think I'm a coward? I need to know."

"No, Abshire, you're not a coward. Now you remember this and remember it well! A coward is one who turns tail and runs away. His fear, in the face of brutal danger, dictates his actions. Did you run away? Did you hide behind any of the other boys during the volleys of fire we gave to the Yankees and they gave to us? Have you ever been labeled a straggler in our company by anyone? Have you strayed from your duties as an infantryman?"

"No, sir, no."

"You stayed with F Company in a time when every soldier attacking Malvern hill, in all probability, either felt like throwing up his guts, felt afraid, felt pain, felt dismay, or felt like running home for good and never looking back. However, you all stayed for the most part. I know from a couple of the companies there were stragglers, but not many from the 26th North Carolina."

"I think I understand. But …"

"Being a soldier is fighting in spite of our fears and timidity. It is human to be afraid in battle, but it is our duty to carry on in the face of uncertain odds and calamities. Be strong, Abshire. When we get back we may face worse conditions as this war wears on and on. We will need more courage. I don't know what lies ahead for us."

"Do you remember, lieutenant, when people in both North and South thought they possessed the best armies and the war would be over in weeks? I remember talking with Krista's brother and father at dinner just before the attack on Sumter; one of my last visits with her and her family. Charles Morris feverishly spoke and justified the superiority of Union forces, saying Southerners had no gumption for military affairs in sustaining their cause."

"Then came Manassas Junction in '61," Harrison said. "We all knew the war was going to be a long one from then on."

Abigail came walking down the stairs from Jesse's room. She asked Harrison, "How is your leg, dear? Can I do anything to help you feel more comfortable?"

"The doctors said to keep the wound clean with this tincture of iodine solution and keep the dressings clean. Do you think I remembered correctly?"

"I will get you well in a hurry. Then you can do some chores on the farm."

"Chores I don't mind, but I don't want to go back to the regiment too soon."

"I agree, lieutenant."

"Boy Alfred; instead of lieutenant, call him Harrison around here. I'm not too fond of army talk, Confederate or Union."

Abby went to the kitchen and finished cooking her soldier's first home-cooked meal; something Harrison and Alfred hadn't eaten in a year. The smell of the cured ham, the sweet potatoes, collard greens and wheat bread overwhelmed the two soldiers with joy and contentment of heart. Applesauce and pie would top off the evening's meal and the comforts of home resonated in Harrison's being like the infinite power of the Blue Ridge peaks and ridges surrounding their home.

– Chapter 4 –
Fading Hope

Fall 1862

Days and weeks went by and Harrison recuperated from his leg wound. Abigail and Harrison felt the familiar partnership in taking care of household chores and farm duties. Harrison's leg continued to heal and strengthen. He felt more useful around the house and farm. Abby spoke again to Harrison about her reservations and consternation concerning the Confederate war effort. Harrison still debated and cautiously argued about the politics of Jefferson Davis and the military campaigns of Generals Lee in the east and Braxton Bragg in the west.

In the early days of healing at home, Abigail and Harrison got along fine until two events occurred that splintered the relationship.

First was news of a second battle fought at Manassas Junction in August 1862. Generals Jackson, Longstreet and Lee routed the new Lincoln appointee, General John Pope, in a repeat victory for the Confederacy. The Union left flank was crushed and the Confederate command now saw a chance to invade the North. An invasion of the North would relieve devastated Virginia farms. Lee hoped for a decisive victory on Union soil in order to send an impending surge of fear and instability into the Union cause. Talk of an invasion upset many people in the South.

This second event, the Confederate invasion of the North, affected the Elington's equally.

Rumors of an invasion North offended Abigail. It brought about much dissension in North Carolina and in the Elington household. Abigail had family living in Philadelphia, Pennsylvania, and she reasoned an invasion by the Confederate Army would be directed right into her native state. This was one event Harrison and Abigail would fuss about during the rest of August and into the middle of September.

"The South, in its secessionist motives, has no right to invade the Union!" Abigail exclaimed to Harrison.

They were both eating breakfast one morning in late September. "When this war started you promised me that the leadership in Richmond, devised in their infinite wisdom, would fight a defensive war! Yes, Harrison, a defensive war where the people of the South would simply strive to protect their institutions and sovereignty against a central government unwilling to recognize states' rights!"

"Calm down, Abby!"

"Don't call me Abby today! It's Abigail to you, my dear!"

"Is this how we are going to spend the last few weeks of my recovery, arguing over issues that don't matter any longer? The war has come and we can't do anything to stop it now!" Harrison said forcefully.

"You betcha, dear!"

"Well, just fine, Miss Abigail Sumner, the Yankee preacher!"

"What did you call me?"

"You heard me!"

"What?"

"I said 'you heard me,' Abigail the preacher!"

Alfred came in the house from Lenoir and couldn't believe what he was hearing. He knew Abigail and Harrison had their philosophical and political differences, but he never thought they could argue with such intensity, especially when Harrison was on furlough. Harrison would soon be back into the thick of it somewhere, most likely in the North itself; then what would Abigail think and say?

"When I get back to active duty I may be wandering North somewhere on a pre-planned invasion," Harrison said seriously.

Smash.

Crash.

Abigail threw a dish clear across the room right at Harrison. It ricocheted off the wall, missing Harrison, but pieces of the dish hit Alfred in the left arm where he had been injured.

"What was that?" Alfred shouted.

"I am sorry, Boy Alfred! I didn't mean to hit you. I meant to hit your precious lieutenant."

Abigail became fixed in a state of vexation. She lamented about how sorry she was to Harrison and Alfred for her present behavior. Alfred was amazed by her sudden and quick change of mood and temperament.

"It was supposed to be a defensive war. You told me! Do you think I want to see you hurt again, or this time even dead! What will I do then? What will the boys do without a father to guide them in life? Will the boys make it out of this war, Harrison? What about them? Fighting for a so-called country, the Confederacy, the Union, whatever it means anymore!" She sobbed.

"Abigail! Abby! Listen to me. I can't predict what the next military plan or action will be. Yes, sometimes I want to agree with you, with all of my heart and with all of my soul. Even during the preparation and troop alignments before the Battle at Malvern Hill and at New Bern I asked myself questions; questions that searched for the meaning of what I was really fighting for, questions about the ability of the Confederacy's military and political leaders, and questions about why men from the South, who mostly do *not* own slaves, would fight hard and brutal for this cause. Why do they fight? Why?"

"Do you still have those questions?" Abigail asked gently. She calmed down somewhat.

"Yes!"

"Sometimes I see myself as a traitor, striving to rid my mind of the guilt of secession and the plague of human slavery. Then in the same flash of thought I see myself leading valiant charges through the heat of battle, with my men and leaders beside me, moving through with undaunted conviction for Confederate causes. What side do I take, Abby? What side is the right course? What does God want us to do in these times of mayhem when men are forced to be individuals they aren't? I am torn! I am tired of it!

"Is Davis a president or a dictator?" Harrison continued. "Is Robert E. Lee a real general or a failed military advisor leading troops blindly into the fire of battle?"

Alfred responded, "Sir, why didn't you ever tell me about your feelings. Although I would argue and debate with Krista's father and brother over the same issues I hear being argued today, I often felt a sense of indecision when it came right down to choosing sides. I do understand, sir, what your going through, but you have to choose sooner or later, or the war is going to entangle you forever in its monstrous clench. You have to feel strong for one side or the other!"

"I am strong for the Confederacy, Alfred, but sometimes I have these endless, nagging doubts."

"I understand, Harrison."

"I need to go and do some work in the barn, Abby. You need to calm yourself, and then maybe we can talk some more!"

The thought of a Confederate invasion had always driven a wedge through their relationship. The invasion came to a head on September 17th, 1862.

*****

An article in the North Carolina Gazette dated September 22, 1862, described to the shocked people living in the state the following events:

"Sharpsburg: An American Tragedy!"

SHARPSBURG, Ma.—The Battle of Sharpsburg, near Antietam Creek, Maryland, has produced the bloodiest single day in American military history, with many sources stating over 20,000 wounded and dead at the end of the day, September 17, 1862.

General Lee, in a daring maneuver of dividing his army to accomplish an invasion of Pennsylvania, pushed his resources and manpower to the limit in the late summer of 1862. Lee had three objectives for his invasion and for dealing with McClellan's cautious forces north of the Potomac River. Get supplies for the Army of Northern Virginia by taking Harpers Ferry, bring the war north to relieve Southern farms, and draw McClellan farther away from his base of operations in Virginia.

General Lee sent a proclamation to the people of Maryland, stating the following:

"Maryland, September 8, 1862, I have the Army of Northern Virginia concentrated in and around the city of Frederick, Maryland. In accordance with President Davis's instructions prior to moving across the Potomac, I have issued a proclamation to the people of Maryland stating what President Davis's objectives are.

"This, citizens of Maryland, is our mission, so far as you are concerned. No constraint upon your freewill is intended; no intimidation will be allowed within the limits of this army. Marylanders shall once more enjoy their ancient freedom of thought and speech. We know no enemies among you and will protect all, of every opinion. It is for you to decide your destiny freely and without constraint. This army will respect your choice, whatever it may be; and while the Southern people will rejoice to welcome you to your natural position among them, they will only welcome you when you come of your own freewill."

The Battle started on the 17th of September, with Yankee General Hooker raking General Jackson's men with horrendous shot and shell, according to reporters and illustrators near the field. This occurred in the Miller's family farm cornfield, where the Union and Confederate forces were pushing and pulling back and forth for control of the cornfield and the areas known as the East and West Woods along the Hagerstown Pike. General Thomas Jackson's men were pulverized by Union Artillery firing from the woods across the Hagerstown Pike. Hooker's divisions and regiments pushed the Confederates from their positions. Stonewall Jackson was reinforced about an hour after the Battle had started, but General Mansfield of the Union Army attacked again into the Miller's cornfield and gained back lost ground that had been bloodied with the hellfire of war and the desecration of the American spirit. Mansfield was killed in action directing his troops toward the woods and cornfield. Numbers of Mansfield's men were cut off near the old Dunker Church—a German immigrant church—from their divisions. General Sedgwick's Union troops went into the West Woods to try and help them, only to be flanked right and left by Jackson's regiments and massed artillery fire.

The fighting then shifted, after hours of heedless carnage in the woods and on the cornfield, to a sunken road where Union forces, under Yankee General French's division, came to support Sedgwick. French would eventually smash into Confederate forces under General D.H. Hill, who thought he and his men were sheltered from the men in blue in the sunken road. The Union Artillery fire raked and busted their positions. When it was over, this newspaper reporter saw Confederate dead stacked three high all along the sunken road. A horrible shame for our beloved country!

The last phase of the battle, according to our sources in Richmond in the September 1862 battle, told of 400 Georgians, the 2nd and 20th Regiments, stubbornly delaying constant attacks from General Burnside's regiments on the south end of the battlefield. The Union troopers made it over the bridge at that part of the battle line by one o'clock in the afternoon, but were driven back by the forces of General Ambrose Powell Hill's Light Brigade, coming from Harpers Ferry. Burnside had to fall back to his position near the Rohrbach Bridge, where hundreds of Union men were killed or injured.

Northern newspapers were reporting the Battle at Antietam Creek may become the bloodiest one-day battle of any U.S. war. Also, the papers were reporting, along with rumors from Lincoln's administration offices, saying the President might free the slaves in the Confederate rebellion states through an Emancipation Proclamation caused by the so-called victory at Sharpsburg. McClellan is claiming victory for simply holding our beloved General Lee from invading the North. President Lincoln became furious over General McClellan's lack of spirit for destroying our great Army of Northern Virginia once and for all. Again, McClellan had the slows. He would not pursue our army in the field. Again, he was afraid to move against our noble generals.

Abigail was distraught over the terrible invasion and news of the battle's details. She contemplated death surely meeting upon her family in some way. She knew many of her friends from college days, up North in Philadelphia, were dead or severely wounded from the devastation of battle. Many Philadelphia volunteers filled the ranks of the Union Army. She pondered going North to find out if her son Jesse was still alive. She hadn't heard from him since before the great battle at Sharpsburg.

*****

Jesse Elington left Granite Falls not long after the Confederate firing on Fort Sumter back in April 1861. Through friends and family relations of his mother, he was able to join the 83rd Pennsylvania Infantry Regiment in order to fight for the Union cause of restoring and saving the United States from secession. He strongly sided with his mother's political views, especially secession and the gradual emancipation of slaves.

Jesse was a hard worker and his habit of hard work and determination flowed into his early working career at the Abshire gristmill in Granite Falls. He also helped his father with the farm work during summers, when he was out of school, and before he was employed at the gristmill as a foreman.

Jesse provided his mother and father with a portrait of leadership, which enabled them to grow confident and secure in his future. Then came Fort Sumter and the secessionist vote, all convulsing on the Southern states like a whirlwind fury, beckoning for independence through war. Jesse didn't see the point of Southern gentlemen going to war over the question of slavery. He believed, adamantly, that slavery was a social ill propagating further distresses on Southern society. He formed his belief about slavery after visiting the Raleigh area when he was seventeen. He saw the slave in his docile and restrained condition, forever doomed to his master for survival. To him, it was moral devastation and moral destruction.

Jesse loved his father, but he couldn't understand why his father would consider fighting for the Confederacy. Jesse heard his father speak of the supremacy of the Union. Abigail recalled a discussion with Jesse, Danny and Harrison just before the firing on Fort Sumter:

"Father! Do you know what you're saying?" Jesse asked.

"Yes, I do know!"

"You would put on the uniform of an army capable of fighting against the U.S. Army; the army you served in for seventeen years of your life!"

"If it comes down to the government in Washington telling us what we can and cannot do, then yes."

"That government is our nation, our history and our life!"

"I have served in the army and I will serve again if I have to. I just hope reason will prevail among the leaders of both sides; then maybe a war will be averted."

"I don't know. Those hotheads in South Carolina are determined to secede if Lincoln is elected President," Danny said.

"Why is it that a small percentage of people owning slaves and a small percentage of people calling themselves abolitionists can start such an argument where the Congress of the United States, the Supreme Court, and the president can't compromise a solution? How did things get out of control?" Harrison asked.

"You're right when you say 'those hotheads.' They will be the ones who start a war. I'm afraid it will be a war bringing much destruction for both the North and for our home here in the South," Jesse said.

"Don't you agree, Father? I mean … with Danny's idea about the radicals in South Carolina. North Carolina has a special heritage and bond with the era of the American Revolution and our founding fathers. Our state helped defeat the British and helped forge a nation we have freedom in today."

"Let's just pray to God in Heaven for His providence and mercy upon our land," Harrison said.

Jesse was there at Sharpsburg. Abigail and Harrison did not know if he survived the great battle. They both felt their sense of loss over Jesse leaving home and his determination to fight against the South. Harrison, though, admired his son's convictions. He had felt guilt and vexation concerning the Southern cause since the war actually started. His doubt built up since joining the 26th North Carolina, but he remained faithful to the cause before him as 1862 came to an end.

*****

Harrison entered the center of town at Granite Falls, riding in his farm wagon and heading for the general store. He needed supplies and tools to get the farm in shape for the winter.

He gazed intently at the people and the little shops operating as if life was just as usual and plain as before the great conflict now raging. It was November 10th, 1862, and things were starting to look up for the Confederacy. Lee brought damage and fear to the North throughout the Antietam Campaign; Lincoln was searching for another general to rid the army of McClellan; and Harrison's wound was getting much better.

Abby can be hard to talk to sometimes, Harrison thought.

He continued down the road.

She has her beliefs just like everyone else does about the war and the many conflicts over secession. Her strong spirit will sustain her through the sorrow we are experiencing. Ah ... her throwing the dish a few weeks back. She always had a bad temper; something I was attracted to when we first met. How I long for those good old college days."

He went over to the store to get a hot cup of real brew; something the army lacked supplies of.

"Lieutenant? Lieutenant? Over here! It's me, Peyton!" shouted the young man from across the street.

"Peyton, how are you?"

"Wounded, sir ... wounded right in the head. Got a pretty bad scrape at Sharpsburg. The general allowed some men to furlough after the horrible butchering in Maryland."

Peyton was in an unusually somber mood. His jovial spirit was injured by war.

Peyton Caldwell, nephew of Dr. Joseph Caldwell, was a former student of Harrison's. Caldwell County was named after Dr. Joseph Caldwell in 1840. Dr. Caldwell served as president of the University of North Carolina, worked tirelessly for a railroad line through to Tennessee and lobbied for a public school system for the county. Peyton was recruited with Danny Elington into Battery D, 5th North Carolina Artillery Battalion back in the fall of 1861. Artillerists were needed desperately after the first Battle of Manassas. The boys joined up out of duty for their new country.

"Were you still assigned with Danny, Peyton? Is he all right? Tell me some information, boy! Abigail and I have been speculating on Danny's condition; Jesse's too. Have you seen him?"

"Yes, yes, sir, calm yourself down. He performed his duties to the utmost of his abilities and with bravery, sir; yes, he constantly showed the other boys what courage is all about."

"That's my son! Always the go-getter in the family. We were glad to hear briefly from Danny a few weeks after the battle, but the letter only spoke of generalities after Sharpsburg and some details of the battle. He seemed to be pressed for time. We didn't know if he survived the terrible carnage before his brief letter arrived. The news stories scared Abby and me."

Harrison stated, "From the newspaper reports, it seems like Sharpsburg was a turning point in stupidity for General McClellan. He had every chance to whip us, but he floundered and gave General Lee the opportunity to escape back into Virginia."

"You're absolutely right, sir. McClellan probably could have ended the war right in Maryland. General A. P. Hill's division was still at Harpers Ferry. Did you hear his division marched all the way from the Ferry, seventeen miles, and made it to the bridge where Burnside was trying to cut off our road of retreat at the Potomac River?"

"Yes, I did hear about the surprise run by good old General Hill against Burnside."

"Speaking of Burnside, lieutenant, did you hear the general was appointed by Lincoln to take McClellan's place as commander of the Army of the Potomac?"

"No, I wasn't aware of the development, but I remember an encounter with Burnside not too long after the 26th North Carolina was placed into service."

"We came across Burnside at New Bern, the rail junction town near Fort Thompson. Colonel Vance formed our line there near the Neuse River. I remember Lieutenant Colonel Burgwyn complaining about the position and wanting to move the regiment to what he thought would be a better site for bivouacking. We broke our backs building breastworks and extending our defenses. Burnside had captured Roanoke Island. What a marshy mess for troop movements. Burnside made his way to the mouth of the Neuse River and secured 10,000 Yankees on land. He directed his troops toward New Bern using the tracks as a guide into town, plus many troops stomped on the Beaufort Road leading there."

"He had 10,000 troops there, lieutenant?"

"Yeah, 10,000 Yankees coming into our homeland. Those Yanks, we were told earlier, carried Enfield Rifles which could pick off our soldiers at greater distances. Some of our guys still held those inefficient, smooth-bore, altered muskets that always gave the fellows problems in training drills. The day before the attack by Burnside's men, it rained like I never saw it rain before. The mud and dampness were overwhelming and agitating for our boys. It was lousy! On the 14th of March, the attack commenced. We were eager to see some action after all the tedious hours of digging and building.

The Union men attacked our left flank, breaking the lines. I remember some of the fellows from the 35th North Carolina firing at the Yankees with their shotguns and hunting rifles and running for their lives. What a sight it was to see. All of us were green in combat, but willing to defeat those Yankees. Burnside may be what Lincoln's looking for in a general, but I don't know. I certainly have my doubts about his ability to lead a whole army. I would say he's a good division commander rather than an army commander."

"How did the 26th do in the battle, lieutenant?

"We never really got into it. We were positioned at the center of the regiment line, away from the action. All the fighting that day came on our left flank. We fared well, though, in our maneuvers and falling back when ordered. Poor Major Carmichael lost his life in the battle; shot right in the head while commanding the left wing. Carmichael was an eager fighter, trainer and overall good officer in our regiment. He is surely missed. We shouldn't have lost good men early in the war, Peyton. I am sure we are going to lose many more."

"When do you go back to duty?" asked Harrison.

"I leave in two days. It's been good to be back home and to see the glorious mountains again. I don't think there is a place, in all the world, having beauty like Caldwell County. It has been peaceful and calm around here, sir."

"Well, I'm glad you can say that. It was peaceful and calm when I first arrived, but Abby, she's having her strong opinions about the Confederacy, again. I was the target of her wrath a couple of times since I've been on furlough."

"The lady of yours, sir, is one opinionated Yankee!"

"Yankee? I wouldn't go that far, Peyton, with your labeling of the woman. You better watch what you say about her; especially around here in town. You and I both know there are Union sympathizers in the western counties, but now we've got a war on our hands and we are fighting for the Confederacy. You need to watch what you say. Do you understand, Peyton?"

"Yes, sir. I was only being sarcastic about the situation."

"Me too," joked Harrison, "a few weeks back I called Abby a Yankee and she threw a plate at me. It almost took Alfred's arm off like a musket shot." They laughed for a while.

"Be careful of your words, Peyton. We both know Abby has family in the North. She supports Lincoln's ideas on gradual emancipation for the slaves down here in the South. She despises the fact of Danny, Alfred and myself fighting a war against her oldest son, Jesse. Anyway, have a safe trip back to the action. I wish you well in the upcoming fights. Take care of yourself and don't get wounded again. We need healthy soldiers in the army. If you do come back home before I do I'll be one jealous fellow. Tell Danny I love him and to keep up the good work firing those batteries."

*****

Slowly, Peyton walked away, contemplating the idea that maybe he would never return to the peace and solitude of his home. He enjoyed being home for a time in the county bearing the name of his relatives. A county in the South forming his beliefs, his skills and his will to fight for a cause. Peyton wondered how all of the confusion would turn out in the uncertain days ahead. He was going back in a couple of days and how could he prepare to fight again after being wounded; after seeing the blood and the carnage at Sharpsburg; and after seeing, with his own eyes, his friends and fellow soldiers killed and heaped in piles like dead animals meaning nothing to the world.

These scenes haunted Peyton and he knew the same scenes haunted Danny, Alfred and Lieutenant Elington. *Would there be more battles like the one at Sharpsburg? Would there be more countless thousands killed on still yet unnamed battlefields? In this momentous conflict, would there be more families torn by the ideas which caused the war in the first place? Could the Confederacy survive the industrial might and numerical advantages of the Union? Would the Elington family make it through the rampage of war; a war bringing inflictions upon Jesse, Harrison, Abigail and Danny?* Peyton thought about all of these prospects. His mind grew burdened.

He was off again to battle.

— Chapter 5 —
Drewry's Bluff and Camp French

October to December 1862

Corporal Lewis Fry was recovering from his finger amputation during the fall of 1862. The 26th North Carolina moved out from Malvern Hill to Drewry's Bluff; a high, steeped bank off the James River and south of Richmond. Drewry's Bluff was used as a defensive wall against Union gunboats. The powerful gunboats periodically bombarded strategic areas near Richmond and the tracks of the Richmond and Petersburg Railroad. The bluff was less than ten miles from the capital.

Corporal Fry still considered himself a loner in the regiment since Harrison and Alfred received furlough for their wounds. He saw a change in command take place in August when the 26th said goodbye to Colonel Zebulon Vance. Vance was elected Governor of North Carolina without campaigning much for the position. Vance seemed to be a shoe-in for the office. His popularity brought him a long way in North Carolina.

He was nominated by quite a few people back home and the election became a successful venture for the colonel. With Vance out, the question now was put forth of who would succeed Vance for the position of colonel of the 26th North Carolina Infantry. At this point in the war, the 26th was one of the largest regiments in the Confederate Army. The regiment members, according to tradition, would elect their officers from the ranks. General Ransom, though, recommended an outsider to replace Vance. He said he didn't want any "boy colonels" in his brigade after getting recommendations from junior officers to nominate Henry Burgwyn for the post. Lieutenant Colonel Henry Burgwyn and his men were furious over the development of an outsider being mentioned to take Vance's place. Through political maneuvers by Burgwyn's father, Henry was placed in command of the regiment by late August.

He proceeded to carry on his strict drill habits with the men to continue preparing them for battle.

Lewis Fry was elated over the triumph of Burgwyn to the position of colonel. Lewis thought all along that Burgwyn was the best officer the regiment had when it came to discipline and guts. He felt the new colonel would be an asset to the development of the 26th North Carolina. Lewis was also overjoyed when the regiment was transferred from Brigadier General Robert Ransom's brigade to Brigadier General Johnston Pettigrew's brigade. The transfer was made final. Ransom and Burgwyn both knew the situation, where a younger officer overruling his older brigade commander might cause future problems and friction in brigade politics. Lewis figured, maybe, there would be more opportunity to fight and destroy Yankees; more than ever after the transfer to another brigade.

He waited for another opportunity to fight and, as he did, times of hard labor progressed for his regiment. Lewis also started to feel a sense of indignation toward Harrison and Alfred. Their recent furlough back home in the pleasant mountain country of Caldwell County still plagued his mind.

Lewis was put to the task of taking F Company troopers back and forth between Drewry's Bluff and Camp French. Camp French was a fortification protecting Petersburg and the path to Richmond from the south. The Confederate Command was wary about Union divisions approaching Richmond from the south. They ordered breastworks and other entrenchments to be constructed. The constant marching and loading of supply wagons with tools and materials was sometimes overwhelming for the troops. F Company worked and worked at their labor. Day after day and hour after hour the labor became more mundane to each member of the company, until they talked about wanting to see battle action again or deserting and going home for good.

Colonel Burgwyn's strict drill instruction and practice was one thing F Company was able to avoid during their labor duties. However, officers were beginning to bring up the issue of re-enlistments, causing interesting conversation during the cool fall nights in Virginia.

*****

F Company sat down one night in early November, 1862, to have rations of fried pork, cornmeal and chicory bean coffee. The men were constantly cursing the Yankee blockade of their ports. They couldn't enjoy real coffee like they used to.

"Did you hear the leaders in Richmond want us to sign on for the remainder of the war?" said Private Jackson Coffey. "They're short on enlistments or something like that. I got kids at home! I got a wife at home, and I need to get back to raise my crop for sale at the market! How do these blundering leaders expect us to keep what we have back home if all the men are fighting the war all of the time? I signed up and I believe in the cause we are fighting for, but some of us need a break! It's been almost a year and a half since I joined the regiment."

His sandy hair flung in the breeze and his youthful blue eyes squinted in anger. He sipped the cheap brand of coffee from his tin cup.

"I'm going to have to agree with you, Coffey," Private Thaddeus Curtis responded. He was drinking some cold water from a nearby stream.

"Shut-up, you darn idiots!" Corporal Fry shouted, clamping down on his corncob pipe; tobacco smoke coiling from the bowl. "If we don't re-enlist, none of you will have a farm or house or a family to go back to. Those stinking Yankees will destroy everything we own and cherish."

"You shut-up, Fry!" Curtis shouted.

"Don't you tell me to shut-up, private!"

"Shut-up, Fry!" Curtis shouted again. "Can you tell us or give us some explanation of how we are supposed to support our families and ourselves without some time off from the regiment, corporal? You know how we fought and performed our duties. We just need to get home and take care of our affairs, especially our crops."

"You darn told me to shut-up again, Curtis!"

Fry then punched Curtis right in the face, picked him up and punched him again. Curtis's nose and lips were bleeding and he spit out a tooth from the back of his mouth. Coffey jumped on Fry and elbowed him to the back of the head. Fry was furious! He picked up his musket he kept loaded at all times and aimed in the general direction of where Curtis and Coffey were standing. Thaddeus's brown eyes filled with tears. His youthful courage shrank. Sweat streamed from his brow where strands of his brown hair settled.

"What are you going to do now, Fry; kill us like we were Yankee enemies?" Coffey said, tending to Curtis.

"I guess you want to kill us like you killed the man who tried to steal your farm horses back home. Yeah, I know all about it from my daddy. He told us the whole story," Curtis said.

Fry pulled the hammer on his musket back and took a percussion cap out of his cartridge box lying near the entrance to his tent. The evening hues were taking over the darkening sky. The other men began to go into their tents for a night's rest. They seemed too tired and ignored the squabble, except for a few of the younger enlisted boys who always enjoyed a good fight.

"You don't think I was right to kill the rascal for taking my property!" Fry shouted, aiming the gun steadily at the two men. He was beginning to sweat from the intensity of the situation. "Why, then, are we fighting this war? Aren't we killing Yankees, in battle, to keep our property, our slave property, our farm property, our darn crop property. Answer me, you idiots!"

"I'll try to understand your point if you put the musket down and if you settle down," Coffey said. Fry slowly lowered the musket and waited for an answer.

"I think I can understand what you did was out of self-defense for your property," said Coffey. "But why in God's name did you have to punch Curtis in the face like you did? We are all fighting for the same country and in the same regiment. Tell me why you did this to a fellow soldier, Fry?"

"Darn it, Coffey, you know we all fight among ourselves on occasion around here. We're not a bunch of schoolgirls, are we?

"Can you put the musket down?" Curtis asked.

"I'll put it down, don't worry. It's just that sometimes I get full of rage. These darn Yankees have really put anger into my heart. Who do they think they are invading our homeland? Our whole lives have been turned upside-down and our souls torn from our insides. Often I can't control my anger. It seems like I have to hit something to get the darn anger out of me. Anyway, you privates get on my nerves with your stupid questions, comments and your fears. Always your selfish fears. Don't you think I have fears too? Don't you think Burgwyn and Elington have fears as we engage in battles? Elington is really going to have me to fear when he gets back here."

"Yes, I understand you and our officers have fears," Coffey replied. "I guess we will all have some extent of fear until the war is over and done with. Fear, though, doesn't give you the right to use violence against us. We can talk more about it tomorrow after you calm down and stop aiming that musket at us like we were Yankees." Blood still smeared Curtis's face.

"You know, Fry, I think you might have to be brought up on charges for these actions you have taken tonight. You know everybody gets mad, but they don't hit people; well, you know."

Shut-up Coffey. It's late and I'm tired from all the darn work we've been doing around here. Come over to the medical tent, Curtis. It's over near the ambulance wagons, where those sawbones work. Let's get you cleaned up for the night, private."

"All right, corporal; thank you."

The men slept under a clear sky. Flames from the army campfires gently crackled in the night air. Men couldn't sleep. Thoughts and memories of home pried into their minds, especially at night. Some sat on logs or on the ground outside of their tents to write letters to families. Sons wrote to their parents. Fathers wrote to their young children, who couldn't understand why their daddy was away from home for so long. Husbands wrote to their new wives, telling them the war would be over soon and the promises they had made to each other would come to pass.

Corporal Fry wrote a letter to his wife, Margaret, telling her of the loneliness he felt during his stay at Drewry's Bluff and Camp French. He asked her in the letter how his three young children were doing without him. He wondered as he wrote the letter what his two daughters were doing, how they were managing without a father around to love and protect them. Then he thought of his youngest, a son named William, who had all the energy a boy could have; energy Lewis missed. His service to the cause and his sacrifice for his country had to come first at this time in his life.

"How much more time will be wasted away from my family?" he quietly asked himself. Fry retired for the night and dreamt of his precious loved ones back in North Carolina, living among the great mountains and sceneries of peace.

The next morning Fry, Coffey and Curtis continued to talk about the situation from the previous night in camp.

"So, men, are you going to re-enlist to fight and destroy those Yankees?" Fry asked. He stared particularly at Coffey and Curtis, watching the expressions on their faces.

"Remember, boys, when you finally decide, think of all the poor boys from North Carolina who have given their darn lives for the Confederacy up until now. All of the boys who have allowed us to continue this fight against the wretched enemy up North. Our cause is a cause to fight and die for, and if any of you don't think what I'm saying makes sense, then you don't deserve to be part of this regiment any longer! I want to kill Yankees! How about you, boys?"

"Let 'em make up their own minds, Fry," Colonel Burgwyn said. "I think in the end they will make the right decisions according to their own consciences."

*****

The men prepared to put in another day of hard labor near Camp French, in order to further the fortifications around Petersburg. Rumors of Union Army movements were starting to trickle in from the northern part of Virginia. The Union Army of the Potomac, under command of its new leader, General Ambrose Burnside, was beginning to target the area at Fredericksburg, Virginia. Burnside envisioned the city being captured easily and the road to Richmond wide open to his army. The capital attacked; the Confederate cause silenced for good.

Along the James River, Union gunboats periodically came up river toward Petersburg to harass camps and supply lines leading to Richmond. With their thirty-pound Parrott rifle guns, their twenty-pound Dahlgren guns, twenty-four-pound howitzers, and two heavy twelve-pound smooth bores, the Union gunboat crews shattered the silence around the James River. Lobbing shells at their targets, they tried desperately to turn the tide of the war through strangling off supplies coming in from other Confederate states and into eastern Virginia. Confederate Naval forces were unable to counter the mobilized blockade that Union Commanders stretched from Virginia to the Gulf Coast. Except for raiders like the *CSS Alabama* and the ironclad *CSS Merrimac*, the Confederate sea forces were weak and few.

F Company began to load the wagons with dirt, sandbags, logs and light stones for the day's work. More breastworks were needed in the area of City Point along the James River northeast of Petersburg. It was a cool November day in Virginia. The ninety-six men of F Company, minus Harrison and Alfred, were ordered to march their supplies to City Point and proceed to build the entrenchments necessary to defend the track connections of the Petersburg and City Point railroads. This railroad was vital for bringing in medical supplies and food arriving by ships on the James and Appomattox Rivers. Medical supplies, food and ammunitions were the things needed to sustain the defenses at Petersburg. The Yankee gunboats caused great interruptions of deliveries along the route. The accessibility to the James River, and their naval commanders' diligence for destroying the Petersburg defenses, combined into a dangerous aggregation of power.

The men continued to load the wagons and complain about their recent hardships, when all of a sudden a deep roar could be heard coming from the northeast. Continuous and ominous, the shelling belted forth without much hesitation. Scouts reported back to General Pettigrew, the brigade commander, of two lone Union gunboats approaching the Jordan's Point and City Point fortifications, about seven miles from the brigade's present position at Camp French.

"We have artillery at those locations, but not enough guns to counter the gunboats," said General Pettigrew to some of his brigade commanders. He was a scholar and always acted as one; refined and precise in his orders. "We have to try and harass the enemy as much as we can by getting at the crew of those ships. Colonel Burgwyn, get Major Jones to take B and F Companies to City Point, reinforce the artillery there and wait for those gunboats to make it from Jordan's Point. When they make their approach I want heavy and continuous fire on those ships from both cannon and rifled musket until they turn around and sail out of that part of the James. We need that supply depot and you have to tell Jones this mission is of the utmost in importance for the survival of defensive position here at Camp French. He must make every effort possible to change the direction of the ships."

"Yes, sir; I'm right on it, sir!

B and F Companies were relieved of their work duties for the day and called to attention by their officers. Major Jones briefed them on the orders from General Pettigrew. The two companies began a quick seven-mile march to City Point. The roads were dry and dusty. They marched in columns and saw a train pass by heading toward Camp French from City Point. When Fry saw the train go by, he perceived the importance of the mission before him. The trains meant life for the Confederate Army. The trains meant life for the whole Confederate cause. The Yankees couldn't stop the trains now. Supplies were always needed in Petersburg and Corporal Fry knew how close Petersburg was to Richmond. Fry thought of how strongly he wanted to win the conflict against the Yankees and now he could taste victory. Even if it was a small victory, he could relish the thought of carrying out his part in the defeat of a Union force. Freedom and a sense of honor protected and encouraged Fry. He continued the march toward City Point.

The sounds of the shells were getting heavier. The two companies saw the trails of smoke and fire from the heavy guns. They were about a mile from their destination. Captain Nathaniel Rankin kept F Company marching in precise time, ordering the double-quick step for a half a mile. The Confederate artillery, now seen by the companies, was firing back at the gunboats. A hiss penetrated the air from the direction of the river. Lewis Fry saw three cannon smashed to pieces. Limbers, spokes and shrapnel flew in the air; giant splinters were created from the wreckage. The fire decimated the artillery crews. The hot metal from the gunboats was relentless and deadly. The Dahlgren and Parrott guns smashed away at their targets; shells screeching, fizzing and whizzing. To Fry, it seemed like the familiar, continuous fire of three shots in a row from the boats, just like it had been on Malvern Hill four months before.

Boom ... boom ... boom...

Boom ... boom ... boom...

The hissing and heat-drenched landscape was magnified by the scenery of the artillery destruction right in front of the two companies from North Carolina. An artillery officer showed B and F Company where to take cover on the high bluff overlooking the river. Construction on trenched breastworks had been started, facing the river, and the high elevation gave the companies' a good position. Major Jones ordered all company officers to position their men in the trenches and to be ready for a massed fire on the ships.

"Steady men!" Major Jones ordered. "Hold your fire until we can see those guns more clearly and then we can inflict damage. We need to have them in closer range, boys."

Loud shrieks and peals of fire deafened the situation in the trenches. For moments at a time, the men could not hear orders from their officers. The roar and continuous bombilations shattered the sky with gray and black smoke. Fry now tried to shout above the noise to help relay orders to the men.

"Get ready to fire!" Fry ordered.

"Take good aim," Major Jones shouted into the stentorian atmosphere enveloping the companies.

"Look, men!" Fry shouted. "I think one of our cannon has made a hit on the boat to the left. I can see fire! It's fire, men!"

When Fry shouted those words, about half of F Company started to fire on the gunboats. A fire had started on one of the guns on deck. The crackle and snapping of the muskets drew attention from the men of B Company. Most of the soldiers in the company began to take aim at the damaged boat. Officers in both companies let the men continue to fire. There was no sense in halting the volleys now that one of the boat's crew was fighting the fire caused by the North Carolinian artillery hit.

"Keep firing boys!" Major Jones shouted. "Aim at the crew! Fire! Fire! Fire!

"Your shooting will help the artillery boys over there!" Fry shouted.

A heavy shell blasted from the gunboat still in good condition. A rumble and then a shriek was heard all the way down the line where the companies tried desperately to take cover. The shell crashed into the center of the line where the two companies met in the entrenchment. Screams and yells were heard. Men in the position were literally shred to pieces by the hot iron passing through them like a knife slicing the air. One private had one of his arms completely ripped from his body; blood splattering all over the other dead and living men around him. Smoke filled the center of the line. The smell of burning flesh sickened other soldiers who were trapped in the firestorm. Officers ordered their men to try and comfort the wounded. All officers told the men to stay in the trenches. Coming out of the trenches would mean certain death.

Boom ... boom ... boom...

Boom ... boom ... boom...

The murderous firing continued from the boats. It seemed like the volleys from the infantry of the two companies did absolutely nothing to weaken the durability and deadly fire from the gunboats.

"Do you think those boats have any ironclad armor?" asked Fry from the right side of the trench line to Major Jones. "If they're ironclad we better darned get out of this position before we get ripped to pieces like those poor fellows in the center." His pipe coiled smoke. He squinted in the face of the bright sunshine, sweating from his brow. The fight continued.

"They're not ironclad, Fry! We had scout reports earlier, confirming the boats are a couple of older wooden gunboats. Continue to have your men on the right fire!"

"Yes, sir, major!"

Volleys endured for another hour against the gunboats. The wounded continued to suffer the pain and shock of their injuries and torments, as if hell had opened up its evil and loathsome gates to swallow the unsuspecting soldiers where they lay. Fatigue manifested itself among the ranks, but the men kept up a good fire. One of the boats started to turn around and, as it did, it came closer to the position of the North Carolinians.

"Fire! Fire! Fire! Poor it on, boys," officers shouted all along the line.

"Send them to hell, those darn Yankees," shouted Fry. "We can give it to them now, men! Reload and fire at will!"

The damaged Union gunboat now flashed into a ball of flame and smoke, explosions setting new blazes. The two companies, along with the remaining artillery pieces, took a heavy toll on the crippled boat. The shelling from the ships finally subsided. The silence brought on by the ceasing of the guns brought on a temporary deafness for Fry and the others in the trenches. It seemed to Fry as if the normal sounds around the river were silenced. The gentle flowing of the waters in the James River, the birds flying north of the river, the rustling of the fall breeze through the trees on the banks were sounds no longer heard.

B and F Companies lumbered with fatigue in their entrenched defenses. Staring with motionless dejection, the private soldiers found themselves in an endless, unreal and belligerent existence, where war now turned to murder at its cruelest. Shock began to overwhelm the wounded and the spared inside the trench. Men panicked, cried and shook with fear. The undamaged Yankee gunboat blasted off one more round from each of its artillery pieces. Again, the repercussions, shrieks and the fury of the howitzers, Dahlgrens, and Parrott guns broke the solitude of the James River, sending soldiers down for cover along the banks.

Then, silence.

Silence upon the whole bank of the river itself.

A manifestation of quietness settled along the fortified position. The day was fading. The men couldn't believe it was already five o'clock in the afternoon. Unexpectedly, the melancholy in the trenches faded.

"I think we got them running or sailing away; well, whatever you want to call it," Fry shouted to the soldiers on the right portion of the line.

"You got it right, corporal!" replied Major Jones, traversing the line for casualty reports.

"Major! We have to get some more help for these wounded and torn-up boys," Fry said. "And I mean immediate help, or many are going to die in the trench!"

"I've sent couriers back to Camp French for more medical supplies; more ambulances are on the way. Keep moving the severely wounded out of the trench and get your men to help you along with Lieutenant Holloway and Captain Rankin."

"We'll keep it moving, sir," Fry answered. "Get some water up here now; send it to the middle part of the line where those two shells hit!"

Fry walked from his position on the right and saw firsthand the atrocities evident in the center of the position. Limbs were strewn, muskets mangled, cartridge boxes burnt and black soot blemished the earthworks. Fry hung his head in despair. *There were many young men who sacrificed their lives for the cause today,* he thought. *The fighting has to progress for us to get our independence from those Yankee pirates, who loot and destroy our sovereign states and our lives.* Fry continued to look into the position and he continued to help the wounded. Privates Coffey and Curtis survived the bombardment and were helping Fry.

"Anyone who thinks secession was a mistake is a darn, fool idiot who should be shot himself!" Fry shouted, looking at the damage and the wounded North Carolinians. "When is justice going to come for these poor souls who die every day in this rancid conflict! I hope General Lee is planning another invasion of the Yankee North, for we can get our justice; yes, justice upon the great enemy who has reduced our capabilities for survival in our own lands. On that day there will be much revelry."

A somber and hushed chant began to rise from the men in B and F Companies. They heard and agreed with Fry and his preaching tone against the Yankees.

It was nine o'clock in the evening when the men made it back to Camp French and rejoined the rest of the regiment. Exhausted beyond comprehension, the men of the two fighting companies ate rations for dinner, washed-up and retired for the night.

The deafening sounds of the day kept many men from sleeping soundly. Fry was one of them. He got up at about 3:30 in the morning, walked outside his tent quarters and lit his corncob pipe, which contained Southern tobacco; tobacco that came from North Carolina in a shipment the day before the horrible defense of City Point. Fry lightly whistled a tune in the early morning, contemplating the regiment's next battle. *Would more immediate fighting stand before me and the 26th North Carolina? Would the regiment continue in the mundane labor at Camp French? When would Harrison and Alfred come back to the regiment? Could the Confederates sustain the war effort and make a successful invasion of the North in the face of massive industrial might?*

Corporal Lewis Fry thought on all of these concerns and apprehensions. He puffed the sweet Southern tobacco in his pipe and slowly started to drift into sleep. His dark brown, almost blackish-colored eyes gazed into nothingness. He got up and made it to his tent before falling fast asleep.

Another day of soldiering left its mark on Lewis Fry.

— Chapter 6 —
Back to Reality

Late November 1862

Harrison recalled his conversation with Peyton Caldwell. Would he see Peyton back home again in peaceful Caldwell County? Would Peyton see Danny again and tell Danny of his conversation with Harrison? When will the war end?

It was November 28, 1862, and it was time for Harrison to return to duty for the Confederate Army. It was time to rejoin the 26th North Carolina Infantry.

With its new brigade assignment, under command of General Johnston Pettigrew; its new regimental leader, Colonel Henry Burgwyn, the youngest colonel in the Confederate Army; and its large muster roll of men, the 26th North Carolina was one of the largest regiments in service. It numbered over 1,000 recruits and officers. The 26th continued to function while Harrison Elington and Alfred Abshire were on furlough; a furlough many soldiers could not get. The new regulations severely limited soldiers' requests for time off, and the regulations were tightly enforced by the Confederate command.

As of fall 1862, one out of every twenty-five soldiers in a company could go home for leave at any given time. The only catch in the system was if a company possessed men who had deserted; no one was able to receive permission for furlough then. Desertions increased after Malvern Hill, Second Manassas and Sharpsburg because of numerous skirmishes and on account of the hard labor of building entrenchments at Camp French and Drewry's Bluff. Colonel Burgwyn posted a reward in the North Carolina newspapers for information leading to the capture of deserters, reporting sixty-two missing from the ranks.

Lieutenant Elington received word from Colonel Burgwyn that the regiment was leaving Camp French, temporarily, to dispatch to eastern North Carolina in order to assist the 17th and 59th North Carolina Regiments in raids against Union forces on garrisons at Plymouth and Washington. Elington was to take the Weldon and Petersburg Railroads to attach to the regiment at Camp French, where the 26th would be returning from Goldsboro to continue their work on building entrenchments.

Elington received his orders two weeks prior to the 28th of November, along with orders for Private Abshire. Abigail was saddened and apathetic to the development. The time she and Harrison spent together was precious, challenging and solemn. The bitter feelings against the Confederate cause rose again in the heart of Abigail, who hated the idea of all of her menfolk being harnessed in an armed conflict leading nowhere for the South. At the same time, though, Abby felt part of herself being torn away again. These were the same feelings she felt when Harrison left in the summer of 1861. Abigail knew she needed to do something to stop the bloodshed. But what could she do? How could she do it? Abigail pondered these questions and emotions since the long ago summer of 1861.

Harrison, a couple of days before he was required to leave for the eastern part of his state, reflected on what he was now going to face when he arrived back with the 26th. *How would the men react to my furlough?* he wondered. *Is Lewis going to give me a hard time about having furlough, when many men in the numerous companies were not permitted to leave over the new regulations? Will I be made to labor for long hours and days? Colonel Burgwyn stated the regiment was mostly involved in digging at Camp French. Can I fight again? Can I lead, again, as I did at Malvern Hill? I hope the men accept Alfred and myself back into the regiment. Is an invasion in the works? General Lee gambled many times against the more numerous Yankee Army of the Potomac. Sharpsburg, along Antietam Creek, stopped his ambitions for a while, but I know he wants a victory in the North, pressuring Union forces to surrender. He wants to send a clear message to Halleck and Lincoln in Washington to recognize Confederate independence and sovereignty.*

What the devil am I going to tell Abby if the 26th joins a possible invasion to Pennsylvania? I have a strong, pernicious feeling Pennsylvania is going to be the next target. Its powerful position, geographically and politically, will enhance any victory there. The Peace Democrats have long been a silent ally for us. I read about their political and military aims in the newspapers. Lee can use the cover of the Blue Ridge Mountains and the Shenandoah Valley to move his armies north like he tried to do before Sharpsburg. Harrison felt himself debilitated from all of the thoughts crisscrossing his mind.

Sharpsburg was an awful struggle of wills, but at the same time, a great spectacle by the Union forces in their lack of command, Harrison thought again, sitting in his oak chair on the porch. *If General Burnside proves to be just as incapable as McClellan was, then I fear many more Southern lives will be wasted over Union incompetence and unaccountability. Through their incompetence, these Yankee generals have forced General Lee to have to stand and fight against larger forces being thrown at him, and these forces only eat away at our Confederate regiments with their shear numbers. Their leaders often have nothing to do with their performance on the battlefield. The number of soldiers makes the difference against us. In another year we are not going to be able to succeed against their armies. We will not be able to find or replace manpower resources.*

Burnside and his bridge. Um ... why didn't he just ford the creek to cross? Instead, he wasted hundreds of Union men to establish lines closer to Sharpsburg, only to be driven back by good old General Ambrose Hill. What a shame! I wonder what Burnside is going to try if he establishes a position near Fredericksburg? I think he is headed there now.

"Well, Abby, it's time for me to get back to the regiment," Harrison said. "Alfred is going back with me, too."

"I can't believe it is time for you to go back. It seems like you just arrived on the train from Virginia not too long ago, when your leg was wounded."

"Can you take us to the train station at Hickory Tavern, Abby?"

"Who else is going to take you and Alfred if I don't?"

"Thanks, Abby."

Harrison took Abby in his arms and held her close. He looked her straight in the eyes with his strong gaze and told her things would be fine. He was back in uniform and looked handsome as ever to Abigail.

"Abby, if there is going to be an invasion of the North, I will let you know as soon as possible. I don't know, to tell you the truth, how I will react to the reality of an invasion; especially if it is directed by General Lee toward Pennsylvania."

"Harrison, don't worry about it now. You need to get back to the routine of the army before you can make any invasion. Remember Lewis Fry is probably going to give you and Alfred a challenge for being back here in Caldwell County on furlough."

"Is Boy Alfred coming back from town soon?" Abigail asked.

"Yes, he should be back within the hour. He said he wanted to check to see if his parents settled in. They came back from their stay in Raleigh last week. It was their third trip to the capital for assistance. They were able to get some promises from the state for aid with the struggling gristmill. He also told me he wanted to stock-up on socks for when we got back to camp. You know, Abby, how socks and shoes are a luxury in the Confederate Army. We are always in short supply!"

"I hope you and your men are not in short supply of leadership and direction when you get back to the 26th. Oh, Harrison, you have to take care of yourself! I can't think of life without you, even if you are a rebel."

"Am I really a rebel at heart, Abby? All I wanted out of life was you and a quiet life in good old North Carolina. I wasn't born to be a so-called rebel. It is a name I am not fond of in this conflict."

"Just be careful my dear and think of me and write to me often, for then I can feel close to you, even though you may be far away."

"I will keep those promises, Abby. We better head to the station soon."

"Lieutenant? Mrs. Elington? Are you ready to go," shouted Alfred coming down the road near the house. He had already put his cleaned uniform on before going into town. His blonde hair and brown eyes blended well with the gray tones of his uniform. Hurriedly, he drank down a real cup of hot coffee made from real coffee beans. This was a luxury soon to come to an end.

"The carriage is ready. Let's go, Alfred," Harrison answered.

The view of the mountains in the west started to fade from Harrison's sight. They headed southeast to Hickory Tavern and the train station. The memories of the last couple of months began to impress the mind of Harrison to the point where he harbored melancholy feelings riding in the carriage to the station. Alfred was in the same mood. Soldiers, who got a taste of being home once again, now had to relinquish their emotions and freedoms of home to the command of the Confederate Army out in the fields of battle.

The morning sun shone brightly with a chilly breeze coming from the west. The smell of the great pine trees from the mountains still lingered in the morning air. The house and the barn faded in the distance. The memories of family were put on hold. Uncertainty filled the minds and souls of Abigail, Harrison and Alfred.

The carriage continued uninterrupted down the winding roads. Silence overcame the riders. The strong shire, Bandit, steadily pulled the passengers toward their destination, hooves clapping the ground. The day seemed to turn to gloom when the sounds of the steam engine echoed against the ridges of the hills and mountains. Harrison broke the silence by saying to Abigail that he loved her above everything on the earth, no matter what the outcome of the war entailed. He continued:

"Our love transcends the division of civil war, proving that human devotion and human character surpass all of the political, economic and nationalistic concerns contained in institutions forged in an imperfect world."

Abigail's tears rolled down her face. Separation, this time, seemed quite uncertain and she knew it no matter how Harrison tried to comfort her.

*****

Lieutenant Elington and Private Abshire were transported from the Weldon and Petersburg Railroad line, by ambulance wagon, to Camp French in Virginia on December 1, 1862. The 26th North Carolina was bivouacked, for it was dusk, and the men put in another grueling day digging and fortifying entrenchments for a possible Union attack, which might come from the south or the east.

Colonel Henry Burgwyn greeted Elington and Abshire. He told them to come over to his headquarters after they were settled. He would brief them on the 26th North Carolina's duties and placements. He also wanted Elington to know what action the regiment had been involved in during his furlough.

Alfred went to his tent quarters and he found himself back with old friends he was assigned with before Malvern Hill and before his injury to his arm. Alfred was greeted by some of his comrades, then was given a tent assignment and rations for the next couple of days. Men were anxious about Abshire being back, just to ask him how things were going at home. Many of the fellows in F Company were from Caldwell County. They were curious about their families and homes. The restrictive furlough regulations of the Confederate Army really made things rough for the younger men of the regiment. They couldn't get home without literally deserting the regiment, as many had done during the previous months.

F Company bombarded Abshire with questions and information about home. Abshire gave his old mates the socks he stocked up on at Granite Falls. The men were overjoyed to have new socks. The commodity had become scarce in the months after Sharpsburg.

Harrison went to his quarters with Captain Rankin and Second Lieutenant Holloway.

"Hey, it's Elington!" Captain Rankin said. "How are you? It's really good to have you back in the regiment."

"I'm doing fine, captain, just fine."

"How's Abshire?"

"He's recovered, sir. I think both of us are feeling awkward about rejoining the regiment. It seems we have been detached from what's been going on in the war since Malvern Hill."

"I bet it was great to be back home, Elington," said Lieutenant Holloway. "We've had it rough here at Camp French. Loading, carrying and digging has been about it. Except for action in skirmishes, we've been mostly involved in fortifying this position with breastworks and entrenchments."

"Tough work being a laborer, Elington. Are you ready for this?" Captain Rankin asked.

"Yeah, I'm ready to get back into the routine. We have to get on with this war and strike a victory against the Yankees. What have they been up to lately, captain?"

"Colonel Burgwyn will brief you in about half an hour. Why don't you get something to eat while you're waiting."

"Good idea, captain!"

Camp French had been fashioned into a temporary home for most of the regulars in the 26th North Carolina. It now seemed as if winter quarters were going to be constructed at the camp. The camp offered the regiment a variety of conditions. The fall was cool and pleasant; however, the men didn't appreciate the constant labor that persisted through those months. The smells were familiar: latrines permeated the atmosphere on certain wind-driven days; the consistent odor of the fresh earth from the continual digging stifled the air; and the stench from the filthy soldiers penetrated the tents and quarters at Camp French.

After a good-sized meal, Harrison made his way to Colonel Burgwyn's log house headquarters in camp. He entered the colonel's residence and noticed his staff working over maps and other papers that appeared, at the time, important to the future of the whole Confederate Army. The colonel always kept a neat and organized appearance and this seemed to carry over from Lieutenant Colonel Burgwyn to Colonel Burgwyn. His education was impeccable and complete at the University of North Carolina. His work habits and meticulous attention to detail made Burgwyn a natural officer, who would undoubtedly rise through the ranks in the Confederate Army. Although the youngest officer in the Confederacy, Burgwyn accomplished discipline, drill and firearms accuracy with the 26th North Carolina since succeeding to colonel upon the resignation of Zebulon Vance. All of these qualities were evident on any average day in the regiment. Harrison observed the activity before him and waited for the colonel to brief him on the duties of the regiment.

"Sit down, Lieutenant Elington," Burgwyn said. "How is your wound?"

"It has healed fine, sir."

"Did you know you were mentioned in dispatches and reports sent to General Lee and General Longstreet after the Peninsula Campaign and Malvern Hill?

"No, I didn't know that, sir."

"I would also like to commend your leadership and bravery in action, lieutenant. That hill was a horrible display of war and destruction upon our forces.

"Well, here is the situation at Camp French, lieutenant. We are to build winter quarters here and continue to fortify this vital defensive position. The men have been involved in hard labor chores for a couple of months, except for short trips away from the camp to harass Union forces in eastern North Carolina. One major fight at City Point required us to protect the railroad junction there. Companies B and F had casualties when they got into a fight with a couple of gunboats that were threatening the railroad lines at the confluence of the James and Appomattox Rivers, targeting City Point. The boys under Major Jones took cover in a fortified trench along the James River portion of the defensive works at City Point. One of the gunboats was set afire by the artillery and musket fire, but it got away back down the river. Your company really took a heavy and direct hit in the trench. We lost eighteen men altogether, dead and wounded in the skirmish. Six of your men died, Harrison. It wasn't a pleasant site for any of us. You will be glad to hear Corporal Fry performed with the utmost of proficiency and leadership on the right side of the line, helping Major Jones in the defense. Since then it has been work as usual for the boys, lieutenant."

Elington, sat looking at the colonel, listening to him, but his feelings were insecure since leaving Caldwell County. He took out some tobacco and placed it in his mouth. Tobacco brought him a sense of security when a situation became tense. Before continuing his conversation with the colonel, Harrison chewed down on the wad in his mouth and rested his jaw.

"It seems like I have missed a lot, sir. Do you think I will fit back into the regiment? And do you think the men are going to respond to my leadership again?"

"You will be fine here, lieutenant. I am sure the boys in F Company will welcome you, especially Lewis Fry; you know the Possum!"

"Yes, sir, I know. Well …"

"By the way, Harrison, the six men who died have been replaced. You have new men to train and to get used to. They are from Catawba County."

Harrison left Colonel Burgwyn's headquarters, headed for F Company's camp to reacquaint himself with soldiers of his command. He spat tobacco juice onto the ground after leaving the headquarters. He walked steadily toward the campsite and noticed Lewis Fry leaning against a tree, whistling as usual, and smoking his corncob pipe. Harrison stopped walking, just stared at the corporal. He thought about what prospects awaited him when it came to Fry.

Fry sarcastically shouted at Elington, "Well, if it isn't a darn lieutenant; a lieutenant from North Carolina; a lieutenant from furlough; a possible Union-sympathizing lieutenant who got wounded and went home!"

"A Union sympathizer! That's what you call an officer in the 26th North Carolina, wounded for his country and almost killed for his country. That's what you have to say to me after four months, Fry? Give me an answer, Fry!" Elington chucked all of the tobacco from his mouth, looking sternly at Fry.

"Yeah! A Union, Yankee sympathizer, who has rested his darn body for four months while we have broken our bodies working breastworks, abatis and entrenchments all around here. We almost had our heads blown off by gunboats!"

"Well, corporal, what did you expect me to do with the wound I received at Malvern Hill?"

"What did you expect me to do with my darn bloody amputated finger? Yeah, look at it, sir. Those sawbones got to me and now I have a little stump on my hand to look at for the rest of my days! I stayed in camp. I recovered in these filthy bivouacs we've been living in for the last four months. I have endured pain by myself and without family. I have worked building endless entrenchments at this stinking camp for an attack that will not come as long as the Union continues appointing incompetent generals. We haven't had one chance to join with Lee's Army and to chase those cursed Yankees all over Virginia. Is that a good enough response to your question, lieutenant, sir!"

"I am sorry you persevered through your ordeal alone, Fry. But you know as well as I that the high command restricted furloughs. The straggling problems and the conscription crisis facing Richmond and President Davis has overwhelmed our ranks. I was lucky to get home. It's the way it goes sometimes, Lewis, and I don't think I owe you an apology or an explanation for something beyond my immediate control."

"Shut-up, lieutenant!"

"What, Fry?"

"I said shut-up!"

"That's not the way to talk to an officer and you know it, corporal!"

"Yeah, I know, but I'm still very angry at almost getting killed while you and Abshire went home to the comforts of your families and houses and food, right lieutenant!"

"I said it was out of my control, corporal! Now you shut-up and carry on with what you were doing while I go and inspect things around here and get reacquainted with the fellows in the 26th."

"Yes, sir, Union man!"

Harrison knew from the beginning he was going to have to set Fry straight to have adequate control and responsibility again in F Company. He grabbed Fry by the arm and squeezed the fingers around where his amputation occurred. He squeezed until Fry was ready to burst in pain and said, "I will rip your other fingers off, corporal, if you keep hounding me about my furlough. I was wounded. Get it through that thick head of yours and get it through by tomorrow. Do you hear me, Fry? I said, do you hear me?

"Yes, I do, lieutenant."

"Now go back to what you were doing and if you want to address me, then you better address me properly or I will bring you up on charges of insubordination. You know I really don't want to do that. I understand the hardships you and the other men have faced these past four months. I know Alfred and I will undoubtedly face the same hardships in the near future. This war doesn't have an end in sight and sufferings will undoubtedly continue. Do you understand?"

"Yes, lieutenant, sir."

Fry seemed to get the message from Harrison for the time being and carried on mumbling to himself about the return of the lieutenant and the others who had gotten furloughs.

Harrison went to see the other privates and corporals in the ranks of F Company. Many were extremely glad to see the lieutenant and congratulated him on his return. The men talked and reminisced about home and family. There were many questions and comments about Caldwell County and if Harrison had seen family members and such. One private inquired about his ninety-year-old grandmother, who Harrison knew for most of his life back home. He said she was still cheering the boys from North Carolina on and she made twenty pairs of new socks for the boys in the regiment, along with whipping up jams for the men.

"You'll be surprised, boys, tomorrow at breakfast when I can give old Grandma Porter's items out," Harrison said joyfully to the men. Others yelled out about new recruits.

"Did you bring any new men with you, lieutenant? You know; some of those boys who just turned of age for enlistment."

"No, private."

"We sure could use bodies in our ranks! We've had a problem with skulkers and stragglers in the last few months around here. Did you hear the number was running at sixty-two men from our regiment! Gone sir! That's a bloody disgrace for all us boys from Carolina! We don't want to be ashamed of our regiment, now do we, sir?"

"You have absolutely nothing to be ashamed about, private! Now that we have Colonel Henry Burgwyn commanding the 26th, we can stand proud and ready for action. I know he will lead us to honorable things in this regiment, boys."

Harrison went on to say, "I heard on the way back that Governor Vance, our former colonel, has issued a proclamation. It states any stragglers who are from North Carolina will be taken back into their units if they return immediately to active duty in the ranks. I think this is a splendid idea for our men."

"I'll kill them if they come back to my company," said Lewis Fry, listening in on the conversation. He subtly made his way over to the area where Harrison was talking to the enlisted men. "Those cowards don't deserve to get a another chance in this here regiment. This unit has worked and agonized too long to become what it is."

"Fry, you will not kill anyone in my regiment," Harrison answered.

"Oh, now it's your regiment! After going back to the county for rest and relaxation, you suddenly come back owner of a regiment. Ain't that just grand news, lieutenant! I hope you are a good owner and master like the masters down here in the old South who own slaves."

"Fry, I don't know what has gotten into you, or what is eating away at your soul, but you better dismiss yourself right now, or else I am going to take disciplinary action."

"Disciplinary action! Well, now, isn't that just some darn, grand officer's talk, huh, 'masser.'"

Colonel Burgwyn came past the tent area where the confrontation was going on and heard Fry addressing Harrison in his sarcastic tone.

"Corporal Fry! Who are you speaking to?" Burgwyn shouted. "Answer me now, corporal!"

"I was speaking to Lieutenant Elington, sir!"

"You will not speak to a superior officer in the regiment in the tone I overheard a few minutes ago! Do you hear what I am saying, corporal!"

"Yes, sir! It will not happen again, sir! I didn't mean to sound the way I did to the lieutenant, sir!" The young privates in the company looked on with quite an interest.

"Tomorrow, corporal, you will be on latrine duty after lunch," Burgwyn ordered. Take three men from your platoon, and I want those latrines buried and new ones dug out so that inexplicable smell leaves our camp. That's an order, Fry. And if this happens again you will be demoted back to private."

The men cheered when the colonel disciplined Fry.

"He's had that coming since after Malvern Hill," one private shouted.

Fry looked dejected and shocked at the consequences dealt out by Colonel Burgwyn. *I thought he would make a good colonel*, Fry thought, walking away from the tent area and the conversing men. *Elington is going to pay for this*.

The evening shades began to envelop Camp French. The first day back for Elington was an eventful spectacle. Elington went back to his quarters, now readied for him. Officers usually lived in wood-framed residences; especially, when assigned to a permanent duty like Camp French. He shared a residence with Lieutenant Holloway and Captain Rankin from F Company. In this atmosphere, officers could converse freely and openly with each other about the coming strategies of the war and about problems in the companies. Elington's quarters was simple: a chimney and stove were located between his and Holloway's rooms, a desk for writing and receiving orders centered the room, an extra table for viewing maps stood in the corner, and a bed was neatly made on the far wall.

Harrison contemplated his future. He felt very gracious to be back in the service of his country, but the old familiar questions began to ring in his mind about his true allegiance. Time would soon reveal what he needed to do if he was to clear his mind of the internal conflicts surrounding him. Reality hit him hard on his first day back.

He checked in on Alfred to see how he fared on his return; back to the reality of camp life, the reality of war, and the reality of work.

— Chapter 7 —
Winter Quarters and
News of Fredericksburg

December-February 1862-63

December winds chilled the atmosphere in Virginia, in the mountains of North Carolina, and in the hearts of the soldiers of the Union and the Confederacy. Winter quarters were established for the second time in the war. Fighting usually came to a halt for the sake of the soldiers in the field, who needed to survive the often-brutal elements of snow, cold rains and cutting winds.

Winter, for some military personnel, was a time for family visits and planning for the spring campaigns. Harrison, Lewis and Alfred established their respective quarters at Camp French. They continued for six weeks to work on the fortifications at and around Petersburg. The men of the 26th also moved to Drewry's Bluff and City Point to help out on more defenses for the rail lines and river docks.

Union forces were also beginning work on winter quarters in parts of Virginia; however, the new general in charge of Union forces, Ambrose Burnside, had other plans on his mind besides comfortable quarters. Burnside had recently taken over for the "slow" General George McClellan and he was feeling the pressure from the Lincoln Administration for action against General Lee in Virginia. Richmond needed to be threatened in order to gain public support for the war effort in the eastern theater. The Union Army wasn't showing what it was made out of, considering all of its training, supplies and number of men.

Beginning around November 19th, General Burnside began to mass his corps in front of the town of Fredericksburg, near the Rappahannock River. The 83rd Pennsylvania made its camp at Falmouth, Virginia, located about two miles northwest of Fredericksburg. Private Jesse Elington was with the 83rd Pennsylvania at Falmouth. He was now part of the 5th Union Corps, under Brigadier General Daniel Butterfield, and he was attached to the First Division commanded by Brigadier General Charles Griffin. The First Division was made up of three brigades. Jesse was part of the Third Brigade commanded by Colonel T.B.W. Stockton.

Jesse Elington figured, at the beginning of the war, he would sooner or later be facing either his father, his brother Danny, or his friends on some battlefield. This prospect haunted Jesse to no end. The last thing he wanted to do was to have a hand in wounding or killing his family or friends in war. Jesse still maintained his uncompromising support of the Union cause, but he did not want to face kin under the present circumstances of violence through battle.

If God can only spare me this agony and uncertainty on these battlefields, Jesse prayed one evening at camp in Falmouth. *Only through Your mercy and strength, Lord, can these horrible devastations of war be controlled or destroyed.*

Jesse was born in 1843, seventeen years after his two favorite founding fathers had died. John Adams and Thomas Jefferson, the towering intellectual emblems of the American Revolution, ironically breathed their last exactly fifty years after the Declaration of Independence was issued and read before a rebellious group of colonists who wanted independence from Britain. Now a boy of nineteen from North Carolina was fighting to keep the experiment in democracy alive at all costs. Jesse knew the foundations of the United States government were bathed in the essence of a miracle. *How could a group of colonists defeat, both in ideology and in battle, the greatest power on the face of the earth?* Jesse thought the United States was destined to be a great power itself one day. How could he let a few states ruin the future greatness of his country? How could he allow or live with the proposition that secession destroyed a people and a nation? His mind never ceased to ponder these ideas. He continued to fight, march and build against the Confederate States of America and he wasn't going to stop until their destruction was complete and the Union secure. But still in the recesses of his mind and in his indomitable spirit, Jesse remembered his mother, the one person who cultivated his strong beliefs and indwelled a sense of heritage for the United States into his soul. *The Union would be a perpetual entity of government and not a temporal experiment in foolish democracy,* he thought over and over again.

General Burnside wanted three bridgeheads to stretch across the Rappahannock River, his armies smashing through the defenses at Fredericksburg, thus opening an uninterrupted path to Richmond. A battalion of men from the 83rd Pennsylvania was dispatched to help the 127th Pennsylvania defend the engineer units who were building the bridges across the river. Jesse was part of the battalion of troopers extracted for the mission. They simply called themselves Sayler's Battalion after their captain, Thomas Sayler.

The Virginia winter was approaching and conditions were not good for working near water. The vastness of the countryside and the flowing river stretched before the men of the battalion, making them appear minute in the overall scheme. Jesse's battalion took positions across from Pitt, Hawke and Faquier Streets, part of the town of Fredericksburg.

Fredericksburg was a serene hamlet; its three church steeples visible on the approach to the town. A sunken road stretched in front of a high elevation called Marye's Heights to the west. The late fall season brought a dissipation of foliage in and around Fredericksburg, giving sharpshooters on both sides of the river the opportunity to pinpoint targets with ease of sight. Any soldier working or guarding the bridgehead locations faced difficult circumstances.

"Boys, we have to get these bridges protected from the sharpshooters as soon as possible," Captain Thomas Sayler yelled to his Pennsylvanians. "Burnside wants us to plow right through this town and then carry on to threaten the defenses of Richmond itself!"

"Burnside! He couldn't even ford a creek at Sharpsburg a couple of months ago," Jesse answered from among his battalion. "He's waited two weeks for pontoon bridge supplies from Washington and all the time, I can bet, those Confederates under General Lee have massed on the high ridge across the river."

"We have to follow orders, private! Let's fan out and take positions along the riverbank; try to find a good tree, if possible, and blend in so you don't become an open target for their guns. We're supposed to have artillery support coming down to lob shells into those buildings across the way. The buildings are definitely making good hideouts for the Rebs."

As the battalion was taking positions, smashes of gunfire crackled intermittently from the buildings on the riverfront side of Fredericksburg. Minie balls sliced the surface of the waters of the Rappahannock. Pockets of dust rose from the drying parts of the riverbank. Immediately six Pennsylvanians thudded to the icy ground. Jesse couldn't believe his eyes. He perceived for the first time the accuracy of the Confederate snipers, secluded from their murderous deeds. Jesse and a couple of other men from the special battalion walked toward the six wounded and dead soldiers, but were forcefully ordered by Captain Sayler to halt. The captain, from his experiences with sniper fire, knew as soon as helpers got to the dead and wounded, those helpers would be either dead or wounded themselves.

Jesse's battalion worked for three days, December 6th, 7th and 8th, guarding the engineers and laborers. The sharpshooters continued to be a deadly force and hard to stop. The work proceeded. The high command of the Union Army wanted a crossing no later than the 11th of December. Corps commanders all down the Union line wanted the town of Fredericksburg flushed of all agitating snipers.

The crossing did take place on December 11th, 1862, with General Burnside sending two of his newly formed Grand Divisions across the pontoon bridges, finally secured, despite the relentless Confederate sniper fire from the other side. Confused orders hampered one of the divisions. Many of the Union troops figured that General Lee more than likely acknowledged the confused orders on the eleventh and employed his defenses more efficiently in the face of the overwhelming Union numbers. Jesse's battalion rejoined their respective companies after the upper river bridges were in place and waited with their brigades for orders from Burnside.

*****

Jesse waited patiently to confront the Confederate forces at Fredericksburg. He kept himself busy discarding things he would have to leave behind when the marching continued after the battle. Soldiers usually lightened their loads, taking things from their haversacks and knapsacks when they knew they were moving to a different location or objective. Jesse was also contemplating writing a letter to his mother. He knew he was going to have to get the letter through to Confederate lines for it to make the journey home to North Carolina. This could be a dangerous venture for a private, but Jesse knew he owed his mother news that he was still alive. With the help of an officer his letter could get through enemy lines.

The 5th Army Corp was positioned back across the Rappahannock and across from where the upper pontoon bridges were made into bridgeheads for the Union Army. Jesse started his letter to his mother. He only got two lines of words down on paper when his brigade was ordered, late in the day on December 13th, to go to the support of General Samuel Sturgis's Second Division of the 9th Corps.

Despite the slaughter of his men from Marye's Heights, General Burnside continued his attack. He insisted on sending more lines of Union brigades into the hail of fire from impregnable artillery positions General James Longstreet had fortified since November 20th. General Charles Griffin ordered his 1st Division across the bridgeheads and to the left of Sturgis's men, who were beginning to weaken in the face of massive fire from the heights. Following Griffin's division were the divisions of Generals Humphreys and General Sykes. Jesse's 83rd Pennsylvania Regiment went in on the left as ordered and received a devastating, reinforced fire from Kershaw's Confederate brigade, just moved into position behind the stone wall in front of Marye's Heights.

The men of Stockton's Union brigade, which Jesse belonged to, encountered sights of hell that would haunt their coming days if they were able to survive the carnage. A cannon blast and then silence enveloped Jesse's mind and being. He was hit by shrapnel in the left side and was bleeding profusely. He knew torso wounds usually guaranteed death for the infantry soldier in the field.

Jesse could only think to himself. He couldn't move.

The battle seemed to freeze in time. Looking all around, he saw the horror and devastation of human loss that went far beyond comprehension. He had seen too many hopeless wounds at Sharpsburg. He never forgot. Jesse lay helpless for a day on the merciless ground in front of Marye's Heights. The slopes were littered with bodies of Union men in blue who had tried fourteen times to charge and take the heights, but would never succeed on December 13th, 1862.

Jesse was eventually taken back across the Rappahannock River to the safety of the Union camps and to the attention of doctors who didn't see much hope for his recovery. Jesse lost a lot of blood and was very weak. After three days, General Burnside ordered a retreat from Fredericksburg. He left behind 13,000 dead and wounded Union soldiers who sacrificed above and beyond their call of duty in the face of military incompetence. Jesse was transported with the main army. His severe condition and his need for constant medical attention required it.

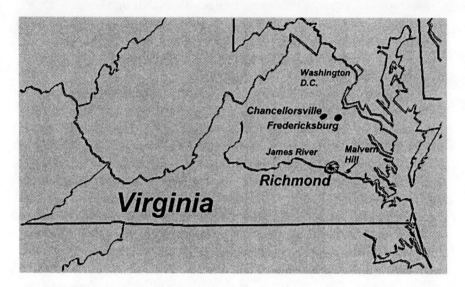

The Army of the Potomac headed northwest from Fredericksburg. Jesse mustered up enough strength to finish his letter to his mother so it could be delivered, possibly, by the time of his death. Jesse thought death had taken its hold on his soul.

December 14th, 1862
Fredericksburg, Virginia

Dear Mother:
I started to write you a letter on the afternoon of December 13th, but was ordered to duty at Fredericksburg, where our honorable and proud Army of the Potomac was engaged in great carnage for the third time this fall. I guess you heard about President Lincoln's appointment of General Ambrose Burnside to relieve General McClellan this past November. I don't know where they possibly can justify the appointment of such military ignorance. For by the grace of God there must be someone out there who can lead our glorious army to complete victory over the inferior forces of General Lee.

Mother, I have been severely wounded in the left side. This occurred in my duties at Fredericksburg when we were ordered to reinforce a division that had been raked over by artillery and musket fire from a place called Marye's Heights, behind the town proper. The only thing I can remember was a blast of flame and then silence. I became unconscious from the pain of injury and fell to the ground. I was not recovered from the field until twenty-four hours later. Some merciful Confederate soldiers passed us water from among the heights where we all fell. I know this will sound horrible for you, but in case I die, I wanted you to know I fought the best I could for the sake of the Union cause. The doctors tell me it doesn't look promising for the recovery of the wound. I think shrapnel went clear through me; there may be some hope if infection can be avoided.

I never wavered in my conviction of spirit for the Union. My hope would be to see my whole, dear family before I pass on, but I know that is impossible under these great and violent circumstances. If I am fortunate enough to be spared by the Almighty in Heaven, I will write you again. It is also my hope this letter will be allowed to pass through Union and Confederate lines to get to you in North Carolina.

Please, Mother, do not worry for me. Remember I did the best I could in my life and in the circumstances of this atrocious war and rebellion. Please give my regards to Father and Danny and Alfred. Please take care of my personal interests back in Carolina. Oh, how I miss the mountains and the fresh country air of home.

Respectfully with love,
Jesse

The letter was handed to General Griffin, who commanded Jesse's division at Fredericksburg. It got to the general through Jesse's commanding officer, Captain Sayler. The letter was stained with blood from Jesse's hand. General Griffin promised Captain Sayler the letter would cross enemy lines under the protection of a truce arranged for the burial of many who died at Fredericksburg and in skirmishes northwest of the town. A courier from General Griffin's staff made many attempts to get the letter to a North

Carolina regiment. On the evening of December 20th, five days before Christmas, the letter was finally given to a lieutenant colonel in the 49th North Carolina under the command of General Robert Ransom, ironically, the same brigade the 26th North Carolina commenced service under. The officer promised that, through the Confederate courier services, the letter would make it to North Carolina along with hundreds of others.

On December 24th, Private Jesse Elington was placed in a Washington, D.C., army hospital for a serious wound in his side. His casualty, like many others before him, worked to nullify the reasons for the war itself. Human life was being sacrificed on a scale unheard of before in the history of warfare. Jesse had just turned twenty-two years old on December 2nd. The war truly made an indelible mark on the Elington family. Family bonds would be further severed. Anguish and pain would haunt the Elington family. Jesse Elington, in his own contemplation, had tried to make his own lasting mark in the war; a mark he saw as an opportunity to save the blessed Union from the rebellion within. Jesse knew the Union cause would go on, even if he died from his wound. Many men had eagerly concurred with the cause from the beginning of the conflict. The Union lost a committed soldier, along with many others, at Fredericksburg, Virginia.

*****

Lieutenant Elington and Colonel Burgwyn heard the overwhelming news from Fredericksburg of another complete victory for Generals Robert E. Lee, James Longstreet and Thomas Jackson. It was December 15th and news traveled quickly from Fredericksburg, which was about seventy miles from Camp French, near the Petersburg area. Elington and the men of F Company continued their duties at Camp French, along with orders to remain in winter quarters there until the outcome of Fredericksburg was decided.

On a chilly and cloudy day near the Appomattox River, F Company was clearing out a new area for additional breastworks for the defenses of the Richmond and Petersburg Railroad.

"I just can't comprehend this," Harrison said to Alfred. "How can the Union Administration in Washington continue to rely on incompetent generals for the execution of the war? I know there are competent people Lincoln could have assume command in the Army of the Potomac. What a waste of young boys and materials at Fredericksburg! General Lee has again proven his flexibility and military prowess."

"I don't know what's going on with those generals, lieutenant, but it has turned out to be surely beneficial to us to have Union leaders who are either too cautious or too careless."

"Darn fools! Stinking, darn fools!" Corporal Fry answered. "The extent of the defeat of those Yankee sons of devils is on their own shoulders, lieutenant. Why do you even show one ounce of mercy to those 'boys and material' you say were wasted in the defeat? I say all of those boys died in the lousy cause of their Yankee Union and they died for their treasonous president, who doesn't know how to run an army. All darn fools! They fight for what? To save the Negro, who could care less if a white man died for them. They fight to keep us from leaving the Union? Let us alone, that's what I have to say."

"Well, Fry, I guess you make some sense about this battle," Harrison answered.

"I agree," Alfred said.

"I just wonder about Jesse," Harrison thought out loud. "I know his 5th Army Corps was there in Fredericksburg at the time of the battle. Intelligence reports from our scouts, who relayed information to Colonel Burgwyn and his staff, verified the 5th's presence there. I hope he is uninjured."

"He'll be fine, lieutenant. Jesse is a good soldier and can take care of himself. I remember my father saying what a good worker he was at the gristmill. Father always thought Jesse would one day manage the mill."

"Your words are no comfort to me right now, Alfred."

"Lieutenant Elington? Don't you find it hard to have a son who is a traitor to the Confederacy?" asked Fry.

"What the devil did you call my son, Fry?"

"You heard it, lieutenant. You just don't want to admit it now, do you? Yes, he is a traitor to the cause of North Carolina, his native home. Why is he fighting for Pennsylvania and the Yankee hordes from hell?"

"Fry, you're dragging personal baggage into this conflict and you know you can't do that. How many families and friends have been split by this war? It's all around us. And I will not. And I refuse to lose respect for my son, who is now old enough to believe in his own causes."

"That's true, lieutenant! I have to say you make a good point. That is, 'it is all around us.' Isn't your wife, Abigail, a Yankee, lieutenant?"

"You scoundrel rogue!"

Harrison plunged forward and smashed Fry in the face with his fist. Fry rolled back and, as he did, Elington kicked him right in his stomach, causing Fry to bend in pain.

"Now you're going to get it, Elington! You know what? I think you're a stinking traitor, too!"

"A traitor?" Harrison asked.

"Yeah, you're always feeling sorry for those Yankees who get their heads smashed in by General Lee. Why is it, Elington? You told me months ago that you didn't know where your allegiances stood in this war." Fry pushed forward and hit Harrison in the gut with his cartridge box and then slapped him with his open hand right on the side of his face.

"I don't care what happens to me now, Elington!" Fry yelled. They can bring me up on any charge they want! I don't care! You have to go, Elington! Go right out of this regiment which is committed to Southern ways!"

"And you are committed to Southern ways, Fry?" The two combatants continued to push, shove and curse each other. Fry continued bleeding from the mouth and Elington's face was scratched pretty bad.

"That I am, Elington; Southern ways, Southern causes and Southern life!"

"The South is my home too, and you know it! It's Jesse's home and yes, it is Abigail's home!" A crowd of privates began to swarm around the fight taking place on the cold December day.

"You don't belong in this regiment any longer, Elington," Fry yelled furiously. "You can't be leading troops who are committed to states' rights, President Davis, General Lee and our history of questioning authority! Do you remember John C. Calhoun, Elington? Do you even know who he was?"

"I know exactly who he was, Fry."

"He is our history and he is our basis for why we fight these no-good, lousy Northerners, who will insist on nothing less than the destruction of our lives and property," Fry yelled.

"Separate, soldiers!" ordered Colonel Burgwyn. "What is going on here? We are supposed to be working on entrenchments. What are you all doing standing around here? Is it another fight, or is it another argument?"

"No, sir!" shouted Alfred.

"We have enough enemies to fight in this war, boys!" Burgwyn shouted. "I can't understand what the problem is, now."

"We'll straighten it out, sir!" Harrison answered.

"When you're out as an officer it'll be straightened out," Fry commented.

"What was that, Fry?" Burgwyn demanded.

"I think Elington is a traitor to the cause, colonel!"

"A traitor! Are you drunk, Fry? What kind of talk is that, corporal!" Burgwyn shouted. "We have gone through these petty arguments too many times. I said the next time you would have to be dealt with more severely than latrine duty. Do you recall this, Fry?"

"Yes, sir, Colonel Burgwyn! But what about traitors like Elington?"

"I have received no evidence from anyone in this regiment that Elington is a traitor to the cause of the Confederate States of America. Am I right, boys of Company F?"

A majority of the company shouted to support their lieutenant, but some began to question the inquiries and comments often made by Elington to some of his men concerning the Yankee soldiers. The men had heard accusations by Corporal Fry and had come to agree with him on occasion at Camp French and at the defenses at Drewry's Bluff. Some soldiers tended to believe that their lieutenant couldn't make up his mind on what side to take in the war. Most, though, still seemed to support and respect Lieutenant Elington as a leader and as a friend they could count on from back home in Caldwell County. After all, many people were torn in this Civil War.

"Corporal Lewis Fry, you are relieved of your duties as a corporal in F Company until you can prove your leadership qualities and prove them in front of your superior officers, including Lieutenant Elington. You are hereby demoted to private until further notice from me. Is that absolutely clear, Private Lewis Fry?"

"Yes, sir, Colonel Burgwyn!"

"Now go and get cleaned up and get back to work on these entrenchments, or else I'll hear it from General Pettigrew that the 26th North Carolina is a bunch of lazy hybrids who can't follow orders."

Harrison was again grateful for the support from Colonel Burgwyn and the men of F Company concerning Fry's allegations. Elington and Burgwyn knew Fry's behavior had to cease. This type of coarse and illogical behavior would surely cause friction and disrespect from others in the future. To Harrison it was like being back at school, where certain students would challenge the authority of the teacher to see how far they could go in instigating the entire class.

After the altercation the officers of the 26th North Carolina began to contemplate the next move of the Army of Northern Virginia, even though their regiment was still building fortifications near Petersburg.

*****

New Year's Day rang in for the second time in the war. The Battle of

Antietam, the bloodiest day in U.S. military history, emboldened President Lincoln to issue his well-thought-out and well worded Emancipation Proclamation. Although the dismissed General McClellan had found General Lee's Order 191 in fields near Frederick, Maryland, he could not organize a complete defeat for the Union. McClellan knew Lee's forces were severely divided during the time proceeding the battle at Sharpsburg. The only positive development from the Battle of Sharpsburg was that McClellan had managed a holding action against Lee, Longstreet and Jackson, preventing an invasion of the North into Pennsylvania. These developments scurried Lincoln into action. For now he saw an opportunity to make the war more destructive for the South by freeing its slaves.

January 1, 1863, would bring many trials and lamentation.

— Chapter 8 —
A Trial of Darkness

January 1863

News, letters and notices were pouring into Caldwell County and into other surrounding counties since the prominent Battle at Fredericksburg, Virginia. Families were receiving words from their native sons and everyone was praying for the best of reports. The stories of Burnside's blunders at Fredericksburg fashioned a sense of awe for the high command of the Confederacy. Generals Lee, Longstreet and Jackson were becoming legends in their own times. Newspapers in the North were reporting the immeasurable logistics and prowess of the Confederate armies. Constantly outnumbered and low on supplies, the Confederate commanders penetrated forward with forceful ambition, guided by a reckless notion of invincibility on the battlefields of Maryland and Virginia.

Abigail Elington tried to carry on with her life on the farm in Granite Falls without the assistance and companionship of her husband and sons. She missed them dearly. Abigail conversed with Mr. and Mrs. Abshire in times of loneliness and worry. She also met with Peyton Caldwell's parents, who Harrison had been close to during Peyton's years at the Academy.

Abigail kept having a recurring sense that something was wrong. She hadn't received letters from Jesse for at least two months. She knew he was in Virginia, but did not gain any other details. Anxiety became an everyday, unwanted nuisance going beyond her control to manage her feelings and resentments. She fell behind with winter chores around the farm and around the house. Milk was spoiling, eggs were piling up and farm tools were being neglected. Many days and nights Abigail simply cried over the horrid circumstances of her life. A trial of darkness set upon her existence.

How are Jesse and Danny getting along in these times of uncertainty? Abigail often wondered. *Their lives mean much to this country. God in Heaven, can you protect and strengthen my boys and my husband,* she prayed on the cold night of January 16, 1863.

January 17 dawned with an eerie calm. Then a cold, stiff wind brushed the landscape of Caldwell County. The Blue Ridge Mountains beckoned stormy weather for the rest of the day. Gray mist and fans of sun streaks hovered over in a gloomy quagmire of clouds.

Abigail made her way out of the house to go and talk to Mr. Abshire about anything he heard concerning the recent battles and skirmishes in Virginia. The gristmill sounded from a distance. Wheat and other grains were being ground for consumer use. Everyday movements compounded the sounds coming from the mill. Abigail went into the entrance of the freshly painted front side of the mill. Mr. Abshire was explaining some procedures to his managers. There had been a high rate of new employees hired in the past three months. The war depleted Abshire's work force and now many women were taking jobs in the mill to supplement income and to simply make ends meet.

"Good morning, Mrs. Elington," said Mr. Abshire.

"And a good morning to you, Mr. Abshire."

"Its not a real good morning for a walk, my lady. It looks threatening atop those mountains today, but how are you doing?"

"I haven't been doing well this week. My thoughts are constantly consumed by the war and the fate of my family."

"It's tough on everyone around here. You know that as much as anyone. You have to keep yourself together and stay positive. Things will turn out."

"My thoughts have been far from positive these days. The Battle at Fredericksburg has gotten me deeply worried. I heard of all the Union deaths against a place called Marye's Heights. Is that the right name, Mr. Abshire, Marye's Heights?"

"Yes, it is. A sad day for the parents up North. Sometimes I find myself caring for those folks in the North. No matter what side you are on in this war, losing a child is just as hard and painful for anyone. I wish Alfred was here working by my side like old times."

"Do you really think they are all doing fine?"

"I can't give you a definite answer. But I do pray and have hope."

"I think a new list of casualties will be listed today down at the town hall building," Mr. Abshire said solemnly. "I find myself praying more often when I know those lists are going to be posted. Even if he was just wounded, I would still be thankful for Alfred's life. I hate when those lists go up. It's often too much for me."

"How are the new workers coming along?" Abigail asked. "Can we work outside of the home and prove our strength in a gristmill?"

"The ladies are doing a fine job in replacing some of the boys serving in the regiments. They are eager, excited and happy to learn the operations of the mill. I can't be any more pleased with their progress."

"I am glad to hear that report, Mr. Abshire."

"Well, I'm sure you will hear more good news about the workers in the local papers and maybe even in the *North Carolina Gazette*."

"Good to hear that."

"When we visited Raleigh for the aid we needed toward the mill, we were able to talk to some reporters about the prospect of hiring woman workers if we procured the aid to carry on with production. Since then I have received notices that one of the reporters, John Earnhart, will most likely publish a story about Raleigh's generosity in giving aid to the mill. Topping the story will be the progressive idea of woman working to compensate for the worker losses in Caldwell County."

"I think it will be welcome and encouraging news for the whole state. Something positive is what we need around here and the Confederate government will also benefit from the news story and the accompanying publicity."

"True, so true."

"Thank you kindly, Mr. Abshire, for taking time from your business to talk with me. It means a lot in these times; thank you. I need to go down to the store for sugar. I was thinking of baking something sweet to lift my spirits on this gloomy day."

"Have a nice day, Abby, and stop by our house soon. Mrs. Abshire would appreciate it."

It was just before noon. Abigail made her way to the general store in town for her sugar when she noticed the posting of the updated casualty list on the front entrance wall of the town hall. She tried to stay away from the building, but her curiosity strongly intervened. She went over to the crowd to see the list. It was difficult and agonizing to see the tears and sadness emanating from the faces of the ones who counted their losses. The Coffey family, from

Caldwell County, lost many thus far in their service. Many Coffey boys were in F and G Companies of the 26th North Carolina, but many were serving in other North Carolina regiments as well. Abigail tried to make her way through the crowd of parents and relatives. She got close enough to see the names. She found no Elingtons on the list. Abigail was relieved beyond explanation, for the last casualty list was posted nearly three weeks ago and the waiting became unbearable.

But what about Jesse? she thought, standing in front of the dreaded list.

Union casualties were not too much of a concern to Southerners, but to Abigail, Union casualties were a concern. *Was he alive after the terrible news of Fredericksburg and Marye's Heights?* she thought. *How could I find out living in North Carolina? I need to know now of his fate. It has been too long since I heard from him.*

Abigail crossed the dirt street again to get to the general store. She was glad to leave the wall and the sorrow surrounding the town hall building. She entered Lockerman's General Store. The store was empty of customers. The casualty list was being read and reread.

Johnston Lockerman, the proprietor of the general store, was a short, lanky man in his fifties who inherited the store from his father. He wore rounded spectacles and had bushy black hair. He was very well liked by the town's people, who depended on him for supplies and mail service even before the war started.

"How are you, Mrs. Elington?" asked Johnston Lockerman.

"Just fine, now, Johnston, since reading that awful list. No Elingtons on it."

"Good news, child!"

"What's on your list today for purchase, ma'am?"

"I need one pound of sugar and one bag of wheat for baking today, sir."

"That will be all?"

"No, you can also give me some of the honey back there on the shelf."

"Just fine, Mrs. Elington."

Lockerman scurried to fill her order, weighing and bagging her items. The store was still quiet and she could hear the crowd outside remaining in its sorrowful mourning. The wind began to pick-up outside the store. The store sign squeaked back and forth over the chatting from across the street.

"Here you are, Mrs. Elington! Everything is ready to go."

"Thank you, Johnston. How much will that be?"

"Well, the price is two dollars for the wheat and twenty-five cents for the sugar. I apologize for the ridiculous prices, but the war has affected wheat prices, especially here in North Carolina. If you need time to pay me, I understand, Mrs. Elington."

"Thank you for your kindness, sir. I will be able to pay you in two weeks. Is that suitable, Johnston?"

"Yes, ma'am. By the way, Mrs. Elington, I received a letter yesterday and it is for you."

"For me?"

"Yes … it was reported to me that the letter came from Union couriers, and then through the lines of the 49th North Carolina Infantry from their position near Fredericksburg. I was going to deliver it right to your house later on today."

"Oh dear! It must be from Jesse! I can't believe on the same day I hear of good news about Danny and Harrison, I get a letter from Jesse. This is too blessed a day, Johnston! Give me the letter!"

"Yes, ma'am!"

Abigail took the letter, grabbed her groceries, and exited the store. She made her way to a bench that sat near the town hall. The crowd had thinned by now. Threatening weather was upon the horizon of the mountains. Abigail sat on the bench and frantically opened the letter and began to read the contents:

> *I started to write you a letter on the afternoon of December 13, but was ordered to duty at Fredericksburg, where our honorable and proud Army of the Potomac was engaged in great carnage for the third time this fall … Mother, I have been severely wounded in the left side … I know this will sound horrible for you, but in case I die, I wanted you to know that I fought the best I could for the sake of the Union cause. The doctors tell me it doesn't look promising for the recovery of the wound … I never wavered in my conviction of spirit for the Union … My hope would be to see my whole dear family before I pass on, but I know that it is impossible under these great and violent circumstances. If I am fortunate enough to be spared by the Almighty in Heaven, I will write you again. It is also my hope that this letter will be allowed to pass through Union and Confederate lines to get to you in North Carolina.*

"Oh Jesus in Heaven," Abigail said out loud. "My Jesse, my Jesse! Is he dead? This wretched and wicked war is unbearable!" Abigail cried out in agony in the emptying street. Some women came to try and comfort her on the cold and gloomy day. Abigail went into a silent mourning upon the street and among her comforters. Only the brick and wood buildings stood with her in her loneliness and agony. The wind rustled through the dirt street, kicking up cold dust, making for an eerie and stoic atmosphere where civilians in wartime grew impassive to feelings; feelings hardened by the constant news of destruction and death.

Ladies from the town walked Abigail back to her house and advised her to get some rest. Abigail went in the house, walked straight upstairs and paused outside of Jesse's room. Her mind became full of the sounds of childhood enveloping the house. She could hear laughter and screams of joy from Jesse as he chased Danny in the hallway. Her memories caused her to smile again. However, reality hit Abigail hard. She ran into Jesse's room and fell face down on his bed in mental anguish. She stayed there for the duration of the night, surrounded by his furniture and little ornaments decorating the room.

*****

During the cold and dark January days in the Confederacy, a strange occurrence manifested itself in the hierarchy of the United States government in Washington, D.C. On January 1, 1863, President Abraham Lincoln issued the Emancipation Proclamation, setting free forever the African slaves living in the states in rebellion. This political tool of war was aimed right at the Confederate States of America. Only the eleven states seceded from the Union were affected by Lincoln's proclamation.

*****

Someone knocked at Abigail's front door the next morning. Abigail got up out of Jesse's bed and wasn't sure she wanted to answer the caller at the door. The knocking persisted and Abigail could hear at least two people talking outside.

"Mrs. Elington? Abigail? Are you inside? It's Mr. and Mrs. Abshire! Please come to the door."

"I will be right there. Please wait a few minutes."

"All right, Abigail." Mr. Abshire answered.

The door opened after about three minutes and Abigail stood in the doorway, her face red and her spirit dejected and depressed.

"Abigail, we heard from some of the ladies in town about the letter you received yesterday concerning Jesse," Mrs. Abshire said. "Can his death be confirmed? There may be hope he is still among the living. Jesse said in the letter he was wounded. At least this is what our neighbor Alicia Townshend told us. She said she helped you get home yesterday after you read the letter."

"The only thing I have to rely on right now is this letter Mr. Lockerman handed me yesterday, Mrs. Abshire. I just can't believe or comprehend my eldest child is gone from us." Mrs. Abshire read the letter Abigail held in her hand from the day before. Abigail kept it next to her.

"Abigail, have you heard anything from Harrison or Danny concerning the matter? They might know more," asked Mr. Abshire.

"No, I haven't. Nothing."

"Have you received any recent letters from Alfred and where the 26th North Carolina is located," Abigail asked.

"No, we haven't heard anything. I think the regiment is still at Camp French in Virginia," replied Mrs. Abshire. The battle at Fredericksburg, I think, has slowed our correspondences. The transportation and sorting of mail has been a low priority since the battle took place a month ago."

"Abigail … dear … you need to take care of yourself despite this news," Mrs. Abshire said. Remember, Jesse may still be alive. My hope is still strong and my faith is persevering in this matter. We will both pray Jesse is alive and well."

"Thank you so much for your comfort. Can I get you anything?"

"No, thank you. You just try and relax and clear your mind of this terrible war," Mr. Abshire answered.

"Oh, Abigail!" Mr. Abshire said. "Before we go, I wanted to ask if you read in the paper about the Emancipation Proclamation issued by President Abraham Lincoln. The Union has freed the slaves in our Confederate states. Now the Union has what they call a moral justification for fighting the war."

Abigail stood by the door, flushed in her anguish, but found the strength to bring a normal tone to the conversation.

"Yes, I am aware of the development. As a Southerner, I have to agree with Lincoln on his political savvy and timing for the Emancipation Proclamation."

"You agree, Abigail?" Mrs. Abshire asked.

"Yes! I beg your pardon, Mr. and Mrs. Abshire, if my thoughts on this subject offend you, but my resolve concerning slavery has not wavered since the time I lived in the North, in Pennsylvania."

"I was not aware of your beliefs about the slave question in the South," Mrs. Abshire replied.

"If Jesse has died in battle, then his death is not marred in futility," Abigail stated. "We will be able to look back at this conflict in the years to come and realize one of us accomplished a purpose through the immense bloodshed that has been pointless. But maybe now there is a point to all of this madness."

Abigail wept. The Abshires tried to console Abigail, but without success, for her mental anguish became insufferable.

"You know, Abigail, I have often wondered about the slave issue, but I have always been afraid to speak my mind," Mrs. Abshire answered. "Slavery is prominent in the eastern part of our state, but it is remote from our lives. Slavery is inhuman! I needed to say that today."

"Well, ladies, I do not want to get into a slave debate. I hope Alfred, Danny, Jesse and Harrison can all come home soon and bring our town back to normal living. I miss many of the men who have been sent to fight. I believe those men are fighting for a Confederate cause worthy to die for. If my age permitted it, I would sign-up in a regiment to fight."

"No, you wouldn't, Mr. Abshire," answered his wife. "Alfred is serving from this family and that is enough for the cause of the Confederacy!"

"She's right, Mr. Abshire," Abigail said. "Sacrifice has been the overriding precedent around here for too long. People need to get on with their normal lives, and oh, how I wish I could do just the same. I am sick and tired of these circumstances of war. The constant sacrifice of lives, of families, of food, and of our resources has made the South wary and tortured."

"But Abigail, remember if slavery is eventually abolished, our whole economy will be affected," Mr. Abshire said. You know how reliant our economy is on cotton production and if Lincoln gets his way, we are going to be faced with massive slave escapes throughout the South and also faced with the doom of economic depression. I know Lincoln has a purpose in mind for only freeing slaves in our states. He did not free the slaves in the border states. I guess he didn't want the slaveholders there to secede from his precious Union."

"I don't care about the economy anymore," Abigail answered.

"But, Abigail, you can't believe that!"

"Why not, Mr. Abshire? It's the greed and materialism in the first place that started the fire of war. I am sick and tired of the politicians who have driven the ideas of industrialism and Manifest Destiny for the United States.

They have ignited a kind of greed never to be satisfied, and I believe Jesse is probably dead because of this ungovernable greed."

"We are going to get back to our house now, Abigail," Mr. Abshire said. "Please try to settle in today. The weather doesn't look any good. Take care of yourself and let us know if you need anything. I will inform you of any new developments as soon as I hear of them."

"I hope Harrison sends his paycheck home soon. The money is getting tight," Abigail said.

"If you need money, Abigail, we will furnish it for you. Don't worry!" Mrs. Abshire answered.

Light snow began to fall outside Abigail's house. The Abshires made their way back to their house a few blocks away. Abigail looked out the parlor window and watched the Abshires disappear from view, their footprints the only part of them left in the fresh snow. She felt saddened by their departure. Abigail pondered her condition sitting in the blue Victorian chair near the window.

"Jesse," she whispered. "Jesse, can you hear me? If you can, I want you to know I love you, son."

There was probably no one there to tell him that, she thought. *How lonely he must have felt. How hopeless he must have been in the hours of suffering and I was denied the motherly right to be with him.*

The mountains radiated down on the Elington home. Abigail remained sitting in the chair near the parlor window for most of the day and into evening. She continued to feel empty inside, even though she saw the beautiful ridges of the Blue Ridge in the distance. Abigail felt a sense of fear for Danny and Harrison, who were possibly her only family left in the South. *God in Heaven, please watch over Danny and Harrison through their journeys. Please spare them from harm and may Your Spirit be upon them,* she prayed.

May Jesse live his life, Lord. I love him.

— Chapter 9 —
My Son

January 1863

January 24, 1863, in Virginia, dawned with sunshine and a lustrous blue sky. The endless rows of tents covered the landscape around Camp French. Fires thrashed in the gentle morning breeze and men began to eat their breakfast before another day's work. The ground was wet and hard from the cold temperatures over the past few weeks. Union gunboats were headed up the James River again, trying to fight a rear guard action to harass and disorganize any Confederate forces attempting to attack Burnside's movements out from the Fredericksburg area.

Harrison, Alfred and now Private Lewis Fry woke to another day of anticipated work constructing, digging and loading materials for the entrenchments and breastworks.

General Johnston Pettigrew's adjutant personally came riding into the quarters of the 26th North Carolina.

He rode into camp on his brown horse, dressed in a new butternut uniform, new hat and buttons shining in the sun. His face was clean-shaven except for a goatee finely shaped on his chin and his expression was serious. He carried with him a letter from the Confederate War Department. The department had been directed by James Seddon since 1862.

"I need to see Colonel Burgwyn!" the adjutant demanded from the men eating their breakfast.

"Yes, sir!" Lieutenant Colonel John Lane answered.

Lane quickly hurried to the colonel's barracks to give him the message. Colonel Burgwyn was finishing his breakfast and reading reports and orders from Virginia.

"Henry! General Pettigrew's adjutant is outside. He wants to talk with you," Lane said.

"I will be right there, John."

"It looks urgent, hurry!"

"I'm coming!"

Burgwyn walked briskly out of his quarters and addressed the adjutant.

"Colonel Burgwyn here, sir! What can I do for you today?"

"I have a letter from the Confederate War Department for a Lieutenant Harrison Elington. Is he part of your regiment?"

"Yes, he is, sir."

"See that he gets this letter, colonel. I don't think it is good news."

"Yes, sir. Give my compliments to General Pettigrew."

"Yes, I will, colonel."

The adjutant rode away from the encampment. Burgwyn pondered about the contents of the letter, but not for long. He walked over to Lieutenant Elington's barracks and found him already outside near the tent of Alfred Abshire sipping coffee from a shiny tin cup.

"Lieutenant Elington, can I see you in private, please," ordered Burgwyn.

"Yes, sir, colonel!

"I have received a letter for you delivered by General Pettigrew's adjutant. He said it was something from the War Department."

"The War Department?" Elington asked. "The only things to come out of the War Department are letters of appointment, orders, or soldier deaths. Oh Lord, what has happened?"

Elington went back to his barracks to open and to read the letter. He opened the letter, his hands beginning to shake uncontrollably. He proceeded to read it.

The War Department of the Confederacy
January 19, 1863
Secretary James Seddon

Dear Lieutenant Harrison Elington:
I am personally writing you this dispatch to inform you that a

letter addressed to your wife, Abigail, was intercepted through a skirmish that took place in Virginia. The skirmish had an affect on both Confederate and Union mail. This particular letter was found in a Confederate wagon and inside a courier's bag that was on a wagon confiscated back in December. Union skirmishers thought the wagon was simply a Confederate supply or ammunition load and took it during the skirmish. The wagon was then returned to Confederate authorities for its contents of mail. Out of respect for the families of soldiers we are in the process of trying to return the letters of soldiers from both sides through a flag of truce and by contacting officers from Burnside's army.

The mail was screened by our intelligence agency. They noticed some pieces of mail were being passed along through Confederate lines from the Union army.

A copy, handwritten by a close aid of mine, of your son's letter is included with this dispatch. The original letter was sent on by this department to your residence in North Carolina in early January. From the tone of the letter, I am not sure your wife knows if your son is living or dead. You may want to contact her.

I know this war has depleted and divided many families from our beloved Confederacy and from the Union. We all understand the circumstances and no one will hold any ill feelings toward you or your family for having a son who fights for the 83rd Pennsylvania Infantry Regiment.

Sincerely,
Secretary of War, James Seddon

Elington read the rest of the dispatch, which included the same words Jesse sent to his mother. He lay face down on his bunk and sank into a deep, depressed state. Harrison, like Abigail, reverted in his mind to the days when Jesse and Danny were infants and young boys. All of the consternation and stupidity of the war at hand was deliberately cleared from his mind and spirit. He hated this conflict that further wounded his family and his pride in his eldest son.

"My son, my son!" Harrison cried in despair. "Jesse, are you really gone? Are you really gone, my son? My boy, who dared to speak against his father, my boy who helped me in life with the farm! My son, who bravely fought for what he believed in! It sounds like your wound is mortal."

Harrison stayed in his barracks until noontime. No officer reprimanded him or bothered him with the mundane chores of Camp French. From Harrison's reluctance to come out of his barracks, the men knew the news must have been bad from the War Department, for Lieutenant Elington never evaded his duties as an officer in the 26th North Carolina.

At about 1:30 in the afternoon, Harrison emerged from his quarters and proceeded to Colonel Burgwyn's barracks, which was across from his own. Burgwyn had gone out to City Point to check on the gunboats that were still harassing the town and the railroad depot there. The rest of the men in the regiment were also on duty somewhere, and Harrison was left for three more hours to grieve alone for Jesse.

Elington walked a couple of miles from the Petersburg area. He followed the tracks of the Petersburg and Lynchburg Railroad for a while and then made his way to the banks of the Appomattox River. There he sat in the dirt and looked at the fading day. The sun started to set and recede in the sky. The gentle breeze made the leaves on the numerous trees near the banks crest with sound, fall silent and then crest again. Like the rhythms of life, the trees confirmed to Harrison that Jesse's crest had come in life and it had seemed now to forever cease on a battlefield of a wretched war. Another life, possibly snuffed out, the result of irreconcilable circumstances between people of the same distinct country, a country Jesse loved and admired through the nurturing eyes of his father, mother and grandfather. A country whose leaders had started an experiment in democracy, but was now on trial by fire. *Would this fire consume all of my family?* Harrison thought, sitting near the river. *Is it true that members of my army may have killed my eldest son?*

"But what about Danny?" Harrison whispered. "He fights in the army that wounded his brother. Does he even know Jesse might be gone?

"Abby!"

How has Abby been getting along since hearing the news about Jesse? I just don't know.

Harrison thought for another hour about his fate in the Confederate army. Could he continue to fight in this army knowing what he knew now? He made his way back to the camp and saw the men of the 26th coming back from City Point. He saw Alfred, Thaddeus and the Coffey boys. He saw Fry, Lieutenant Colonel Lane, Major Jones, and Colonel Burgwyn. He paused for a moment and stared thoughtfully at the busy men of the regiment. He then glanced up and saw the young enlisted men of the regiment; young men like his sons,

Jesse and Danny. Privates Jackson Coffey and Thaddeus Curtis marched among the men and Harrison thought more of Jesse.

These men are my family, Harrison thought. *They are my strength and my reason for going on. They have led me through fire and death, through sadness and friendship. How could I have ever thought about leaving or deserting my regiment and thus support the Union? I love Jesse with all of my heart; my son. Jesse fought for what he believed in, but he still respected Danny and me for fighting for what we believe in concerning this war. I know he wouldn't want us to change sides.*

"My strength will now stand on the rock of my son and his example of courage and fortitude he has shown me," Harrison said out loud. "I will fight now, for my cause. May God guide my decision upon this day. Amen."

Harrison felt an inner strength like nothing he felt before. He didn't know for sure if Jesse was dead or alive, but he had to carry on. The war created in him a paradox; on one hand wanting to fight and win for the Confederacy, but on the other hand sympathizing for the Union cause. Now was a time for decision and faith. Jesse's predicament continued to haunt Harrison, but now relinquished Harrison from his divided allegiances, washing him from the guilt he felt for years. Peace of heart possessed Harrison and he felt secure in his thoughts for the first time. He felt an inner peace in the midst of war.

"Lieutenant Elington, how are you doing? We missed your help today in the trenches," Alfred said as he returned to camp from his day's work.

"How are you, Alfred?"

"Just fine, except for these relentless jobs we got swindled into. Was it real bad news, lieutenant?"

"Jesse was either killed or wounded at Fredericksburg, fighting for the 83rd Pennsylvania. At least this is what they think and this is what they are telling me from a letter found on a Confederate supply wagon in Virginia."

"Do they really know if he died?"

"No. I can't believe this whole situation, Alfred!"

"I am sorry, Harrison … lieutenant."

"The time for grieving will have its place, Alfred. But for now we have a war to win and many battles to fight before us. Jesse's situation, I believe, has sealed my fate for the Confederacy and the Southern cause. We must prevail in this conflict or else the revolution of our grandfathers will fade away without a vestige. Future Americans will never know the sacrifices and the convictions of heart felt by those revolutionaries. We must carry on the revolution of old for the new future of our governments and state sovereignties, for our heritage, for our families and our property."

"But, lieutenant, what about your own grieving for Jesse?" Alfred asked.

With tears enveloping his bloodshot eyes, Harrison responded:

"My heart is broken, Abshire. But I believe Jesse would want us all to go on living and fighting for our cause like he may have died for his cause. A parent should not have to see the death of his child. I have to get in contact with Abigail concerning this matter. Let me go and see what I can do to send her a message. Have a good evening, Alfred. Remember, we must press on..."

Harrison wept, not allowing anyone to notice him as he tried to show his strength in leadership with Alfred. He moved away from Alfred and the other men of the regiment.

"I will pray for you and Abigail, lieutenant."

Harrison was soon able to get a letter out to Abigail back in Caldwell County. He ruminated the almost certain possibility that Abigail left Caldwell County and North Carolina altogether after hearing of the wounding of Jesse. She wouldn't be able to confine herself to the four walls of the house knowing that her son may have been wounded. The brigade courier service got hold of the letter. They told Harrison it would get to Caldwell County in about three or four days. There happened to be many deliveries waiting to be sent home.

The fortitude shown by Harrison in the face of possibly losing his son began to encourage and invigorate the men under his command, especially Alfred. Private Fry came to Elington the next day after all of the news spread around camp. Fry expressed his pity concerning the rumor of Jesse's mortal wounding. Fry knew Jesse as a young boy back in Granite Falls. Despite all of their confrontations and differences of opinions, Fry knew deep in his heart that he cared immensely for the Elington family.

"I'll never know how it feels, Elington," Fry said, standing in the light drizzle of the day. "My son, I hope, will always be too young to ever enter this war, lieutenant. It may go on, though, for longer than any of us can ever foresee. It's a darn waste of life to die in a war. Are you sure he died?"

"No, Lewis. I don't know what the whole story is. Fragmented information on this matter will undoubtedly torment me through the upcoming days."

"I can understand, lieutenant. I am sorry for this news."

"Thanks for expressing your pity for my situation, Lewis."

"Remember, Elington, those Yankees still need to be whipped!" Fry said, walking away from the front of the officer's barracks.

"That makes even more sense to me now, Fry. I have had time to rethink my convictions about the war and I have concluded we have to win in order to survive as a culture and as a government."

Fry stopped walking and said, "Darn glad to hear that, lieutenant."

"Jesse has taught me to let my mind be eased from my recent internal conflicts of Union verses Confederacy. I told Alfred I believe Jesse would want us all to continue in our cause as he did in his cause. He often challenged me back home about the correctness and resolve of the Southern position. I know he would not respect indecision and inaction from anyone. He fought for a cause and we must continue in ours."

"I hear we may be going back to eastern North Carolina for some military action against Union forces there," Fry said.

"I hope we can get to the fighting soon," replied Harrison.

"Jesse is a good young man, Harrison," Fry solemnly said.

The drizzle fell all day. January turned damp and cold and uncertainty entered the ranks of the 26th North Carolina. Although Jesse was not a member of the regiment, his father was. That alone made deep impressions on the other men who surrounded Harrison in his everyday duties as an officer. The men sympathized with his foreboding. They understood that even though a member of the 83rd Pennsylvania Regiment was down, he was a relative of a Southern officer who they respected.

He was also a member of the same country they all once belonged to, the United States of America now divided in minds, bodies and souls.

— Chapter 10 —
New Bern and D. H. Hill

March to June 1863

Major General Daniel Harvey Hill, brother-in-law of the infamous General Thomas "Stonewall" Jackson, was a conscientious and loyal officer under General Robert E. Lee. With the conclusion of Burnside's Fredericksburg folly in Virginia, D. H. Hill, as he was more commonly referred to, took command in North Carolina. His main mission was to recruit new troops for the Confederate army, which was slowly being worn down by the more numerous Union forces. It was plain from the field commands in Virginia that the Confederate army possessed better and more daring generals. The Peninsula Campaign, Second Bull Run, Antietam Creek, and Fredericksburg all proved General Lee and his officers could out-maneuver and out-general the Union commanders. However, soldiers were needed to replenish the ranks and to give rest to the war weary men constantly marching, building and fighting.

General D. H. Hill had other plans for eastern North Carolina. He wanted to attempt to retake New Bern, the indispensable port and trading facility of coastal North Carolina, for the purpose of re-establishing coastal operations for the Confederacy. He also wanted to clean out threatening Union forces making their way down the Virginia, North Carolina and South Carolina coasts.

During winter camp, desertions again increased in the ranks. Recruitment was a priority for General Lee. Operations were beginning to generate more regularly by March 1863. Men were needed to fill the ranks for these operations. Even the grand 26th North Carolina was in need of more men to fill its ranks. Sixty-two deserted through the winter months.

The North Carolina Home Guard regiments were on full alert for deserters from the Confederate army. Boys and older men alike, who grew weary and disillusioned with Confederate objectives and leadership, were trying to make it home. Many were merely in want of survival, hiding in caves and in the mountains of the Blue Ridge. Governor Vance, the former colonel of the 26th North Carolina, wanted enforcement of desertion laws; so as a result the Home Guard troops were looking out for any suspicious men walking the river roads or lagging in towns or villages.

Pettigrew's brigade left the Petersburg fortifications by way of the Weldon and Petersburg Railway. They were transported to Weldon, North Carolina, along the Roanoke River. The brigade then transferred to the Washington and Weldon Railway and headed straight for Goldsboro.

"These train transports can be brutal," Corporal Lewis Fry said, puffing his corncob pipe. Fry had been reinstated as corporal after a period of better discipline in the ranks. He and Harrison had patched up some of their disagreements and Fry was drinking less and showing more leadership qualities.

"You ain't kidding," Alfred replied. The rail cars moved rapidly and wildly down the tracks.

"I think I'd rather march back to North Carolina, then I wouldn't get so stinking sick," shouted Private Thaddeus Curtis.

"I'm sick, too," Private Jackson Coffey replied.

"I have a headache! A bloody headache! It is really irritating me," said another private from F Company.

"I think I'm going to throw up, corporal," Alfred said. "You are corporal again, right, Fry?"

"That's right, Abshire! Make sure you don't throw up on me. Did you hear me?"

"Yes."

Complaints continued through the couple of more hours the men traveled before arriving at Goldsboro.

It was mostly the younger privates who continued their chorus of agony:

"My ankle … it's killing me!"

"My fanny hurts from sitting on this train for so long!"

"What kind of word is that for a soldier to use, you idiot. My haunch hurts!"

"What the crap is a haunch? You moron."

"Shut up, privates!" a sergeant ordered. "You sound like two sissies whining."

"I got a bellyache, boys, and I think I'm going to stuff my pants if I don't get off of this stinking train."

"I wish I was going home now, boys, back to the mountains, to the home-cooked food, and to my girlfriend, Ellie."

"I beg your pardon, boys, but we're headed off to North Carolina. That *is* home, you senseless lunkheads," another corporal shouted in reprimand fashion.

Soldiers continued their list of agonies:

"Are we there yet?"

"No!" Corporal Fry answered.

"My hand is cramping. I don't know how I'm going to load and hold my musket if we get into battle!"

"Musket! I think I left my musket back at Camp French in Virginia! Do you think they'll turn around to go and get it for me."

Laughter filled the train car.

"You're an idiot, private!"

"So are you, man!"

"I got the screamers ... screamers, darn it!"

"All right! Everybody shut up so we can at least get some rest before we march into Goldsboro when this cozy train adventure ends," Fry ordered.

Men fell asleep. The clattering of the train caused soldiers to go into a daze that enabled them to finally stop complaining. Corporal Fry was satisfied and he tried to get some rest on the train.

On March 7th, Pettigrew's brigade made it into Goldsboro. The men proceeded to set up a temporary bivouac in the town, still firmly in Confederate hands. From the area of eastern North Carolina, Pettigrew followed General Hill's orders to proceed to New Bern with General Junius Daniel's brigade. Pettigrew would approach New Bern from the north side of the Neuse River. Daniel's brigade would approach New Bern from the south, coming along the Trent River. The intention and hope of the plan was that Fort Anderson, at New Bern, would be approached and attacked from two directions simultaneously.

March 9, 1863, dawned as a rainy day. Mud was the normal condition as Pettigrew's brigade exited Goldsboro to proceed to New Bern and the Union defenses there.

"Now we go from a train ride of sickness and agony to a mud march through our home state," shouted Alfred, struggling through the thick dirt.

"We have endured this marching for three days and I'm tired of it, boys," Harrison shouted. "I am also tired of the complaining from you boys! Or is it schoolgirls?"

"We're not schoolgirls, lieutenant," Coffey said. "On the other hand, maybe Curtis is a schoolgirl, hey, boys?"

Laughter streamed down the columns of marching men from F Company.

Pettigrew's brigade crossed bridges and creeks without bridges. Often the bridge supports collapsed as a result of the extreme weight crossing them. Cannon, men and wagons caused many other collapses. Fording creeks was another hardship for the men of the brigade. Soldiers walked through high-rising waters with their muskets held high along with their haversacks or knapsacks. Ammunition could not get wet in the crossings, for it would fail in battle.

On March 14, the sounds of Confederate cannon could be heard smashing into Fort Anderson, which made up the main Union garrison at New Bern. Four Union gunboats were beginning to take formations heading northwest along the Neuse River. The deep roaring of the heavy guns shook the area where the 26th North Carolina began to take position near a causeway leading toward the fort. Pettigrew observed this route to be the only viable entry into attacking the garrison. Along with the 11th, 44th, 47th, and 52nd North Carolina Regiments, the 26th North Carolina waited for direct orders from General Pettigrew.

"That garrison has been a thorn to our defenses for over a year now," General Pettigrew complained to Colonel Burgwyn.

Cannon continued to fire at the garrison of Fort Anderson, with its jagged walls and entrenched earthworks. The day was calm compared to the stormy calamities the brigade faced over the past four days of marching.

"Colonel Burgwyn, place your regiment before the causeway leading to the fort," ordered General Pettigrew. "I see it as the only approach to the fort for a charge against the fortification itself."

"Yes, sir, general!"

Burgwyn shouted above the artillery fire: "All company commanders! Order your men to a quick march to the causeway for a charge against the fort. Do it now! Keep your columns straight, men!"

"Sir! The causeway is only the width of a supply wagon! How are we going to get the regiment over the causeway span to attack?" Harrison asked.

"Just take the position, lieutenant," Burgwyn replied. "We are under orders directly from Pettigrew to charge the fort after the artillery breaks-up their defenses.

"But what about those gunboats?" Elington asked. "The boats are only going to come closer to our positions, and it is going to mean more deadly fire from the big guns on those boats."

"They could become problematic, lieutenant. I 'm going to get some heavy fire to bear down on the gunboats. We had some experience with gunboats when you were on furlough. We actually caused a fire on one of them. Maybe we can do it again here today."

After Burgwyn gave the orders to sustain fire on the gunboats using the artillery, the men fostered more confidence in their ability to charge the fort. Smashes of solid shot were heard booming over the Neuse River toward the gunboats. The heavy guns from the boats took aim right back at the North Carolina artillery and broke two guns to pieces, killing five of the crew. Two of the other guns in the battery were having problems with axles and one gun's barrel exploded, causing more sustained injuries to the Confederate crews. The companies of the 26th North Carolina waited for a few more hours to receive orders to charge the fort and make a difference in the war. The orders never came. The continuous and lethal fire of the gunboats continued. The unrelenting aim of the heavier guns eventually overwhelmed the brigade and a retreat was ordered.

The blue sky of March over Fort Anderson again was blackened with ornaments of war fire and smoke. The water from the Neuse River glittered in the afternoon sun when the firing finally slowed. The 26th was given the job of covering the retreat for the rest of the brigade from the areas of the fort. This occurred while the Union gunboats continued a pounding, disseminating fire.

"Hold, men! Hold your position! We are not charging the fort. Artillery malfunction and that God-awful gunboat artillery upon our position has hampered our progress," shouted Burgwyn to the regiment. Burgwyn gathered his company commanders and said, "We have been given the honor of covering the retreat of our brigade. Just hold your position and fire at will at any musket counterfire coming from the fort!"

"Is this really an honor, sir, or is it a fool's mission," asked Fry.

"Just follow your orders!" Burgwyn answered.

The gunboat artillery continued to crack the clear skies over the 26th.

"Take cover, boys," Elington shouted to his company along with Captain

Rankin. Some men of the other regiments, especially the 11th North Carolina, retreated in a frenetic melee across the causeway and back to safety.

A loud shriek, then a violent hissing and finally a thud of smashing, burning metal hit right into the right flank of the regiment. Several men went literally flying through the air, screaming in pain and agony from the direct hit. The gunboats had clearly found a target.

Harrison ran down the line to the area of impact to try and help the boys. He found thirteen dead soldiers and five wounded. One was a captain, another a sergeant, and the rest privates who on this day met their deaths for the Confederate cause.

Harrison belched forth in an angry tirade at the sight of his fellow soldiers lying on the ground either dead or wounded. His determination and resolve for the mission of the 26th North Carolina intensified. He now was sick and tired of the stupid and mundane holding attacks.

These attacks seem to mean nothing militarily, he thought, watching the rest of the brigade withdraw from Fort Anderson. Harrison thought about requesting to have either a transfer to another regiment to be attached to General Lee's Army of Northern Virginia, or to suggest Pettigrew's brigade be attached to Lee's forces. Elington was now ready, beyond any reasonable doubt, to make a contribution to the Confederate cause. This meant taking part in a decisive battle against the Union, an invasion if possible; a specialized mission, or a major campaign. *This had to happen soon,* Elington thought, or else he would finish the war as a failure; a failure because he had done nothing since trying at Malvern Hill to further the resolve and the strength of the Confederate States of America.

General Lee knew what had to be done in order for the Confederacy to rise above its circumstances of being out-numbered, Harrison thought. *Lee could justify a plan to win a decisive battle in the North. Pettigrew's brigade needed to be part of this. The brigade had the ability to contribute a large number of needed men who had some combat experience. The men of North Carolina volunteered many boys to the army, and now North Carolina has to make a difference.*

Elington said softly to himself, "But who will ever listen to me? I am only a measly lieutenant trapped in an army with many generals who can override me."

The final remnants of the brigade retreated from Fort Anderson and New Bern. Many soldiers in the brigade, especially from the 26th, complained along the way back to the safety of Goldsboro. Most reflected the same attitude of Lieutenant Elington.

"Where is General Lee? We need to join him, then we can fight like real darn soldiers."

"Will there be another invasion of the North, like at Sharpsburg?"

"How many times will we have to take the train back and forth from Virginia to North Carolina?"

"I want out of North Carolina. The real fighting is in Virginia!"

"I think this whole darn army has to invade and defeat the Union Army in the North, then we can show the Yankees we are capable of threatening and destroying their lands and property like they have constantly done to us! Virginia is devastated!"

"Yes, but when will all of this happen? We have heard rumors of another Northern invasion for months ..."

*****

Word came to camp at Goldsboro, on May 5, of another Confederate victory in Virginia by General Lee. A battle in the wilderness near Chancellorsville, Virginia, had taken the new Union General Joseph Hooker by storm. The storm carried a high price on the Confederate army, though. General Thomas "Stonewall" Jackson was killed by his own men while conducting a reconnaissance in the area at dusk. General Jackson had become the heart of the Army of Northern Virginia. His prowess and determination on the battlefield had enabled numerous Confederate victories over flustered Union commanders.

What would General Lee do now without his most daring associate in arms?

The time for a Confederate sweep North seemed at hand for the second time in nine months.

– Chapter 11 –

Isolation, Deprivation, Anxiety of Heart

May 1863
Fredericksburg

General Robert Edward Lee contemplated his next strategic move after the costly victory at Chancellorsville, Virginia. He sat alone in his headquarters, now established in a farmhouse near Fredericksburg, where part of his army had positioned itself. It was May 10th, 1863. It was the day the beloved and revered General Thomas "Stonewall" Jackson suddenly died from pneumonia after being wounded in the woods near Chancellorsville. Lee, after hearing of Jackson's left arm being amputated, said, "He has lost his left arm, but I have lost my right arm." Lee knew Jackson's death would effect the next move of the army and possibly the outcome of the war.

Looking out the opened window of his headquarters, he could see the new and splendid vegetation of springtime all around. He could smell the grasses and the trees in late afternoon, fresh with foliage of lush green tones filling his eyes and his mind with new hope. But how could he have hope when his best lieutenant general was now dead and gone forever from the ranks of the dwindling Confederate army. *The muster roll of future recruits was fading,* Lee thought inside the farmhouse.

Will the good Lord in Heaven allow my army to finally be defeated, he pondered? *Lord, have I gone against Your will in ordering the deaths of so many of my own men and the men of the Union? My God. I always thought You gave me a clear conscience and boldness in the causes we have set forth these past two and a half years. I have never strayed from Your will, my Lord. Is it Your will for us in the South, in Virginia, to have our own way of life and our own government? You know the wretched "peculiar institution" has not been my reason to fight this awful conflict against many men who I have known; men who I served with in Mexico and who I met at West Point. I have looked to Your word, Lord, and I see nothing saying our cause is a mindless venture or a ruthless game. We want to preserve our families and our heritage that You, Lord, have bestowed upon us in this great country forged by men of the South and men who always held You high in their thoughts and decisions. I have sacrificed much for this cause, dear Jesus. My wife is sick and I pray You, Sir, that she can recover and live out her years without the worry and torment of her sons and her husband being trapped in this endless conflict of wills. Lord, You alone have allowed the nation of America to exist and to prosper. I pray You, Sir, that You will find the meaning in our cause of freedom and will bless the remaining boys in our Confederate armies. I pray these boys will not lose faith in You, or in the ideas we have sacrificed much for these past couple of years. Amen, my Lord.*

General Lee began to realize in his heart that the leaders of the Confederate States of America would have to gamble and expose themselves in a different manner in order to insure victory for their cause. Something had to be accomplished outside of the devastated Virginia countryside. With the Battles of Manassas, the Peninsula Campaign, Hampton Roads, Fredericksburg, Chancellorsville, Salem Church, and other skirmishes around northern and eastern Virginia, the South needed to be spared from another growing season of Union ravages and property destructions.

The people were beginning to feel the toll of economic, physical and mental hardships and it went beyond anything they were used to. Lee was feeling their pain and their anguish through all the occurrences of war in Virginia. Confederate commanders knew the high casualties in recent battles had weakened their army, even if they were counted as victories. This meant the manpower problem in the South was eventually going to cripple the army. Northern and Southern populations differed substantially when the war began and this was one of the reasons for the defensive posture of the Confederate high command.

Colonel Charles Venable and Colonel Walter Taylor entered Lee's farmhouse headquarters. They came in to check on their beloved general, for there were no words or orders from him in the past few hours. Lee continued to procrastinate, brood and mull over his next move; an innovative move now needed in this great chess match of maneuvering armies.

"Is there anything we can do to be of service, sir," Colonel Venable asked Lee politely.

"No, there isn't anything at this time, colonel. I have been in here praying to my God for strength and help in our cause. It seems the time for great decision is upon us in this theater of conflict. I believe we must induce a very well-planned invasion of the North, particularly aimed and directed at Pennsylvania; specifically the capital, or maybe even the city of liberty, Philadelphia."

"Yes, sir, it sounds like a logical inducement for the army," Colonel Taylor responded, "but, sir, you know with General Jackson gone, many of our high command would not be comfortable or possibly willing to plan and carry out such an offensive movement to the North."

"They will follow, colonel. They want this war and this destruction to come to an end and I know they would be willing to invade Pennsylvania for the sake of foraging for precious supplies and food sources. A man can go hungry for only a short period, gentleman. But hunger isn't the point here. The good Lord has provided us with adequate food for the time we have been in conflict and I believe He will continue to provide. We need to be faithful to Him, gentleman. Do you understand?"

"Yes, general. I know we can survive and we need to break through with something different in strategy, especially after another earned victory against Hooker," Colonel Venable responded in kind.

"I see what you're saying, general, but do you think you can carry through with an invasion of Pennsylvania and the long journey it will involve?" asked Colonel Taylor. "Your health hasn't been the best these past few months, sir."

"My health is not an issue either, colonel. I have been appointed by President Davis and by God in Heaven to carry out my orders, and orders will be carried out in spite of me, Colonel Taylor. I have appreciated all of your support and help in the past few months, gentleman. I thank God for the men of our army and the faith many of them have in the Lord above. I will miss Jackson. He probably is commanding in the heavens about now and is in a much better predicament than we are."

"Amen to that, General Lee," Colonel Taylor said. "We will see you in the morning, sir. Maybe we'll take a stroll and talk more about the army tomorrow."

"Sounds fine, colonel. Have a good evening."

The silence of the room again crept into the mind and physical being of General Lee. He continued to think on the proper way to finish off the war, a war he had grown used to in the preceding months as commander of all Confederate forces in the east. He began to think of the early morning when he would rise for the day's missions and adventures, still seeing the men sound asleep in their bivouacs. That was his favorite time of day, a time before the sun was strong and the darkness of night was just beginning to fade into the mist of the coming day. Coffee was brewed by the early risers and Lee quoted the scriptures in the joy of the morning. He longed for joy and he experienced it every waking morning from the Lord, but he knew much needed work had to be done before he could experience extended joy.

For now, though, Lee rested in a cozy room of the farmhouse near the wilderness of Chancellorsville. Thoughts of Mary and his sons consumed the remainder of his waking minutes. The faded, filtered sound of skirmishers kept waking him as he tried to get much needed rest. Birds and an owl could be heard. He rocked in the wooden chair, blanket as usual covering his lap and legs for the night. Often times he felt guilty sleeping in someone else's bed. He felt guilt any time he deprived one or more of his citizens the simple luxuries of their own homes. *After all, wasn't the war about the preservation of states' rights and the procurement and preservation of individual rights and decisions?*

Lee fell asleep and dreamt of General Jackson.

"General Lee, what are my orders on this glorious morning, sir?" Jackson said to him in the dream.

*****

The next morning General Lee woke at his usual early morning hour and ate a light breakfast of biscuits and jelly. *Another spring day brought forth more blessing from the Lord,* Lee thought. Trees of green, colorful wild flowers, and sunshine filtered his mind. The early mist and the unpredictable journeys of the day stood before him like many other days during the war. He ate his biscuits and jelly and drank a piping hot cup of coffee as he recited a Psalm to himself and to his God in Heaven.

"Create in me a clean heart, O God; and renew a right spirit within me. Restore unto me the joy of thy salvation; and uphold me with thy free spirit."

He remained seated at a table outside of his headquarters where he was eating and meditating on scripture from memory. He wrote a long message to President Jefferson Davis, in Richmond, regarding the state of his army after the death of General Jackson. He wanted to go to Richmond to meet personally with Davis for the sake of convincing the president of his intended invasion plans into Pennsylvania. Lee knew many of the high command in the Confederate army wanted to concentrate in 1863 on the Tennessee theater of operations over the threat by General Ulysses Grant at Vicksburg. The city was under siege by Union forces there and the citizens were having a hard time of it, trying to survive and keep the city from falling into Union hands. If this happened, the great Mississippi River would be totally controlled by Union forces and a virtual split would be accomplished upon the Confederacy. The threats worried the Confederate high command, especially General James Longstreet, who thought operations in the west were more pressing than in the eastern theater. Longstreet figured Lee's forces could fight a defensive action in Virginia after achieving victory at Chancellorsville, thus giving more priority and manpower to the forces in Tennessee, who were fighting the ruthless General Grant. Grant continually pushed the Union forces to their limits in victory after victory in the west.

In a few days the meeting with President Davis did occur. Lee justified and won approval for the reorganization of his army and received permission for his advance into Pennsylvania for the sake of convincing the Peace Democrats in the North that the war needed to end. A Confederate victory in the North might indeed accomplish the recognition of the Confederacy by the United States government and thus end the bloody conflict.

Lee knew he had to reorganize his army. The numerous amount of men who made up each of the two main infantry corps made it difficult to command in battle. After the death of Jackson this became an easier thing to do.

He told Davis in Richmond, "The army needs a more tightly manageable system of operations when on the field of battle. Corps commanders have a hard time seeing their orders carried out since 30,000 soldiers is a lot of men to command at one time on a battlefield. I want to create a third corps of infantry and along with Stuart's calvary brigades the army will be more manageable and more efficient in battle."

Davis agreed with the plan.

The Confederate army would be organized with three infantry corps each containing three divisions and artillery support. Lieutenant General James Longstreet would command the 1st Corps. His corps would be made up of McClaw's, Hood's and Pickett's divisions. Lieutenant General Richard Ewell would command the 2nd Corps. His corps would consist of Rhodes, Early's and Johnson's divisions. Lieutenant General Ambrose Powell Hill would command the 3rd Corps. His corps would be made up of Anderson's, Heth's and Pender's divisions. Finally, the cavalry command would be led by Major General J.E.B. Stuart consisting of Stuart's and Imboden's divisions.

Lee seemed content with his reorganization plan and was confident now in the invasion plans for Pennsylvania.

"We must give Virginia a reprieve from the destruction of property these past two years," he told Davis when he was in Richmond. "I know my plan for an offensive maneuver sounds as if I am contradicting Confederate war strategy, but if we can get the Union command to attack us on land of our choosing, then we will secure our strategy upon the enemy's own land and bring defeat upon the Army of the Potomac once and for all. We will carry the day, sir. On top of this, the Peace Democratic movement in the North would gain much needed momentum, especially in Philadelphia. I have heard and read the peace movement and Southern sympathies lay waiting in the city."

The 26th North Carolina would finally get its orders in a few days to join with the Army of Northern Virginia for a mission yet unknown to the common infantry units. The 26th would be assigned by Lee to the division of Harry Heth under A.P. Hill's 3rd Army Corp. His division contained many other North Carolina brigades and regiments.

Fredericksburg

The war-ravaged countryside of Virginia met the gaze and minds of Danny Elington and Peyton Caldwell. They were assigned to defend the Confederate holding positions at Fredericksburg after the Battle of Chancellorsville. They were placed by their divisional commander, Lafayette McClaws, back on Marye's Heights behind the infamous stonewall west of the town where many Union men met their deaths in December 1862. This place was where Jesse Elington of the 83rd Pennsylvania Infantry also fell upon the cold Virginia ground of winter.

Danny and Peyton were now experienced soldiers and artillerists who had been through all of the major battles up until the spring of 1863. They fought in many skirmishes since leaving the confines of Caldwell County in North Carolina back in 1861. The two boys, nineteen years old, were considered excellent military men by their divisional and regimental leaders. They knew the call of duty and heard the call loud and clear back in the days after Fort Sumter.

Danny, the son of Harrison Elington, and Peyton Caldwell, the relative of the founding father of Caldwell County, knew each other since they were four years old. Both boys had the pleasure of having Harrison Elington as their high school teacher and also as a mentor in their lives.

Danny, a bright-eyed and articulate boy, was rather quiet as a soldier since joining the 5th North Carolina Artillery Battalion, Battery D, along with Peyton Caldwell. Danny's blue eyes, black hair and slim form made him a standout young man back in Caldwell County, especially with the girls in his high school class. Danny liked to read and dream of adventures he could one day encounter away from Caldwell County. He respected both his mother and father, who inculcated into him a spirit of patriotism and ambition. Like his brother, Jesse, he held strong convictions about the sectional strife that tore the United States into two fragments. Danny, unlike his brother, conformed to the ideas and the aspirations of the Southern cause. He could not fight against his family. He never found in his heart to hate his brother, though. Danny respected the convictions of his brother for the Union cause.

Peyton, a mellow and shy fellow, had seen and talked to Harrison Elington a few months back when he was on furlough for his head wound at Sharpsburg. His light brown eyes, light brown hair and his boyish features stood out as characteristics. Peyton's comical expressions and skinny form made people laugh when he talked and joked back in Caldwell County. His wound brought a more serene and unnerved soldier back to the 5th North Carolina in November of 1862.

"Can you believe we are back here on these heights again, Danny?" Peyton asked in a surprised tone.

"No, I really can't believe we are in almost the same position as we were on December 13, where all of the carnage was caused upon the enemy. My father's letter from a couple of weeks ago out of coastal North Carolina said this is where Jesse may have been fighting with his 83rd Pennsylvania Regiment when he was wounded. Oh man, Peyton! Do you think I could have seriously wounded or even killed my own brother with our cannon fire?

Father said he was shot, but he didn't specify how or with what."

"Could be, Danny. Almighty in heaven! I am sure feeling bad about Jesse. I was thinking the same thing as we approached this position, having the knowledge of where Jesse was wounded in my head. Almighty! Almighty God! Please don't let this be!"

"This war has taken its toll far worse than I ever expected," Danny said. "I remember arguing with Jesse and my mother a couple of months before Sumter. My father was thinking about the grave possibility of war upon the South and he stated to Jesse he would fight for the South if needed. Jesse couldn't believe hearing talk like that from my father. Dad had spent much of his life in the United States Army. How time has gone by and how things have changed."

"You're right!"

"I can't believe Jesse may be gone," Danny said in a low tone.

"Danny, you know death is part of war and it's not going to change with this war. We have to win the conflict in spite of Jesse's situation. The South has invested too much to lose or give up now."

"What do you mean 'in spite of Jesse's situation,' you stupid braggart! I told you before you can really get on my nerves when you preach your know-it-all philosophies to me!"

"Whoa, Danny, you can't talk to me like that just because it regards your precious family! Jesse was a good person, or *is* a good person; I don't know! My parents adored him and were jealous that the Abshires wanted him to manage their gristmill. My father wanted Jesse to help him come up with ideas for his farm inventions back home. It was always 'Jesse this' and 'Jesse that!'"

"How in the world and under these circumstances of war can you be jealous, Peyton? I'm tired of it, boy! I am really sick and tired of it. Do you hear me? Now go and get some more friction primers out of the caisson. We can unlimber this piece and defend the position. Maybe we will kill more Yankees today and you will be happy with your little darn war; your war of cause and conviction; your war of valor and honor. Right, Peyton!"

"Please shut up now, you big idiot. You know I was only trying to redirect your thoughts away from your brother's misfortunes. I know it has hurt you deep inside, but what are we going to do, stop the fight? Are we going to abandon our cannon over Jesse possibly being killed in action? Think about it, Danny. You're acting like a child. The facts still remain in this war and a resolution has to be at hand soon."

"I need to fight and to kill even more, that our cause may be accomplished," Danny said angrily. "We deserve independence. It is our God-given right!"

The rumble of cannon was heard from across the Rappahannock River, where General Joseph Hooker's corps organized positions after their route at Chancellorsville. It was an overcast day and the fire from the cannon could be seen clearly. The Confederate command wanted to secure and guard the position at Fredericksburg and force all of Hooker's army across the Rappahannock at least until Lee aligned his next move for the Army of Northern Virginia.

Hiss … smash!

The blazing convergence of Union artillery fire raked the Confederate positions on Marye's Heights. A couple of cannon were blown to bits just to the right of Danny and Peyton. Men entrenched themselves in the face of the terrible fire that harassed the lines of gray and butternut.

"Load!" said Major Franklin Sayre of the 5th North Carolina Artillery Battalion. The men scurried to secure solid shot from the caissons for the six cannon in Battery D. Barrels were swabbed, solid shot rammed into place. Using a vent pick, one gun crewmember from each of the six-cannon batteries perforated the powder bags, which were set and attached behind the shell, while another crewmember placed the friction primer attached to a lanyard in the hole from where the vent pick was removed. Elevations were measured by another crew member for better aim. The crew waited its turn to fire the gun. Battery D liked to fire in three shot intervals using the six cannon. Peyton was on the same gun crew with Danny and their timing was impeccable and precise in loading, aiming and firing their piece. This resulted from many battlefield experiences together through the two and a half years of the war.

"Fire!" ordered Major Sayre. Three guns belched forth shells.

"Fire!" he ordered again. The other three cannon shot in a salvo across the Rappahannock and into the blue lines of the Union corps.

The major used his small telescope to survey the damage, or lack of, upon the enemy. "Keep the guns aimed as is," yelled Major Sayre. "We got ourselves a destructive line of fire! Look at those Union caissons blowing up. I think we hit a couple of supply wagons, boys. Good job!"

The loading and firing drill continued for about three hours upon the enemy. Not many Union guns were firing back or hitting targets. Then all of a sudden, as Battery D fired its six guns in its three-gun rotation, a Yankee shell made a direct hit on one of the caissons in the rear of the battery's position. The explosion ripped through three crewmembers standing near Danny Elington. Cries of pain and sprays of blood, all twisted in the mass confusion of the moment, were seen by Danny and Peyton. They hit the ground hard to escape any repercussions of the blast. As they were lying on the ground a second Yankee shell hit one of the guns of Battery D and the hot barrel exploded into the back of Major Franklin Sayre. The major fell to the ground without a sound and appeared to die on the spot. One other crewmember from the battery had his arm torn at the biceps and was screaming in pain next to the cannon that exploded.

"Somebody get to the major!" yelled Lieutenant S.A. Sanders. We got to help him before it's too late!" Cannon fire continued to hammer the Confederate positions on Marye's Heights.

"I'm going, lieutenant!" Danny responded.

"What do you want to do, get yourself killed?" asked Peyton angrily. "Wait until the firing slows. We have fought too many engagements to have you die or get yourself wounded over somebody I think is already dead. Look, the poor major hasn't moved since he went down."

"I have to try and help him, Peyton. How can you be so cold, boy!"

"Almighty in heaven. How many officers have we been through?"

"Five!"

"So, what's the point? We will get another major. Maybe you can be our next one, Danny!"

Danny went over to the dilapidated gun where Major Sayre fell. There was no response and Danny yelled for stretcher-bearers to take the major away from the position. Danny had grown fond of Sayre for his fairness and honesty with the men of Battery D. Now another terrible casualty made its mark on the Confederate army.

Nightfall began to creep onto the battlefield and the cannon fire kept up, but at an intermittent rate. Danny and Peyton got a chance to sit down and eat some supper. Peyton ate biscuits left in his haversack from breakfast. Danny and Peyton both had some salt pork left in their haversacks. They made a fire and cooked it up in the pan one of the soldiers carried in his mess kit. The pork was tough to chew and it seemed, Peyton thought, as if all of this battling, killing and wounding on the part of Battery D upon their Yankee enemies entitled the boys to at least a decent meal.

"We can't even get real coffee around here," Peyton said to the other members of Battery D. Many of the other fellows were discharged of their duties for the night and began to gather around where Danny and Peyton were eating and complaining.

"This stinking chicory coffee is a literal disgrace," Peyton continued. "How are we ever going to win the war when the Yankees have us efficiently blockaded from getting basic supplies? Sometimes I think we have all lasted long enough in this army and before more of us common soldiers get killed we better get a furlough or run home. What do you say, boys? Aren't you tired of this mundane and futile existence in our own country? Say something, you idiots, instead of just stuffing your faces! Look at you all, like animals!"

"Peyton, stop harping on us like an old woman," shouted a private.

"Yeah, you do sound like a woman," Danny concurred.

"I am just sick of army life," Peyton said. "When I was home on furlough it was great, just like old times back in the Tarheel state. The comforts of home, nothing can compare to it. I think I'm leaving for home tomorrow, Danny."

"Oh yeah, that's really nice now," Danny replied quietly. "And how do you plan on accomplishing this?"

"I think General Lee wants to invade the North again. He's been itching to do it ever since Sharpsburg, back in September. I can just feel it coming. When we begin the march north, I'm going home, back to North Carolina, Danny.

"Well, just great," said Danny. "You're gonna go home a deserter! And what will Caldwell County think of that piece of information? I can see it now, in the papers: Caldwell County Founding Father's Nephew, a Deserter from the Confederate Cause; a Coward!"

"What do you say to that, Mr. Caldwell?"

"That's all a sham, Danny! No one is going to label me a coward or a deserter after my record of service in this army. I will explain to the town fathers the situation and the awful circumstances of our plight in this stinking war and they will understand. That's what I have to say to your charge, Mr. Elington."

"Fine, Peyton. But what about the Home Guard? Ah."

"Come on, Danny! You saw today how I didn't even care or flinch when Major Sayre was killed right in front of me, right before my eyes. In the beginning of this wretched, stinking war I would have gotten sick to my stomach when I saw a man killed or even wounded. Now I just don't feel anything. It's not a good thing when a man becomes callous toward killing and murder. I feel like an animal, not a person. Are we murderers, Danny?

"Not at all. We are fighting a war, not committing the savage crime of random murder."

"Is that so. Then what do you call what we did to those poor Pennsylvania and New York boys right here at Fredericksburg? What was that? Give me an answer!"

Danny bowed his head in contemplation and stared at the ground. "Well, it wasn't murder, Peyton, it was war. It's war for a cause."

"Is there a cause any longer in this madness?"

"Yeah, there is. It's known as independence and self-preservation."

"I have to have some privacy now. I can reside on my escape plan from this wounded army. I am tired of the killing, or whatever you want to call it."

"Pleasant dreams, Caldwell."

The pitch-black sky, illuminated by the blue sparkles from heavenly stars, hovered over the Rappahannock. The wary boys of the 5th North Carolina Artillery Battalion settled in for another night of guessing and waiting for orders. The smell of gunpowder stifled the air around the camp and the scent of dirty soldiers coupled with burning fires made the camp hot and uncomfortable for the men.

*****

Would General Lee order the invasion of a Northern state? Danny wondered during the night. *Which state would be the target of the Confederate thrust? Did Peyton make sense at all concerning an invasion, or was it just mere speculation? Is there a cause left for us? Where is father now? Will he be part of an invasion with the 26th North Carolina or not? He was determined after news of Jesse to be part of something where a difference could be made for the Confederacy. Where is mother? Jesse's situation, I know, has devastated her beyond belief. In her state of anguish will she leave our home in North Carolina to go and be with grandpa Sumner in Pennsylvania? Will Peyton carry through with his plans of going home, and if he does, what will I do? I wish I could be home now, back in the mountains of Caldwell County and in the freshness of the mountain air. I get sick of the war too, but I don't know if I am able to desert.*

Lord, as I look up to the stars tonight help me see Your divine purpose in this crazy and deadly war, Danny prayed. He never was one to go to church often after high school, but upon hearing that General Lee was a devout Christian and serious about his faith, Danny wanted to model his Christian beliefs after his revered general. If Lee was admired for being overly religious, then Danny thought God could answer his questions of destiny also.

"Well, reveille will come soon in the morning," Danny whispered. "I better get some sleep."

*****

The orders from General Lee came clamoring down the columns of the marching men in the 26th North Carolina.

"We're finally going to join General Lee, boys! We're going to Virginia!," yelled Lieutenant Elington.

The 26th North Carolina was on its way into another skirmish with Union coastal forces near Kinston. They were leaving Goldsboro and then were abruptly redirected to the rail station at Raleigh. It took the 26th a couple of days to reach their new destination in the capital. It seemed to the men the long wait was over and something big was coming down the line. The 26th North Carolina was ordered to Richmond and then to Hamilton's Crossing, located in the area of Fredericksburg. The men knew their daily destinations, but the overall picture was kept from them for the sake of surprise upon the enemy.

In the confines of his ever-obtrusive mind, General Lee secured the invasion plans for Pennsylvania

Lieutenant Elington, Corporal Lewis Fry, Private Alfred Abshire, Private Jackson Coffey, and Private Thaddeus Curtis had now been given a chance at joyously joining the armies of Robert E. Lee. After weeks of speculation, skirmishing and bottleneck operations, the men became enthusiastic and energized by the prospects of fighting with the main eastern-theater armies. New uniforms, courtesy of Governor Vance's uniform factory endeavor, also made the 26th and other North Carolina regiments overflow with a new determination of honor and duty for the cause set before them back in 1861.

"You look great in the new officer's frock, Lieutenant Elington!" said Alfred.

The men were getting ready to march again from their assignment at Harrison's Landing.

"Same with you, Abshire. It was real considerate of Governor Vance to appropriate these here uniforms for us." Elington chewed part of his week's ration of tobacco and straightened his new jacket.

"You better not compliment yourselves to death," Corporal Fry said, climbing out of the breastworks. "We are sure going to get into a big fight and you men better stop worrying about what you look like and start concentrating on the battles ahead of us, for God's sake. I can feel something different coming our way. I hope this feeling is right!"

"It seems like we are holding a position again, lieutenant," Alfred complained. I heard Longstreet's and Ewell's corps have moved out and are heading north. What's going on?"

"I don't know for sure and I don't think we will be staying in the vicinity for long. After all, we are getting ready to move out of here, private."

The mid-June day was unusually warm for springtime. The 26th was ordered to remain with General Harry Heth's division under A.P. Hill's 3rd Confederate Corps as they marched out of the Fredericksburg area. The marching of thousands of soldier's feet clamored in rhythmic intervals, caissons barreled through the dusty rutted roads. Officers ordered their troops to be as quiet as possible, thus Union spies would be deceived of the numbers of men and the smell of many horses confronting the senses. This characterized the next move of the 26th North Carolina Infantry.

"Where are we moving now?" Private Thaddeus Curtis shouted among the clinking, clattering and turmoil caused by the distinct movement of an army corps. Curtis gained respect in F Company after confronting Corporal Fry back at Camp French.

"Colonel Burgwyn stated this morning we are headed to the Culpeper courthouse, where we will then proceed north along with the rest of the army," Harrison responded solemnly. "If we are headed toward Pennsylvania or any other Northern state, I am going to have the devil to pay with my wife. She has clearly been against any invasion of the North in the war." Harrison felt the pain of his digestive disorder flare up the pain in the breadbasket as he thought about the consequences of his Confederate cause.

My wife left Caldwell County and I don't know where she fled to, Harrison thought. The marching began for F Company and the day turned blasted hot. Harrison ordered his company, along with other company commanders, to form columns and march. He then continued in absorbed thought, appraising his life and the effects the war had on it. He marched near his friends, his Possum.

My son Jesse has been sacrificed in this conflict. I can feel it. My property is abandoned in North Carolina. What am I to do? I cannot bear the waiting any longer! Speculation was the norm for most of the men of F Company.

Questions abounded for days at a time on the fate of the army. After their long winter encampment crossing between Virginia and the North Carolina coast, doubts and perplexing thoughts still confronted the regiment.

"Those darn deserters have to be dealt with once and for all!" yelled Fry. "Can you fellows believe that sixteen potbellied pigs left the 52nd North Carolina this morning. Some of my new friends from the other regiments in the brigade informed me of the news earlier. I say firing squads for all deserters; no more leniency."

"Corporal, don't rile the men up right now. We have a lot of marching ahead of us and I don't feel like having the men sick with your preaching about deserters," Harrison shouted.

"Here we go again, lieutenant. Around and around in our little endless circle of debate and conflict. Why do you always see it as your place to monitor my every word and move? Leave me alone, will you!"

"Its just that the brigade officers are expecting a visit from our new divisional commander, General Harry Heth. We want to make a good impression on our new command since we are all anxious to join the Army of Northern Virginia. We don't want to come across as a bunch of whining, blathering idiots. Does that make sense to you or not, corporal?"

"I can't say right now, lieutenant. I have to go really bad, if you know what I mean!"

"You better get going in the woods, Fry," Alfred said.

"I would agree," Curtis added, holding his head in disgust.

On June 16, 1863, Johnston Pettigrew's brigade, under the divisional command of General Harry Heth, made its way into Culpeper courthouse. The 26th North Carolina and the 52nd North Carolina bivouacked near each other when evening came and before moving onto Chester's Gap.

Over the next couple of days, the men felt like they were home in western North Carolina. The majesty and stunning opulence of the Shenandoah Valley, with the Blue Ridge Mountains in view, cast a dreamy blur upon the minds of the men.

Memories of home cascaded like an incoming artillery shell for the soldiers, but the explosion contained life instead of death. Explosions of colors, fresh scents and peaceful sounds permeated the senses. Life seemed new again. Hope caused smiles to break the solemn expressions of stoicism. Among the men of the 26th North Carolina especially, happiness pushed its way through the concreted hearts abused by war and stained with filthiness. The trees of the Blue Ridge cast a spell upon the regiment. The greens of the blackgum, sourwood and dogwood splashed the horizons stretching over the scabrous peaks. The russet maroons of the red maples interspersed the scenery to give it a touch from a master artist. The master artist was God himself as some of the men commented to each other. *It makes you want to get on your knees and praise God for the earth,* Alfred thought. He saw chipmunks and squirrels playing randomly with no worries of war and broken families, sorrow and broken dreams, death and sadness.

Skirmishes, non-stop, continued through the march north. Minie balls and the clamoring of muskets always replaced the solitude of the precious, peaceful moments. The 26th North Carolina hated when this happened, for it was the only peace many of them had had since the war started. The marching continued, though, through all of the skirmishing.

An engagement at Winchester, Virginia, between June 13 and 15 and heavy skirmishes at Berryville and Martinsburg finally cleared the way for the Army of Northern Virginia to proceed without further infractions to the North. Confederate Cavalry units not attached to Stuart's brigades had been effective in clearing enemy skirmishers from the mountains, and General Lee now depended on his cavalry more than ever.

The Confederate army moved slowly, but determinedly, through Virginia and toward Pennsylvania. They marched through Front Royal and Winchester; Berryville and Charlestown; Shepherdstown and Sharpsburg; and then finally to the gates of the North, fording Antietam Creek into Pennsylvania itself. Pettigrew's brigade crossed into enemy territory at about one o'clock in the afternoon, on June 25, 1863.

The minds of the many in the brigade sensed an eerie gratification that filled the soul. Here they were in the enemy's territory, but this territory looked beautiful and peaceful. The acres and acres of undisturbed farmlands, the many domesticated animals waiting to be feasted upon, and the gently flowing streams of clear sparkling water made men feel like they inherited the promised land streaming with milk and honey. The mind also began to focus on the great task ahead of the Army of Northern Virginia. *What would be the mission? How will the objectives of the high command be carried out? Can we escape if the Army of the Potomac sets us in a Yankee trap?* Many of the men in the brigade pondered these questions.

"I heard from the colonel, gentlemen, that our mail service has been discontinued until further notice in our operations," Lieutenant Elington said to his gathering of men. "Communications with home are to be cut in order for resources to be utilized elsewhere." *Abby is going to love this,* he thought. *She'll find out about our invasion from the newspapers. I will not have a leg to stand on if I make it home to her after the war.*

The brigade came to rest at Fayetteville, Pennsylvania, on June 26, 1863.

The 26th bivouacked there on a Friday night and hence the silliness of young men pervaded the atmosphere in camp. Rations were consumed with lots of coffee confiscated from various places in Pennsylvania and enjoyed by the men. Many chickens and other delights were brought into camp against General Lee's strict order not to confiscate property without payment. Lee made it clear to his officers that the men of the Confederate army would not behave as the men of the Union army did when they occupied Virginia. Compensation would be made for the materials needed to support the army while in Pennsylvania, or else punishment would follow.

Civilians would not be random victims of war, according to General Lee.

"What do you think is going to happen next, Lieutenant Elington?" Alfred asked.

"I am not supposed to discuss this at length, but our plan as of now is to entice the Union army to attack us on ground General Lee sees fit for us to fight on, and then to proceed in annihilating that army."

"That sounds like a mighty blessed plan, lieutenant."

"Yes, I think so too."

"May God be with us, sir."

"You keep on praying, Alfred, for we will all be safe and protected in our mission."

"I will, sir."

"Do you really think God cares about us? Especially when we are invading territory not belonging to us?" Fry asked. "Darn boys!"

"Yes, Fry, he cares about us beyond anything in your feeble mind," Abshire answered. Alfred's blonde hair was drenched with sweat from his work loading canteens for his company and from the long march.

"We will see, Alfred. The Yankee army and President Lincoln aren't going to just stand by while we forage in their country. They aren't going to let us darn Rebs devastate their homeland, even if they can't find a decent general to command their sorry butts."

"Enough, men. There will be services the day after tomorrow, this coming Sunday," Harrison said, "and I want the whole company there to stand in unity of prayer for our cause in this land."

"I guess you're being sucked-up by the revivals among our Southern brethren, hey, lieutenant?" Fry asked.

"Maybe so, corporal, but at least it gives us hope and strength in the things we can't understand, like this here war. God is for sure more powerful than us. I have truly come to believe that. I have been feeble in my beliefs. It is about time that I embolden my faith."

"I've known you a long time, Elington; the big military man of the Yankees for a good part of your darn life. An academic who taught a lot of the boys here in the regiment. And most of all, a darned good father who I always saw caring for his family back in the county. I never thought I would see you as a religious man; a Christian. I, for one, want no part of it. God doesn't care for us."

"Kind words from a man who wanted to take my head off when I returned to the regiment."

"Watch it, lieutenant; it could still happen."

"Very funny."

Elington and Fry bonded as soldiers since Harrison's return from furlough.

"God does care for us, Lewis. Remember that. It is not His purpose for man to fight wars and kill each other."

"Keep talking, lieutenant."

"You should try, at least, to turn your attention to God and Jesus once in a while. I think it might flatten that sharp attitude of yours, corporal. We can use less agitation during this invasion." Elington spit tobacco juice from the portion he was enjoying, rubbed the tip of his nose and ran his hand down his face and continued to say, "I hope all of us are able to conquer our inner fears and our outer weaknesses in order to carry out a victory in the land of the Yankees. For if we fail, I fear our cause will be over and done with."

Fry, Abshire, Curtis and Coffey all stared at Elington as if they all wanted to say something. No words came out. There was a peculiar silence within the Possum. The only sound heard was the crackling of the fires where rations were being prepared. Each man bowed his head and contemplated the words of their lieutenant, who for the first time seemed to draw from his closest associates in the company a respectability that enhanced his authority as an officer in the Confederate army.

*****

Philadelphia, June 26, 1863

The evening air sunk down into the great city of the North. The city symbolized liberty, justice and revolution. The American Paris, with its high society populations, its arts and entertainment, its leanings toward Southern sympathy, and its contracts of business and industry established a social fabric that became exclusive and discriminatory among its members.

A naval yard, arsenals, railroads, iron foundries, the Morris Ironworks at 16th and Market Streets and the Robert Wood Company Iron Foundry at Ridge Avenue and 12th Streets, engendered much for the war effort in weaponry and transportation equipment. Sugar refining, textiles in the Kensington section, and omnibus transportation systems throughout made Philadelphia a cog in the wheel of industrial growth and developments.

The captains of industry, with their greed for perpetual materialism and their grand expectations for the future, had for a long time spread their roots in the city of brotherly love. With their stupendous business attachments and their tendencies toward supporting the South on the slave question and race, Philadelphians posed as a paradox to other Northern cities in 1863. Ever aware of the rising African population, many Philadelphians saw emancipation as a destructive force for the future of the city. At the same time, though, Philadelphians stood as the protectors of liberty and equality for all men. Politically, the city had to defend the tenets of Union for the sake of the Declaration of Independence and the great United States Constitution, both products of the city. Once the capital of the infant United States, Philadelphians secured a history of freedom and they knew the world looked upon them for courage and stability in a global society poised for more democratic revolution.

Presidents and congressman, kings and queens, artisans and peasants, saw the city as a bastion of pride for the cause of democracy and republicanism where the average person could make their viewpoints known to governments without deadly reprisals. This was the city that formed a son of English immigrants and a United States Senator from Pennsylvania, Robert Sumner. His daughter Abigail arrived in Philadelphia to secure, with the help of her father, the fate of her son Jesse.

Senator Robert Sumner made a name for himself in the high society of Philadelphia. Extracting many business ventures with Robert Wood in the iron foundry sectors, Sumner became an efficient representative for the Wood Company. Making deals and contracts for sales across the city and across the country, he invested much of his money into sugar and textile industries throughout other parts of the city. A Democrat for most of his life, he switched to the Republican Party after the 1856 election of President

James Buchanan. Sumner once said of Buchanan, "The man has no courage. He lacks the political and economic abilities to be President of the United States. He displays no loyalties and conforms to the bidding of his cronies. I must say the Democratic Party blundered beyond comprehension in this bid for office."

Sumner was a Republican who shared the ideas of gradual emancipation for the slave. He believed forced and immediate emancipation by the federal government upon the states would cause racial, economic and political upheaval beyond the nation's ability to handle and repair such damage. His political and social views were transferred to Abigail at an early age when the senator and businessman saw the impeccable qualities and abilities of his only daughter.

Their family house, located on the block of 20th and Pine Street, stood out with its deep red brick exterior, its four massive chimneys marking the sky, and an ever-present American flag hanging from a pole beside the front door at a forty-five degree angle. The neighborhood breathed with the essence of culture and well-to-do airs.

Assisted by Mr. Abshire with transportation details back in Caldwell County, Abigail trekked through the dangerous war-torn country of the South and then passed over into the strange enemy towns of the North. Abigail Elington was in Philadelphia for about a week now, and her father's political strings failed to locate her son, the young boy who dared to venture to the North and fight for the 83rd Pennsylvania Infantry.

Wounded at Fredericksburg during the cold and dark battle back in December of 1862, Jesse remained missing. His friends from the regiment stated repeatedly that Jesse was transported to a Washington, D.C., army hospital for care of his wounds through immediate medical attention. This occurred in December of 1862 after the battle at Fredericksburg. His friends also stated to investigators from Senator Sumner's office that they saw a doctor, though young and inexperienced, sign orders for the transport of Jesse to the hospital. This also occurred after part of Burnside's armies moved out of Fredericksburg. Jesse's friends said, obviously, they did not oversee what happened to Jesse after his transport, presuming all of the necessary arrangements would be carried forth by the ambulance and the army staffs. Some of his friends stated paperwork errors were common in the transport and registering of wounded soldiers at military hospitals, especially after the carnage and confusion of a major battle.

"We have to get to the bottom of this, Abigail!" her father said. His daughter sat by the window in the parlor, wearing a beige Garibaldi blouse and matching petticoated skirt. She was looking at the seemingly happy and content people walking along Pine Street. "I can't believe this Union army loses many worthless battles against this Robert E. Lee fellow, and then they lose wounded soldiers who are committed to fighting the cause of the same army. I am furious over this! My grandson deserves at least an honorable and proper burial after his service in the Union cause. That is, if he is deceased."

Tears fell down Abigail's face. She sat and listened to her father's complaints, but had no strength to add to or embellish his arguments. She was tired of arguments, war and death. She traveled from the South, dirtied and hungry along the way, trying to prove to herself the fate of her son. She gathered no evidence of his death, yet. She was not convinced of her tragic circumstances befalling her since the letter arrived in Caldwell County.

Does Danny know his brother is supposedly dead? Abigail thought, continuing to stare in a melancholy state out the window. *How has Harrison dealt with this situation? Has he come to grips with the apparent death of his oldest son? Is Jesse dead at all? Has this been one big error on the part of the Union army, just like many of the battles have been? Is my son alive somewhere in the North or the South?*

"Oh my," she thought out loud, "has he become a prisoner of war, locked away in one of those devastating prisoner of war camps? Father, I cannot bear these thoughts any longer. What am I to do?"

"We cannot give up hope, my child. Hope is the lifeblood of our souls when we are faced with afflictions and unbearable junctures in life."

"Why has God allowed these things to occur in our family, Father? Not only are we literally at war with each other, but we have family members who take different sides in the war. Fathers against sons, brothers against each other, and wives who are caught in the middle of the turmoil and ruin of it all."

"Do you really think God is the author of this mess we have found ourselves in, Abby? I really would doubt if God could be the creator of slavery or secession. This is a man-made hell, reminiscent of the days in England when kings ruled with iron fists and did it in the name of God; when English tyranny tried to subjugate our thirteen sovereign colonies with Parliamentary actions unrepresented in our own lands."

Abigail looked at her father and saw tears flowing from his blue eyes as he tried to hide his emotions from his daughter. The senator was a tall man, serious looking and professional in all of his mannerisms. His graying hair made him look distinguished among his peers. However, for the first time the strong man of politics and industry came to realize his precious grandson, who he admired for his courage and conviction, might be lost to the Civil War. Men made of intelligence and passionate convictions of heart, like Robert Sumner, could not hold back their emotions when news came of one younger than themselves being sacrificed on the altar of war.

"Father, I can't remember you ever crying in my presence. Let us try to have hope like you said earlier. Maybe Jesse is alive somewhere and God has spared him for a purpose we don't understand right now. I heard a sermon one Sunday back in Caldwell County about the timing of God. 'He doesn't work according to our finite timetables,' the minister said. 'He does things in his own good time upon the earth.' We need to stand back sometimes in our lives and give our circumstances to God."

"I guess that is why he waited for me to marry your saint of a mother before she died. I have always considered meeting your mother and having the short time I spent with her as the most blessed of things in my life. For look at you, my daughter; you have developed into a lady that I and a lot of other people consider ahead of her time. You are a lady who is not afraid to express and admonish her opinions and convictions upon society and upon her family. You need to be proud of the boys you and Harrison raised. They have both achieved honor and a sense of duty from their parents, especially their mother, who bestowed her rich beliefs and traditions into their souls."

Rain began to fall on the rooftop of the Sumner house. With every drop of rain gently falling onto the house and the street outside came gentle thoughts for Abigail of the many days taken for granted before the war when her family was together and free.

Nighttime, with all of its solitude, encompassed the Sumner house. A temporary peace slid into the minds of Robert Sumner and his daughter. *Being with family can cause outside fears and harborings of doubts to subside for at least a while,* Abigail thought. Like the rain washing the city streets and the polluted air, tears and conversation along with the presence and the security of family gave Abigail sleep like she hadn't had in months. A refreshment of life, a cleaning of her war-torn spirit and travailed mind was charged temporarily at home in Philadelphia.

In all of her dreams, Abigail reverted to one common place; a place where Jesse was safe and all of her men were back in Caldwell County breathing, living and relieved from their fears of battle and war.

Abigail's father looked in on his daughter the night of June 26, 1863. She slept in the bed of her childhood, wrapped in the assurance of her heritage and the love of her father. As the rain fell and Mr. Sumner watched his daughter sleep in peace, the news of invasion began to trickle in from western Pennsylvania. Men in gray were poised at the foot of South Mountain, encamped at Fayetteville, west of the mountains, where General Robert E. Lee had already sent Ewell's 2nd Army Corp toward Harrisburg in an effort to cause mayhem upon the Yankee North.

Not knowing, whatsoever, her son Danny and her husband Harrison were in Pennsylvania, Abigail Elington continued to rest in her secure surroundings in Philadelphia some 140 miles to the east. All efforts by Harrison to inform his wife of the impending move by Lee to the North failed. Abigail had left North Carolina, where Harrison sent all of his letters to her, and now the mail delivery service was on hold until further operational notice.

*****

Fayetteville, Pennsylvania, June 26

The transfer occurred smoothly. Danny and Peyton, along with the rest of the 5th North Carolina Artillery Battalion, were ordered to leave Longstreet's corps, McClaw's division, and join with A.P. Hill's corps, traveling in advance of Longstreet's corps in case of contact with the enemy along the Chambersburg Pike in southern Pennsylvania. This long and straight Pennsylvania road was now occupied by thousands of Confederate troops moving east toward a battle destined to turn the tide of the war one way or the other. The colors of gray, butternut and red canvassed the road as the uniformed soldiers marched, rode and carried regimental flags.

The 5th would be attached to Heth's division and Johnston Pettigrew's North Carolina brigade. Would fate now unite father and son? After two years of separation in the same army, Danny and Harrison could possibly look forward to being near each other in battle that was bound to come soon. The great Confederate endeavor on Union soil was well underway.

The hour was getting late and pickets were spreading out to guard the night position of the Confederate 3rd Army Corps on both sides of the Chambersburg Pike. Lieutenant Elington and his men spread out their bedrolls. Tents were ready to take in the tired soldiers for a night's rest. The coming lightning flashes of battle set into the minds and the dreams of the troopers late in the June evening. Coming out of the western mountains, like a fast rising rain and lightning storm heading east, Harrison could see himself leading charge after charge of Confederate gray against inferior Union lines and positions. He could see General Lee forging the army ahead to victory. Danny was there to fight the cause next to his father, with cannons blazing and cavalry charging. Suddenly, Harrison was awakened by the noise of twenty-four limbered and rolling cannon artillery from the road to his right. It was a unit consisting of four batteries of artillery.

"What in the world could that be?" asked Lieutenant Elington, lurching from his tent quarters. He startled Captain Romulus Tuttle, who had replaced Captain Rankin. Others in F Company were awakened by the commotion late in the evening. General Pettigrew was seen by many of the men coming out of his tent quarters to receive artillery units for the brigade. Questions pried the officers of the companies, for many enlisted men and boys thought the brigade would be moving to a destination for battle during the late hour:

"What's going on here, lieutenant?"

"Is it time for an attack, sergeant?"

"Are there Yankees near our position here at Fayetteville, captain?"

"Are they Yankee prisoners over across the road there?" asked one private from company G who looked about 13 years old.

"Calm down, men!" Colonel Burgwyn whispered as he walked around the camp of F Company. "Show some restraint and order, boys. I think we have artillery units being attached to our brigade for the upcoming fight. I heard General Pettigrew talking to his staff the other day before breakfast about the possibility of having more artillery attached to our division as the 3rd Army Corps makes its way down this turnpike."

"Well, it looks like the artillery has arrived and there is a heap of a lot of guns there, colonel," said Captain Tuttle.

Lieutenant Elington stood outside of his tent and appraised the possibilities that one of those batteries might be from Danny's unit of the 5th North Carolina Artillery Battalion. Battery D was part of the artillery reinforcements sent to bolster the brigade for the imminent fight against the Yankees. As Elington stared across the road, he felt he should go and investigate the identity of the artillery units. He requested permission from Colonel Burgwyn to inquire about the units and made his way over across the pike. He moved slowly through the many tents and dying fires encircling the bivouac of the brigade. He kept his eyes on the target of his investigation.

Pulled by their black horses, the caissons and the limbered guns moved toward the front of the brigade. Elington ran toward the men of the artillery units and tried to study the men to see if he could recognize anyone resembling his son, Danny.

The darkness of night on the Chambersburg Pike and the mud-splattered uniforms of the gun crews made it hard for Elington to focus on anything.

"Hey, hey, can you men halt for a minute," shouted Elington, hatless and without his officer's sword. He saw some of the men stop, but the lead gunners kept on going.

"What can we do for you, sir? Is it lieutenant?" asked one of the privates from the artillery units.

"Yes, it is. I am Lieutenant Elington. What is the name of this artillery command?"

"Our unit is the 5th North Carolina Artillery Battalion, consisting in this present service of Batteries A, B, C and D, sir.

"The 5th North Carolina!" Elington said with surprise.

"We were transferred a few days ago, by orders of General Lee himself, to reinforce your brigade under General Pettigrew and Heth's division. I think the ball is about to open in a big way, lieutenant!" From the darkness another crewmember joined the conversation.

"Hey, Lieutenant Elington? Do you by chance have relatives in the 5th North Carolina?"

"Yes, I do. Who is speaking to me?"

"Is this relative a good soldier and a favorite son of Caldwell County back in the good old Blue Ridge hills?

"Who is that? Show yourself, will you? Danny, is it you, boy?"

"You bet, Daddy!" Danny answered from the darkness along the Chambersburg Pike.

Danny ran out of the darkness, tripping over the ruts and crevices in the road made by the cannon wheels. He embraced his father, slapping his arms around him in utter joy and compassion.

"How are you? Corporal Danny Elington it is now, my boy?"

"That's right, Father, or shall I call you lieutenant?"

"How long has it been, son? How many battles have you been through in this cruel war?"

"Well, its been over two years since I saw you last, back in Lenoir when we were being shipped out of good old North Carolina. Peyton and myself have fought in almost every major engagement up until now. It's been hell."

"I talked to Peyton when we were both home in November. We were both on furlough for injuries.

"He told me all about it."

"Where is he now, Danny?"

"He tried to desert when we started the march North, said he had had enough of soldiering and the war. Me and four other boys from the battalion chased him down and roughed him up a bit. We didn't want to see him shot by a firing squad. We risked our necks to go and get him."

"Good thing you did, son."

"He's quite mad at us for dragging him back to the war. He is serving with some of the distraught boys of Battery C for a while. He'll get over it. He had a hard time with all of the killing going on, especially among our officers. He was starting to think in his mind that we're committing murder on these fields of battle. He began to question if we have a cause left at all in this Confederate army."

"I can understand his dilemma, son. Its been hard for all of us. Have you been injured or cursed with dysentery or anything like that?" Harrison asked.

"Only the dysentery, 'screamers' as the boys refer to it, which knocked me out of commission after the Battle of Sharpsburg. The green apples and corn did it to us."

"You've been blessed, son. This war continues to destroy human life at a disturbing rate and without regard to who you may be in this world. Did you hear of your brother's wounding at Fredericksburg?

"Yes, I did, Father, from Mother. I am sorry."

"No one really knows for sure if he is dead or alive, according to the War Department dispatch I received. Even poor Stonewall was killed not two months ago."

"Father, I have to continue on to our new position down this pike. I can't hold up the guns any longer. Please be careful, Dad. Maybe we can talk more in the next few days; I hope."

"May God be with you, Danny. Stay out of danger as much as you can. Remember, we are in enemy territory now and I don't think General Hooker is going to stand by and let us stay."

"I will see you, Father. Take good care of yourself."

With that, Harrison and Danny parted ways again. A brief encounter between blood relatives produced only a fleeting memory; *a memory that should have had more time to flourish,* Harrison thought. A father and son were subjected to the thief of war. A thief has no care or sensitivity for human relationships. He robs the feelings from one's soul while in its weakest form. How long would this thief be allowed to roam, devour and steal the human spirit? It was like Satan himself maneuvered his way, through war, into the confines of human existence; not using his demons or his legions, but himself to possess the relationships of men.

Harrison went back to his tent quarters across the pike. He continued to ponder the thief of war until he saw his colonel and his friend. He saw Colonel Burgwyn standing in a silent state of prayer and reflection. Still, being up at a late hour was unusual for the colonel. Burgwyn, Harrison thought, had a lot of responsibilities to think on and to handle in the next few days. Death was always on the minds of the men and particularly on Colonel Burgwyn's mind before a battle, but he knew what had to be done.

With the events of the night and the short visit of Danny still fresh in his mind, Harrison retired for the evening to his quarters.

It was a night to remember.

— Chapter 12 —
Caldwell County

June 1863

Rumors around Granite Falls and newspaper reports told of an invasion by the armies of General Robert E. Lee, late in June 1863. The home county of many men in the ranks of the 26th North Carolina and the 5th North Carolina Artillery Battalion was another oppressed Confederate tract of economic distress and military threats.

Caldwell County, known for its Union sympathies, would not escape the cruelties of civil war. The mountain scenery could do nothing to ease the tension and calamities caused by the great conflict.

The stone and white-shingled farmhouse sat on the street's edge, silent and void of activity. The thieves of war intruded and pillaged the property of the once perpetual family. Abigail had left Granite Falls for Philadelphia in mid-June to try and relieve her desperate agony over the fate of Jesse. The house and the farm were left unattended. No life or happy dramas between a family existed there any longer. The hopeless restrictions of war finally came to rest on the tranquil surroundings of the Elington homestead.

Mr. Abshire tended to his duties at the gristmill and tried to keep an eye on the Elington residence. He secured passage of Abigail to Philadelphia by way of carriage and railway. He wanted Abigail to be satisfied in her quest for Jesse's whereabouts. He also wanted Abigail convinced that Jesse was really dead, or if he was still alive. But Mr. Abshire was also concerned about Abigail traveling through the South with all of the raiding, stealing and destruction going on all over the Confederacy. Summer was near again and military activity began to convulse upon the countryside.

Mr. Abshire, immersed in his responsibilities, could not get over the events of a month earlier.

In May, the elements of a Union raiding party crossed the Blue Ridge Mountains at Blowing Rock Gap in Watauga County. Invading from Union-entrenched eastern Tennessee, Yankee marauders made it a habit of entering the western counties of North Carolina to steal horses, take prisoners from Confederate training camps, destroy troop training facilities, burn mills, rob civilians, and recruit Union-sympathizing North Carolinians. However, one of the most important jobs of the raiders was to destroy the transportation and refinement of salt in the Confederate states.

Many deserters from the regiments formed in North Carolina often joined Union-raiding regiments to fulfill their ever-changing loyalties. Like Harrison Elington, many questioned the authenticity of the Confederate cause and determined to go to the other side. Mr. Abshire despised these "gutless traitors," as he called them.

Major Benjamin McQuade commanded 600 organized marauders from the ranks of the Union army. Known as the 9th North Carolina Mounted Infantry and attached to the 23rd Union Army Corps, Major McQuade was given the primary duties of causing havoc behind Confederate lines, concentrating his forces in the western counties of North Carolina. Intelligence gathering and stealing horses for his men to ride characterized his initial actions in North Carolina. As the raids progressed, looting and personal wealth became the new agenda of the regiment.

Destruction of rail lines and train freight confiscations brought much harm to the logistical operations of the Confederate forces. Like the Jayhawkers of Kansas and Missouri, these raiders got what they wanted from the enemy.

Clad in their blue uniforms and trotting on stolen property from the Tarheel state, this 9th North Carolina Union Regiment frightened and humiliated the proud people of the mountain counties.

Back in May the terror hit Caldwell County. The terror always began with the name of the mounted infantry unit; a unit carrying a Southern name in blue uniforms.

"Halt!" Major McQuade shouted to the drivers of three wagons. He turned south into Caldwell County to loot from the citizens there before continuing on to his main mission of destroying the salt works in Smyth County,

Virginia. Like lightning from the western skies, flashing and flickering before a summer storm, the 9th North Carolina Mounted Infantry of the Union army converged upon Caldwell County.

"I said halt, or I will blow those wagons to kingdom come!" The wagons halted immediately. McQuade and his troopers made their way through Granite Falls and took everything they could get their hands on during two days of pillaging property and threatening citizens.

"What do you want with us? Is it major, sir?" asked one of the drivers in a cautious tone.

"I want to see the contents of the wagons. What kind of contraband are we hauling today, you Confederate rats?"

"We are carrying three loads of salt to the center of town, major. It can be distributed to farmers to add to their livestock feeds. You know very well, major, that we need this salt to preserve our meats and vegetables."

"Too bad, Rebel scum! That salt is being confiscated by me and my Yankee infantry."

"Now that's a rotten thing to do to us. You know we need the salt!"

"By the time we're finished in these parts of this traitorous country you call North Carolina and Virginia there won't be any salt left for you, for your families, or for your stinking Confederate armies. Do you hear what I'm saying, Reb?"

"Yeah, I hear what you're saying, but I don't care anything about what you're saying. I'm not a Reb and I don't care too much for you or your stinking Union army, major."

The driver then pulled out a shotgun and fired toward Major McQuade, who was sitting on his horse. The shot missed the major, but took out three of his men who were mounted near him. The other two drivers and a bunch of other men came from under the covered wagons of salt and began to fire at the 9th North Carolina Mounted Infantry. Shots rang out and blasts from shotguns and hunting rifles repeated in the afternoon breeze. Mr. Abshire ran out to see what was going on, for the incident was taking place just near his gristmill. He went back into his mill and grabbed his shotgun and a few of the younger male workers to come out with him. He told the women workers to stay inside.

The fire on the streets intensified as Abshire and his small contingent ran out to help their fellow citizens. McQuade organized a line of his men on the street and they were pouring fire into the wagons. All of the drivers were killed with the Spencer carbine rifles the Union infantrymen were firing. Mr.

141

Abshire began to fire his shotgun at the Union raiders from behind the wall of Lockerman's General Store. Rapid and deadly fire answered his and he fell wounded in the arm. His employees quickly carried him inside the general store, where Johnston Lockerman was hiding behind his counter. One of the employees told Lockerman to help Abshire down into his store basement. Abshire's employees did not want him to be captured or executed for resisting Union forces. Lockerman was successful and Mr. Abshire was spared from the iron fist of Major McQuade for now. Abshire had shot at least one of the raiders.

The 9th North Carolina regrouped after couriers went out to bring the whole regiment together. The rest of the regiment was out foraging and destroying other towns in the county. The officers in the regiment were very concerned that the 200 men with Major McQuade were going to be completely ambushed by the townspeople and possibly Confederate Home Guard troops. The dust from the roads was kicked up all over the center of town by the galloping horses. The afternoon sun was shining brightly in the midst of the commotion and confrontation. A crowd, including family members of the wagon drivers, was screaming and yelling at the Yankee hordes from hell. A sense of panic gripped the town of Granite Falls.

"You're criminals! You Yankees! Why are you killing civilians trying to do their jobs?" shouted one townsman. Cries and yells of rage continued.

"Scoundrels!"

"Rats!"

"Devil Yankees!"

"Murderers!"

"Pigs!"

"Why don't you all go back to Yankee land, you traitors."

"Yeah, we know a whole bunch of you over there are from North Carolina. You're traitors!"

"You're worse than the British Lobsterbacks we fought in the old revolution."

"Why aren't you fighting with Confederate North Carolina regiments?

"Traitors!"

"Why do you even want our salt?" yelled one woman from near Lockerman's store. "Since when does the military ravage and destroy the needs of civilians? Leave us be!"

"That's enough!" yelled Major McQuade. He ordered his men to form double lines up and down the main road through Granite Falls. Their rifles were aimed at the crowd. A few minutes after the shouting from the citizens started, the rest of the mounted infantrymen joined the ranks and the files of their regiment. With five dead from the regiment, it now totaled 595 men. Twenty-one townspeople had been killed and ten others were wounded in the confused and shocking melee.

"What's enough?" asked one of the wounded citizens sitting up on the road.

"If you will disperse immediately, there will be no other retributions against this town," ordered Major McQuade. "Go back to your homes and we will get some of the men in town to get the bodies of these traitors off of the road. You all know the wagon driver fired on me unexpectedly. I did not intend to kill civilians in this raid. We are here only to pillage and disrupt any Confederate army supplies."

"You're a liar, major!" shouted a young man who was on furlough for a wound he received at the Battle of Chancellorsville.

"Liar! Scoundrel!"

"All Yankees are liars! Get out of our town and leave us alone."

"You enjoy destroying our lives and property! We have heard about your army's actions and conduct in Virginia; all of the pillaging, raping and plundering of our country. You want personal wealth off of the hardworking backs of Southerners."

"Get out of our town," another bystander yelled with strong conviction.

"We will, if you comply with my orders," McQuade said sternly.

The crowd dispersed after the response from the major. They did not have the weapons or the manpower to make an attempt at overpowering the mounted infantrymen. Mr. Abshire tended to his arm, with the help of Johnston Lockerman, in the basement of the store. His wound was only a graze, causing bleeding and initial discomfort for Abshire. Now Mr. Abshire wanted to confront the Yankees who had caused calamity and terror in his town and country. He figured, as he listened to the orders of the major from the basement, none of the Yankees would recognize him as one of the shooters. He left the basement and went out onto the street in the center of town.

"Major!" shouted Mr. Abshire. "I would like a few words with you, please."

"No, I am sorry, but I cannot listen to more of you Rebs complaining. I have work to do and raids to plan, sir. There is more salt to confiscate around these parts."

Woman from the town were still crying and screaming insults at the Union regiment. Many of their husbands and sons lay dead on the ground in front of the whole delusional episode.

"I am only asking for a few minutes, sir."

"I said no!"

McQuade, a stern-looking blue-eyed officer with a deep, bellowing voice, continued to order the civilians. His pristine uniform was accented with a yellow sash and he now stood proud and defiant in his demeanor.

Mr. Abshire ran over to the major and grabbed him by the arm to have a word with him. One of the sergeants from a company of the infantry smashed Abshire with the butt of his rifle, hitting him in the shoulder. Abshire went down to the ground in pain and pulled at the legs of the sergeant.

"What do you want me to do with this scoundrel, major?" the sergeant asked.

"Take him over to the town hall building across the road there, sergeant. Tie him to that flagpole and flog him like we do to those dirty, deserting, Irish immigrant soldiers who cause us trouble. Do it now, sergeant!" The crowd reformed over the incident between Abshire and Major McQuade. Everyone became curious and at the same time angry toward the actions of the major. The sergeant dragged Abshire by his wounded arm over to the flagpole and tied rope around him. Abshire faced the pole and he could see the latest list of Confederate casualties posted on the front wall of the town hall building behind him. He tried to ease the pain in his shoulder and arm, but could not do it. His blue eyes welled up with tears for Alfred and he thought, looking at the list, how much he missed his son. He still had hope for his son. Alfred's name hadn't shown up on the list. He thought about how he had seen many families crushed and torn by the war. Now he thought about this raiding, no-good major who was terrorizing civilians for the cause of his Union.

"Major! Can I at least say something in my defense?" Abshire asked.

"You have two minutes, Reb. And I want your name. What is your name?"

"The name is Alfred Abshire, Sr."

"All right, proceed with your statement, Abshire." The crowd became intently quiet. Mrs. Abshire ran from her home to come to the center of town and now saw her husband about to be punished. She stood across the road from her husband and wept at the sight of his poor condition.

"Major, why are you carrying out military operations against civilians? I thought military men fought against other soldiers on battlefields."

"That is all changing now, Abshire. Our commanders want an end to this war and they want it now! All elements serving or supplying the Confederate army in any way must be destroyed. This is a new policy of General Grant out west and President Lincoln himself. You Rebs and any civilians who help or aid in the rebellion must be dealt with at all costs."

"All costs?"

"Yes, Abshire. Is that all, man?"

"Do you have children, major?"

"Yes, I do. What is it to you?"

"I have a son, Alfred, whom I haven't seen in over two years. And now you have the audacity to come into my town and disrupt the lives of the poor people who aren't even fighting the war, major?"

"You are all fighting this war in your own way, you Rebs. You are all traitors to the cause of the United States." McQuade looked about, up and down the street, like he was preaching a political sermon upon the heathen of the South.

"You are traitors to the revolution that gave us this country through bloodshed and sacrifice. I may seem like a hard man, Abshire, but I cannot stand the sight or the smell of rebellion against my country. It's a dirty business, rounding up rebels. It stinks and it has to be disposed of. Do you think everyone should be fighting for your rebel causes. You better look straight to your own towns. Many Southerners, especially from your Confederate state of North Carolina, have joined our cause for the Union and are joining as we speak, man. Do you understand what I am saying?"

"I hate you and your Yankee soldiers and your Yankee politicians, major! I thought I could try to reason with you, but I guess I was wrong."

"You understand correctly, Mr. Abshire."

"I just wanted to try and spare my town from further raids from your Yankee herd of horsemen, who just want to make themselves rich from our misery. I thought we could talk and act as human beings, as Americans. But no, major. War has blinded you and every one of your men. Greed and power have manipulated your souls beyond repair. Isn't that right, major?"

"Don't preach me a sermon, Reb. I want this war over as much as you do, Abshire. But if it has to go on, what is the problem with me and my men gaining some of the spoils of war?"

"I'll say it again. I hate you, major, and your Yankee soldiers and your Yankee politicians who steal and kill our sons. You are killers for profit."

"That's a shame, Mr. Abshire. I was only going to give you twenty lashes with the whip, but now I think you can have full military honors, Reb. Give him forty lashes, sergeant."

The crowd began to hiss and slander the men of the Union regiment with more vehement anger and insolence. The confrontation continued, with the men of the 9th North Carolina Mounted Infantry readied with rifles, again, pointing toward the hostile crowd.

The sergeant whipped Mr. Abshire. Mrs. Abshire could do nothing. Woman in the crowd tried to console her, but to no avail. From the window on the second story of Lockerman's General Store, some of the crowd could see the barrel of a musket peaking out and pointing toward the flagpole. No one said anything. Mr. Lockerman took aim at the sergeant who was beating Mr. Abshire. He thought about how he could not betray his friend and business associate. He thought of all the sons of the South on the many lists always posted on the wall of the town hall building. He thought of the Elingtons and their pillaged property. Lockerman had seen Major McQuade and about fifty of his men descend upon the Elington residence earlier that day and take everything of value from the farm and from the house. Johnston Lockerman, with his small frame, lanky form and dark hair and eyes, had always been mild-mannered and gentle in his dealings with the citizens of Granite Falls. But now he had had enough of the war and the abuse from the Yankees and their egocentric leaders.

He aligned the sights on his musket and put the sergeant's head right into aim. Lockerman pulled the trigger and hit his target with devastating effect. Multiple shots rang out from the street below, from the soldiers of the 9th North Carolina Union Infantry, blasting Johnston Lockerman's insides to pieces. His body came crashing through the window of the second floor storage room where he was perched. The force of the shots pushed him violently backward; he fell into solid crates that were behind him and close to the window and then he was hurled out of the window and down onto the road for all to see.

"Second sergeant, resume the punishment," Major McQuade ordered. He seemed to ignore the firing and the death of one of his company's first sergeants. The blood flowed freely down the gutter of the street. The blood of Johnston Lockerman and the unnamed first sergeant mingled on a road of a town in the Confederacy. The mingling of the blood had a strange effect on the crowd and on the common soldiers in the 9th North Carolina. For a fleeting moment, Mr. Abshire's words made sense. The sons of Americans were being sacrificed on both sides of the conflict. American civilization was destroying itself town by town and man by man with its own sons. *What a catastrophe this all is and continues to be,* thought many in the crowd and in the battle lines of the 9th North Carolina.

Mr. Abshire received his forty lashes as ordered by Major McQuade. His back was a bloody mess of open wounds and torn flesh. Mrs. Abshire ran to her husband after the beating was over and with the help of friends carried him back to their home near the Elington residence on Sunset Street. Major McQuade coldly resumed his duties after the flogging, ignoring the help Abshire was getting.

He could hardly make it into the house. Mrs. Abshire noticed on the way back home that the Yankees had stolen all of her horses. Furniture was destroyed inside the house and personal belongings were pillaged. The town doctor tended to Mr. Abshire.

"He'll recover, Mrs. Abshire, but it is going to take a while for the healing of those abrasions."

The next morning, Mr. Abshire heard hundreds of horses moving and trotting. Major McQuade and his Yankee hordes were done with Granite Falls and other parts of Caldwell County. They were off, according to Mr. Abshire's conversation with Major McQuade, to Virginia to destroy the elements of more life. Salt was the target. Used to preserve, clean and medicate, the Union command knew salt depravations could cause more harm and destruction to the Confederates than artillery shells hitting direct targets. This was a cruel human fate. *What would be next?* Mr. Abshire thought as June came to Caldwell County.

The war went on and now news of an invasion to the North by General Lee filled the town conversation. *Will Northerners now face the same treatment as we have had in the South?* Mr. Abshire sympathized for the dead on both sides in the war, but now he wished the same treatment on Northern civilians. Treatment of humiliation and depravation needed to be forced on Northerners, for they might give up their operations in the war.

General Lee had everything to prove in his quest to Pennsylvania.

Mr. Abshire continued to ponder the invasion. June came to a close and as he went back to the operations of what was left of his gristmill, uncertainty filled his mind.

Before McQuade left Granite Falls he found out Abshire owned the gristmill in town. He ordered his men to burn the mill's storage warehouses, but for some reason did not order the total destruction of the mill itself.

Mr. And Mrs. Abshire took from the actions of Major McQuade some hope in humanity. They also began to communicate more with Abigail

Elington in Philadelphia. Senator Sumner was able to get messages through Confederate lines back to Granite Falls. Abigail and the senator were curious as to what was going on in the South during the Confederate invasion of Pennsylvania.

*****

News of invasion spread all over the North and the Union command was debating what course of action to follow after their defeat at Chancellorsville in early May. Harrison Elington and the men of the North Carolina regiments were cut off from communicating with their loved ones. Lee wanted no distractions in his plans toward a victory on Northern soil.

He wanted to build upon the Peace Democrat's confidence in ending the war and bringing closure to the status of the slave question in the United States.

– Chapter 13 –
The Arsenal

June 28-29, 1863
Fayetteville

He entered camp on a shiny black mount, saddlebags packed with unknown contents, an expression on his face of utter seriousness. The chaplain was giving a stirring Sunday sermon to the men of the 26th North Carolina. The unfamiliar officer trotted past the 26th. He listened to parts of the sermon as he sat upon his horse. Few of the men noticed him passing by, for they were intent on absorbing and concentrating on the words of the chaplain. The officer, dressed in a charcoal-gray major's uniform, stood up straight in his saddle and trotted by the other encampments. He gazed intently upon the men of Pettigrew's brigade. In his forties, his crystal blue eyes, blondish hair and muscular build gave him a presence later noticed by the other men who were tending to the morning duties of the brigade. He wore a black slouch hat sloped over his eyes, but his gaze still penetrated from beneath the brim of the hat to reveal someone who commanded attention. Lieutenant Elington was the first to notice the officer after the sermon ended.

"Hey, boys! Who do you think that is on the black horse over there?

"Looks like a Yankee to me in the dark uniform," Corporal Fry said. Laughter filled the area around where the Possum was sitting. They had all gathered together to hear the sermon near a fire where a pot of coffee was brewing. Tents were still perched and the common designs of a bivouac surrounded the men. They were in good spirits after the sermon and they wanted to forget the horrors of war for at least a day.

Fry, usually confrontational in his demeanor, knew when to say something to lift the spirits of the men. He acquired this gift after his injury at Malvern Hill. As the anniversary of that battle crept up on the men of the 26th North Carolina, a new sense of hope entered their minds.

Corporal Fry, Privates Abshire, Coffey and Curtis, and Lieutenant Elington—the Possum—laughed at the prospects of the officer being a Yankee.

"If he is a Yankee, corporal, then I guess we have lost the war, or we are all a bunch of traitors for having the fellow in our camp," said Private Thaddeus Curtis.

"Let's stop being silly here, men," Lieutenant Elington said. "I am sure the gentleman officer is a Confederate and we haven't lost the war yet. I will find out later, I am sure, who he is and what his business is here in our camp."

"Do you think Pettigrew or some other high-ranking officer in our brigade has been replaced by that fellow?" Private Abshire asked.

"No," Private Jackson Coffey answered. "Why would they replace good officers such as Pettigrew or Heth? They are men distinguished in honor and duty in the war and I, for one, don't want to see them go. For God's sake, we are in enemy territory! Why would Lee change officers now?" Speculation continued among the Possum despite Elington's words of assurance.

"Sometimes I wonder if our leaders in Richmond have their heads on straight."

"I often have the same thoughts, Alfred," answered Thaddeus. "My daddy always said that politicians can't run a war from far-off places. They don't know what the soldiers really need and they don't know what the soldiers go through in battle. Hell, we're lucky if we can get more food rations sent to us from Richmond, let alone worry about a change in officers."

Jackson listened to the conversation at the campfire and said, "Why do you think General Lee was the choice to replace General Joe Johnston back a year ago? The politicians in Richmond did know something about war, for what better general could we have gotten than Robert Lee."

"That's a good point, private," Fry said. "General Lee and all of our leaders are the best in both armies. I can't believe on this Sunday, in enemy Yankee territory, these darn idiots are questioning and doubting the leadership of the Confederacy. What is wrong with you, Abshire and Curtis? I can't figure you out."

"Let's calm it down, boys," Elington said forcefully. "Remember, we are all on the same side and we are in enemy territory, like Fry said. The politicians have their jobs to do and we have our jobs to do out here in the field. Let me go and see what's going on with this fellow."

The men of the Possum remained conversing and sipping coffee by the campfire while Elington went to Colonel Burgwyn's tent. The mounted officer was waiting outside of the tent and looked over to Elington. Nothing was said between the two. Elington asked Lieutenant Colonel Lane if he could speak to Colonel Burgwyn for a few minutes. Lane said he would see what he could do. Lane knew the colonel was quite busy this Sunday morning.

Elington continued to observe the mounted officer. The stranger to the camp made distinct observations. Elington thought the officer had a way of studying people and their actions with an efficient aptitude. *What does he want from our brigade?* Elington thought.

"Good morning, gentleman," Colonel Burgwyn said, emerging from his tent quarters. "That was a fine sermon today. Would you agree, Lieutenant Elington?"

"Yes, sir. A fine sermon on this beautiful day."

"Lieutenant, I will call for you later. I need to meet with this gentleman, General Lee, General Heth and General Pettigrew first. Important and urgent business has come to my attention and it can't wait. However, I will do my best to speak with you at your request as soon as I can."

"I understand, sir."

Colonel Burgwyn mounted one of his prized horses and made his way with the major to meet with the other officers. Elington did not know where the meeting was to taking place, but he speculated it would be wherever General Lee's headquarters was located at the time. Elington went back to his men and the daily regimental duties were carried out: men washed their clothes, extinguished unnecessary campfires, cooked rations, received couriers, foraged for more food and some of the men of the 26th were ordered by Pettigrew's staff to go out and round up Alabama and Tennessee men from Heth's division who were outwardly violating Order 73. General Lee had made it clear to his officers to make payment for confiscated supplies while in Pennsylvania.

Elington and the men of the 26th North Carolina could see the range of the South Mountains east of Fayetteville. What was waiting for them beyond the mountains? Elington thought about this question as he watched his men busy themselves with their daily camp chores. *Can General Hooker maneuver into a position to destroy the Army of Northern Virginia? Where is General*

Stuart? Will he help us in our time of need upon the ground of the enemy?

Sunday, June 28, proved to be another day of thinking for Harrison Elington and his men. Sacrifice dominated his thoughts. *Jesse is in some type of peril, I suppose. Abigail has left Granite Falls, as far as I know, and my property has been abandoned. I have seen Danny, but I pray he will be safe. His battery of artillery is sure to be present when the shooting first starts in this coming battle. Danny, whether I like it or not, is going to be on the front lines of the fighting. I don't want to lose another son to war. I have sacrificed too much as it stands now.* Looking east toward the South Mountains, the mountains that seemed to reflect much about home in Caldwell County, Elington continued to wonder and contemplate his fate beyond the elevations. Questioning voices soon overtook his thoughts and he could hear the sincerity wading through the camp.

"Are you all right, sir?" Alfred asked.

"I don't know. I have too many unanswered questions floating around in my mind today. Questions I haven't thought about for a while have swept my mind like a Union skirmish line."

"When will our questions be answered, lieutenant?" Coffey asked.

"When we win this battle in the North and end the war. You and I know it is the only blessed thing that will answer all of our questions. Then we will truly find out about our families, our homes and our lives, private."

The Possum finished up their daily chores and sat down for a rest and for some lunch. Fresh chicken was on the menu for the day, along with corn and tomatoes. The rich and fertile Pennsylvania countryside continued to provide the men of the 26th with a vast amount of varied foods. Elington and his Possum sat around a small fire where more coffee was being brewed and each man took a piece of the chicken that had been roasted by the regimental cooks. The men enjoyed their usual ration of cornbread and molasses along with some bacon. Apple butter sweetened the meal, but nasty mosquitoes tried and failed to take the joy from the soldiers.

The heat of the day wore on the men. Water was fetched by some of the privates in B Company and distributed to the regiment. The cold water from the creek reminded Elington of the carefree days back in the mountains where he would take big gulps of mountain water after journeying through the trails as a young man.

"Can you believe all of the men from the Confederate army who have died at such a young age?" said Corporal Fry directly to Elington. "All of the men who will never have an opportunity to have a wife, to have their first home back in the mountain country, or to own their own land for tending crops. Men who have been denied the pleasure of having their own children and their own feelings toward those children."

"I sometimes can't believe it, Lewis. Thousands have died for our cause and how many thousands will still die in the battles to come. I hope General Lee can accomplish what he wants to do in this invasion. We are running out of men everyday and we can't replace them."

"I hope to God we can win a battle here in Pennsylvania, lieutenant."

"Did you hear it, boys!" Alfred shouted. "Corporal Fry has asked God to help us. The God he doesn't believe exists. The God he thinks doesn't care for us. I think the Almighty has something special in store for our regiment after the corporal's leap of faith today. Was it the sermon, Lewis, that changed your thinking?"

"Will you stop your bragging, Alfred? I was only speaking in a common expression. I still don't believe your Christian God cares about us or this stinking war. He has abandoned us, private."

"That's a downright heathen statement, man. You better ask the Almighty for forgiveness, or else I would be fearing for my life if I was in your shoes, Lewis."

"Fearing for my life! Come on, Alfred, we have all feared for our lives since New Bern and Malvern Hill. Darn! I have feared for my life ever since joining this regiment, having been shot at from muskets, cannons and, for God's sakes, even gunboats. I have had one of my fingers sliced off by those gutless sawbones and I have been demoted once in my service to this regiment, for my opinions and beliefs. We constantly fear for our lives."

"Victory will bring the greatest blessings and joy to this army," Elington said solemnly. "I believe God will grant us victory in this land. Keep praying, Alfred, and seal our victory."

Late afternoon came on Sunday with a bright shining and blazing sun. The men were given extra rest for the heavy marching they endured through the Shenandoah Valley. Their marching was plagued by an early spring heat wave giving the men further burdens of stress. Sunday was a blessing for the 26th and they knew it, for battle was close at hand, enveloping the mind and soul of the men from North Carolina. Elington sat down by an old maple tree and realigned his sight and his thoughts toward the South Mountains to his east.

Danny must be closer to our destined battle upon this ground of the enemy, he thought.

I just pray to you, Jesus, that my healthy son can endure and persevere through the upcoming firestorm. I pray, Lord, Your guiding hand can be placed on his soul and let him rely on You for strength and hope, for You are his only hope in the madness we are fighting through. I am sorry for ignoring You, my dear God in Heaven, through all the years of my life. I have taken too much for granted. I have become ashamed of myself to now come to rely on You in my time of trouble, confusion and heartache. My faith has become stronger for You in this war, Lord, and I thank you for sending Alfred our way. He has been a mighty witness for You through this struggle of civil war and murder. Bless Abigail, my dear wife, and send her hope wherever she may be. Amen.

*****

They came rushing back to camp at about five o'clock that evening. Colonel Burgwyn and the dark-suited major trotted briskly through camp and toward the colonel's tent, which was located on the northern side of the regiment's bivouac. Burgwyn's fellow officers and staff joined him on his return to see what the new orders were for the 26th. Lieutenant Colonel John R. Lane, Major John Jones, and a few of the regiment's company captains came to greet the colonel and to see what the long meeting had been about. After all, it was quite unusual for General Lee to meet with specific regimental commanders in the field. Lee always entrusted his corps and division commanders to discharge his orders to the brigade and regimental levels.

There was much talk among the crowd of officers and among the enlisted men, who again tried to speculate what was going on. Colonel Burgwyn sent his couriers out to each company captain in the regiment to say there would be an urgent meeting outside of his quarters in half an hour. Only Burgwyn's officers and company captains were to attend. Questions were now running wild to what was to unfold at the meeting. Anxiety was at its highest, for many of the men knew something big was coming, but they just couldn't pinpoint it as of yet.

At six o'clock the meeting began. To everyone's surprise, around Burgwyn's tent quarters, the sound of horses interrupted the solitude of the camp. The men of the 26th observed the trotting horses bringing Generals Lee, Hill, Longstreet, Heth and Pettigrew into the bivouac of the 26th North Carolina. The conversation among the men increased until they were called to attention by General Pettigrew himself.

He stated to the men that, "pressing matters necessitated a meeting of high-ranking officers and I would appreciate your quietness and cooperation as the meeting commenced."

The enlisted men gave a loud and pompous cheer to their officers and then efficiently went back to the work of readying themselves for battle. Tent encampments of some privates and corporals were moved temporarily away from the front of Colonel Burgwyn's tent. The officers could then converse in private and without interruption or delay.

General Ambrose Powell Hill opened the meeting by introducing Major Frederick Albert Fincannon. The major's habit of folding his arms while standing and listening to people was evident this day. The major strolled into camp that morning, but no one had met him in Pettigrew's brigade. General Hill pulled a map out of a cylindrical case. The map displayed a town called Gettysburg and it contained traces and markings of roads leading to Philadelphia, clearly labeled. The map was placed on Burgwyn's observation table and the officers poured over the contents.

"Gentleman, study the map before you," said General Hill. "General Lee has anticipated, without reconnaissance information from General Stuart, that it would be best to march toward the junction town of Gettysburg, which we estimate is probably less than twenty miles from General Pettigrew's present location." Looking down, pointing to the map and appearing to have every officer's attention, Hill continued. "We are here, in the encampment of the 26th North Carolina at Fayetteville, Pennsylvania."

"I think we all know that by now, general," answered General Longstreet in his usual dry manner. The other officers laughed at Longstreet's comment, which broke the tense mood, but then they seriously turned their attention back to the map.

General Hill proceeded with his explanation.

"Our objective for a victory in Pennsylvania is to agitate General Hooker to advance against us in his home territory. Hooker, being under pressure from Lincoln in Washington, will be forced to attack us without hesitation. We can then maneuver to force the Union corps to attack us on defensive ground of our choosing. We must try to preserve the army, the ammunition and the morale of our men during this campaign."

General Lee stood unusually quiet as Hill continued his explanation of the plan.

"General Lee placed me in a position before we left Virginia to recruit a brigade of men from the western theater of operations. The purpose of this brigade is to assemble an intrepid force of men who would not decrease the numbers of our three present corps, and have this force invade Philadelphia, hopefully at the same time we engage Hooker's units somewhere near Gettysburg. This brigade will be led by Major Fincannon, who has had much experience in scouting and raiding communications facilities for our army, especially in Tennessee and Kentucky. We want to do extensive damage to the Frankford Arsenal in the northeastern part of the city. Its mass production of percussion caps, cartridges and timed fuses supplies many Union soldiers in the field. Major Theodore Laidley has procured the annual production of some two-hundred and fifty million percussion caps in a factory built on the grounds of the arsenal. He also has ordered the production of three million friction primers for artillery and twenty million cartridge assemblies for various guns.

"The Frankford Arsenal also has a 50,000-pound powder capacity; it stores more than 18,000 muskets for new recruits and replacements; it produces timed fuses for various artillery shells; stores horse equipment for mounted cavalry units; and through the work of Alfred Mordecai, a native North Carolinian, has attained some abilities to apply scientific methods to munitions production. Mordecai has enabled many weapons to be mass produced in the North, thus giving the Union army an infinite supply of munitions for war.

"We believe an attack on this facility will cause a concentrated blow to the Union army, and it may promote the political movement and philosophies of the Philadelphia Peace Democrats to push for an end to the war and recognition of the Confederacy as a legitimate country. Civilians will not be attacked in this raid unless they purposefully try to suppress the mission. Then action will have to be taken. The last thing we need, though, is a massacre of Northern civilians that would cause a reversal in our strategy toward Philadelphia. The situation is a delicate one. It needs much in the way of coordination. I know Major Fincannon can be trusted to maneuver into the situation using his 3,000 man brigade to attain the objective.

"A simultaneous victory on a battlefield in the fields of southern Pennsylvania, coupled with a massive explosion and destruction of the Frankford Arsenal, could achieve great psychological, political and military effects on the enemy. The people wouldn't be able to predict what would happen next after the explosion at the arsenal. The Peace Democrats will criticize the Republican administrations of Governor Andrew Curtin and

Philadelphia mayor, Alexander Henry, for not supplying an adequate defense for the city of liberty. You understand, gentleman, there can arise many complications in this raid and attempted battle plan, but General Lee and President Davis himself have endorsed the strategy and the guerilla-type tactics involved here. We have studied, intently, the Spanish guerilla tactics against Napoleon in the Peninsular War back in the early part of our century. Those 'little wars' produced many casualties for the French and I think it can work in this situation upon our present enemy. General Lee, do you have anything to add at this time?"

"Gentleman," Lee said, "this plan has been well thought out and gone over many times before we left Virginia and many of our scouts have kept us abreast of any changing situations in Philadelphia. We have been fortunate to secure the work of scouts who have infiltrated the arsenal in Philadelphia. They were able to do this back in the winter and with the help of individual Peace Democrats in the city who warranted jobs for a few of the scouts in the percussion cap factory. These people have been paid in gold and can be trusted. Also, we have acquired information from Josiah Gorgas, the former superintendent of the Frankford Arsenal, who is now Confederate secretary of ordnance in Georgia. Gentleman, this mission has to work, or we will be forced back into Virginia with no alternative plans for victory. I believe it would only be a matter of time before our great and brave army would be worn down by the industrialization of the North. We all know this to be true and we have to realize how important a victory is for all of us. The things discussed here today will go no further for the sake of the raid on Philadelphia. Captains, you may inform your officer staffs about the agenda, but that is it. I am issuing this under the guise of Order 75. 'Arsenal' is the code name of the order. I want Major Fincannon to now brief you on the locations, roads to be used by the brigade and building facilities at the Frankford Arsenal. Major."

"Thank you, General Lee. It is my honor to be among the corps commanders of the Army of Northern Virginia. Your victories and your plentitudes of leadership have been well known throughout our armies in Tennessee and Mississippi. You, my fellow officers, have been an inspiration to the Army of Tennessee." Major Fincannon looked intensely around the map table and tried to look deep into the eyes of every officer present. His blue eyes seemed to cast a sense of sagacity and unexplained insightfulness upon the other officers, except for General Lee, who already knew the mission by heart.

"General Hill, is everyone present who will join my brigade on the journey to Philadelphia?"

"I believe everyone is here, major."

"General Pettigrew, is your explosives man here to be briefed on this mission?" Fincannon asked.

"Please excuse my oversight, major, General Lee. Colonel Burgwyn, please go and get Lieutenant Elington. We need to bring him here to see if he will help in this raid on the arsenal. Please get him now!"

"Yes, sir, general."

"Gentleman, again, please excuse my oversight on bringing Elington to the meeting. I have no excuse to offer except for my forgetfulness. Colonel Burgwyn graciously suggested and recommended the lieutenant a few weeks ago after I briefed the colonel on the updated information concerning the raid. Elington has had seventeen years experience in the U.S. Army and during his service to the army he worked on explosive technologies."

"No need to apologize, General Pettigrew," said General Hill to his brigade commander. The other officers agreed and tended their understandings to Johnston Pettigrew.

"It has been a stressful time for all of us, Johnston," General Lee added.

"Thank you for the words of confidence, sir."

Colonel Burgwyn came back to his tent with Elington beside him. Elington was in awe as he approached the map table surrounded by the high command of the Confederate army. He observed General Hill with his red battle shirt under his gray jacket. The general seemed pale and sickly as he spoke among the other officers, but his speech and his forcefulness of words blended into an air of confidence. Elington looked at General Longstreet, Lee's Old War Horse, who was staring at the map and its markings of the city of Philadelphia, his gaze casting doubt on what was being discussed. Longstreet smoked a big cigar. It often calmed his apprehensions, according to rumors from his staff. He looked over and saw Major Fincannon, who he had run into outside of Colonel Burgwyn's tent that morning, never guessing he would be asked to serve on a mission right from the top of Confederate command. Then he gazed at General Robert E. Lee, the great warrior general, who had outmaneuvered four Union generals at battles on the Virginia Peninsula, at Second Manassas, Antietam, Fredericksburg, and most recently, Chancellorsville. He couldn't believe he was standing before the great leader, the man of God, the consummate optimist, who always saw a way around a larger army than his own.

Elington felt a sense of embarrassment standing among the great commanders. He thought immediately of all the times he questioned and ridiculed the very leaders who now were before him. *My God, I have committed treason in my heart, against these men of honor and courage. I have faltered in my dutiful respect. I can see in their faces the storms and the unrest of war. These men have been faced with the plain horrors of leadership where they have to order the deaths of many comrades upon the hallowed fields of this war. If they only knew the betrayal I have committed in my soul when I thought about going over to the Union cause with Jesse, when I argued with Lewis about our leaders, and when I agreed with Abigail on occasion in degrading General Lee and our politicians in Richmond for being committed to a possible treasonous cause. Please Lord, forgive me in the face of these tested men and help me to do what they ask of me.*

"Lieutenant Harrison Elington of Granite Falls, Caldwell County, North Carolina; is that correct information?" Major Fincannon asked.

"Yes, it is, major."

"By the way, Elington, my name is Major Frederick Albert Fincannon out of the Army of Tennessee and born in the grand old state of Louisiana."

"Glad to be of service to you, major."

"Lieutenant, please be introduced to General Lee," Fincannon said. "Also, this is General Hill, General Longstreet is here to my left, and I am sure you already know General Pettigrew and Colonel Burgwyn."

"How do you do, gentleman? It is my honor to be here among you and at your service," said Elington. He looked at each officer and made sure he presented a demeanor of confidence and ability to his superiors. After all, he was approaching these men with an overriding feeling of guilt. He needed to hide his former feelings, even though no one present could ever read his mind.

"Lieutenant, you have been recommended by Colonel Burgwyn and General Pettigrew to accompany a raid into the northern city of Philadelphia in order to cause massive destruction upon the Frankford Arsenal located in the northeastern section of the stated city. All of us around this table plan and hope to have this raid take place simultaneously with a grand battle against Hooker's Union corps, who are tracking our movements at this very hour. Do you understand this, lieutenant?"

"Yes, I do, major, but ..."

"No questions or inquiries at this time, Elington. You will be presented with the plan and then you will have until tomorrow evening at around

159

suppertime to give Colonel Burgwyn your answer. Other prospective officers who have had work and experience with explosives will be informed of the plan and some have already been informed of the duties required. However, with your experience in U.S. Army explosives and timing fuses, you come highly recommended from your superior officers. They have reported you are not only experienced in what we need, but you are committed to the Confederate cause and your loyalty cannot be questioned. Is this clear to you, lieutenant?"

"Yes, sir. I appreciate the confidence of my superior officers in this matter of recommendation. I thank you both, Colonel Burgwyn and General Pettigrew."

"All right! Enough with the formalities and gratitudes. We have business to take care of and I want you, especially, Elington, to listen to the plan and the modus of operations for this raid. Then you can mull it over in your sleep tonight."

Again, laughter from the officers interrupted the flow of conversation, but then the major got everyone back to the pressing matter at hand.

Evening fell upon the brigade bivouac of the North Carolinian regiments. Soldiers lit new fires to cook supper rations and to brew a last pot of coffee for the day. Coffee became popular again since entering Pennsylvania. Foraging and confiscations by Confederate soldiers enabled the supply of coffee to grow.

A peaceful atmosphere descended on the camp and officers continued their conversations and planning for the Philadelphia raid. Cooks from the 26th North Carolina brought coffee to the officers still assembled around the map table. The officers refused a meal that evening. The pressing business before them was enough to fill their stomachs with anticipation. However, many of the enlisted men were again enjoying meat from pigs and from chickens. They were able to boil vegetables to their liking and then topped off their meals with biscuits and apple butter washed down with coffee. Men enjoyed and appreciated a new pair of shoes supplied from Chambersburg and York, Pennsylvania. The shoes were confiscated by General Richard Ewell's corps. His corps was well in advance of Lee's army and they had already threatened and taken over some towns containing crucial supplies for the Army of Northern Virginia. These supplies trickled back to the 3rd Corps.

"All right, let's go over the strategy and tactical information one more time for the sake of Lieutenant Elington," Major Fincannon said enthusiastically. "Then we'll retire for the evening."

"That would be just fine, major," General Longstreet answered tiredly.

"If you look at the map you can see a road leading out of Gettysburg. The town is surrounded by good roads and railroad junctures. The road that will be initially used by my brigade is the York Road, which extends northeast out of Gettysburg and to the town of York. If General Hooker doesn't march toward Gettysburg, then he has a problem. He would just wear his army out marching it off major roads like the ones on this map. Consequently, General Lee is counting on the Union army to use these roads so an engagement can be commenced at or near Gettysburg. Our scouts from Ewell's corps have informed us there are many good high ground positions south of Gettysburg that could serve as Confederate defensive positions; a dug-in position where artillery could make quite a difference upon the enemy.

"Our brigade would then make its way onto the Philadelphia-Lancaster Turnpike coming out of York. We have to get there before the Philadelphia defenses come out and burn the bridge at Wrightsville and Columbia, which crosses the Susquehanna River. The bridge is vital to the plan of operations. The turnpike will take us right onto Lancaster Road in Philadelphia. We have been consistently informed that Governor Andrew Curtin of Pennsylvania and General Napoleon Dana, in charge of the defense of Philadelphia, have been unable to mobilize people to protect their own city. I think Philadelphians are sure we are not going to invade their city. They have grown insusceptible toward seriously defending their environment from our army. Real troop strength is at around 600 trained troops and maybe 400 more who could be mustered out of other duties in and around the city. Artillery would not be a problem. Our scouts have doubly verified to General Lee and myself there are approximately ten guns present for defense. It is to be concluded Philadelphians are apathetic toward an invasion. We could have Lincoln totally embarrassed if the city of brotherly love, the city of the Declaration of Independence, and the city of the U.S. Constitution was marred and violated by the enemy in a surprise raid. I think the people would literally throw him out of office."

"That would be a blessing, now, wouldn't it?" replied Longstreet. "I am getting tired, fellows. Will this be much longer?"

"No, general. Just a few more minutes," Fincannon said. "Once we enter the city near Hestonville and Ardmore along Lancaster Road, we will destroy the line of weak defenses set there by General Dana. We will then proceed to the Market Street Bridge crossing the Schuylkill River in downtown Philadelphia. Let's count on the bridge being intact there when we enter.

Fording the Schuylkill there is not going to be possible.

"If we make it cleanly to the Market Street Bridge, we will immediately proceed to the Frankford Arsenal, which is situated along the Delaware River on Bridge and Tacony Streets. Our brigade of 3,000 will make its way from the Market Street Bridge to North Broad Street and then to Girard Avenue. From Girard Avenue we will then be on a straight route to the arsenal by way of Frankford Avenue. We will enter Tacony Street, where the arsenal is situated on the banks of the Delaware River. I suspect resistance will be light there. The utter fear we will cause by the initial invasion and raid into the city itself should throw their defenses off line. We cannot be sure of the regiments who may challenge our arrival, but our scouts assure us the Philadelphia Home Guard is weak. Count on casualties, Elington.

"My men have trained and have been completely briefed on the planned raid. They are considered a brigade of mounted infantry who are efficient in cavalry and infantry tactics in the field. They know how to operate and discharge any type of artillery we can confiscate along the way. We are still contemplating the idea of bringing our own battalion of artillery with us. It has been suggested the guns will slow our progress, but I haven't ruled this possibility out yet. Lieutenant, are you familiar with timed fuses and artillery pieces?"

"Yes, I am, sir. I had extensive training in the use of artillery and timed fuses in the U.S Army back during the time of the Mexican War. You know, major, when our armies assailed the devastating heights of Chapultapec."

"Tomorrow, if you agree to accompany us and help us on this mission, then we will go into the details of the methods in destroying the arsenal. I am still waiting on a diagram of the arsenal from one of our scouts in the city. When I get it, I will be able to quickly put the pieces together for an attack which will wreck the Union's capacity to fight us. I know destroying one arsenal isn't going to completely cripple the Union armies, but we all think it can have the psychological effects upon the people and leaders of our enemy. All right, gentleman, I am through for today. Get some sleep, Elington, and I will be looking forward to hearing your answer on the mission by this time tomorrow. Is that clear, lieutenant? We need soldiers willing to volunteer."

"I will see you tomorrow, major."

"I hope so, Lieutenant Elington. You can ask questions tomorrow if your response is satisfactory to us."

The officers said good evening to each other and then they headed out of Pettigrew's camp to ride to their own headquarters. Elington seemed sad to see the great leaders go from his camp. He still was struck by the presence of the Confederate high command who stood around a map table for a couple of hours and who were interested in his skills for the proposed raid to Philadelphia. Suddenly, Major Fincannon came trotting back into camp by himself and rode straight up to Elington.

"Lieutenant!" he said. Fincannon dismounted his horse and folded his arms. "Is Senator Robert Sumner going to be a problem for you if you decide to carry through on this raid?"

Elington felt the pain in the breadbasket. He was surprised Fincannon investigated his private life without him ever knowing it. *What else did Fincannon know about me and my family,* he thought silently. *Did he interview Lewis? Oh man, what in God's name am I to do now? How should I answer him?*

"Are you sick, Elington?"

"Not at all, major."

"Answer me, then. I don't have all night."

"The Senator is my father-in-law, sir. He will not be a problem for me at all. I haven't seen him or talked to him since the war began."

"Is that right, lieutenant?"

"Yes!"

"Were you aware your wife is in Philadelphia at this very moment and she is staying at her father's home on Pine Street? Twentieth block to be exact, lieutenant."

"What! What did you say, major?

"You heard it, lieutenant."

"No! I was not informed of her location since winter. I know she took the news of our son Jesse's wounding hard back in December. He was wounded in action at Fredericksburg."

"Hmm … and what side of the war was he fighting on, lieutenant?"

"I am sure you know by now what side Jesse fought for, or is still fighting for, major."

"Are you ashamed of the fact you couldn't keep your oldest son from fighting for the dastardly enemy we now face?"

"No, I am not ashamed. He did what he wanted to do and my wife has done what she needed to do in this time of war and hell on earth, major. No. I am not ashamed to say my son fights as a member of the 83rd Pennsylvania Infantry Regiment. He fights for a cause he believes in. He may even be dead. We are not sure what happened to him after Fredericksburg. Danny and I believe in another cause. A cause of states' rights and independence from an abusive central government."

"This has been an interesting conversation, Elington. Are you prepared to sacrifice, again, for the Confederate States of America? I want to know, lieutenant!"

Elington stood there, studying the intensity on Fincannon's face. Elington couldn't understand why he asked him a question that didn't need to be asked.

"My answer is due tomorrow, isn't it, major?"

"Make sure you can be trusted," Fincannon said. "Remember your decision will effect many people both in the North and in the South. Thus far you haven't evaded the truth of your family. That is good, Elington. If you agree to go on this raid, then I will go over the plans of the arsenal with you and we will have to try and accomplish the destruction of the arsenal with the least in civilian and Confederate casualties."

The major mounted his horse and continued out of the bivouac of the 26th North Carolina. It appeared to Elington, Fincannon set forth his first test to judge the character of the prospective raiders. *What would come next?* Elington thought. *How can I know what decision to make about this raid if Abby is in Philadelphia? Should I go on the raid at all? Can I trust Fincannon? What do I do?*

Elington went back to his tent where Fry, Abshire, Curtis and Coffey were waiting.

"What's going on with all of the high command coming to our camp?" Alfred asked.

"Yeah, I can't believe General Lee himself was present here, among all us peons!" Thaddeus said. "What is he like, lieutenant?"

"Hold it!" answered Elington.

"Who was the fellow on the black horse?" Jackson asked. "He looked pretty mean and serious, lieutenant."

"I said, hold it! Give me a chance to explain the situation here. I am overwhelmed with the proposed plans for this upcoming battle. These plans affect me beyond your understanding."

"Have some coffee, lieutenant, and relax," Alfred said. "I hope you can find it in yourself to tell us what in the world is going on. We are anxious, lieutenant."

"Do the plans you were discussing include any of us in the regiment?" Lewis asked. "Come on, man, we have to know what's going on. We are in enemy territory and we desperately want to engage those darn Yanks to try and end this war."

Elington splashed his cup of coffee onto the ground in disgust. He then got up off of the crate he was sitting on and went into his tent. The Possum was surprised and angry at the actions of their lieutenant, but there was nothing they could do.

Evening had fallen and the humid conditions tired everyone out. The other officers of the regiment were still quietly conversing among themselves, standing outside of various company tents. The summer fires of military camp spread through the horizon west of the small town of Gettysburg. Elington had hard decisions to make and he didn't have a lot of time to make them.

*****

The blue stars of early morning twinkled in the black summer sky. The only sounds were men serving picket duty from one of the other regiments in Pettigrew's brigade, various insects and the crackle of dying fires around the bivouac. Time appeared to stand still in the firmaments and in the war itself. The stars shone soft light on the earth, light brightening the violence of the many battles fought thus far in the war.

Men suffered and died in unbelievable numbers. The dreams of many were put to rest or put on hold for the sake of two differing causes. Marriages were denied to soldiers not old enough to even care about such things. Generations of various families ceased to exist. Social life for soldiers in the war froze in time. Only persistent memories gave some solitude to the minds of the men in the field who were constantly away from their loved ones back home. The thoughts of home usually ventured into the minds and emotions of soldiers. As they slept in their tents, they could dream of home.

The expansive calmness of the Pettigrew bivouac soon gave way to the haste and clamor of couriers dispatching new orders before sunrise to the brigade. Knapsacks were rolled and prepared for a move, tents were struck, fires extinguished, horses and supply wagons reattached to each other; men discarded unnecessary materials to lighten the load of marching as they talked about and deliberated the situation. Getting orders to march early wasn't unusual for the men of the brigade. The recent heat forced commanders to order early morning marches to prevent heat sickness. This was a usual thing since leaving Virginia. The thought of being in enemy territory and the perpetual hazard of imminent battle caused men to become nervous and somewhat confused.

Messages were sent to the companies of the 26th North Carolina that the brigade and the regiment would be continuing their march east out of Fayetteville, Pennsylvania. Colonel Burgwyn had the honor of having his regiment ordered to lead the brigade on the march east. Daylight emerged when the 26th began its march on Monday, June 29, 1863. It took a few hours for the brigade to ready itself for the move. Word was coming down the columns that the Union Army had shuffled another general to lead the Army of the Potomac. As the soldiers made their way down the Chambersburg Pike and into the elevations of South Mountain, they felt a sense of pride for all of the confusion and incompetence they caused in the political and military organizations of the Union.

"Lieutenant, I hear they got another general hired to lick us good," said Corporal Lewis Fry.

"That is the word."

"He is a Pennsylvanian, General George Meade. Can you believe they fired Hooker already? What a darn shame. They should have kept him in longer. We could have defeated the Yankees once and for all, and on their own land."

"Yes, I got the message about the change in command from Colonel Burgwyn. Meade could be a problem. He is now defending his own land in Pennsylvania. You saw how hard we fought in Virginia and in North Carolina to protect our own property and our rights. I am sure Meade doesn't want to lose a battle in his home state. It could be a real bad thing for him and the Union army to get whipped. I think we are going to have to fight mighty hard in order to bring those blue bellies down this time."

The men continued their march east. Through early morning clouds they saw the sun begin to break in the east, but only for a short time. The morning vowed to be overcast and gray. Elington and his men walked up the rise of the South Mountains, seeing the valleys and the apple trees perched on slopes, creating a beauty and an adventurous feeling for the men. *What lies ahead?* Elington thought. Are *we to enter the decisive battle of our fates?* The ridges and the inclines on both sides of the regiment, again, reminded the 26th of home and the Blue Ridge. They weren't home now, and every tick of the clock, every forward step they marched along the pike, brought them closer to battle and maybe death upon enemy soil.

"I really can't concern myself with Meade right now, Lewis," Elington said.

"What do you mean?"

"I still have to make up my mind about this upcoming raid to Philadelphia."

"What raid? You didn't tell us anything last night, remember?"

"I didn't get a wink of sleep over this. Not that we had a whole lot of time to sleep anyway. But I don't know what to do! Major Fincannon told me Abby is in Philadelphia. He's been doing some investigating on men being considered for the raid."

"What raid is it, Harrison? You're ignoring me. Who is Major Fincannon?"

"A mounted infantry raid into the city of liberty, Philadelphia, with the motive of destroying an arsenal to cripple Union army logistics."

"Why were you considered?"

"Because of recommendations by Colonel Burgwyn and General Pettigrew for my experience with explosives in the U.S. Army. They want this raid, consisting of 3,000 men from the western theater of operations, to blow up the Frankford Arsenal in Philadelphia."

"What? That's a great idea, lieutenant."

"You think so, Fry?"

"What could be better than causing destruction on those no-good Yankees, who have devastated our homeland and without remorse to anyone of us. Do it, Harrison! Go on the raid and give it everything you have, man. Give them hell! Do it for the sake of the cause, man.

"It's not that easy. According to Fincannon's intelligence information, Abby is now at her father's house in Philadelphia. What if something happens to her during the raid? What if she finds out I am on the raid to her native city? That will be it between us, Lewis. We had a conversation about the Confederate command's earnestness to invade the North back when I was on furlough. Boy, did we start some heated arguments. I can't believe she has left Granite Falls. How in the world did she get there in the first place? I've been thinking on that all night."

"You can't worry about it now."

"But she's my wife, Lewis, and I love and respect her beyond anything else in this stinking world and in this stinking war. I do not want anything to happen to her. I have possibly lost Jesse. Don't you think that's enough?"

"I do understand, Harrison; but the fact is, we have to win a victory here and now, or our whole world as we know it will cease to exist. It will come crashing down in eternal flames. Don't you remember what you told me after we had the fight and then heard of Jesse's circumstances?"

"Yes, I do remember."

"You said you had to do something so Jesse's situation and the cause he stood for would not be wasted. You wanted our regiment to be attached, as it is now, to General Lee's army. We have that now, Harrison, and we have to make the best of it, or else we are doomed to subjugation by the Yankees. Think of it, man. The dream and the hope of independence gone!"

"I can't believe I am in this predicament; stuck in this war for over two years, separated from my entire family, still mourning over the possible loss of Jesse and no longer able to tend to my own property I have toiled over for many years. This is a disgraceful situation for a man to be in, Lewis. And now this mission!"

"I finally have to totally agree with you. But what about this invasion? What about the plans of General Lee? We have to do something now. We have the whole darn Confederate army in enemy territory. We have close to 75,000 men here in Pennsylvania. I heard the numbers from one of the officers in the 11th North Carolina. We are ready to take action, Harrison, and you have the chance to be involved in a special way. You don't have to be stuck in this Godforsaken infantry, at least during this upcoming fight, if you go. You can do something different for a change, like destroying Yankee property as they have done to us these past three years. Think, Harrison! You can be a hero, man."

"Yeah, I've been thinking ever since the meeting yesterday and I am still having doubts. It's only over Abigail, though, and nothing else, for I am not a hero of any kind, Lewis."

"How is your wife going to find out you are one of the raiders? She knows you are part of the 26th North Carolina Regiment and not part of a mounted infantry or cavalry unit. Come on, you know that!"

"I think you're right, Lewis. How will she ever find out? If I am killed or have to stay behind for some reason, or if I am taken prisoner, she will find out only then."

"There are risks you're going to have to take if you decide to go on the raid, Harrison, but remember courage is rising up in the face of risk, doubt and fear. Courage is what has made this whole Confederacy. Think of all the men who have given their lives for the ideas of our Confederacy. Think of all the sacrifices of the generals you met with yesterday. It's overwhelming to envision the raw courage and idealism before us now. We are here in Pennsylvania, a Yankee Union state, wide open for battle; a final battle, Harrison. A battle that could end the carnage and the bitter taste of loss we have felt for too long."

"Nice speech, Lewis," Elington said. "I didn't know you could be sympathetic and convincing. You sound like some patriotic preacher speaking to a school child."

Elington and Fry continued to converse. The 26th North Carolina led Pettigrew's brigade, on June 29, farther east and closer to the junction towns of southern Pennsylvania. Fry smoked his familiar corncob pipe. Smoke from the tobacco puffed up into the enemy's sky and Fry straightened out his uniform while the march continued. Pride filled his mind as he thought of a final victory upon the enemy.

Elington marched and felt the burning in the gut. He placed his right hand down on his Colt Navy revolver and began to tap his hand on the gun. He pressed his black slouch hat over his brow and continued to ponder the immediate questions circulating through his brain and soul. Elington, like Fry, pulled his cadet gray officer's jacket tight to straighten out his uniform. He also felt a sense of pride rising in his head. He was asked, by the high command of the army he loved, to go on a raiding mission to one of the most important cities in the North. The war brought an immediate urgency to Elington.

He alone would make the final decision to go forth on the mission; a mission that could forge an apocalypse for the Union.

— Chapter 14 —
The Spires of Gettysburg

June 29 –30, 1863

The day remained overcast, gloomy and gray. General Pettigrew's brigade continued to lead the march through the South Mountain pass. Green valleys and small farms remained in view. Chambersburg Pike rose into the mountain and the men of the South, clad in butternut and gray, climbed the elevation with ease and confidence of heart. The soldiers were gliding along, anticipating a battle and at the same time thinking of final victory for their cause.

Some Confederate enlisted men, by this time in the war, had gotten rid of their knapsacks. The men had become used to marching with a haversack containing basic necessities: a blanket with a rubber ground piece, or oil cloth rolled and tied at both ends and carried over the left shoulder; cartridge boxes; cap boxes; and a good tin cup. Canteens became cumbersome and many soldiers replaced it with the cup. Rations were in plenty supply since the army entered Pennsylvania and Lee's Order 73 had been, for the most part, obeyed by the men.

The 26th North Carolina marched in with the rest of the brigade. Colonel Burgwyn, Lieutenant Colonel John Lane, Major John Jones and the company commanders marched their columns forward toward an unknown destination, reining their horses in the direction of the pike.

"I will go on the mission to Philadelphia," said Elington to Lewis Fry. They marched at a brisk pace along with the thousands of other men in the Confederate ranks.

"I knew you would make the right decision, Harrison. We need to end this fight and you can now contribute to a possible end to the war."

"An end to the war. Wouldn't it be nice to hear the silence of peace? Wouldn't it be grand to go home for good and have our families reconciled and happy once again? The carnage and destruction has weakened the spirits of too many in these three years of conflict, Lewis. I pray the end is near before our end comes and the joy of life is gone forever."

"Concentrate on the mission, lieutenant. Yes, the end can come if those sympathetic Peace Democrats get their way. Word is out that General Lee himself destined this invasion to appeal to those Democrats who want an end to the war through recognition of the Confederacy. You have to understand that a lot of people in Philadelphia don't care if we keep slavery. They see the Negro has inferior, tied to the menial tasks in life. I read a quote from a Philadelphia newspaper we had traded with a Yank a while back and it stated the people in the city are discouraged by the increases in the Negro populations across the city. They see the Negro as necessary labor. Many of them work in the homes of wealthy businessmen in the city, but other white citizens see them as a 'disturbing presence' living among the inheritors of colonial independence."

"You have been informed and educated on the matter of the Peace Democrats, Lewis. Your patriotic fervor has come to settle me in my decision. I hope and pray for the Peace Democrat's support."

"We have to give them something to support. If we can win a great battle on Northern soil and if you can carry out this mission to Philadelphia and the arsenal, then I think things will be placed in motion."

The two men talked to each other as they began the descent from South Mountain. From the brow of the mountain they could see a tiny inn on the left side of the road. The brigade was entering Cashtown, a small village hamlet at the eastern foot of South Mountain.

They could see ridges in their front toward the town of Gettysburg, the same town mentioned by Colonel Burgwyn as a possible stop over for supplies. Maps showed Gettysburg to be a junction town where numerous roads collided into a hub. The town would make for good transportation, Burgwyn had thought, when he and Elington discussed the possible movement of the army through Pennsylvania. Elington and Fry dropped out of column for a few minutes to see how the boys were holding up. They saw the Possum coming straight at them on the Chambersburg Pike, chewing tobacco, eating rations, drinking from their canteens and cups, and talking non-stop. They marched along, in youthful vigor, with the regiment. Alfred didn't look too happy, though. The sun made a brief appearance through the clouds and the summer heat reminded the men of the continued struggle before them.

"Lieutenant Elington!" shouted Thaddeus Curtis.

"Hey, it's the lieutenant, Alfred. Maybe he can explain what happened yesterday evening," Private Coffey said.

Elington and Fry joined the Possum on the march toward the ridges ahead. From the elevated slope of South Mountain, the Possum saw the steeples of churches and the cupola of what seemed to be a school or college of some kind.

"What a beautiful sight before us," Elington said. "Look at that town, men, sitting there among the heights. How are you all this morning, men?"

"Just fine," Alfred answered in a stern voice.

"Not bad today, lieutenant," said Private Curtis.

"I am hungry, lieutenant," Private Coffey complained. "Getting up early for this here march has robbed us of a time to eat, sir."

"You'll live, Coffey," answered Elington. "None of us really had time to eat anything this morning. It seems to me, boys, we are headed toward some kind of fight."

"At least we know you're headed for something, lieutenant," said Private Abshire.

"Alfred, I know you are upset from last evening, but I had a lot on my mind. You see, I have been asked by the high command of our army to go on a mission to help blow up some arsenal over in the city of Philadelphia."

"What!"

"Yeah, Alfred, an arsenal … Philadelphia … where Abby is right now. The Colonel and General Pettigrew recommended me for my experience in the U.S. Army using explosives."

"You're lying, right, lieutenant?"

"No, I am not."

"Do you know for sure Abby is in Philadelphia?"

"Major Fincannon, who is to lead the 3,000-man mission to the city, has been doing some investigation of possible recruits for the mission and he informed me last night Abby is at her father's house in the city. She finally left Granite Falls and Caldwell County. I guess she couldn't take any more of the speculation about the fate of Jesse. Major Fincannon wanted to know if Senator Sumner and the fact that Jesse is part of a Union regiment would be a 'problem' for me."

"It sounds serious, Harrison, I mean, lieutenant," Alfred said solemnly.

"Yeah, it is serious, Alfred, especially if Abby gets wind of the mission and somehow finds out I'm part of it."

"You have made up your mind over this, hey, lieutenant?" Alfred asked sarcastically.

"It's made up. I hope God will have His purpose through me in whatever I have to do."

Elington saw Colonel Burgwyn riding on his horse by the side of the regiment. He called to Burgwyn to tell him of his decision. He wanted Fincannon to know as soon as possible his mind was made up. Elington was curious as to the details of the attack on the arsenal and he wanted a review of how the brigade would make it into the city.

"Colonel, sir. I wanted to inform you of my decision concerning the raid. I will be honored to go on the mission. I want to also thank you again for your recommendation to General Pettigrew. I appreciate your confidence in me and I will do my best to carry out my responsibilities during the mission, sir."

"Glad to hear of your decision, lieutenant. You will be an asset to Major Fincannon's brigade. I will pass on the news of your decision to the major as soon as I can find a courier. There are so many couriers with messages going up and down our columns today that I am getting dizzy. I will see you this evening, lieutenant."

"Thank you, colonel."

Elington contemplated his action. He knew he was now committed to the mission. He couldn't turn back after telling the colonel of his choice. He thought on the details of the mission. *How will the defenses be set upon us in Philadelphia?* He knew Fincannon would brief him again on the plan, but he started to worry. As an officer, he worried for the safety of his regiment and about the location of General Stuart and his brigades of cavalry. Elington figured that without cavalry, the infantry would be going into battle without pertinent intelligence information needed to make quick strategic decisions. *Where is Stuart?* Elington thought as he walked with Fry and the Possum.

The regiment continued on the Chambersburg Pike. The conversing between the men had subsided for a while as the march of the columns stupefied each one. The rhythmic trotting of the horses and the constant marching of the men often times caused Elington to just stare at the man in front of him on the march. He would stare for minutes at a time in a tranquil haze, trying in some way to relax his mind from all of the pressures of war, to ease the conflicts in his heart concerning his family and to make the pain of emotional stress fade from him.

At about two o'clock, on the afternoon of June 29, the rest of Hill's corps crossed South Mountain without incident. General A. P. Hill, leading the 3rd Corps, made his headquarters at the Cashtown Inn. Wagons loaded with plentiful supplies slammed along the pike, racing, it seemed, to get to the regiments before nightfall. Many of the wagon and supply units were ordered to stay to the rear of the marching columns in case battle commenced, or Union cavalry tried to steal the supplies.

Word came down to Colonel Burgwyn and Lieutenant Elington that General Lee had issued new orders for the three corps of the Confederate Army. After learning from a spy of the Union army's locations, General Longstreet informed Lee of the closeness of the Union forces. Lee now ordered his generals to move their armies to the town of Gettysburg. With its good roads it would be easy to centralize his forces there. Lee was being uncharacteristically cautious as he moved his army through enemy territory and into a major battle. Lee cancelled the invasion of Harrisburg in his new orders. He approved the invasion of Philadelphia and he directed his commanders to force a battle on Meade's line of march. Order 75 was finally mandated and it began to direct the Confederate forces to their destiny.

*****

The 26th bivouacked on the right side of the Chambersburg Pike. Elington and the Possum stretched out their blankets and raised their tents along the patches of clover near a wheat field. Fires were sparking all over the encampment as evening approached and brought an end to another day in enemy territory. The evening was humid, but the temperatures had cooled. Men took their rations and ate like it was their last supper. Young North Carolinians and men from Alabama and Mississippi sat down from the day's march to write letters, play cards and pray. Some soldiers tried to clean themselves with bars of soap they purchased from the Sutlers back in Maryland. Sutlers followed armies, as did lice, in order to profit from the desperate soldiers who only longed for the comforts of home. Water from nearby streams and runs could help the soap along.

Elington was sitting down, trying to write a letter to Abigail. If he died on the mission, or in battle in southern Pennsylvania, Harrison wanted his wife to know what he was involved in since talking to her back on furlough during the pleasant fall months in North Carolina. He leaned on his portable writing desk that was on the table in his tent. Dipping the nib of his quill pen into the umbrella-shaped ink well, Elington contemplated and strained for the correct and appropriate words he could place down on the damp paper before him. *How do I start this letter? How do I begin to explain this raid into Philadelphia to destroy part of the North? Lord, please give me the words and the inspiration to tell my beloved wife what I need to inform her of, especially if she gets this letter and I'm dead.*

Corporal Fry came to the outside of Elington's tent and placed his face near the front flap to tell the lieutenant some soldiers were approaching from the western horizon of South Mountain.

"Do you hear the rumbling, lieutenant?"

"Leave me alone, corporal, I am busy right now."

"There is sure a lot of darn dust being kicked up by the approach of what looks like some of our cavalry."

"I said I am busy, corporal."

"Busy you may be, lieutenant, but I think you had better come out of the tent and take a look at this horde of horsemen."

"A horde, Fry?"

"Yes, sir!"

The flap flung open and Elington came out of the tent in a depressed mood. He was sweating and itching at mosquito bites on his arm. He looked ragged and dirty. The western sun shone upon his face.

"I said I was occupied with something important, man, can't you understand what I mean?"

Elington turned and looked toward the western horizon where the 26th had marched from South Mountain. He saw the horseman. Black and dark brown horses, beige and gray dappled animals with riders directing the animals in column form toward the bivouac of the 3rd Corps. As the riders got closer to the bivouac, Elington could see Major Frederick Fincannon leading the men. The continuous rhythmic roar of 3,000 horsemen coming toward the camp caused the guts to smolder. Elington thought he would never be able to forget this sight and the sounds of the movement of men and beast. A strange rumble of the earth.

"I apologize, Lewis. I was trying to write a letter to Abigail in case something happens to me in battle or on this mission I volunteered for."

"No need to apologize, lieutenant; Harrison."

"Those horsemen are going to be my new, but temporary, brigade mates for this mission. The officer in front with the Yankee-looking uniform is

Major Fincannon. I am sure he is going to pay a visit to me soon in order to review the details of the mission to Philadelphia."

"Quite a scene, lieutenant. The major looks serious enough in front of his brigade."

"Well, Lewis, let me go back to writing the letter to Abigail. I know the mail service has been put on hold since we entered Pennsylvania, but I still want to write her. You make sure the letter eventually gets to Abigail if I should fall in this conflict. Can you do that for me?"

"Yes, Harrison. Give me the letter when you are through with it."

"I will."

Elington went back into his tent, took the tin cup from his table, sipped the coffee now cold from sitting too long and again contemplated the words. He quickly went outside of his tent and poured the cold coffee out of his cup. He glanced one more time at the galloping 3,000 and worried more on the mission. Elington went back inside. The taste and grit of the dust settling over the bivouac enmeshed Elington's mouth. He sat down and picked up his quill pen to write. But again there were no words. Elington felt a sting of shame toward himself. Abby would never understand the meaning of the mission he was about to embark on to Philadelphia, even if he did explain it in with the best of words.

He dropped the pen onto the table and just stared at the silhouettes outside his tent quarters. His stare was then interrupted by a large silhouette growing as it came toward the tent wall, illuminated by the setting sun and flickering fires.

"Lieutenant Elington, are you available for consultation with Major Fincannon?" asked Colonel Burgwyn from the flap of the tent.

"I will be right out, sir."

"No, lieutenant, we can talk in your tent if that is all right with you. Major Fincannon is in somewhat of a hurry this evening. He needs to meet with Generals Hill and Lee after he speaks with you."

Elington came out of the tent and invited the colonel in. "Fincannon will be right over, Harrison."

"Do you think, colonel, I made the right decision to go on the mission?"

"Yes, Harrison, we need this mission. I think the overall plan is beneficial to our cause here. I also have much confidence in Major Fincannon. I know he seems arrogant and pugnacious, but the fact is, he is committed to our cause and he has many battles and raids behind him to serve as experience as a leader on a crucial mission like this one."

"That is good to know, colonel."

"Just focus on what you have to do after Fincannon briefs you on the details."

"Do you think you and the men of the regiment will be all right in the upcoming fight, colonel? I will not be here for the duration of our next battle. I have a feeling some of the Yankee army is just over those ridges to our east. The town they are calling Gettysburg, in my estimation, is too important in topography and roads. The Yanks are going to go for that terrain, colonel. I may be here if a battle commences, but please take care of the men, sir. You know I have always looked after the men in battle. Watch out for the Possum, especially. Alfred, Thaddeus and Jack are young boys who have their whole lives ahead of them. I wouldn't want to make it back from the city there in the east and see that something terrible has happened to them, sir. As for Fry, well, he can take care of himself in battle. He is a fierce man and a fierce fighter. I will miss you all while I am away."

"Don't worry, I will see that the Possum and all the men of the 26th have their provisions and dispositions ready for any battle."

"Colonel Burgwyn, Lieutenant Elington, may I come in?" asked a man from outside the tent. It was Major Fincannon, ready to tell Elington about some of the other details of the raid.

"Yes, sir, major. Please come in," Elington answered.

He entered the cramped quarters, still looking spiffy and stylish in his dark Confederate charcoal gray uniform. The crystal blue eyes penetrated through Elington, seeming to tell the lieutenant what the major was already thinking.

"I do not have much time tonight, gentlemen. I need to meet with Generals Hill and Lee later on to discuss the timing of our departure to Philadelphia. It seems new information on the locations of General Meade's Union forces has been updated by a scout General Longstreet has employed. This valuable information may alter the day we leave to blowup that infamous Yankee arsenal."

"Yes, sir," Elington answered.

"Let's get right to the plan, Elington."

"All right, major."

Colonel Burgwyn stayed with the major and Elington as the meeting went on.

"Just to review what you were previously privy to from the contents of General Hill's meeting, you know the Frankford Arsenal is a heavy producer of percussion caps, cartridges, timed artillery fuses, and it is used for the storage of muskets and powder. Previous scientifically minded commanders of the arsenal have procured many other capabilities for the facility and it needs to be eliminated now.

"You were also informed by General Hill of the attitudes of the Peace Democrats, many of whom reside in the city. This invasion will entice their appetite for a recognition of the Confederacy. If we are successful, they will undoubtedly strive for peace in the face of the many casualties sacrificed by Union divisions. Information for us has been obtained from employee spies who have infiltrated the arsenal walls and the arsenal administrative buildings.

"Later on tonight I am going to recommend to Generals Hill and Lee that we depart for Philadelphia on July 2, early in the morning. I want to make sure we can get out of the Gettysburg area without too much harassment from Union corps coming up from Maryland. I don't see too much of a problem as of now, Elington."

"I understand, sir."

"Look at the map, gentlemen. Again, we will take the York Road out of Gettysburg to begin our trip. We then connect onto the Philadelphia-Lancaster Turnpike, which is located here. Can you see the location of the turnpike?"

"Yes, major."

The men stared down at the map and concentrated on the network of roads coming out of Gettysburg. They noticed the towns of York and Lancaster. Elington saw how far away even those towns were from the base of Confederate operations and the burning came upon him like never before. The breadbasket pain that had haunted his existence for over twenty years made his guts smolder. He tried his best to cover the pain from the major and Colonel Burgwyn. The wide distances between towns made him anxious.

The major continued his review of the mission.

"The brigade will travel to the Wrightsville and Columbia Bridge. The crossing of the Susquehanna River will take place there. Let's all hope the Home Guard forces don't burn the bridge. Again, it is vital to our operation. Advance skirmishers will try to harass any attempt to destroy the bridge.

"When we cross the bridge we will continue on the Turnpike, through Lancaster County, and connect onto Lancaster Road in the suburbs of Philadelphia. From there we will enter the city and cross the Market Street Bridge over the Schuylkill River. If you look at the map of the city, Elington, you can see that the arsenal is in the northeastern part of the consolidated city. Philadelphia has expanded its territory in recent years by consolidating other townships and boroughs into its borders. At this point we will cross the bridge and connect onto North Broad Street and then onto Girard Avenue. From Girard Avenue, here, we will be on a straight course to the arsenal by way of Frankford Avenue and Tacony Street. I suspect we will hit mild resistance as we ride through the city itself, lieutenant. Riding through the city will serve as a mental strain on the citizens and it is imperative we ride through fearless and with great confidence of heart.

"All right, Elington, take a good look at this diagram of the Frankfort Arsenal. You can see in the upper left part of the map or northwest corner of the facility there is a square parade ground surrounded by the quarters of officers stationed at the arsenal. The commanding officer's house is there. We will execute the commanding officer as a requirement of war. His capabilities must be destroyed. Two store houses and the original arsenal building are also located in the area of the parade ground. In the middle of the arsenal stands a T-shaped machine shop and an H-shaped percussion factory building, which houses the percussion cap machine. If you look to the right of these buildings you can see laboratory buildings where experimentation is done to better the production of arms and ammunitions. The big U-shaped building stores muskets, cannon and artillery ammunitions. All of the buildings I have shown you on the diagram will be destroyed by fire when we reach the arsenal grounds.

"Lieutenant, do you have any ideas on how to blowup and destroy those buildings with minimal loss of civilian life or loss to our soldiers? You can imagine the explosive force that will form from the powder and powder residue all over the arsenal facilities."

"Major Fincannon, as I see from the map and diagram, it would be best to fire one artillery shell into each building at a range of 100 yards. The Federal Schenkl shell with a percussion fuse, in my opinion, would do the job, sir. I am sure the arsenal will have three-inch ordnance rifled cannon on hand for us to confiscate, along with the shells for use in the destruction of the said buildings. The impact of those shells will have an ignition effect on any powder residue in those buildings, especially the machine shop, the percussion factory and the laboratories. The store houses and the U-shaped building containing any other weapons or powder will naturally be destroyed using this simple artillery method. We must make sure the commanders or the employees of the arsenal do not get those darned guns fixed on us first, major. If we fire the same cannon at the officer's housing buildings and the mess hall, those structures will be ignited by the exploding shell itself and I am sure will render much havoc and damage to the facility. I would hope, major, to secure at least four guns for firing upon the arsenal. Our timing needs to be quick and efficient, and we need to exit the area as soon as possible to avoid casualties. I have heard and read about many riots in the city of brotherly love, sir."

"Yes, I am aware of the worker unrest in many of the city's industries. This factor could possibly work to our advantage. Could stir up some needed confusion when we attack."

"Maybe, sir."

"Your idea sounds very efficient, lieutenant. We had gone over a plan back in Virginia, but we weren't sure of the range figures and fuse types as you are, Elington. It is good to have you going with us."

"Thank you, sir ... but, sir, you're telling me you couldn't find another former Union artillery man in the whole Confederate army who could have told you the same information pertaining to the shelling of the arsenal? Many in our ranks know how to operate Union guns."

"True, Elington. However, there are other reasons and circumstances that drive officers to make personnel decisions."

" I see, major, but I am still confused about my so-called expertise."

"Enough with your questions, lieutenant!"

"Yes, major. By the way, sir, if we can't get a hold of those three-inch ordnance pieces, I am sure we can cause damage with other types of guns they have on hand at the arsenal."

"I understand, lieutenant. Hopefully our retreat will be smooth. We will follow the same course out of the city and then we will do our best to rejoin the base of our operations somewhere near the area of Gettysburg. I hope and pray General Lee will have a victory celebration waiting for us either here or somewhere else in Pennsylvania."

"I pray, major."

"Gentlemen, I need to leave now. I do not want to keep Hill and Lee waiting too long for my arrival. Like I said earlier, I believe tonight we will change and approve the mission to leave early on the 2nd of July."

Major Fincannon left Elington's quarters, gently saddled his black horse and rode into the twilight. The gentle gallop of the horse faded onto the Chambersburg Pike. Elington and Colonel Burgwyn were left outside the tent. They stared at the major until he disappeared down the road.

Major Fincannon and his brigade bivouacked to the left of the Chambersburg Pike on the night of June 29.

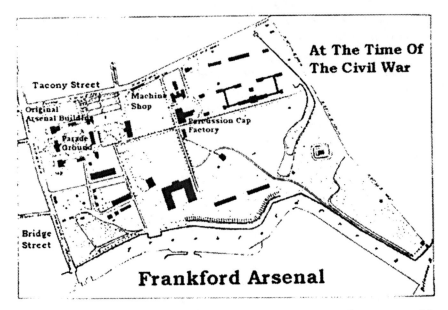

At The Time Of
The Civil War

Tacony Street

Original
Arsenal Building

Machine
Shop

Percussion Cap
Factory

Parade
Ground

Bridge
Street

Frankford Arsenal

Meanwhile, the new general of Union forces was preparing to move his corps to Gettysburg. Reports from his cavalry scouts mentioned a concentration of Confederate forces on the Chambersburg Pike west of the town. General George Meade knew he had to defend his native Pennsylvania soil and the honor of the Union cause. Not since the War of 1812 had enemy forces attacked a Union state. Meade had to make sure his army would defend the citizens of southern Pennsylvania.

*****

Elington said goodnight to the colonel, went into his tent and tried to resume the writing of his letter to Abigail.

> *Dear Abby:*
> *At the time I am writing this letter to you, I am sitting in my tent quarters in your home state of Pennsylvania. The 26th Regiment is about ten miles from a town called Gettysburg. I know you will be upset by this development, however, I needed to tell you the truth about my participation in this invasion. It seems that at any time, now, we could engage Union corps coming up from Maryland. Your father's friend, George Meade, is now commanding the*

Union army. I don't think a Philadelphian like Meade will allow us to sit tight here in his Home Guard state and not do anything.

Abby, you need to know I love you above all else in this world. I am truly sorry about whatever has happened to Jesse. I know you have blamed the Confederacy for his fate, but you can't blame me. You know we each have had our causes to bear and to sustain in this awful conflict of arms.

I have been asked by the high command of Confederate forces to go on a raiding mission to the city of Philadelphia in order to cause destruction to the Frankford Arsenal. I have been informed as of yesterday that you are at your father's residence in the city and that you had left Caldwell County. Why did you leave our house, Abby? Our property will be in ruins without someone to care for it. What will we do when this war is over and we have no home to go back to. Please be careful wherever you are, my dear. I hope you do not hate me for going on this mission to the city. This arsenal has been trouble for the Confederacy and we believe the Peace Democrats, there in the city, may call strongly for an end to the war and recognition of the Confederacy. This is why I am going, Abby. I want an end to the war now, today. I am not being vindictive toward you in any way.

I saw Danny a couple of nights ago. He has joined our corps to supplement our artillery needs in the field. I will do all I can to watch out for him. He looks great and is as patriotic as ever. He feels much sorrow for Jesse.

If I should die during the mission, please keep this letter for the rest of your days to remember our struggle in this confused but culminating time in history. I believe history will remember this great war for a long time to come because of it being a civil war, where many of our countryman have been killed.

I am somewhat afraid of the mission to Philadelphia. I really can't express my fears to any of the men in the regiment. Alfred, Thaddeus and Jack are all too young. I can't talk with them. I may break their confidence in me as their officer. It is hard to talk to Colonel Burgwyn, for he is so noble and committed to the cause. He wants to make a difference, but he is only twenty-two years old. Word is that he is the youngest colonel in the Confederate Army of Northern Virginia. Lewis has been the only one I have had a chance to talk to concerning the mission and my feelings toward it. We have become closer friends since our arguments and fighting transpired when I first got back from furlough. My most pressing fear, Abby, is losing you. I don't want that to ever happen. Please understand what we have gone through in this army of the South.

We have had low supplies for too long. Ammunition runs out on a daily basis now. I don't know if we even have enough artillery ammunition to last us while we are here in the North. You probably don't want to hear all of this military talk from me, but I need to talk to you. You are my truest friend beside being my dear wife.

Well, I am glad I have finally found some words to say to you before the mission proceeds. May God be with us no matter what transpires in the coming days. These next few days, I believe, Abby, will resolve our intentions in this war one way or the other.

With sincere love and devotion,
Harrison

Elington placed the letter down on his portable writing desk after he reread it. Night had fallen around the bivouac. He came outside to get one more comforting cup of coffee from the pot sitting on the fire near his tent. He rubbed the tiredness on his face and spat the last remnants of tobacco from his mouth. He looked around at the encampment and saw the majesty of his resting army, an army ready to inflict a decisive victory upon the men in blue. He said a simple prayer of protection as he continued to gaze at the bivouac and toward South Mountain to the west. A flash of summer lightning caught Elington's eye over the horizon for a split second. He thought, *That is how fast our fates could change in the next few days here in Pennsylvania.*

– Chapter 15 –
Blue Ghosts

June 30,1863

The videttes loomed in the distance. Attired in blue shell jackets and sack coats, heads covered with forage kepi hats, and mounted on strong, well-fed horses, the picket lines of General John Buford's Union Cavalry division appeared on a ridge just west of the town of Gettysburg. Other Union riders were noticed by the men of the three North Carolina regiments, who made up Pettigrew's reconnaissance mission to the Pennsylvanian town. The men of the 26th North Carolina had been on the road to Gettysburg by 6:30 in the morning. Another gloomy-looking day with intermittent showers welcomed them onto the ridges of the junction town. Pettigrew had been ordered to scout the town for General Heth, who was attempting to acquire shoes and other stockpiles for the under-supplied Confederate troops.

Yellowing wheat, fields of oats and orchards were seen by the men of the brigade as they moved east. They marched at a steady pace down the Chambersburg Pike. Again, the thoughts of battle penetrated the mind. They tried to talk to each other, but were ordered to keep the conversation down over the uncertainty of the situation ahead. The solemn clanking and rustling of the march continued. The men tried to adjust to the road and elevation conditions.

As a specter perturbs the unstable mind, the ghostly figures of the blue cavalry, fading in and out of the morning mist, flustered the minds of the soldiers in gray and butternut. Were those mysterious riders Union regular troops, or Pennsylvania militia? Colonel Henry Burgwyn and Corporal Lewis Fry studied the movements of the cavalry riders and asked each other that question. Sketched maps were made by officer's staffs. General Pettigrew would be able to make a full and efficient judgment of the topography to General Heth.

"Colonel," said General Pettigrew, "I need to send a courier with a message to General Heth concerning those blue riders who seem to be Union cavalry in our front."

"Yes, sir, general. Get me the message and it will be sent."

"I don't know if we should continue forward, colonel. My skirmish line is moving in our front and I haven't received any reports from them of immediate danger from those boys in blue."

"We are not to bring an engagement of battle during this reconnaissance mission, sir. They were orders directly from General Heth."

"You're correct, colonel, but I want to try and get those supplies for the men. Some of our soldiers desperately need shoes and other accoutrements for their continuation of service to this army. Besides, I can't ponder the thought of our infantry backing away from a cavalry picket."

"Yes, sir, I do understand."

"What would you do, Burgwyn?"

"I would try and find out more about the enemy guard in our front."

"Maybe we can do it after we hear from Heth on this matter."

"All right, general."

The men of Pettigrew's brigade began to move over a ridge locally known as Herr Ridge after descending from Knoxlyn Ridge to the west. They crossed over and found another high ridge in front of them. The blue cavalry picket lines stayed entrenched where they were and seemed to examine the Confederate brigade line coming up on them from the west. The brigade kept up its march, steady and confident. The courier had beckoned to Pettigrew earlier and Heth's response was to continue the reconnaissance. After the line of blue horsemen disappeared over what was known as McPherson Ridge to the east, Pettigrew called back his skirmish line and ordered his brigade back to Cashtown. Even though he felt foolish backing away from cavalry, Pettigrew did not want the responsibility of commencing a grand battle which could alter the course of the war for the Confederacy.

The men of Pettigrew's brigade marched west along the Chambersburg Pike and settled a few miles outside of the town of Gettysburg. Pettigrew continued back to Cashtown in order to report to General Heth.

"General Heth, I am convinced the Union army is in force and is strengthening behind a ridge just before you enter the town of Gettysburg."

The two generals got a chance to meet about the reconnaissance mission not long after the brigade's return.

"General Pettigrew, with all due respect to your opinion, I cannot make the same conclusion about the location of the Union Army. As of yesterday, I was under the impression the Union Army was still making its way out of Maryland and trying to shadow our movements into Pennsylvania. Meade is not so fast."

"Sir, I saw experienced blue riders out there today and they didn't look like state militia. They looked and acted like seasoned veterans who could be a definite threat to our army and to our positions here in Pennsylvania."

"I want you to make another reconnaissance tomorrow, general, with your brigade, along with other brigades from General Dorsey Pender's division of the 3rd Corps. General Hill has given the order to have our division reinforced with Pender's division. Archer's and Davis's brigades have been informed and ordered to lead the reconnaissance tomorrow into Gettysburg. I guess we will solve this little mystery for ourselves. We'll hit them hard and in force. Good day, General Pettigrew, and thank you for your work."

"Thank you, general."

Pettigrew's brigade bivouacked closer to Gettysburg on the evening of June 30. They set up near the Marsh Creek Bridge, about three miles west of the town, in the vicinity of a smaller town called Seven Stars. Columns of men began to fall out to the right and left of the Chambersburg Pike into their bivouac. Tents were set, bedrolls unbundled and haversacks were emptied in order to get to rations and utensils. Water was fetched from the nearby creek. An old stone bridge crossed over the creek and soldiers were able to relax and dream with the sound of the streaming water easing their minds. A grove of trees was near the area where the 26th North Carolina had settled in. Even though the sun wasn't out for much of the day, the men did get to enjoy a sunset that evening.

Did the sunset bring hopes for the Confederacy, or did it bring omens of destruction? Could the sunset be a sign of the fading away of the Confederacy, or the dawn for a new nation conceived in blood; a second revolution?

Lieutenant Harrison Elington contemplated these questions as he rejoined his regiment after its mission earlier in the day. Elington was spared the reconnaissance over details related to his upcoming mission to Philadelphia and to the arsenal. Preparations had to be made and supplies had to be secured for his temporary assignment.

"Colonel Burgwyn!" yelled Elington.

"Yes, lieutenant!" The two officers, along with the Possum, came together beside the Chambersburg Pike and began to converse and joke like there wasn't even a war going on. Lewis Fry, Jack Coffey, Thaddeus Curtis and Alfred Abshire, along with their lieutenant, were all together again. They sat around a small fire for cooking, trying to keep their distance from the fire. The heat of the day and their annoying wool uniforms aggravated their situation.

"How is it down the Chambersburg Pike, colonel?"

"It seems we have enemy cavalry posted on a couple of ridges west of the town of Gettysburg. Blue riders, as General Pettigrew called them, were spotted today and it looked as though those riders were scouting our positions."

"Sounds serious, colonel."

"You can verify what I saw from your buddies in the Possum, lieutenant. Go ahead, Alfred, tell him what's going on."

Alfred sat down on the grassy area where the bivouac was and explained, "Those soldiers we saw today, lieutenant, were not state militia as General Heth and General Hill think. They were full fledged cavalry units. We all can't understand why both generals are being so sure about the situation and thinking only militia are present over those two ridges east of here. Come on, Harrison, you remember when we encountered those Yankee blue-coated horsemen at Malvern Hill. Wouldn't you be able to tell the difference between them and militia?

"I believe I would, but the generals may have more updated intelligence on the whereabouts of the Union army."

"Do you really believe that, lieutenant?" Thaddeus asked.

"Yes! I don't think the high command of our army would be risking our positions here in enemy territory. After all, don't you think they want to believe their own intelligence reports for the purpose of strategy when battle does arrive?"

"I guess, lieutenant," answered Thaddeus.

"I sure pray General Heth is confident in his intelligence information about the location of the Yankee corps," Alfred said to the Possum. "General Pettigrew was mighty sure of what he observed today and he told Generals Hill and Heth."

"I pray, too," Jack Coffey said, swatting at some flies, his blue eyes squinting in disgust. "I hope this here upcoming battle in Northern country can be a success and not a massacre for us."

"You boys better start concentrating on battle again. Concentrate on your dispositions and weapons to get ready for the fight," Corporal Fry said in a demanding tone. "You are always talking on some other darn subject other than the subject at hand. Stop second-guessing your generals and start knowing your orders, your drills and your own hearts. Time will prove our cause and that's all we need to be concerned on right now. We are soldiers and we fight for a living. Why don't you all shut up and get some preparation done for battle."

Fry sat there in the humid evening air. He was sitting on a wooden crate used for supplies when he reprimanded the rest of the Possum, who were all by now sitting in the grassy patch near the fire. Time seemed to move slowly for the men on the night of June 30, 1863. Camp responsibilities were carried out by many different regiments, including the 26th.

Artillery units, again, were rolling forward on the Chambersburg Pike. The guns, Napoleons, three-inch ordnance, and Parrotts, were being placed in limbered positions spanning across the Pike in front of the 26th North Carolina's bivouac. Soldiers from the 26th were placed in charge of picket duty for the night. Lieutenant Colonel John Lane commanded the detail. Danny Elington's 5th North Carolina Artillery Battalion was one of the battalions set across the pike by General Hill. Battery D, with its six guns, joined Pegram's artillery units there on the road and pointed east toward Gettysburg. In the morning the gun battalions would move closer to Gettysburg.

"Something has to happen tomorrow, boys," Fry said solemnly.

"You can count on it, corporal," Alfred replied nervously.

The heavens stood silent above the men of the South that June night. God in His infinite wisdom knew the destruction that would come on the morrow. He had seen the destruction in many battles thus far in the war. Even though they were led to confidence and redemption by their chaplains as they progressed into Pennsylvania, many men still held one question in their mind. Why must the war go on? They rummaged this spiritual dilemma through their wearied minds again and again. The only conclusion some came to was the fact that the world was a world of sin and disease. Man would only find true peace in the afterlife, in heaven. Part of hell had already eaten away at their bodies and souls through the ravages from the disease known as war.

Truculent circumstances had destroyed humanity thus far in the conflict between North and South, Yankee and Reb, and between Blue and Gray. Among the tents and bedrolls, picket lines and camp fires, privates and generals, and among the young and old soldiers, prayer became the order of the night for the 26th North Carolina.

— Chapter 16 —
Ridges of Destiny

July 1, 1863, early morning
Gettysburg

The break of dawn pierced the halcyon darkness of night on Wednesday morning. At around 4:30, the men of the 26th North Carolina and their brigade mates were roused from their nervous slumber and ordered to prepare for the march to Gettysburg. Glazed eyes and aggravating aches and pains greeted many of the soldiers. Haversacks and knapsacks were piled up and loaded onto wagons to be held for the men, when and if they returned from battle. The Possum could hear the sounds of artillery caissons pulled by horses trotting and clanking their way east on the Chambersburg Pike. It seemed as if the artillery boys were up and ready to go, way before the infantry. Danny's 5th North Carolina Battalion and Major Pegram's battalions were on their way toward the town. They would go in front of General James Archer's brigade of infantry, who would lead General Heth's division back for supplies at Gettysburg. Heth wanted cannon up front in order to flush and scour any enemy regiments who might be waiting for him on those ridges he observed west of the town the previous day.

The 13th Alabama led Archer's brigade east on the pike. General Joseph Davis's brigade followed behind Archer. Heth had ordered these two brigades to be the head of the march into Gettysburg. The soldiers of the two brigades marched toward the town in columns, four men across. He would deploy them as necessary as the march continued and pressed on toward the east. The two brigades passed the 26th North Carolina at their bivouac site.

Showers had fallen at about six o'clock, but then cleared and most men could tell it was going to be a sweltering day. The lingering humidity and rising temperatures caused the men of all regiments to begin sweating under their uncomfortable wool uniforms. Some of the men had adapted to this combination of hot weather and wool uniforms, but others had not.

The onset of heat exhaustion percolated the bodies of officer and enlisted men. Sudden bouts of dizziness and faintness made soldiers afraid to go into battle. To them it was like fighting two foes, the blue uniformed soldier and the mysterious sickness that always got in the way of a man's thinking. Headaches and rapid heartbeats made routine movements seem like endless, contorted ventures. However, most men tried to endure and carry on through their ill symptoms, not wanting to become a liability to their regiments. This behavior displayed the character of men such as Colonel Burgwyn, Lieutenant Colonel John Lane, Major John Jones, Lieutenant Elington and the boys of the Possum. They knew what their duty was and sickness was not going to stop their mission.

Heth's division stayed the course along the pike. Archer's brigade and the men of his 13th Alabama Infantry continued to lead the division toward their destination east on the Chambersburg Pike. Davis's brigade still followed second in the column. By this time in the morning, seven o'clock, Pettigrew's brigade joined the march and fell in behind Davis's as reserves for the lead two brigades. The men of the 26th North Carolina were on their way, bringing up the rear of the brigade as the last regiment in Pettigrew's line. Watching Archer's brigade cross the Marsh Creek Bridge ahead of them, the rest of the men of the 26th gathered their possessions and began to fall in behind their division. Colonel John Brockenbrough's brigade filed up next in the column, also serving as a reserve brigade for Heth's division. For additional security, on this reconnaissance-in-force, General William Dorsey Pender's division was ordered to follow behind Heth's division to supply additional units, particularly artillery, to be placed in support of Confederate infantry. Men from North Carolina, Alabama, Tennessee, Mississippi, Virginia, South Carolina and Georgia were now ready to do battle upon the Yankee enemy.

Gettysburg 1863

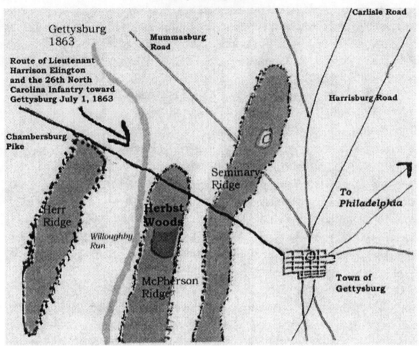

As Archer's brigade made its way across the Marsh Creek Bridge, clanking and kicking up the dried dirt on the road, a Union cavalry patrol spotted the brigade. Pickets from the 8th Illinois Cavalry, sitting three-quarters of a mile east of the bridge, observed the Confederates coming up the road. At around 7:30, on the morning of July 1, 1863, a shot pierced the air three miles west of Gettysburg, near a little-known rise of earth that carried the name Knoxlyn Ridge. A Union carbine fired a round at the men of the 13th Alabama. No one was hit in the regiment, but the ball had opened on another battle between Johnny Reb and Billy Yank.

Men had finally heard and "seen the elephant."

With muskets shouldered, cartridge boxes full and uniforms still relatively in good condition, the soldiers in the 26th North Carolina Infantry Regiment, the men from the mountains and ridges of Caldwell County, the young and the more mature fellows, pressed forward into an unknown destiny. Many of the soldiers in the 26th asked themselves poignant questions that cut right to the heart of the expectant battle ahead. Reminiscent before each horrible engagement, soldiers would think of the little things important in their lives. Things taken for granted before the war between the states had started were now present like a treasure box of relied-upon memories; food for the souls of boys and men alike who might never return to their former lives.

Soldiers would ask or say to themselves and to each other:

"I wonder what's going on in Caldwell County right now."

"Betcha Daddy is smoking his pipe on the front porch, watching our stupid dog do some kind of cheap tricks."

"Wonder what Ma's cooking tonight."

"I can see the lake down near my house as clear as day. I wonder if anyone is catching a fish right about now."

"Bet my wife is cooking for the children."

"Oh, how I wish I could be home right now, looking at the beautiful mountains God gave us back in the Globe."

"If only I could look at Grandfather Mountain, I would praise the Lord in heaven."

"I want to go home."

"I don't want to die before my time."

"I wish I could just get under a blanket and hide from all of this carnage and destruction of mankind. I just want to be a little child again."

"I hope Abigail, Abby, is all right over in Philadelphia with her father, the senator," said Lieutenant Harrison Elington to Corporal Lewis Fry. The men headed east with the rest of Pettigrew's brigade. Dust covered their passage as they marched. The 26th was the last regiment in the brigade.

"Lewis, today is the day of our accounting for what we have done thus far in this war. We are about to find out if we can fight these no-good Yankees on their own soil."

"You have a darn good point there, lieutenant. I would guess we are going to jostle right into the whole Union infantry, who are in all probability over those ridges in our front."

"You think so, corporal?"

"Yes, lieutenant. I believe General Pettigrew was right about what we reconnoitered yesterday on those ridges. I think General Meade has better intelligence information than we do and we are going to pay for it if we don't get some reconnaissance from General Stuart and the cavalry."

"You're right on about that, Lewis. We have to know what is in front of us. In my opinion, those Union men you said you saw yesterday were there to scout the ground around Gettysburg in order for the main Union army to move north into Pennsylvania. I can't see how any military commander could ignore the importance of the junction town. Whatever army takes control of that town will be able to control maneuvering and transportation abilities for their troops. This, corporal, will determine the outcome of any battle fought in this area of enemy territory."

"I agree, sir. I would also agree that Archer will send skirmishers out soon to press those Union troops, whoever they are."

Archer's skirmishers did deploy and were successful in pushing and jostling General John Buford's cavalry screen farther to the east and back toward Gettysburg itself. After sweeping the Union videttes further from their original positions, General Heth deployed his two leading brigades on both sides of the Chambersburg Pike. Buford's cavalry then redeployed on Herr Ridge closer to Gettysburg. Archer went to the right and Davis went to the left of the pike. With Pegram's guns and the guns of the 5th North Carolina Artillery Battalion moving in front of Archer's and Davis's infantry, the Confederates grew more confident in their venture forward.

Spread out into a battle line running five-eighths of a mile wide across the pike, the gray and butternut regiments made good, solid progress in the face of an enemy still mostly hidden.

The Confederate division then headed on to Herr Ridge, where Colonel William Gamble of Buford's cavalry division had formed his entire line. A piercing volley of musket fire was heard as Archer and Davis's brigades pressed and harassed the Union cavalrymen on Herr Ridge. The Yankees retreated farther east after the Confederate brigades attacked. Running to their rear and firing their carbines as they went, the blue cavalry men focused on delay. Gamble's men were doing just what they were supposed to do: slow the advance of the Confederate division. Archer was then able to deploy his brigade on the eastern slope of Herr ridge. It was a good launching point for an organized and sustained attack upon Buford's forces.

"I can hear the volley and peppering sounds of battle," said Elington to Colonel Burgwyn.

"It sounds as if we have made contact with the enemy, lieutenant. Archer must have finally pulled his skirmishers in and attacked."

Archer and Davis, after securing Herr Ridge, redeployed skirmishers to press the enemy further and move into the targeted town beyond the next ridge. General Heth ordered his two brigades to gain as much ground as possible toward the town.

At around ten o'clock in the morning, Heth's orders were put into effect, in force, by Archer and Davis. As double lines of Archer's brigade moved forward from Herr Ridge, Union cannon fire raked their right flank, causing early casualties. The cannon fire was coming from a stand of woods known as Herbst Woods, located on another rise of land called McPherson Ridge. A stream ran through the base of the ridge and the Union soldiers continued a steady fire from the eastern side. Pegram's cannon opened up on the Union cannon across the way and a brief artillery duel sounded and blasted through the countryside. Corporal Danny Elington's 5th North Carolina Artillery Battalion answered the bombardment of Union guns along with Pegram's men.

"I know Danny is in action now," Elington said to Lewis.

They continued their march behind the main battle line.

"Those guns firing are definitely cannon from his battalion. I guess we are headed into it next. Here we go," Elington said.

"Our turn will surely come before we know it," Lewis answered.

The heat of the day intensified upon the field of battle. The ill symptoms of heat exhaustion arose throughout the field. Men on both sides had the two great enemies to fight once again: their mortal enemies and the mysterious enemy of sickness. On the Southern, or left, side of the Chambersburg Pike, Archer's brigade pressed forward under heavy Union fire. The brigade crossed Willoughby Run and double-quicked up a steep slope into Herbst Woods. On the northern side of the pike, Davis's brigade pressed forward, making better progress in the absence of wooded areas there. They passed along an unfinished railroad cut that ran parallel to the pike. Artillery fire continued louder and louder across both Herr and McPherson Ridges. The men of Archer's brigade could see blasts of shrapnel hitting the ground before them. The men were sweating as if they had been drenched after being thrown in a lake. A gap soon developed between Archer's and Davis's brigades near the Chambersburg Pike. It looked as though the two brigades might be flanked by the Union 1st Corps.

Soldiers in the 26th North Carolina could now see the coiled smoke of destruction and decimation. They could hear calls for help and for relief.

Elington thought of his analogy for gruesome battle from his journal:

The dead, hot led of Minie balls again smashed the flesh, men shrieking with pain and agony. The shrieks and calls for help did nothing to stop the awful engine of human battle.

The familiar sounds of the engine were all over the field and in the minds of Confederate and Union soldiers. Opening volleys raked the fields with musket fire. Cannon fired rounds of solid shot and case shot to try and soften the resistance from the other side. The combination of rifle and artillery fire generated the great engine into a seething quagmire, where death and mayhem persisted upon every breathing moment.

The engine functioned efficiently for hours at a time. Its iron fuel, fired from the bowels of hell from hundreds of muskets and tens of cannon made the exhaust hot and loathsome. The exhaust, the waste of the engine, the ingredients the engine no longer needed, was the dead soldier who laid upon the field of battle. The dead could no longer produce the spark that in turn produced the projectile that ultimately entered human flesh, tearing and severing the vital organs of the creator of the engine itself. For men became killers of other men upon peaceful fields of golden wheat and oats polluted by the human exhaust of death.

The soldiers of the 26th could hear and see the smoke and they had to wait before they could enter the great engine of battle.

How long would it be until we could add a spark to continue the engine's operation? Elington considered this as his regiment reached the shade of Spring Hotel Woods on the eastern slope of Herr Ridge.

For now their march halted and the soldiers of the 26th waited patiently for their role in the mayhem.

As the hot day wore on, the men of Archer's brigade were pressed and probed by the men wearing those big black hats. It was the 2nd and 7th Wisconsin, the 19th Indiana, and the 24th Michigan Infantry Regiments, better known as the Iron Brigade. Their vigor and strength in previous battles had acquired the label for the regiment and they were known by men of both armies. These regiments almost surrounded Archer's regiments, causing the brigade leader to call for a retreat across Willoughby Run and back to Herr Ridge. Word came down to the 26th that Archer himself was captured during the brief battle on McPherson Ridge. Davis's Mississippians in the meantime were being cut to pieces in a railroad cut dug out for new track that ran along the pike. Rebel fire that had been as hail in a windstorm slowed to a peppering of fire. The rail cut was to high for the Mississippians to fire out of, thus suppressing their damage to the enemy. Men from the 6th Wisconsin had the rail cut in direct aim from the southern edge of the Chambersburg Pike, and many Confederates threw down their muskets and surrendered or retreated. A hollow of death and confusion marked the great battle.

The engine of battle was finally dissipating upon the fields near Gettysburg. The dead and wounded from Archer's and Davis's brigades muddled the grounds in Herbst Woods, on McPherson Ridge and across the railroad cut. The McPherson family farm buildings were surrounded by wounded from Union and Confederate regiments. Activity slackened as the noon hour approached. The sulfuric smoke, mixing with the hot and humid air, engendered an atmosphere almost unbearable to the men of both armies. Those ill symptoms, the headaches, faintness, nausea and dizziness kept a relentless hold on the soldier. He often seemed trapped in his own body and limited by his own will, where change could not take place.

The 26th along with the 11th, 47th, and 52nd North Carolina Regiments continued to wait for orders, now arrayed in double battle line formations. Even though the musket fire dampened, the artillery, both Confederate and Union, continued to rumble. This caused the air to stifle and the body to quiver. Colonel Burgwyn grew impatient over the hesitation of orders from his superior officers in the field.

"What could Hill be thinking?" Burgwyn said to Elington.

"We weren't supposed to bring on an engagement, colonel. Do you remember those orders we got from Pettigrew and from General Hill himself?"

"Yes, I do, Harrison, but why don't we continue to bring up more artillery? This ridge is an excellent positioning point for more cannon! Can't they see this?"

"I don't know, sir. I hope Stuart shows his sorry face before General Lee and our divisions face more Union infantry."

"I can't believe he hasn't gotten his men to us yet. Stuart has to realize we may have been engaged by now. But why doesn't Lee utilize Jenkin's cavalry for reconnaissance. He surely can be of some help to us!"

"Sir, I did hear early this morning from some of the officers in the 52nd that General Richard Ewell's corps is going to be attacking somewhere north of Gettysburg and it's going to happen soon. They said General Robert Rodes is leading Ewell's corps down from Carlisle. You know how Rodes is. He will not hold back when he sees Union corps entrenching in his front. I know he will try to take the high ground when he comes."

"Rodes. Hey, Elington, that sounds good for us. If he can concentrate an attack from the north, maybe we will get a chance to attack from the west again. I can't see how Lee could resist such an attack."

"We can stand here and dream all day, sir. But I'm going back over to the boys in F Company. They are in the shade now and I have to cool down before I get the heat sickness."

"All right, Elington. I will see you soon. Stay low, friend."

The early afternoon came and went. The intermittent pounding, shrieking and crashing of artillery shells remained upon the field of battle in front of Pettigrew's brigade. Smoke still lingered in the afternoon air. The sun blazed its summer fury on the wounded and dead strewn on the green grasses, fields of oats and fields of winter wheat. The remnants of Archer's brigade began to filter through those fields and some blessed men made it back to the safety of the eastern slope of Herr Ridge, where they had started their advance a short time before. General Heth ordered Archer's fragmented brigade to position on the right flank of Pettigrew's brigade. Davis's brigade was ordered by Heth to stay where it was and try to rally stragglers and rescue men who had been wounded near the railroad cut. He eventually pulled his brigade back to an area a few yards in front of a farm and its surrounding buildings.

"Get down on the ground, men!"

Orders were disbursed through the chain of command in the 26th and in other regiments in Pettigrew's brigade.

"Lieutenant, make sure our companies stay in battle line, but on the ground!" Colonel Burgwyn shouted with ripe intensity to Harrison and his other company commanders. "There are enemy sharpshooters on the roofs of those farm buildings, just ahead and to the right of our position, Captain Tuttle. They are a problem. That darn artillery fire from the pike is beginning to scour us like autumn leaves."

Romulus Tuttle had taken over as captain of F Company after Captain Nathaniel Rankin left the regiment. Tuttle was from Caldwell County and had relatives in the 26th. An innocent and young-looking man with sandy brown hair and blue eyes, Tuttle was respected by his company.

"What should we do, colonel?"

"Send a courier to the 5th North Carolina Artillery, over there on our left, and tell them to blast canister fire toward that farm. In the meantime I will get some of our own sharpshooters from E Company to take those rogues out of that place. They're hitting our men and we haven't even gotten orders to advance on the enemy yet."

"Yes, sir!"

Captain Tuttle grabbed Private Jack Coffey and told him to deliver the colonel's message to an officer in the 5th. Coffey ran off into the woods behind the regiment's line of men crouching and lying on the ground. He ran faster as he heard the peals of case shot fly overhead. He made it to the pike and asked the artillerists where their officers were. A tired and gritty young man came over to Coffey and said he was the man in charge; a major by rank.

"Colonel Burgwyn needs canister fire on those farm buildings.

Sharpshooters are harassing our regiment from the right flank. Can you help us or not? I need an answer."

"Tell the colonel I will fire rounds over there in a few minutes."

"Thank you, major."

Coffey ran back toward the 26th amidst the smoke and metal flying through the sulfuric air. He approached the rear of his company line and a Minie ball nicked him in the right thigh. He fell to the ground in pain and yelled for help. A small spattering of blood stained his trousers. Private Thaddeus Curtis ran to his aid, helped him up and got him into the cover and safety of the company line.

"Those no-good sharpshooters got me," he said.

"You will be all right, Jack," Thaddeus answered.

"Thaddeus, you have to get the message to Burgwyn. The major of the artillery told me that the colonel's request will be carried out in a few minutes. Those men are under heavy counterfire from across the ridge. The Yankee guns are blasting away over there. But he said he could help us."

"I will go right now, Jack, don't worry."

"Thank you, Thaddeus."

After a few minutes the belching fire of canister shot was heard by the left wing soldiers of the 26th. The 5th kept its promise. E Company sharpshooters dispatched by Burgwyn rattled the farm buildings with accurate shots from the Springs Hotel Woods on Herr Ridge. The sharpshooters in blue were silenced and the soldiers of the 26th continued to wait for their battle orders. The summer heat made it quite uncomfortable for the men.

Time dragged on with an incredible sluggishness, aggravating the temperament of everyone.

– Chapter 17 –
A Stealthy Advance

July 1, afternoon
Gettysburg

The blue battle line swerved into a semicircle formation. The Union 1st and 11th Corps furnished a line extending from the northern ridges of Gettysburg, turning left in an arc, and continuing south across the Chambersburg Pike anchored on McPherson Ridge in the wooded enclave of Herbst Woods. Artillery continued its hot and inclement inferno upon the areas of Herr Ridge, McPherson Ridge and along the Chambersburg Pike. The torrid sun withered the spirits of the soldiers waiting for their orders to advance on the enemy. Dire circumstances surrounded the ridges west of Gettysburg. The Confederates knew they had to press the Union corps again. General Lee wanted a victory and now a battle had started toward that victory. Even though Archer and Davis failed to break the Union lines, Heth knew a second wave attack would break those same lines and force the blue coats to retreat.

Like a grandiose juggernaut, resplendent in countenance and gloriously set upon the heights of Oak Hill and Oak Ridge, General Richard Ewell's corps, led by General Robert Rodes's division, stealthily advanced out of the trees from Carlisle to the north. A clash of fire reverberated through the town of Gettysburg from the northern heights and the frightened citizens became even more disconcerted in the midst of the rising storm of battle.

"Look at that magnificent sight to the north of the town, Elington. It's

Rodes and his division," said Lieutenant Colonel John Lane. Waiting and commanding the right flank of the 26th North Carolina, he could see the grand approach of his comrades in gray and butternut, convulsing into the fusillade of battle. The thin and gritty lieutenant colonel was a well-trusted and respected part of the 26th. His picket detail and skirmish line duties were always trusted by Colonel Henry Burgwyn. As an officer, Lane's ability was always effectual to the men of the 26th.

"They are attacking, John. The Union formation in their front doesn't have a chance now. Rodes will do his job and perform his duty," Elington said.

"Our boys are getting restless. They want to get into this fight, but I can't imagine why we haven't received orders to march to that yonder ridge."

"Colonel Burgwyn has to get orders soon, John. With Rodes attacking we can decimate their lines from the west. We can be like lightning, hitting them from two directions—north and west."

"When we go in, Elington, we have to make sure the younger boys keep their bearings and comprehend the enemy's positions. Do you understand?"

"I will be right on it. Remember Malvern Hill last year when we went through that hellish inferno of artillery fire from McClellan? The boys stood up pretty well and I think they will do the same today."

"Good, Elington."

"Let me go over to the center of the line to see what our situation is, John."

As Elington said those words to his friend and fellow officer John Lane, Colonel Burgwyn was heard from the center of the regiment line shouting orders:

"Attention! Attention! Men of the 26th North Carolina, rise from your positions. We are ordered by General Pettigrew to advance to the next ridge and engage the enemy."

"Move, boys! Move and dress on the colors. File closers, take positions!"

Lieutenant Colonel Lane, along with Major John Jones, who commanded the left flank of the regiment, aligned their men into a solid battle line. The men rose in majestic splendor, joining the rest of Heth's division, ready to commence their mission. Colonel Burgwyn mounted his horse and rode up and down, behind the regiment's battle line, to urge the men on and to pour confidence into their hearts and souls. Elington always complimented Burgwyn on how he accomplished the intense onus of keeping the boys steady in a battle line and in battle itself. Captain Romulus Tuttle, Lieutenant Elington and Lieutenant John Holloway ordered F Company to position itself for the advance and shoulder their muskets. Sergeants helped relay orders to the enlisted men.

"Forward, march! Forward, march!"

The command was heard down the regiment and brigade lines, traversing through the woods as company officers formed the entire division together into a battle line of nearly 3,000 men.

Pettigrew ordered his brigade to move by the "left flank in echelon formation." This made the North Carolina regiments appear to be moving in numerous staggered lines toward the Union troops on McPherson Ridge. Union regiments became concerned about the seemingly endless lines coming at them. Eventually, Pettigrew's brigade would form into one battle line as it moved down Herr ridge and into the field of oats before Willoughby Run and McPherson Ridge.

"File closers, dispatch," shouted Colonel Burgwyn from the center of the line. "Dress on the colors. Steady boys!"

"We have to keep together," Private Curtis said to Alfred.

"We have to keep alive!" Alfred answered solemnly.

The repercussions from the sustained cannon fire along the pike made Private Abshire nervous again. He was beginning to shake in his shoes.

"I can remember the same type of fire at Malvern Hill when I got shot right in the arm," Alfred said to Private Coffey. "It seems like it was just yesterday when I shivered from the artillery blasts coming from that hill in Virginia."

In their line of march, the Possum stood side by side. Corporal Fry was on the left flank of the company and then Alfred, Thaddeus and Jackson fell in on his right. Elington would always position himself to the left-center of the company battle line. Captain Tuttle liked to use Elington as his left flank lieutenant and anchor.

The men marched steadfast toward the water of Willoughby Run and the edge of McPherson Ridge. The high oats brushed their uniforms. The smoke and smell from the gunpowder hung in the hot, thick, humid air. Soldiers licked their dry lips. Many brushed the sweat from their brow with their free hand. Yells for help and cries of pain sliced through the sounds of the artillery barrage. The Possum saw the dead and wounded of Archer's brigade in front of them and they were shaken to the core.

"I can't believe we are here again in these awful scenes of battle," Abshire said. He continued an unfinished prayer as he marched.

"You better start believing it, Abshire, for we are about to witness it again any minute now," Corporal Fry answered from his position near the color guard.

F Company was formed to the right of the color guard, a bull's-eye for the enemy. Fry was right there. He was the left flank soldier of F Company and positioned to the right of the colors.

"Thanks for the warning, corporal."

"Keep your head up, Abshire, and you'll be fine."

"Do you think we'll make it out of here today, corporal?" asked Private Coffey. He was really becoming nervous from the anticipation of battle. He was also feeling quite sick from the heat of the day and from his wound earlier as a courier. His sandy hair was drenched in sweat and his face was becoming white from sickness. Faintness, nausea and dizziness followed his footsteps toward the enemy up on the slope.

"We can make it, private. Make sure you load your musket properly. Remember your training. Don't go putting three cartridges into the muzzle all at once before you fire the first one. Do you hear what I'm telling you, private?"

"Yes, corporal, but I think I forgot what you said already. My head is beginning to spin. What the heck!"

"Steady, boys!" ordered Burgwyn, sitting upon his horse. "Keep your lines together. We are about to form on the bank of the run in our front."

"Steady, F Company!" ordered Elington from the left. "Those black hats are right in our front, formed at the top of that slope across the creek. It's that darned Iron Brigade. Be prepared to take fire from those boys and then we'll give them a volley they'll never forget."

"We'll give it to them," Private Curtis commented as he formed along the bank.

The rebel yell was employed loudly and forcibly by the 26th. *The red battle flag of the regiment looks larger than usual,* Elington thought, standing among the briers and underbrush along Willoughby Run. The smells of tree wood decaying and moss growing in the small valley penetrated the senses of the men. The summer humidity saturated the air. Thorns pricked the soldiers and officers waiting by the creek for their orders to march across and attack those black hats of the 24th Michigan.

An earsplitting, stentorian blast of fire, lead and tree bark shattered the lull of the afternoon on July 1. The Union Iron Brigade opened a horrendous conflagration against the 26th North Carolina. Flashes of musket fire bursted from the trees in front of the 26th. The water in Willoughby Run splashed from the searing Minie balls aimed at the Confederates. Tree bark scattered through Herbst Wood, flying in every direction from the force of the massed shots fired from atop the slope east of the creek. Men in gray fell in the oat field from random hits. Some fell into the twisted brambles of the creekside underbrush, becoming severely entwined and left to suffer from the hot lead; the dead metal bullets flying across the fields taking precious life from the 26th North Carolina.

"Hold the line, boys!" Elington shouted to his company.

"Don't retreat, boys; steady!" yelled Colonel Burgwyn from his central position in the regiment. "Ready! Get your muskets ready! Aim! Fire! Fire! Fire!"

Burgwyn got down from his mount to observe the outcome of his regiment's volley at the enemy and to protect himself from enemy fire.

An officer on a horse during battle made a pretty target for an infantryman.

The 26th returned a covering volley across the creek and up the slope. The 11th North Carolina, from their left flank, sent another searing, massed fire toward the Iron Brigade. The 26th crossed the run. Boys in blue fell to their deaths and shrieked in pain from the two massed volleys launched from the west bank of the run. Acrid smoke filled the canopy of trees in Herbst Woods. Men on both sides felt the heat of the day and smelled the odors of battle as the artillery fire and musket fire continued.

Burgwyn, Lane and Jones closed their ranks and compensated for their loses. They had to press on through the woods and now was the time.

"Dress on the colors, men," ordered Lane.

"Color guard, advance!" shouted Burgwyn.

Sergeant Mansfield of E Company proceeded and was immediately shot down. The red battle flag of the Confederates fell to the ground.

Sergeant Johnson of G Company picked up the battle flag and proceeded with the color guard across the creek, amidst raking artillery fire.

"Advance!"

Officers down the line shouted and directed their companies to proceed across the shallow run.

Boom ... Boom ... Boom ... Boom ...

Artillery fire focused in on the 26th and tore it apart. Parts of uniforms and human bodies were dispersed through the line of battle. Holes opened in the ranks and men cried in pain and agony upon the once peaceful and pleasant ridge. Case shot exploded above the regiment line of the 26th North Carolina. Hot pieces of metal rained down on soldiers who by now were desperately trying to cross Willoughby Run and reform on the other side. The aroma of burning metal seared the nostrils. Men looked up past the green trees, lying on their backs, and trying to pray their last words to God as exploding case shot plummeted from the blue, tranquil sky.

Heaven watched the carnage, but there was no effort to stop the wreckage of battle, no response. The engine had started again, the sparks resupplied, and the exhaust of human carnage resulted in a vehement and hideous display of man's invention of war.

As the soldiers of the 26th crossed the run they swelled together, the fire of the Iron Brigade was hectic and uncontrollable. Men tried to find cover where there was none. Company lines tangled and a salient formed along the line of the regiment. This had also happened to the regiment line at Malvern Hill in Virginia, one year ago to the day.

A thud trickled through the 26th's line. The men reformed and aligned on the eastern edge of the run. Private Jackson Coffey fell into the run. Face down he did not move an inch as the splashing and current-driven waters rippled over his body. Bullets and soldiers continued to crash into and across the run. His blond sandy hair skimmed the surface of the water and his blood surrounded his body.

"Coffey is down!" yelled Private Thaddeus Curtis to Lieutenant Elington.

"You have to reform with F Company, Thaddeus. Get back to your position on the left side of the battle line, boy. It looks like poor Jackson has had it."

Elington stared for a moment at Coffey lying face down in the water and he saw three other young men beside him. The four men lay in stillness among the intense movements of the regiment and the brigade.

"What in God's name are we doing here?"

Elington then coldly turned away from the dead soldiers and shouted for his men to align themselves for an assault on that no-good blue line up on the slope, the devilish line of Yankees causing mayhem among the ranks of the 26th.

"He's dead, lieutenant?" Private Abshire asked. "That's it for young Jackson? We just leave him there in the water? I have to go back and see if he needs help!"

"No, Alfred!"

"We can't leave him there. His wounds might of just knocked him unconscious, lieutenant. I have to see if he is alive."

"Stay in line, Alfred, or you're going to get it next."

"Listen to the lieutenant," shouted Corporal Fry from the far left of the company line. "Darn! Stay where you are! Coffey will survive if he can. He's a darn tough buck, Abshire. Now don't move from your position or I will knock you out. Do you here me, private?"

"All right, corporal. Whatever you say."

With the color guard somewhat intact across Willoughby Run, F Company did its best to reform, straighten its line, and reposition to the right of the flag.

"Dress on the colors!" Captain Tuttle shouted above the crashing, shrieking and crackling arms fire.

Rodes was still advancing from the north of Gettysburg. His juggernaut kept pressing the brigades and regiments of the 11th Union Corps. His cannon were now perched on Oak Hill, sending a blistering fire through the ranks of the Union divisions. Men and artillery pieces on both sides were caught in a caustic system of destruction.

"Dress on the colors!" Lieutenant Elington shouted from the center of F Company's line. He had been shifted away from the left while seeing if Coffey was alive. "The colors are there before us. Let us drive the enemy to hell. Let's break their cursed lines to pieces!"

The cool waters of Willoughby's Run gently passed some yards behind F Company. The refreshing waters could not be noticed by the soldiers reforming for a massed and murderous attack. The simple pleasures of life, like a fresh running creek, could not be appreciated by men on this day. Battle persisted from every angle. Cannon fire from the north and east, musket fire from the front and reserve troops from Pender's division waiting from behind made the 26th North Carolina a battle line saturated in combat.

"I pray to God in heaven that He will keep us safe and look down on us with His mercy," Alfred prayed.

"Don't forget to deliver a darn prayer for me, Alfred," Corporal Fry said solemnly.

A harsh, crackling sound emanated from atop the slope where the black hats were fixed in position. Alfred, Thaddeus, Lewis and Harrison, the Possum minus Coffey, all wavered as they tried to keep their positions in F Company's left flank. Other men fell around them from the deluge of ardent lead hissing through the trees. Smoke and metal fragments whistled through the thick air.

"This is hell!" cried Thaddeus.

"I think the end is near, boys," Corporal Fry shouted. "I haven't felt fear in battle as of yet, lieutenant, but today I have been introduced to unknown trepidations in my heart."

"Don't break on me now, Lewis," Elington shouted from the left center. "I need your leadership. The men need your leadership. Please, Lewis, don't abandon your mission. Steady! Keep your eyes on the colors and on Colonel Burgwyn when you falter. All right, Lewis!"

"I'm trying, lieutenant."

Lewis saw the flag go down again and he felt dizzy. Private John Stamper raised the flag for the honor of the 26th and he was quickly shot. Private George Kelly took the colors and he was shot and fell to the hallowed ground.

"We're being torn to pieces, Captain Tuttle," Elington shouted over the blare of muskets.

"We have to hold our line together, Elington, or we will all perish. We have to charge that murderous black hat position before they cut us up. Casualties are mounting in every part of our regiment."

"I'll try to keep the remaining boys together, sir, on the left. We have to keep the flanks of this line strong so the center doesn't cave in, sir."

"Good, Elington. Do your best for the honor of North Carolina upon the ground of the enemy. We have to be victorious, or our cause will falter; it will be lost forever."

Private Larkin Thomas of F Company now held the colors high.

"Color guard, advance!" Colonel Burgwyn again ordered in the midst of smoke and heat.

The color guard took its six steps forward, signaling the start of another advance. Burgwyn stayed in the center of his regiment, Lieutenant Colonel John Lane continued to bring up the right flank of the regiment and Major John Jones led the boys on the left flank of the 26th North Carolina.

Like tens of trees falling and stalks of corn crackling in fall fields, the men in blue, atop the bloody slope on McPherson Ridge, unleashed another devastating onslaught of scorching fire. White smoke cascaded through the ridge line, expanded gaps were ripped open among the company lines of the 26th and human death was heaped in full view of the struggling soldiers.

"We can't get the gaps and holes in our company filled fast enough," Elington shouted to Colonel Burgwyn, who was still showing his cool and collected demeanor under intensive enemy fire.

"Keep your company steady, Elington, along with Captain Tuttle. We are going to return fire in a minute. We'll have those blue bellies on the run before you know it. Go back to your post, lieutenant!"

"Yes, sir!"

Crackling, piercing, shrieking storms of lead and coiling smoke characterized the sights and sounds the soldiers encountered. Muskets fired sounding like hail in a storm.

Smoke and the sulfuric smell of gunpowder overwhelmed the soldiers of the 26th, but they pressed forward under the steady direction of their twenty-two year old colonel, the boy colonel. Muskets flew through the air, young soldiers grappled at each other and at the ground for the sake of acquiring a sense of security.

Confederate attire was saturated with blood. The oat field was stained with human slaughter. Willoughby Run ran red as crimson from the continual supply of flowing blood upon its waters.

"Ready! Aim! Fire! Fire! Fire!" charged Burgwyn.

Scores of men in blue tumbled from their defensive line up on the slope of McPherson Ridge. Some of their black round hats bounced and toppled down the slope and into the ranks of the 26th.

The soldiers of the 26th continued their ascent toward the enemy. Elington fired his prized Colt Navy .36 caliber revolver straight at the standing officers commanding the 24th Michigan in his front. Alfred, Thaddeus and Corporal Fry repeated their loading regimen with their muskets that by this time in the attack were as hot as coal burning in a furnace on a winter's night. Grabbing cartridges from their boxes, the soldiers handling the muskets tore the end of the paper from the cartridge, poured the powder down the hot barrel, placed the Minie ball into the top of the barrel supported by their thumb, detached a ramrod from the bottom of the musket and rammed home the lead ball. Ramrods were returned to holders. They then raised the gun to place a percussion cap on the nipple of the nose cone under the firing hammer. They cocked the hammer halfway back, placed the cap on the cone, cocked the hammer fully back, aimed and then fired their round. The men had to accomplish this great loading task while under enemy fire and while sweating profusely, making the ramrods almost useless. Many soldiers could not ram the rounds down the barrels. Their hands slipped while trying. Many soldiers used tree trunks as back stops to push their lead down the barrels with their slippery ramrods.

Volleys and men firing at will continued and repeated back and forth, back and forth upon McPherson Ridge. Loading and reloading of muskets continued as the ascent by the 26th endured the murderous, raking fire coming down the slope in their front.

"They're breaking, boys!" Elington shouted as loud as he could. "We have them now! F Company, charge! Charge!"

The men in the company already had their bayonets fixed and they began to fall in a straight line, ready to charge the enemy line that was breaking apart and falling back. The 19th Indiana black hats, formed on the left flank of the 26th North Carolina, were the first to fall back from their original battle position. Soldiers in blue started to retreat in good order considering the circumstances of intense and fierce battle.

"Captain Tuttle, do you agree that we should charge that retreating regiment," Elington shouted. "Their line is bending. We can break'em, captain."

"We'll have to wait for orders from Burgwyn, Elington."

"But we can all see them now, captain. They're running. We can destroy them upon their own ground."

"All right, Elington. Let's do it."

"Good, sir!"

"F Company! All bayonets fixed, now! On the order, charge the flanking companies of that regiment falling back in our front."

"Charge! Charge! Charge!"

F Company began the charge toward the Iron Brigade and they saw the 24th Michigan boys along with the 19th Indiana get up and run for their lives from their original battle line in Herbst Woods. The crackling of tree branches and the rustle of men sweeping forward covered McPherson Ridge. Firing continued as the Union men fell back to another battle line. The Confederate red battle flag flew among the trees, among the dead, among the wounded and among the living from the 26th North Carolina. Smoke filled the area and the hot, humid air continued to stifle men on both sides.

"Charge! Charge!" Colonel Burgwyn shouted when he saw F Company take the initiative toward the enemy.

Bending and curling up the slope, the 26th North Carolina chased the Iron Brigade through the trees. Private Thomas of F Company fell to the ground. He was shot in the left arm by one of the blue bellies falling back on the ridge. Private John Marley of G Company picked up the colors without hesitation and ran toward the enemy. The regiment followed as Burgwyn urged his troops to decimate the enemy ahead. The 26th, along with the 11th, 47th and 52nd North Carolina Regiments, continued to press, prod and pummel the enemy line. Hundreds of Confederate soldiers lay dead in the path from

Willoughby Run to Herbst Woods on McPherson Ridge in a remote town in south-central Pennsylvania.

War had come to the North, to the Union. The fresh fields and the tidy barns were now trodden under the feet of massive armies. The only goal of those armies was victory at all costs, victory to end the ravages of war.

Parched rounds of musket and artillery fire continued to come across the ridge. The Union Iron Brigade, wearing their bloody blue, re-established a position in Herbst Woods. The 19th Indiana and the 24th Michigan again kept up a steady, streaming fire toward the 26th North Carolina. Many of the men in the Iron Brigade hid behind trees of all sizes in Herbst Woods to cover themselves from the relentless cauldron of battle. Explosions of arms fire breached the lines on both sides. Officers fell to the ground, leaving whole companies leaderless and abandoned. Privates from the 26th crunched down behind trees, dropped their muskets and faltered, exhausted from the intense and horrible minutes it took to get as far as they had made it to on the ridge.

General Johnston Pettigrew, perched on Herr Ridge in the rear of his brigade line, sent a staff officer to Colonel Burgwyn. The staff officer carried a message from Pettigrew, telling the leader of the 26th North Carolina, "Today your regiment has covered itself with glory."

Burgwyn was inspired and now motivated to sweep the Union line off of McPherson Ridge. In the midst of intolerable battle conditions characterized by dense, coiling smoke that dried out mouths; hot lead that splintered trees and bones all around; artillery shrapnel that bursted above and in front of the lines; smells of sulfur; burning brush and human death all around, coupled with the hot temperatures and high humidity of the day, Colonel Henry Burgwyn continually reformed his regiment and carried out his duty for the honor of the Confederacy.

"They're reformed in our front, sir," Elington shouted to Burgwyn. "I can see the two regiments that retreated from the brow of the slope and they are now entrenching firmly across our front in the woods. We're going to have to break that second line, colonel, in order to win this day."

"Pettigrew has sent us a message, Elington. He has stated that our regiment has 'covered itself with glory' today. Did you hear what I said?"

"Yes, sir! That is good news, but we haven't won anything yet. We haven't earned any glory in the sight of that enemy, sir. Those boys are putting up a tough match for us. We can prevail, though, sir."

Elington chewed down hard and rhythmically on his tobacco. His right hand was blackened from the powder discharged from his Colt revolver. He had loaded and fired his gun time after time as he made his way up the ridge.

Some boys in the 26th went down to the ground and tried to rest from the sustained terror, from the carnage and from exhaustion. Unlike Archer's and Davis's brigade, Pettigrew's brigade was making better and more deadlier progress against the enemy lines. Colonel Brockenbrough's brigade continued the assault of the Union line closer to the Chambersburg Pike on the left flank of the 26th. His regiments smashed through the Yankees like artillery shot smashing through a barn.

"Dress on the colors, men!" ordered the colonel. "Steady the lines. We're going to give them fire they will never forget as long as those blue-coated Yankees live. Advance to the enemy, 26th! Fire at will as we advance, boys."

"Thaddeus, Alfred, stay near me and Corporal Fry," Elington said from the left of his company line.

"All right, sir, but where is Corporal Fry?"

"He's coming up right behind us. I think he was trying to get some water."

"Lewis!" Elington shouted. "We are going to try and stay together as we go into this next assault. We have to try and protect each other. Look at the trail of our dead behind us. I never imagined in my life I would see so many dead and wounded people at one time. This attack is turning horrendous for our companies."

"Those poor boys are going to be missed by their families back in Caldwell County, Harrison. What a waste!"

In the face of the inferno churning upon McPherson Ridge and across the pike on Oak Hill and Oak Ridge, the soldiers of the South continued their stealthy advances toward the enemy regiments. Firing, reloading and advancing, the 26th North Carolina, along with its flanking regiments, pressed and prodded through the woods, sustaining more losses as they trekked.

"Get ready for a volley, boys," Burgwyn ordered over the smashing sounds of battle.

"Fire! Fire! Fire!"

Another blistering volley of lead, from the aimed muskets of the 26th, ravaged the lines of the 24th Michigan and the 19th Indiana in Herbst Woods. Shrills of agonizing sounds rose from the woods like a specter haunting the unstable mind. Soldiers wavered in their steps. Their legs became like logs, forcing many to fall to the ground for cover and for rest. The haunting screams were ignored by the able-bodied soldier, for the battle had to be won at all costs, despite the tiredness of the men. General Lee wanted victory and the boys of Elington's unit wanted to give it to him. Sacrifice, above all they ever dreamed of, was now being offered for a cause of independence.

Like the fathers of the old Revolution of '76, the ancestors now fought in a second revolution parched by fire and stained in blood.

– Chapter 18 –
The Crest of Betrayal

July 1, 1863
Philadelphia

"March!" ordered General Napoleon Dana to his Home Guard troops. "We need to defend this beloved city to the end, gentlemen. This city represents to the world what democracy is. We are the protectors of history, culture and liberty."

In Philadelphia, General Dana tried his best with who he could muster into service to defend the sacred Union city. Listlessness and denial had foreshadowed this city of subtle incongruities. Philadelphians never seemed to take serious a Confederate invasion of the North, or more directly, an attack upon their own city of finance and industry. Citizens of the city continually conversed on the prospects of civil war, abolitionism and the Peace Democrat Party, but they couldn't believe in their hearts that General Robert E. Lee would attack and desecrate Philadelphia.

As news of the Gettysburg battle rustled and wound through the corridors of the city, people went about their everyday lives. Factory workers produced, politicians wrote resolutions, omnibus drivers rode, butchers sliced meats, and arsenal workers constructed and supplied Union armies. One prominent citizen was said to remark that in Philadelphia, "Everything Southern is exalted and worshiped here."

Many businessmen in the city wanted no parts of the argument over slavery. To most of them this argument needed to be settled by Southerners, through their experiences and their attitudes, over the issue itself. Southern culture and goods were very much welcomed by Philadelphians. Exchanges of ideas in science, especially in medical educational programs, promoted travel and written correspondences between Philadelphians and the Southerners of many states.

In the midst of apathy and incongruity, General Dana delved into the building of entrenchments and fortifications for the city of brotherly love. With Governor Andrew Curtain as an agitator for defenses throughout Pennsylvania, Dana was able to get Mayor Alexander Henry to procure the services of 300 volunteer workers to dig fortifications in and around the city. Dana carefully targeted three main areas for entrenchments and the placing of artillery. The Falls of Schuylkill was one area of defense that blocked the northwest entrance into the city from Confederate marauders. Fortifications on a confined hill near the Gray's Ferry Bridge would impede an attack from the west. Finally, the southwestern approach to the city could be cut off using entrenchments on the east side of the Schuylkill River near Gray's Ferry Road. Avidly, Dana provoked the citizens to protect themselves against attack and intrusion from the Confederates, however, the people of Philadelphia continued their rejective attitude toward a real attack.

*****

Two citizens of the American Paris in Pennsylvania did contemplate and attend to the possibility of General Lee amassing an invasion and subsequent capitulation of their city. On Pine Street, off of South Broad Street, toward the center of Philadelphia, Senator Robert Sumner and his daughter Abigail Elington of North Carolina engaged in more conversation concerning the plight of their divided family.

"Betrayal, father! That's what it is," yelled Abigail from the luxurious parlor of her childhood home. "The Confederate high command has reneged on its own strategy and tactical ambitions. Robert Lee should be hanged for treason and other crimes of war."

"Settle down, Abby. You know what the Confederates are driving at. They want the Peace Democrats to call off this ghastly war. If they can win in the North, they know enough people might get tired of the war and force President Lincoln in Washington to recognize the legitimacy of the Confederate States of America. Slavery will prevail and the great experiment in democracy will falter and disintegrate into ashes. The renowned experiment in democracy will fall upon the failed pages of history."

"What you're saying does make sense, father, but what about all of the men who are following General Lee. Do they really believe they can win a substantial battle or series of battles in the North. Do you think Harrison and Danny can believe this kind of propaganda from General Lee and his president?"

"Yes, I do."

Senator Sumner was a tall man with blackish-gray streaked hair, a squared chin, and deep-set hazel eyes. Abigail had the same eyes that pierced at you when you spoke to father or daughter.

"Leadership is a complicated piece of human endeavor. People can lead or they can't lead, Abby. Lee has proven time and again that he is capable of almost pristine leadership when it comes to fighting against the Army of the Potomac. On the other hand, our Union generals are a disgrace here in the eastern theater. General Lee can convince his army of almost anything, in my opinion."

"What about Harrison and Danny, and even Alfred?"

"I believe they are here in our state as we speak, my dear girl. Do you really think any of the soldiers who have made it this far in the battles against the Union forces are going to quit now? They are all here and I don't know what is going to come out of this battle. According to my sources, a battle has already started and it doesn't appear promising for our Union boys."

"What did you say, Father?"

"I said a possible defeat of our forces may have already occurred. Telegraph communications have been sputtering back and forth across the state all day long. It's almost two o'clock in the afternoon, and as a member of the Senate I have heard nothing positive in the way of reports from Gettysburg."

"Where in the world is Gettysburg?"

"It is a town in the south-central part of our state where many roads converge. Sources are saying this is the reason the battle started in the area."

"Do you think Harrison has betrayed me, father? Before he went back to the ranks from his furlough, he told me he would inform me of Confederate operations in the North."

"I am sure he has tried to contact you, Abby, but he doesn't even know you are here. He probably thinks your still home in Caldwell County. His letters are probably piling up at Lockerman's store."

"Lockerman, Mr. and Mrs. Abshire, the Caldwells; I hope they are all doing well. We had heard of Union raiding parties coming out of eastern Tennessee with the intention of confiscating property and salt supplies from the Confederate mountain counties. I remember talking to Mr. Abshire about the situation, but our town, he said, was spared up to the time I left for Philadelphia."

"I hope this all ends soon."

"Me too, Father. Me too."

"We have to keep trying to find Jesse."

"Now I have the safety of Harrison and Danny to worry about. I can't stand it any longer, Father! Why have our lives come to this? What a useless and pathetic existence we have."

"Why don't we go for a walk, dear, and get some fresh air. I think it will clear our minds for a little while."

"No, Father. I need to go and rest until this battle is over and I know the fate of Harrison and Danny. Why don't you go for a walk? I think it will do you good."

"Are you sure?"

"Yes."

The fighting continued in Gettysburg as Abigail rested and her father walked in Philadelphia. Harrison, Danny and Alfred, along with Lewis and Thaddeus, still had hell to go through before the first day of battle was complete.

Abigail tried to think of the hardships of battle. She tried to place herself in the midst of her son's and her husband's circumstances. This, however, was an area of life she could not comprehend. It was beyond her mortal soul to digest what it was like for a man in battle. Only the few woman who had experienced nursing work could come close to understanding the battlefield.

The afternoon wore on and Abigail waited for her father to return from his walk. She knew he most likely went to his office to get the latest reports on the place called Gettysburg.

Time would eventually provide answers to many of Abigail's questions and ponderances.

— Chapter 19 —
Upon the Altar of Fiery Battle

July 1, 1863, late afternoon
Gettysburg

Belly down, he was lying on the ground upon McPherson Ridge, a mile west of Gettysburg. He pushed himself up, looking around to find his commanding officers, but the smoke was too thick and the eyes too watery. Gray uniformed soldiers and friends were disseminated all over the ridge, between trees, on top of each other, mangled into briers, and submerged in Willoughby Run. He could see the horrors of war, horrors conceived in hell, for God himself was not the creator of such human carnage. Private Thaddeus Curtis stared at the unbelievable and unforgettable sights that formed in his eyes and in his mind.

Apparently dead, Private Jackson Coffey floated on the surface of Willoughby Run. He couldn't see Jackson's body any longer. The 26th had pushed its way further through the woods and the storms of battle on the ridge. A bellowing flash of sharp, concentrated fire came from the newly formed lines of the 19th Indiana and 24th Michigan Infantries. Blinks of fire penetrated the dense smoke from the Union positions and Curtis could still see intermittent pulses of musket fire coming through the smoke and trees of Herbst Woods. Coupled with the musket fire was case shot being blasted from batteries somewhere on the Chambersburg Pike and from the northwest of the 26th's position.

Is this what destiny has called me to? Curtis asked himself in a low tone among the sounds of battle. *This is murder at the highest level. What, then, is war? It has to be considered murder and I am deep in it; trapped in it.*

Thaddeus continued to hold himself up, still down on his belly and still trying to find someone who could tell him what to do next. "Where in the world is everyone from my regiment? Are they all dead?"

"No, private, we're not all dead," shouted Lieutenant Elington from behind Curtis. "Get up before you get yourself shot to pieces on this Godforsaken ridge."

"Yes, sir, lieutenant."

Private Curtis made his way back to the 26th's diminishing battle line. The last round of firing caused him to lose his bearings and sense of direction. He rejoined F Company, which by this time was fragmented by high casualties thus far in the engagement. Elington led him back to the left flank of the company and the soldiers reformed a line. Lewis, Alfred and Harrison were still alive among the carnage and Thaddeus was glad to see his comrades.

Sweat poured from the faces of the soldiers. The heat and humidity of the July afternoon didn't make things any easier for the troops of the South. Uniforms reeked with odors. Mud from the run splattered men's faces, shoes and boots. Foliage colors seemed blurred and faded. Farm houses and buildings burned on the horizon. Human senses became overwhelmed and agitated from the pollution of war; civil war.

The battle lines of the 26th North Carolina and the 24th Michigan stood about twenty yards apart. The boys from the 26th could now see the black hats clearly. On both sides, each line of soldiers tried with great effort to out-load each other. Clamor and clatter, rattling and bickering were heard from the opposing lines. Soldiers used every drill technique they could muster in order to be the first to fire their muskets. The distinct sounds of metal hitting metal rose to a pitch that became frightening for the soldiers. Death lay on the other side of the trees in a matter of minutes.

As the men loaded and continued to fire at will toward the 24th Michigan, General Pettigrew's courier Captain McCreery, who had delivered Pettigrew's compliment to Burgwyn earlier, picked up the battle flag after Private Marley went down. He was the eighth bearer of the colors for the 26th. He heard the order to charge the Yankees in the woods and he immediately stepped forward to lead the regiment and was shot through the heart. His body slammed down to the ground.

The colors fell under his lifeless body. McCreery's blood soaked the red battle flag as he lay among the casualties on the field of glory and honor. Human, red lifeblood, now stained the material of the starry cross. Humanity, in its frail state of being, was forever consumed by an idea so essential to a cause that men were willing to die for that idea in the bloodbath of civil war and fall upon the altar of fiery battle.

The ninth color bearer pulled the flag from underneath McCreery's body. Lieutenant George Wilcox of G Company tried his best to redirect the charge of the 26th, but was only able to take a few steps before he was shot. The battle line surged forward past the fallen color bearer amid the sounds of the ear-piercing rebel yell. Colonel Burgwyn hurried to the fallen colors and retrieved them himself.

"Dress on the these colors, men! Let us press the charge and defeat our enemy."

The battle line of the 26th took on new life. The men watched in awe as Burgwyn risked his life to carry the colors and lead the charge of his regiment. They knew he had seen nine color bearers go down this day, either dead or wounded, but he still pressed on in courage and determination, now the tenth color bearer himself

Private Franklin Honeycut of B Company ran over to Burgwyn's side and offered to take the colors from his colonel. The firing kept up at an awful and deadly pace. Smoke dried the throats of the soldiers. Water was now in short supply. It was almost three o'clock in the afternoon and devastation reigned on McPherson Ridge. The dead and wounded cluttered the steps of the able and living soldiers, who in the heat of battle ignored the sanguine conditions. Lieutenant Colonel Lane came from the right side, tripping and staggering from the heavy metallized fire of Minie balls.

"Colonel, how are you doing in the center? Are you all right?"

"We have to press this charge and sweep them off of this ridge before we lose our whole regiment, John."

"Give up that flag, colonel. We need your guidance today."

"Take the flag, Private Honeycut," Burgwyn said with great emotion. "Take it for the courage, honor and valor of the regiment, for the honor and glory of the South, and for the honor and glory of our brigade."

Burgwyn relinquished the flag to Honeycut. At that moment, a horrendous and galling volley of musket fire hit the center of the 26th's dwindling battle line. Again, smoke, tree bark and lead plunged into the North Carolinians, ripping and tearing holes in the line. Ricochets from rocks and stones hit bones and flesh. A consummation of battle fire, without

219

precedent, scoured the regiment, officers and enlisted men alike.

Honeycut, the eleventh color bearer, was hit and killed on the spot where Burgwyn had handed him the flag. Colonel Burgwyn saw Honeycut fall on the now hallowed ground and thought of retrieving the colors again.

He did.

"Press on, men! Charge! Close ranks," ordered the colonel.

The hot, dead lead ripped his cadet gray frock coat. Flesh was torn and the Yankee Minie ball plunged through both lungs. Gasping for breath, Burgwyn was spun around by the force of the musket shot. After turning from the uncontrollable force, he fell. He could see the smoke-filled gray-blue sky through the canopy of trees and dark smoke on McPherson Ridge. The colors of the 26th wrapped around him as he fell.

In his pain, Colonel Burgwyn thought about the bravery of his men this day in Pennsylvania. He thought of his fiancée back home in North Carolina. He thought of his commanding general going out of his way, in the heat of battle and planning, to send a courier to compliment his regiment's service to the Confederate Army. Tears fell down his young face. Breathing became increasingly difficult for him. Death seemed to be calling inside of him. Burgwyn knew his Savior and he believed in the salvation of the soul. He knew Jesus would welcome him into his kingdom for his faith. *But what of all the killing?* The colonel became afraid for a moment. He didn't really know what Jesus would think of all of the killing, destruction and war. He prayed to himself and felt the comfort of the Lord upon his being. The Spirit moved within his soul and gave him a peace he never felt before. He knew he would die for his cause and never thought of himself as any kind of hero. He thought of himself as a man who did his duty for his country and the cause of independence. Tyranny had to go. It was disposed of by the old revolution of his forefathers and now tyranny would be defeated once and for all, even without his presence. The momentum the Confederate cause had begun would not slow down over his death. He would die, but life would proceed and the dead officers and enlisted men of the Confederacy would forever be remembered and seared into the minds of the living.

A colonel was fading away far from his homeland. He was hanging onto life in Pennsylvania, the land of the first rebels, who had forever made the first revolution succeed above and beyond all expectations.

Not many on the battlefield knew the fate of their colonel or their friends or their brothers. As in life without war, the regular hustle and bustle of everyday existence goes on in the face of death. Only the family and truest friends suffer real loss. The earth still turns, the days proceed in unending fashion without regard of who has died. People still marry and still laugh. Life, in its mysterious abundances of twists and turns, goes on in the cities and towns even in the midst of battle.

"Colonel Burgwyn! Henry!" yelled Lieutenant Colonel Lane, who had been at the center of the line when the burst of fire and lead hit the area where Burgwyn was standing.

Lane proceeded to tend to his colonel. He took the colonel's hand and looked into his brown eyes and saw the bravery and determination that was always present. The fire, though, was being extinguished. That fire of endless resolve Burgwyn had carried with him was fading; it was weakening beyond his control.

With all of the confusion surrounding McPherson Ridge between two American army regiments, the 26th North Carolina and the 24th Michigan, the men continued to fight with miraculous abilities. Successive musket shots still ripped through the air. Men were still falling all around each other, the living among the dead. Artillery fire still belched forth shrapnel, exploding from various rounds of case, solid and canister shells.

The mangled and bewildered battle line of the 26th North Carolina continued to assault the Iron Brigade, which by now had fallen back to its fourth line of the day, toward the Lutheran seminary where devout Christian men were taught peace, not war.

Lieutenant Elington and Corporal Fry ran over to the fallen colonel, where Lane was trying to comfort him. It was an area in Herbst woods that would soon be forgotten, possibly tread on by curious battlefield tourists one day or worked by loggers cutting trees from the wooded area. There was a swale of land where Burgwyn fell. Indented into the earth and into the hearts of the 26th. Farmers in the area would soon go back to their daily chores on this land, but for the men of the 26th North Carolina Infantry they would always think of this area of common woods as hallowed ground where their friends, brothers and comrades lost their lives for a cause of freedom and self-determination.

"What can we do for you, colonel?" asked Elington. Burgwyn couldn't speak. In all probability, his lungs collapsed from the force of the shot. He could only stare at his officers and nod his head in response.

"I can't believe he has been hurt this bad," Fry said emotionally. "He doesn't deserve this. He has his whole life ahead of him. He is an educated man who could submit essential leadership and character to this rotten world.

He is a shining star that could always light the world. What has happened? What are we to do now?"

Lewis fell to the ground and wept. His sadness was multiplied by the abundance of killing and mayhem this day. He then moved forward and back to his position on the left side of F Company, now made up of only five soldiers.

Ninety-one of F Company's brave sons had either been killed or wounded severely. Their bodies littered the ground between Willoughby Run and in Herbst Woods. Lewis, Alfred and Thaddeus waited for Harrison to come back to the line and give them orders. For the sake of all the boys and men who had fallen this day, the Possum would continue on to victory through the further hell of battle.

Elington and Lane saw there was nothing medically they could do for the colonel. Stretcher bearers were sent for. Hopefully, men from another company could get Burgwyn to the rear of the battle lines expanding through the woods.

"Lieutenant Elington, we need to press this attack and head right for the center of that no-good, blue-bellied battle line near the seminary," Lieutenant Colonel Lane said. "Are you ready to drive those lousy people from the woods and take that high ground?"

"Yes, sir, John. We need to achieve victory for Burgwyn today. It has to end here! I am sick of this fighting and killing and mayhem."

"Men of the 26th! Men of the 26th!" shouted Lieutenant Colonel Lane. "Form your company lines now! We are going to charge that regiment one more time and we are going to sweep them into oblivion. Their regiment will no longer be remembered. Do you hear me?"

A perforating rebel yell was heard from the meager remnants of the 26th.

"K Company, dress left! That gap in the line must be filled!" Lane ordered.

Lane ran to the left flank of the regiment and ordered Major John Jones to have his companies fix bayonets.

"All companies fix bayonets! We are going to charge and break right through the regiment in our front, along with help from other brigade companies. Does everyone understand!"

Cheers rose from the ranks. Lane felt a surge of patriotism and honor in leading the regiment. Soldiers commented to Lane:

"We can do it, colonel!"

"Let us do this for Colonel Burgwyn. I heard he was shot."

"For North Carolina, our home."

"For General Lee."

"For the Tarheels of North Carolina, and for our families back in Caldwell County."

"Charge! Charge! Charge!" Lane yelled above the battle sounds.

Lane picked up the regimental colors and shouted with distinct determination and fortitude, "26th, follow me! 26th, follow me!"

General Pettigrew, observing his men in action back on Herr Ridge, commented to a staff officer:

"It is the bravest act I ever saw."

Checked by the continuous metal firestorm from the edge of the woods, the soldiers of the 26th tried their best to further engage the enemy and destroy them, this enemy which had brought much destruction, turmoil and death upon the men of the South.

The remnants of the 26th's line, in their dirty gray uniforms, tired, sweaty and angry, charged the current line of the 24th Michigan and 19th Indiana Regiments. With Lieutenant Colonel John Lane leading the regiment, the 26th finally accomplished sweeping the Union forces from Herbst Woods. The Yankees were running toward the Lutheran seminary, trying to take cover behind trees and a post and rail fence bordering the grounds of the institution.

The light of the sky could now be seen by the men in Yankee blue retreating from the woods. Smoke and acrid fumes of sulfuric poison fomented the air between McPherson Ridge and now Seminary Ridge. Soldiers wanted water desperately. The wool uniforms irritated their skin. Bleeding, wounded men trekked on both sides of the lines, trying to make their way out of the living hell of battle. But the gray Confederate line swarmed near the edge of Herbst Woods. The men gave the retreating Yankees one more good volley of forced lead.

Lane pushed the 26th forward. As he did, a rear guard skirmisher from the 24th Michigan shot Lane right through the neck.

Lane fell.

The twelfth color bearer was down. The 26th North Carolina Infantry stalled and then stopped their charge. Three brigades of General Dorsey Pender's division rushed up behind the wrecked 26th Regiment and continued to push the Yankees back toward the Seminary and eventually through Gettysburg itself, thus securing victory for the Confederate cause on July 1, 1863. General Rhodes and General Early continued to press and push the 11th Corps of the Union Army back from Oak Ridge and Oak Hill to the north of the town. The Yankees were now on the run.

Lieutenant Elington saw what was transpiring in front of him. The Union forces were retreating, but they had good, high ground to retreat to.

"John! John!" shouted Elington to Lane. There was no movement form Lieutenant Colonel Lane's body, which had fallen like a rag upon the cauldron of battle.

"Lieutenant! Get down. Those skirmishers are still active in our front," Private Abshire yelled.

"Lieutenant! Take cover, man, or we're going to lose everybody in the company," Private Curtis yelled.

"Boys! We have to get word back to Pettigrew that the high ground south of Gettysburg has to be secured. If we don't, well … I don't know!"

A crackle of musket fire smashed into the 26th's line again, just after Elington had given his warning.

"No! No! No!" Elington cried in agony. "My God, what has happened?"

Alfred and Thaddeus fell to the ground, shot through by the fire from the dwindling number of Union soldiers retreating back toward the town.

Thaddeus was lying on his back and there was no movement. Alfred was lying on his side, curled up in pain and shouting out for help.

"Jesus in Heaven, where are You? Save us from this wretchedness and carnage," Elington cried out among the many dead and wounded in the woods of McPherson Ridge.

Elington dropped his precious Navy Colt revolver and sword and ran over to Alfred first. Blood soaked his gray uniform and perspiration drenched his face. Alfred stared into Elington's eyes. His face glared with a youthful state of fear and he knew something was terribly wrong with his body. Alfred clutched Elington's hand. He tried to keep his breathing even, for the wound was in his chest, causing sporadic contractions of air to run through his mouth.

"Hold on, Alfred. You will be all right. Please, Alfred."

"I … I … can't breathe right, Harrison. How could it be that our whole company has been shot to pieces? We are all gone this day. F Company of our beloved 26th North Carolina Infantry has fallen today on this Pennsylvania ground. Why, Harrison, has God allowed this? Harrison, He has spared you."

"Try to rest yourself, Boy Alfred. You and I know God is not the author of this confusion and war, this whole stinking mess. He will help you and me to live through what many of our friends and comrades haven't lived through."

"I am not going to make it, Harrison. I can feel the Lord's breath on me. I can feel it. I can feel it is my time, lieutenant; friend."

"No! No! Alfred, it is not your time to leave this earth, to leave me or the boys in the regiment."

"Yes, Harrison, it is. Please tell my parents that I love them and I fought for our cause to the best of abilities and courage. Tell them how the men from North Carolina, from Caldwell County, fought with bravery and honor."

"I will."

His eyes closed and his breathing slowed. His mind sensed that his physical death was near, however, he knew his Christian beliefs and that a spiritual inheritance in heaven awaited him, even upon this Pennsylvania battlefield.

Harrison gazed upon his young friend, his adopted son. He thought of his own two sons, Jesse and Danny, and how he had sacrificed his family and friends in this terrible armed conflict of civil war. *What do I do?* he thought as he again looked upon the dying face of Alfred and then looked over to Thaddeus Curtis to his right in the torn-up woods. Muskets were strewn all over. Haversacks were twisted among the dead and wounded men in gray, in blue and in butternut. Soldier's hats and belt buckles laid between the brush of the summer trees. Tin cups, rations of food and canteens were spread all over the place. *What have we done to ourselves? We, the American ancestors of the first and glorious Revolution of '76? This cannot go on. Tomorrow I will go to Philadelphia and end this war,* Harrison thought to himself.

"Harrison! Harrison!" Alfred cried out. "Did Thaddeus make it through that last round of fire?"

"He is lying to our right, Alfred, over there by the big maple tree."

"Go and see if he needs help."

"No, Alfred. I will stay with you."

"Tell Krista in a letter, Harrison, that I loved her to the end of my life and I am sorry for going back on my promise to marry her."

"It will be done."

Flashes of musket fire continued to pierce the woods where Harrison was holding on to Alfred. Pender's men had flushed the woods of Yankees and the fire of battle seemed to push more toward the town of Gettysburg. The rebel yell could still be heard from the north and now from the east of the 26th North Carolina's ragged position. The waters in Willoughby Run continued to move and Harrison tried to picture in his mind the gentle flowing waters. He thought about how Colonel Burgwyn was doing back near the run. He saw men from other companies tending to Lieutenant Colonel John Lane. It looked as if John was trying to talk to the men helping him. *This is a good sign, concerning Lane,* Harrison thought as he held his dying friend, Alfred.

"The cannon, lieutenant! I can hear the rumble and fire of shells! For I am no longer afraid. I have crossed to the other side; my fears have subsided."

With those words, Alfred quietly passed on from this world. Harrison gently closed Alfred's eyes. The lieutenant bowed his head and wept in silent prayer and sorrow for Alfred and for all the pain and loss of the day. His young friend had now become a martyr for the Confederate cause of independence. He would be missed by his family and friends back in North Carolina.

Harrison was exhausted from the continuous heat of battle. He leaned back with Alfred still clutched in his arms. He closed his own eyes and thought on all the men of F Company.

After about fifteen minutes, Harrison moved Alfred's body onto the ground, ground that had become hallowed among the annals of history, for too many had perished with a blind faith in a cause of Southern independence. Harrison looked at Alfred one more time, tears streaming down his face. His breathing became heavy as he choked with emotion at the loss of his friend and fellow soldier.

He turned and walked back toward Willoughby Run. He saw ghastly sights. He made his way back to inquire on how Colonel Burgwyn was doing. He stepped over bodies and brush, over wounded boys and tree branches, and over discarded ammunition and cartridge boxes. Then he saw from a distance three soldiers in gray standing over the body of Colonel Burgwyn. Another soldier cradled the colonel.

"Colonel Burgwyn! Elington shouted.

Elington made his way over to the bank of the run where the men were. As he did, one of the soldiers in gray said to him, "Lieutenant! The colonel died about fifteen minutes ago. There was nothing we could do for him. He said to all of us that he was happy and proud of what the regiment had accomplished this day. He had no regrets that he died doing his duty. His very last words were, 'Our regiment has performed its duty today. The Lord's will is done through my life and through my death. I surely have no regrets.' Then, lieutenant, he passed from us."

"No!" Harrison cried.

The anguish of the situation overwhelmed him. Alfred and the colonel had died at about the same time, gone from this world together and into the Lord's peaceful presence. A few of the soldiers with the colonel tried to comfort Elington in his grief.

The 26th moved back. It moved from the position it had achieved this bloody day. Graves needed to be prepared, for the dead were everywhere to be seen. The wounded needed to be taken to hospitals. The young men needed to be comforted from all the horror. Ambulances began moving forward upon the battlefield and the cries of the wounded echoed through the woods, through the ridges and through the mind of Lieutenant Harrison Elington, one of the only men left standing in F Company from the 26th North Carolina Infantry.

Captain Tuttle had been wounded severely in the leg. The other corporals, sergeants and lieutenants had either been killed or wounded. Elington was the only soldier left standing from F Company as he could see. He helped get Colonel Burgwyn onto a stretcher to be transported to the rear, back to Herr Ridge. Burgwyn had been told by Captain Joseph Young, the 26th's quartermaster, that if anything were to happen to the colonel in battle, he would take care of all details. Burgwyn and Young were longtime friends and a bond of trust had been formed through their friendship and trials of army life. The promise was kept.

"My God! What has happened to Lewis?" Elington shouted as he turned from Colonel Burgwyn and the stretcher bearers. "He was with me, Alfred and Thaddeus when that surge of musket fire hit us. What has happened to him?"

Elington made his way back up the slope of McPherson Ridge. He retraced the regiment's steps toward the former position of the enemy line of the 24th Michigan, which had mauled the 26th but had not defeated it. He ran, looking for Lewis, and he checked to see if Lewis was hopefully walking back with the living remnants of the 26th.

"Lewis! Corporal Lewis Fry! Have any of you men come across a corporal from F Company? Skinny, dark hair and dark eyes."

"No, lieutenant. We haven't seen a living corporal anywhere," a private said from E Company.

"No, lieutenant. I haven't seen Lewis anywhere," another private answered from among the shaded woods.

Elington continued his search, winding back around to where Alfred and Thaddeus were still lying dead. No one had made any attempt yet to take them somewhere to be buried. It would be hours and, in some cases, days before all of the dead could be buried. *I will get help later to come and get these bodies,* he thought. *They will be sent home under my command. Mr. and Mrs. Abshire will be grateful for the return of their son's body. They will be devastated by his death, though, just as so many parents have already been.*

He slowly walked over to Thaddeus's body to finally see for himself what had happened. Harrison walked over and knelt down beside young Thaddeus. He determined that his young friend from the Possum was shot clear through the chest. A gaping exit wound was visible in his back. There were no signs that Thaddeus suffered or even knew what hit him in the storm of battle. Harrison gently closed the eyes of his other friend as he had done with Alfred. His hand felt Thaddeus's face and Harrison wept again. He wept for the overwhelming loss of life, from the Possum to the colonel. He wept in agony for the tremendous loss of life in F Company. He wept for the brave display of courage and determination of his officers and enlisted men of Pettigrew's brigade who from the early hours of the morning engaged in battle upon McPherson Ridge. His tears billowed forth and fell upon the body of Thaddeus. His emotions overcame him and Harrison sat on the blood-stained ground. He could not move to do anything of use for his regiment.

His tears clouded his vision for moments at a time. He still could see the human destruction all around him, but it now seemed as a dream, a nightmare of sorts. He tried to compose himself and as he did his teary eyes glanced over to a black walnut tree over to his left. There, perched against its trunk, was Corporal Lewis Fry. His head was hanging down, with his chin upon his chest, like he was taking one of his common afternoon naps. Harrison immediately got up from where Thaddeus was lying and ran over to Lewis. Harrison knelt down to see if Lewis was all right. He tried to listen for any breathing. He couldn't hear or feel anything. However, he did see a bullet hole that went through his shirt. Lewis had taken his jacket off and it was still laying next to the walnut tree. Harrison shook Lewis, but again there was no response.

"They are all gone," Harrison softly said out loud.

And so the Possum was gone. Lewis lost his life trying to save a cause. Lewis had been killed in battle and for the first time he had been afraid on this particular day of battle. He died under a walnut tree where, in life, he loved to take a nap or rest, where he would reflect on life and on the war and where he felt the most comfort during his time away from home. The black walnut tree was his favorite tree in the world. He always found a walnut tree somewhere to take a nap under.

Harrison sat on the ground, teary-eyed, exhausted and now depressed. He felt a tap from behind on his right shoulder. He turned around and saw Sergeant Robert Hudspeth of F Company. One other soldier from the company had made it without wounds or death. The two men embraced and then sat for a time on the stained ground of McPherson Ridge.

*****

The hustle and clamor of men bristled through the woods. Orders were given from officers and sometimes private soldiers to the men of the 26th Infantry to retreat back to Herr Ridge where they might reform and recover. The devastating toll would not be truly known until later that evening, when many soldiers failed to arrive for evening roll call. Friends and comrades could not believe the loss of this day. Officers, including General Pettigrew, tried to mask their horror and sadness by thinking on what had to be done tomorrow in the enemy territory of Pennsylvania. The cause would be won or lost in this Union state. Most of the Southern soldiers knew this by now and they had to deal with fighting as sure as the sun would rise on July 2, 1863.

Time seemed to stand still in the woods of McPherson Ridge. Harrison was trying to think clearly, but he could not. The thought of the mission to Philadelphia, in the midst of all the death, haunted his spirit.

How can I function after this day of ruination? he wondered. *How can I ever muster enough strength to carry on and be successful? God, help me in my desperation to do what You want me to do. Help me to be confident in my mission as Colonel Burgwyn was in his duty to this army and in his duty and obedience to You.*

"The altar of fiery battle must go on until we are victorious."

— Chapter 20 —
Sacrifice and Honor

Evening, July 1,
Morning, July 2, 1863

The full moon on Herr Ridge cast an eerie solitude among the soldiers of the Confederate army. Devastation had come upon the ranks of the 26th North Carolina and no one could believe the loss of life. Evident among the camp this night was the missing personnel: officers, enlisted men, Southerners from many different states and counties throughout the homeland. Coffee helped subside the sadness for short moments at a time, but the lingering depression set in as the night wore on in Pennsylvania.

"Water! Someone bring me some water," cried one wounded Yankee from the Iron Brigade.

The moans and cries were repeated for hours under the white, shiny moon of summer. Union prisoners were marched away from Herr Ridge to be sent out of future action in Gettysburg. Torn uniforms, bloodied flesh and dirty faces characterized the Union prisoners in blue, who stared into a void as they marched west. Many voids had been created on this hot summer's day.

Major John Jones now commanded the 26th North Carolina. After the death of Colonel Henry Burgwyn and the severe wounding of Lieutenant Colonel John Lane, Major Jones was the highest ranking officer ready and qualified to fill the unfortunate holes blown through the 26th upon McPherson Ridge. The 26th had started July 1 with more than 800 officers and enlisted men. At roll call in the evening it was determined that 212 men reported. The attack on McPherson Ridge lasted thirty minutes, but the affects would last a lifetime. Companies E and F were virtually wiped out. Through the night, ambulance crews and medical personnel worked diligently to care for the wounded and sick.

Those Michigan and Indiana boys must be suffering as we are, Elington thought. He looked over to a hill where the Union army now secured a position. He sat by himself and near a tree he could rest his back on. He couldn't see it now, but he realized the Yankees were moving and setting their reinforcements on Cemetery Hill, closer to the town. The locals called the hill by that name. The town cemetery was located there. The rumble and rustling of wagons moving and couriers galloping sent his mind into a haze. *I am tired. I can't even move my legs or my arms,* he thought. *I can't believe that they are all gone. The colonel, Lewis, Alfred, Thaddeus and Jackson; all dead. Why am I here? Who am I, that I should still be breathing, Lord in heaven? John Lane might even be dead. I don't even know where they took him. This has to be a nightmare. It can't be true.*

Harrison Elington began to weep again for his lost friends and leaders. The shock of their deaths became too much for his mind and his spirit to handle. He always was able to bounce back from the events in life that tore at the fabric of his being. However, this event of July 1, a battle beyond all other battles, caught him in a trap of despair where normal functions lost meaning.

In his apathetic and hopeless state of mind, Elington managed to get some sleep on Herr Ridge, a few miles outside of Gettysburg. At about 2:30 in the morning on July 2, a courier came to Herr Ridge to inquire about the location and condition of Lieutenant Harrison Elington of the 26th North Carolina. The courier was actually part of Major Frederick Albert Fincannon's brigade of 3,000 mounted infantry. They were about to embark on the secret arsenal mission to Philadelphia. The Major's brigade was now called Fincannon's Titan Brigade. General Pettigrew directed the courier, Captain Nathan Lockert, to Lieutenant Elington.

"Lieutenant," Lockert whispered to Elington, still asleep near the tree he was leaning on. "Elington, we have to move out. The major wants us to get our supplies. Lieutenant, can you hear me?"

"Yeah, I can hear you. I'm not dead yet, like the rest of my comrades and friends. Who are you, man?"

"Captain Nathan Lockert, lieutenant. Part of Major Fincannon's staff commissioned to help on the mission to Philadelphia."

"You mean it is already time to go? Right now, tonight?"

"Yes, Elington, tonight. We need to get our horses ready and our supplies secured, then the major said we can all get a little bit more sleep. He wants us out of here by five in the morning."

"Now how do you figure, captain, we can get any more sleep if that is truly the plan the major has for us." Elington looked at the captain, hair amiss, hazy-eyed and desperately longing for rest.

"We have to go. I didn't come here to argue with you. Let's get going, soldier."

"I don't think I'm going on the mission, sir. I have just been through the most horrendous battle anyone as ever fought in and I think I am entitled to make a decision to pass on the mission. Do you understand, captain?"

"I heard the fighting was brutal here yesterday, lieutenant. Did your regiment incur many casualties?"

"Casualties! We were just about slaughtered here on these ridges. I lost five of my closest friends, captain. What fighting have you been involved in?"

"Only skirmishing in Tennessee and action in Kentucky. Nothing like what happened here."

As the captain spoke, Harrison bowed his head, showing despair and heartache over his losses. He didn't seem to care about the officer's answer to his quick question.

Looking back up at Lockert, Elington said, "That's a good thing for you, sir. No one should have to go through what we went through yesterday. What did you say your name was?"

"Captain Nathan Lockert."

"Well, Captain Lockert, let me go back to sleep and you can go and tell your major that I am staying put, right here near Gettysburg. My regiment needs me now. We only have 212 men fit for duty and my company, that I help command as an officer in this army, is in dire need of men."

"The major isn't going to like this news one bit, Elington. He told me he was really counting on you for this mission."

"And why is he counting on me, captain? What in the world do I have that some other lieutenant in this whole Confederate army doesn't have? Come on, captain, tell me! I want to know now. The fact of me being chosen and investigated by Major Fincannon has bothered me since I met with him. Tell me, captain."

"It is your Union artillery and explosives experience. This is what I was told by the major and that is it."

"Sure, captain, I'm sure that is what you were told. But I say there is something else behind this whole thing."

"There is nothing else. We need to get into the city and blow that arsenal simultaneous with General Lee securing us a victory on this ground. The Peace Democrats will be forced into action to help the Union recognize our sovereign independence. We are wasting precious time here, lieutenant, and I am sure Major Fincannon is wondering where we are."

"All right, Lockert, I will come. But I am doing this for the memory, for the honor and for the sacrifice of my friends and family who I have lost in this wretched war. This conflict, like I have said many times in the past, has to come to an end or else the South will cease to exist. Our way of life will surely disintegrate."

*****

Thursday, July 2, came upon the Pennsylvania countryside gray, gloomy and grim. The sun was nowhere to be found. The early morning hour was very quiet, for the men on both sides of the ridges were worn-out and dead tired from the marching, fighting and killing of July 1. As the morning wore on, General Pettigrew tried his best to bring his brigade together and refit it with men and supplies. Regular army chores were carried out in order to have the men dwell on their routines instead of the horrible losses of the previous day.

Lieutenant Elington was now with his temporary brigade stationed north of Gettysburg near the town college. He was about a mile and a half from his regiment on Herr Ridge.

Fincannon's Titan Brigade had been drastically reduced to 1,500 men and officers by General Lee. More men were needed now to fill the ranks of infantry, like the 26th North Carolina and other regiments ravaged by the first day's fight. General Lee knew the fight would be renewed this day. The special brigade would have to be reduced and most of the 1,500 men would be assigned to General Imboden's mounted infantry to guard the Confederate escape and supply routes back toward Cashtown and Chambersburg.

The situation grew tense among the ranks of the Titan Brigade north of Gettysburg. The remaining 1,500 men didn't think they had a good chance to bring the arsenal down with the cut in personnel. Lower-ranking officers pleaded with Major Fincannon to ask General Lee to reconsider his options for the mission. They wanted Lee to at least give half of the men back to Fincannon's command.

"Gentlemen, I have spoken with General Lee. He is very concerned about the location of General Stuart's cavalry. You know how the general has relied steadily on the work of Stuart to screen the movements of the enemy and to secure the movements of our infantry. Without Stuart here, General Lee feels he is blind to the enemy, who are now, in all probability, stacking their corps on those hills south of the town."

"We can understand that," one corporal said, "but, major, we have to make sure we have enough reinforcements ourselves as we enter into this mission. We need as much firepower and men as we can muster into service. We don't know what those Yankees are going to hit us with, if and when we enter the city on the Delaware."

"I agree, sir, with the corporal," a sergeant said. He stood there in his butternut uniform, which looked relatively new despite the long marches and riding he had been exposed to.

"Major," Captain Lockert said, "I think we better get this mission underway before we are unable to even move from the vicinity of this here town. There are reports that more Union corps have been on the move toward the hills and high ground south of Gettysburg."

"Sir! A courier from General John Gordon's brigade is approaching from town," Captain Lockert shouted.

Lockert always looked pristine and efficient in his cadet gray officer's uniform. He wore a black sash around his waist, a black slouch hat that looked a little big for his head, but handsome in appearance, and a revolver similar to Elington's Colt Navy revolver holstered around his waist. The captain had a mustache of sandy brown hair, a good head of light brown hair, and brown eyes. He was a graduate of West Point and his home was Virginia. He was twenty-eight years old and committed to the cause of the Confederacy. Always, though, he had a boyish look on his face like he was interested in everything that came his way whether it involved him or not. The captain liked his tea instead of the usual coffee most of the soldiers preferred.

"What is it now?" Fincannon asked out loud. His mood was pessimistic.

"Major Fincannon! I need to see the major, is he here?" asked the courier.

"I am Fincannon. What is it, son?"

"General Gordon is on his way to talk with you, sir. It is important information that you and General Lee need to hear pertaining to your mission to the arsenal in Philadelphia, sir."

"Do you have the subject of the message, at least, lieutenant?"

"I was with our brigade a few days ago. I think it was the 28th of June, sir, and we were all together with General Gordon. We were ordered by General Early, while in York, Pennsylvania, to take our Georgians and go and scout the Wrightsville and Columbia Bridge, which spans the Susquehanna River. We did this in case General Lee wanted our whole army to cross the bridge and threaten Philadelphia. When the state militia troops observed us coming to capture the bridge, they proceeded to burn the structure, thus cutting off a way to cross the river. Without that bridge, sir, I don't see how your brigade can threaten Philadelphia or the arsenal there."

"I will verify this with General Gordon when he gets here. Thank you for your information, lieutenant. It looks like the character of our whole mission will change now."

Lieutenant Elington listened as the courier relayed his message from General Gordon to Major Fincannon.

"What are we going to do, major?" Elington asked intently. "What are we to do without a bridge to travel across?"

"Keep it quiet, Elington. I will let you know, along with the rest of the brigade, what our next plan of action will be."

"Yes, sir, major."

Precious time was ticking away. It was now after six in the morning and General John B. Gordon approached the grounds of Gettysburg College on the western edge of town. Fincannon's brigade of Confederate troopers was watering horses, readying them for the long journey. The soldiers were busy with the extra time cleaning guns and stocking haversacks with rations, for they knew supplies would run out before the end of the mission and foraging would have to re-supply their ranks. Bacon and salt pork, beef or salt horse, cornbread and real coffee were hoarded like bankrolls. Money meant nothing to these troopers now. Food was the capital for survival.

A mixture of dissimilar equipment was also being stacked and loaded by the mounted infantry: Carbine ammunition boxes; various types of sabers; revolver ammunition boxes; arsenal belts and holsters; cap pouches and infantry cartridge boxes; bayonets and scabbards; extra canvas haversacks loaded with additional supplies; drum and wooden canteens; and tin cups. The men were struggling with loaded saddlebags to be placed on their horses. Various saddles, Jenifer and McClellan type, were strapped tightly to the tired animals. The brigade's distinctive beige and dark blue stars and bars flag was rolled and covered, ready to be used when the attack came; the attack that hopefully would make a vital difference in the war for the Confederacy.

All the remnants of camp were gone now on the grounds of the college.

General Gordon had arrived and he and Major Fincannon stood alongside the Mummasburg Road.

"Glad to meet you, Major Fincannon," Gordon said, gasping for breath after his hurried ride over to the college. Gordon and his brigade had played a key role in attacking the 11th Union Corps on July 1, north of Gettysburg.

"Tell me straight, general. Is the bridge burned? The bridge crossing the Susquehanna at Columbia and Wrightsville."

"I am sorry to inform you, major, that this is true."

"Darn it! Now we have to find another route. I have been anticipating this and the only other alternative is to ride north into Harrisburg and cross the camelback bridge my scouts have told me about. It runs along Market Street, through the city."

"Have you talked to General Lee about this change?"

"No, I haven't seen the general yet. Captain Lockert! Get a courier to General Lee's headquarters and inform him of our situation concerning the bridge. Ask him if he can ride over to our position and give us orders to proceed through Harrisburg. Go, captain!"

"Yes, sir, major!"

"We'll have to wait, General Gordon. Do you think General Lee will approve this move north?"

"I believe he will, major. I suggest that he give back to your command at least 700 men from the 1,500 he took, plus a battalion of artillery. My staff informed me on the way here that your force had been reduced. You're going to need firepower to take the militia guards away from the bridges you will approach, both in Harrisburg and in Philadelphia."

"That sounds like a wise idea. I will propose this to Lee when he arrives."

The two officers continued to converse for about twenty minutes. General Lee and his staff road up the Mummasburg road, riding over McPherson Ridge and Seminary Ridge to get to the vicinity of the college.

"Major Fincannon!" Lee said as he climbed off of Traveler. "I hear that the bridge at Wrightsville is gone."

"Yes, sir, general!"

"What do you propose we do? I need this mission to take place, major. We are ready to engage the enemy again today. General Longstreet and General Ewell are going to attack the flanks of the Union's high ground positions, for we have to move those people off of the heights there, south of Gettysburg. God's will, major."

"I understand, General Lee, that the situation is fluid. However, with you striking the enemy and removing him from those heights and our brigade sending havoc through Harrisburg and then Philadelphia, we are sure to appeal to the Peace Democrats and convey to the enemy to recognize our country."

"Harrisburg, major?"

"Yes, sir, General Lee. With advice from General Gordon, who I know you respect as an officer in this army, I have concluded that we need to travel through Harrisburg in order to get to Philadelphia. This plan may work even better than the original plan, which had us crossing the Susquehanna at Wrightsville."

"Explain to me quickly, major. We are wasting precious time here."

"General, the plan now is to move the brigade north on the Harrisburg Road, move into the southern edges of the city and secure the Market Street Bridge there. We then cross the Susquehanna and ride our way to Philadelphia. Gordon's scouts and my scout have concluded that Governor Curtain of Pennsylvania has had a hard time stretching adequate defenses through Harrisburg. Lincoln's call for militia troops to stay in the army for 90 days hasn't been received well. The newspapers are reporting dissension among recruits, for these men are unable to leave businesses and jobs for that long. Harrisburg, sir, is weakly defended. We can hit them hard for the sake of that bridge and then move on to our original objective."

"Yes. It sounds like a good alternative plan, Fincannon. Good advice also from General Gordon."

"Thank you, General Lee," Gordon answered.

"General, there is one request that we need you to strongly consider. After much discussion, I recommend that you turn over at least 700 of my original 1,500 men you took from my ranks. We need more men for this mission, especially now that we are to enter upon the Pennsylvania capital. Before you answer to that request, I also need a battalion of artillery. We're going to need firepower, sir, in order to secure the camelback bridge in Harrisburg and the Market Street bridge in Philadelphia. I hadn't planned to take artillery with us at first, but I have changed my mind. They'll have to keep pace with us. I know this sounds like a lot of men and equipment, and I know you're engaged here with the enemy, but think of the confusions and disruptions our forces will render in this state. They won't know where we're coming from, or what our main intentions are. Lincoln will be thrown into disarray. Union commanders will possibly divide their army here in Gettysburg to try and chase us through the rest of the state. We can really be a factor, general."

General Lee, who looked ragged and pale, stood in front of Major Fincannon and General Gordon and stared at the two men, thinking how brave and committed they were to the cause of the Confederacy. He looked at Lieutenant Elington, who was standing by Fincannon and Gordon and with his new friend Captain Lockert. Lee seemed to prod and ruminate all of the information in his mind. He closed his eyes as he tried to imagine the results of such a divided army in enemy territory. His gray uniform showed signs of past perspiration and dirt. His hair was ruffled in spots. He placed both hands over his face and bowed his head into his hands as if he was asking God to direct his thoughts. A commander, beloved by his men, was now faced with a life-altering decision. He looked up, his hands dropped back down to his sides. When he came out of his silent motions he looked over at Elington.

"How was the fighting for your regiment yesterday, lieutenant?"

"Horrible, sir."

"I remember, lieutenant, when I met you at our meeting to discuss this mission to Philadelphia. You are part of Pettigrew's brigade, aren't you?"

"Yes, general. Lieutenant Harrison Elington, Pettigrew's brigade, 26th North Carolina Infantry, sir."

"I have heard from Pettigrew that your regiment 'covered itself with glory yesterday.' I am aware that our young Colonel Burgwyn was killed doing his duty on McPherson Ridge."

"Yes, you are correct, sir," Elington said with solitude. I have lost a close friend and the best fighter in this army. Many of my close friends from North Carolina also perished yesterday, sir."

"You have my regrets and prayers, lieutenant, and I personally thank you and your comrades for your service to this army."

"Thank you, General Lee, I appreciate your condolences."

"Major Fincannon, you may take back the 700 men. I will also assign you one battalion of artillery. I think Lieutenant Elington will be happy to know that his son fought with valor yesterday along the Chambersburg Pike, covering our infantry. The 5th North Carolina Artillery Battalion will accompany you gentlemen."

"Thank you, sir," Fincannon replied.

"Thank you, General Lee, for a chance to be with my son, Danny," Elington said. "In my depressed and saddened state, I forgot that Danny was even here in this fight."

"Well, major, it is after seven now. You have to get this brigade moving. I need to get Longstreet moving to take the Union left flank."

"Yes, sir! May God go with you, General Lee."

"I pray, major, that you and your men will be successful. However this turns out, I will look forward to seeing you back in the vicinity of this town on or around the 5th or 6th of July. I pray that I will have a victory waiting for your men, major."

"Yes, general," Fincannon said as he shook Lee's hands with solemn emotion and gratitude.

"Will you be all right with the procurement of supplies, Major Fincannon?" asked Lee.

"We will have to forage when the supplies run out."

"I understand."

General Lee knew that this mission, without victory, would leave a bitter taste in his mouth. For when the excursion began in Pennsylvania, he issued a general Order 73 requiring compensation with confiscation of materials from the enemy. He always wanted to prove to the Northern mind that his army would not ravage through civilian institutions, causing massive losses as the Union Army had continually done in Virginia and Tennessee. His reputation as a fair commander was important and he wished to continue with this practice. However, he had to weigh in his mind the victorious results which could flourish from his decisions and the current battle, compared to a few instances of armies foraging in enemy territory.

Lieutenant Elington, still overwhelmed in sadness from the loss of his colonel and the Possum, mounted a reddish-brown colt requisitioned to him by the brigade. Elington had placed his saddlebags upon the horse. He now had a breech-loading rifle holstered on the right side of the horse. He waited for his orders to begin the anticipated mission. Elington looked around at the college grounds and thought back to the days of his schooling back in North Carolina. He thought of military training and teacher training. He thought of all the students he had had in various classes and he tried to think of how many were still alive. The birds sang and chirped on this summer day. The green trees, the wheat and oat fields and the buildings of this snug and quaint town stood silent, but now it was on the brink of historical importance where the blood of many would rectify the war one way or another.

History, once again, waited for sacrifice and honor from men who had displayed these attributes many times before.

*****

Harrison sat on his new horse along the Mummasburg Road.

In a clearing off of the Chambersburg Pike, the men of the 26th were about to bury their colonel and other men who had sacrificed for the honor of the Confederacy. West of Herr Ridge, where the 26th had valiantly commenced their operation against General Doubleday's force on July 1, one of Burgwyn's friends prepared the colonel to be buried, temporarily, about seventy-five yards to the north of the Pike. Burgwyn's friend was sure the family would want to return the colonel's body after the war to North Carolina, where he would finally come to rest in peace in his beloved Southern home.

Expressions of sorrow and loss were shown by all of the men present at the burial ground. Burgwyn's commitment was continually praised and reviewed by those present. A red woolen blanket had been tightly wrapped around his body and the colonel's remains were set in a wooden gun case, used now as a coffin for the young officer. The colonel could now rest in the presence of his Savior, but he was forever removed from his regiment.

Removed in body, but never in spirit.

– Chapter 21 –
Harrisburg, A Change of Plans

July 2, 1863

Major Fincannon quickly advised his regimental commanders of the change in route for the mission to Philadelphia. The commanders and staff members of the Titan Brigade mounted their horses. The 2,200 men formed into two columns and paused to verify last-minute details on the Mummasburg Road. It was now going on eight in the morning and time continued crucial for the brigade.

Major Fincannon briefed his commanders concerning the last minute changes approved by General Lee. He also pointed out the new route. The route would start on the Harrisburg Road. Fincannon pressed the issue with his waiting officers that they would now be attacking parts of Harrisburg in order to secure the Market Street Camelback Bridge, which would connect them onto Tulpehocken Road and then back onto their original route of the Philadelphia-Lancaster Turnpike. The brigade would bypass the Wrightsville and Columbia Bridge. It had been destroyed, burned in the presence of General John B. Gordon's brigade on the 28th of June.

Officers seemed apprehensive about attacking the Pennsylvania capital and Pennsylvania's American Paris, Philadelphia. Many of the officers were beginning to think this mission as a diversionary tactic in order for General Lee to achieve victory in Pennsylvania at their expense. But orders needed to be followed. The skulkers, stragglers and cowardly complainers had left the Army of Northern Virginia by now. The same seemed to be true in

Tennessee, where many of Fincannon's brigade originated.

"Brigade! Move out," ordered Fincannon.

The hoofs of hundreds of horses rumbled upon the ground. Dust parched the air. Black and gray, chestnut and brown, dappled grays and dappled browns, light beige and reddish, the horses carrying the riders of the Titan Brigade rustled and galloped by on the Mummasburg Road and headed to their connecting point of the Harrisburg Road about a half-mile away to the northeast of Gettysburg.

Lieutenant Elington, part of Fincannon's staff now, rode toward the front of the brigade. He tried to see Danny earlier in the morning, but time and circumstances did not allow it. Mentally, he began to try and prepare himself for yet more battle and death upon northern land. *The thirty-six miles to Harrisburg will not be a difficult task for us today*, he thought, *but what will be waiting there when we try to take that bridge?*

Corporal Danny Elington performed with courage and absolute efficiency on July 1. He now rode on his limbered cannon, still part of Battery D, and ready to take on the job of assaulting two major Pennsylvanian cities.

*****

The Department of the Susquehanna, under General Darius Couch and under the guidance and fortitude of Governor Andrew Curtain, issued calls for the defense of Pennsylvania when news of Lee's invasion hit the wires and newspapers. Many men answered the call, but most of the militia were poorly trained and inexperienced soldiers.

General Albert Jenkins and his cavalry brigade made substantial progress into Harrisburg on June 28, skirmishing with New York and Pennsylvania militia who fell back upon Jenkins's attack. Jenkins's and his cavalry moved back when ordered by General Lee to concentrate in Gettysburg.

Fincannon's scouts and General Jenkins's intelligence reported civilians were being used to dig entrenchments on the opposite side of the Susquehanna and the capitol building. Most of the fortifications were constructed near a dominant defense called Fort Washington and an outwork called Fort Couch. These heights and forts guarded the western approached to the bridge Fincannon needed to cross. The two forts were hastily constructed in June of 1863 as news of General Robert E. Lee's invasion rippled through Northern newspapers.

Fort Washington stood on sixty acres of land and it sat upon Hummel's

Heights, overlooking the river and the Camelback Bridge. The bridge also crossed City Island Park, an actual island supporting parts of the bridge. The pinnacles of structures in the city, the steeples of church buildings, the apexes of factory smoke stacks and the vertices of roads merging into one another could all be seen from the heights of the redoubt. The fort contained earthen embankments for its parapet with a surrounding berm half-completed, and gabions and sandbags for reinforcement. Twenty-five cannon, mounted behind stone and soil fortresses and placed on wooden platforms, served as artillery defenses for the forts and the surrounding bridges.

Fort Couch, named after the former corps commander of the Army of the Potomac, was located on 8th and Indiana Streets. The fort was positioned one-half mile to the west of Fort Washington, occupying higher ground, and to the Union militia offered a defense for the main stronghold. The Harrisburg Road turned into the Harrisburg-Carlisle Turnpike as one approached the capital and the turnpike passed right by these forts.

Lieutenant Elington, Captain Lockert and Major Fincannon all relied on the intelligence information from General Jenkins and their scouts.

The forts are inadequately armed and the troops are too green to give us a problem, Elington thought as the brigade approached the spires of the state capital. New York militia units made up the bulkhead of the defenses in the capital. *I don't think those New York boys are going to have their hearts in defending the state.* Elington continued in thought. His horse took him closer to his new mission in enemy territory.

Elington remembered a cherished Biblical verse Private Alfred Abshire had associated with the war, especially when the South was ready to attack and force judgment upon the extremely confused Union generals back in the spring and summer months of 1862:

"For as the lightning cometh out of the east, and shineth even unto the west; so shall also the coming of the Son of man be."
Alfred thought God Himself was on our side, Elington thought; *on the side of liberty and self- preservation as the Gospel message rings truth today of how Jesus brings liberty from sin and preservation of one's soul.*

*****

The sweltering heat and humidity slowed the ride of the mounted infantry. The sun blazed in the afternoon. Men drank away their rations of water, but more water was still plentiful along the route to Harrisburg. Soldiers ate food right from their haversacks as they galloped along the road. The columns of riders swerved through the green and lush countryside of Pennsylvania like a steady moving railroad train headed for its depot. The Confederate soldiers continued to be amazed at the tidy and organized farms throughout the state. Corn, wheat and orchards speckled the many fields along their journey. Animals grazed in fenced areas and farmers tried to tend to their chores in the midst of an invasion.

No time to forage now, Elington thought. *Our first priority is to take the bridge and thus complete our missions through Harrisburg and then onto Philadelphia.*

He thought about the Possum, again. He thought about their lifeless bodies back on McPherson Ridge, hoping they were now interred in a temporary grave and not left out for the hogs and the vultures to consume. Tears filled his eyes, but were quickly dried by the hot air on his face and the drying effect of riding into the breeze.

The letter next to Alfred's body, he thought of as the ride continued. It was from Krista Morris, his beautiful Yankee fiancée, from Maine. Elington had taken the liberty to read the letter, stained in the blood of his friend. He hadn't heard Alfred talk much concerning Krista in the days leading up to Gettysburg. She said, in the letter, how she had regretted not hearing from Alfred. She said it was very difficult to get letters through to the Confederate soldiers from Maine. She contemplated the love and affection she still felt toward Alfred and how she longed for the day of their reunion, perhaps in the form of a quiet picnic under some large shady trees on a warm summer's day. She wrote one thing in the letter that impressed upon Harrison's mind.

Alfred, she said, *it is hard to realize that a war is going on in America. I am removed from the events of the fighting and I sometimes forget we are in the midst of a horrible civil war. Life goes on here in Maine, as usual, except when the sad news of a local casualty, a Union son killed or wounded, hits the newspapers. Mourning fills the homes of the dead, but if it is not your own family member it doesn't affect one too much.*

Harrison thought how easily people of the two countries could forget the sacrifice, honor and bravery of what the average soldier in the field was doing for the cause of his nation. *How could people ever forget a war is going on? It must be the naïve notions of a young girl. This cannot be the thinking of most people. If I live through the rest of this madness and horror, I, for one, will teach people to remember. I will make sure monuments and remembrances of this conflict fill the summer air every year in time of peace.*

The brigade continued the ride toward the capital of Pennsylvania. The heat of the day began to affect the men and the horses, but no orders were given to halt. Major Fincannon wanted Harrisburg over with as quickly as possible so Philadelphia could be set upon his sights.

*****

The skirmish line approached the capital from the southwest as the rest of the brigade left Mechanicsburg. Major Fincannon sent the boys out to feel for the enemy before the main body of the brigade reached Harrisburg. The two columns of horseman veered into aim toward the capital. It was early afternoon and the artillery was ordered to come up the road and unlimber about a mile from the bridge, near the west side defenses overlooking the Susquehanna. Major obstacles, especially in the way of state militia, did not hamper the brigade's move into the capital city.

Harrison glimpsed over to his son Danny. The boy ordered the private soldiers in his battalion to unlimber the cannon. The sun started its decline toward the western sky. The spires of Harrisburg loomed on the horizon and citizens were told by the militia to stay out of the way. The twelve cannon from the battalion were lined across the Harrisburg-Carlisle Road.

"Fire! Fire!" the major of the battalion ordered.

Fincannon ordered fire placed on the fort west of the bridge to clear out the militia and scare them from their fortified positions in the main structure, Fort Washington. The twelve guns fired case and solid shot toward the fort. The rumblings and thunderous repercussions didn't even make the hardened veterans flinch. The fire and smoke, the blasting sounds of targets hit, and the maimed cries of the receivers of the shrapnel had become routine for Lieutenant Elington and his new comrades, especially his son Danny.

Corporal Danny Elington fought with distinction at First Bull Run when the confused Confederate lines were re-established by the arrival of the great Stonewall Jackson. Danny heard the booming guns there for the first time. During the Peninsula Campaign he saw the carnages of war firsthand as a young private. The mangled bodies of his school mates and the wounds of countless others calloused his mind to death and destruction. At Second Bull Run and at Sharpsburg, along the Antietam Creek, he saw the gates of hell prevail upon the sickening butchery of war. Men with gaping wounds and fatal gunshots in their flesh taught Danny that war, in its raw condition, is the worst of earthly domains, but at the same time one who fights the war cannot be consumed by the frailties of its human cost. *If we wanted this war,* Danny would say, *we need to fight it full-heartedly, never shrinking from our duties for the cause we enlisted to defend.*

Danny fought on the first day's battle at Gettysburg. It was a victory for the Confederates, but at a cost no regiment had incurred before. He knew the 26th North Carolina had been massacred and he prayed his father was all right after hearing of the devastation. Destiny favored him today, for he fought along with his father.

Harrison thought, watching the tenacity of his son manning the guns of his battalion, *He is only a young man in his early twenties. He has seen things our youth shouldn't have to see. How will he deal with such images after the war? He must survive. I cannot bear to lose him. Abigail cannot lose him. She grieves for Jesse. Where are you, Jesse? What has happened to my eldest son?*

A general store, a carpenter's shop, and a bookbinder's establishment sat on both sides of the road where the brigade gunners took aim at the fort. People inside closed their doors and locked the Confederates from their world. Many workers and proprietors ran out the back doors of their establishments, fleeing from incoming shells from their own militia.

The brigade fanned out into an established battle line broken into short segments with some regiments moving forward and some taking flank positions closer to the bridge. It was an array of noncontiguous lines. The brigade's artillery continued its rhythmic fire toward the fort and its outwork, Fort Couch. A huge explosion rumbled through the streets of the city when a shell hit an ammunition depot near the fort.

"Good work!" yelled Major Fincannon. He was watching the affects of the artillery for a few minutes when the depot blew up. "Keep up a good fire on that position, major. I am going to get two of our regiments to storm the bridge and permanently relieve those green militia."

"Yes, sir, Major Fincannon!"

"Elington!" Fincannon said. "Organize our two lead regiments and storm the bridge."

"Yes, sir, right away."

"Lieutenant, I have promoted you to captain and you will be officially part of my staff on this mission. Do you understand me, Captain Harrison Elington?"

"Yes, major. Thank you, sir."

It looked as though Major Fincannon knew how to lead. In the short time Elington had been with Fincannon, from Gettysburg to Harrisburg, the major's command structure and flexible attitude gave men new confidence toward the mission. For the first time since yesterday, he felt he could truly trust and rely on another person to be his superior officer. *Colonel Burgwyn was irreplaceable, but Fincannon possessed a tough, honest spirit and he can be trusted,* Elington thought.

"They are reinforcing, sir, from their right flank," Captain Lockert said.

"We'll get'em, captain. They're green and they're ready to run, I can feel it. We're making direct hits on the walls of that fort there overlooking the bridge and the approaches to the city. I know when Elington leads the charge he will lead in fury. His devastating losses of yesterday will reinforce his will to succeed against the Yankees. He needs to get that out of his system."

"Isn't that risking failure, sir, when a man is fighting for revenge."

"You have so much to learn, captain. Hate and revenge are the fuels for this war. It is part of what allows us to function on the field."

"Lockert! Go and tell Elington that I want the charge first to be a cavalry charge at the enemy, and then I want the charge to halt in mid-stream, about a 100 yards from those entrenchments. Finally, have the mounted infantry dismount, followed up by the second regiment on foot and attack and clear those works. Men from the second regiment can hold the horses and tie them by threes. Now go, captain!"

"All right, major!"

The orders were dispersed and Captain Elington arranged his units to attack the way Fincannon ordered. He thought it was a grand attack plan. One regiment of the Titan Brigade formed close together along the road, spanning into fields that were on both sides of the road past the stores. The men of this first regiment, named on the spot by Elington as the 90th Tennessee Mounted Infantry, sat on their horses with carbines ready for action. Captain Elington assembled his second regiment, the 91st Tennessee Mounted Infantry, behind the 90th. Their horses were sent to the rear of the battle lines on the Harrisburg Road and held by the third and smallest regiment of the brigade. Elington had gotten permission from Major Fincannon, through Captain Lockert, to name the regiments for easier deployment and for identification of officers and enlisted men throughout the mission. The smaller regiment was named the 125th North Carolina Mounted Infantry. A large number of North Carolinian soldiers made up this regiment.

Earlier in the war many of these men headed west to help fight in

Tennessee under Major Fincannon. Fincannon organized his men into regiments, but he never gave them official names. He would remember each regiment by its officers and that was enough for him. All of the fancy names and battle flags in the ranks didn't interest him. On raids into enemy territory, he figured, who would care about names and flags?

Like a finely crafted clock, the brigade moved in precise time, filing into battle lines, holding horses and marching toward the bridge. Dust and sunbeams cascaded through the ranks south of the target. Captain Elington configured his regiments according to plan and informed the regimental officers, mostly lieutenants, of the attack.

The bridge stood before the Titan Brigade. The unusual humpback structure resembled a monstrous, serpentine dragon meandering through the countryside. One hump of the bridge spanned from the Harrisburg side to City Island and another hump arched from City Island to Bridgeport. Constructed of wood and covered by trusses of timber to protect the deck from weathering, the bridge stood as an engineering accomplishment and a money maker from tolls collected.

The engine was ready to start anew. The engine of battle. The engine of human destruction. The engine which produced exhaust of wasted lives and tattered dreams. The engine, adrift in a tide of destruction and removed from normal life, caused men to become like animals, either fighting for survival or fleeing in desperate fear from their predators.

The 90th Tennessee rode toward the bridge. First riding at a quick gallop, then ordered to charge, the men in the saddle resembled the horsemen of the apocalypse eager to bring down destruction upon their enemy. About a 100 yards from the bridge the mounted infantry soldiers dismounted and quickly formed a battle line on foot. They readied their carbines and had some of the men from the 91st Tennessee behind them restrain their horses and hold the animals in place while the other men of the 91st got ready to support the 90th. At the double quick, the 90th Tennessee began its march toward the bridge. The men in the regiment could see their artillery support continually hitting targets. The shells made harsh piercing howls passing over the heads of the soldiers from Tennessee. Rolling explosions filled the afternoon air. The regiment was ordered to march at the quick step as they got closer to the bridge. Their battle line halted around forty yards from the target.

"Volley fire on command! Ready! Aim! Fire!" Officers shouted the command down the line.

The stentorian crackle and gut-popping fire of carbines could be heard and felt by the citizens of Harrisburg. The fire was murderous upon the inexperienced Pennsylvania and New York militia units trying to protect the bridge. Fort Couch, occupying the higher ground of the two forts, was obliterated by the rapid and continuous fire from the hardened and experienced artillerists in gray and butternut. With flags and colors flying in the hot sun, the outwork was quickly taken by Fincannon's men and they proceeded to move on the main entrenchment, Fort Washington.

The carbine was a weapon having advantage over the common musket used by most of the infantry soldiers on both sides in the war. The rifles were breach loaders and the soldier handling the gun could get more shots off per minute than the soldier handling a musket.

The militia in blue dispersed from Fort Washington and its modified fortifications. Shells from the 5th North Carolina Artillery Battalion and the carbine fire from the mounted infantry regiment moved the green Union troops into an agitated and confused frenzy. They tried to fire at the Confederates as they retreated, but with little affect. A stray cannon shot made a hit on the left flank of the 91st Tennessee, following in support of the 90th. Some men went down in the regiment, but weren't seriously hurt.

Union militia tried to defend the fort as others ran from the more experienced Confederate raiders. Earth, planks of wood, sprays from exploded sandbags, and logs rose into the air and then fell back to the ground in bits as the artillery shells made their desired imprints upon Fort Washington.

"Steady, boys!" ordered Captain Elington.

"Feed them with the fire of lead!" a sergeant yelled in a sermon-like tone.

"Volley; give them more volleys of lead and they'll run like there's no tomorrow," a lieutenant hollered from the 91st Tennessee. The rebel yell ensued over the landscape of dust, humidity and boiling temperatures.

Other Confederates commented as they closed in on the fort, "Flank them green, unseasoned blue bellies!"

"We're going to whip them today, major."

"Let's charge that bridge and the fort now, Captain Elington. We can take 'em. They're running back to New York, man!"

"I can see 'em."

"We all can see 'em, private."

"Halt!" ordered Elington.

"Let's give them another volley, sir."

"That's just what I was about to order, sergeant."

"We're going to give them another round, men," Elington said.

"Yes! I like those volleys," shouted one brazen private.

"Ready! Aim! Fire !" Captain Elington shouted above the tumult of battle. Artillery fire persisted. Volleys blazed through the ranks of the falling Union militia. The depot burned with black smoke. All of this desiccated the Union defenders.

"Forward march!" ordered Elington to his men in the three regiments positioned to pursue their main target. Fort Washington was all but vacated. A few sharpshooters tried to stifle the advance of the brigade, but to no avail.

"Halt, brigade!"

"Ready! Aim! Fire!"

Another ruinous volley was fired into the fort walls, bullets and exploding shells penetrating deep into the weakened parapet of the structure. Dirt continued to fly and burst over the fort.

As Captain Elington saw the damage over the fort, he directed his brigade to get ready to charge the bridge.

"Sergeant!" screamed Elington. "Go and tell the 125th North Carolina to fall back to the artillery line. Then ..."

"Wait a minute, captain. I want to write these orders down."

"All right sergeant, but let's make it quick. We have to take that bridge now"

Continue your orders, captain."

"Tell the 125th to fall back to the artillery line of battle. Then order the artillery battalion to limber up and along with the 125th move closer to the bridge. Tell the officers and Major Fincannon to bring up the rear of our brigade and position the two units at around fifty yards from the bridge. Tell Major Fincannon to clean out any further opposition from the fort and any reinforcements of the fort immediately. Did you get all of that, sergeant?"

Yes, sir, I am on my way."

The sergeant mounted one of the horses the 91st was holding in place and charged back to the artillery line. He arrived in a few minutes, out of breath and awful excited about the movement of his brigade toward the bridge.

"Major Fincannon! Major Fincannon! I have orders for the rest of the brigade from Captain Elington."

Fincannon and Captain Lockert were positioned behind the artillery battalion, the 5th North Carolina, and watching the action through their field glasses.

"What are the orders, sergeant? Give them over to me," Fincannon said in a demanding tone of voice.

"All right, Captain Lockert. We are about to move from this position in order to support Captain Elington's move on the bridge."

"Yes, sir, major! What do you want me to do?"

"Order the 5th to limber up and move to within fifty yards of the bridge and as close to the bridge as possible. When they get there have the major of the battalion unlimber six of the guns to support the crossing of the bridge and to fire on that no-good militia on the other side."

"On the other side, major?" Lockert asked, looking toward the bridge.

"Yes, captain. I guess they're going to try and attack us as we cross, or they're going to try and torch the bridge to prevent our crossing."

"All right, major!"

"I hope Captain Elington has a plan to take those militia off of the bridge," the major said to Captain Lockert before he galloped away.

"Men of the 90th and 91st Tennessee," Elington shouted over the soldiers falling into their battle lines. "We are going to secure the bridge now. As you can see, we have visitors trying to come over and harass us. Well, we're going to harass them first and get them off of the bridge before they go and try to burn the structure like the cowards did at Wrightsville."

"Yes, sir," shouted the men in the ranks.

"We'll charge across the bridge in two columns, running as fast as we can. Load those carbines and watch out for shooting your own men. We can't spare any today. We still have to make our way into Philadelphia."

"We'll make it, sir," one private shouted.

"Yeah, we'll get across that bridge as fast as you can say charge, sir," another private said from the ranks. The soldiers were severely sweating and about to run out of water.

The men wanted to get across to get their supply of water intact and secured for the next phase of their mission.

"We're doing fine under your command here today, Captain Elington," said one of the lieutenants in the 91st Tennessee. "We are glad to have you as an officer on this mission. You have displayed pristine leadership and encouragement to the men."

"Thank you, lieutenant, but the time for compliments will come another day. We have to move across the river and to the other side of our destiny."

"Forward march!" Elington shouted the order to his regiments.

The men, still mentally and physically capable after the battle for the forts, marched with determination and a sense of self-respect toward the bridge.

The soldiers all knew how vital the mission they were carrying out was to the Army of Northern Virginia and to the outcome of the war itself. General Lee needed a victory on Northern soil like he needed his next human breath, commanding the great Confederate Army of Northern Virginia, a proud Southern army that invaded Maryland upon the bloody fields of Antietam Creek in 1862.

"At the double quick step," Elington ordered as the regiment entered the ramp of the bridge.

Union militia fired at the 90th Tennessee, which led the attack. The 90th returned fire with efficient results. The firing continued back and forth as the opposing Union militia unit packed more determination than previous militia units to defend their post. Hot lead blared through the ranks on both sides. Union soldiers fell from the bridge and into the rushing waters of the Susquehanna.

"Watch out ahead," Elington yelled to his leading regiment. He saw the militia lining up to send a volley of musket fire from the other end of the bridge while the militia on the bridge hunkered down upon the structure. He could also see four pieces of artillery ready and unlimbered to take action against his men.

"If those guns fire on us and hit us, it will be too devastating for our ranks and for our mission," Elington said to his lieutenant.

"Halt the brigade, men," Elington ordered. "All men, lie down on the bridge, lie down where you are. I am going to get artillery fire to take that militia unit and its artillery pieces out of action."

The men followed their orders and waited.

In a few minutes a searing blast of fire erupted from the western edge of the bridge. Corporal Danny Elington and his artillery battalion fired murderously into the poor boys on the other side. Limbs flew, smashing into the sides of the bridge. Red sprays of blood, rising up over the deck of the bridge, were observed by the Confederates lying down on their bellies. Seven cannon were now in action to clear the bridge.

Captain Elington met up with Captain Lockert and they devised a message system using signal flags. The two officers needed to communicate so each knew when the artillery needed to fire and when infantry support was appropriate.

The 5th North Carolina Artillery Battalion worked their guns for about fifteen minutes without interruption. Three of the Union militia guns were destroyed. One gun fired at the Confederates. The shell flew, burned and shrieked over the mounted infantry's heads, landing straight into one of the guns of the 5th. Three crew members were instantly killed by the shot from the stubborn militia.

"Hurrah! Hurrah! Hurrah!"

"Hurrah! Hurrah! Hurrah!"

The Union men delighted in their victory over one of the Confederate's guns.

As the cheers continued, Captain Elington took advantage of the lull in the fighting and ordered his two regiments to stand and charge the militia's position on the eastern end of the bridge.

"Charge bayonets! Get ready to charge to the other side of the bridge," Elington ordered.

"We're going to do something now," one private shouted.

"They're dead men if they stay on this bridge," yelled another soldier.

"The wrath of God is coming upon their souls and their bodies," one other enlisted man lamented to his comrades.

Like an anaconda moving as air toward its prey, the battle columns of the 90th and 91st Tennessee Regiments coerced the Union militia, trampling their remnants and removing their force from the bridge with bayonets and Bowie knives. The last piece of Union artillery stood alone on the road before the east entrance to the bridge. It stood alone from the living. Tens of young militia recruits, compelled by old Abe Lincoln and the confident Governor Andrew Curtain, lay dead or severely wounded and mortified by the Confederate attack, an attack that became the second victory upon the enemy's soil. July 1 was the initial, costly victory by the Confederates in achieving their cause, an objective to finally be recognized by the North as an independent country, free from the reign of the United States government and free from the death of three years of fatal war.

Many Confederate politicians also longed for recognition from the British and the French. Sporadically, negotiations occurred in England since the beginning of the war. The British and the French held the position that the Union would not be able to conquer the Southern government and its 750,000 square miles of territory.

Smoke smoldered on both sides of the enemy bridge. The Titan Brigade's artillery and the 125th North Carolina passed over the bridge without resistance and the two units joined together with the 90th and 91st Tennessee Regiments. Horses were reunited with their riders and water became the target of the men's interests once the bridge was ensured.

"All men of the brigade," Major Fincannon ordered, "get ready to fall into column formation for a resumption of our mission. Fall in!"

The brigade aligned into columns to restart their ride to Philadelphia. The soldiers rode for the remaining daylight hours. It was three o'clock in the afternoon when the brigade fell in across the bridge. The major directed his officers to find the Tulpehocken Road. The road led the brigade back onto the Philadelphia-Lancaster Turnpike beyond the Columbia-Wrightsville rail bridge.

The Union militia retreated, skadaddled from the scene of the bridge. Many of Major Fincannon's men looked back at the bridge, wondering if it would be there when the brigade returned from Philadelphia.

Unpredictable, they thought. *Unpredictable.*

"How will we get across and back to Gettysburg if they burn the bridge, Major Fincannon?" Captain Lockert asked, sitting on his horse and ready to proceed.

"In all probability, captain, we will not be coming back through Harrisburg in order to regroup with the Army of Northern Virginia and General Lee. We will have to hear of news from Northerners, or read in their newspapers pertaining to the fate of our army in south-central Pennsylvania. We will make a determination for our trip back upon the outcome of the remaining conflict in Gettysburg. If General Lee sows victory we will reap a safe return through Pennsylvania to seek our victorious comrades. If General Lee sows defeat in the Pennsylvania town we shall seek an alternate route of escape from enemy territory. A crossing of the Potomac, perhaps, through Maryland, could be our escape route if General Meade defeats our army."

"I understand, major. I guess we can't worry about it now."

"Let us proceed, captain. Inform Captain Elington of the plan of action for our exit out of Pennsylvania if Lee is defeated and see if he has any ideas. We must keep all of our options open. He will ride in front of our brigade and I will ride toward the middle for a while. I can help keep the boys online. You can ride at the rear and keep an eye on the artillery. Make sure they hustle to keep up with the mounted infantry."

"But, major, the dust."

"Follow orders, captain. We will go to the front as we close in on the Turnpike to Philadelphia."

"Yes, major."

*****

The brigade made its way southeast of Harrisburg. Passing through Middletown and approaching Elizabethtown, the mounted infantry rode steadily toward Lancaster, where the army foraged and feasted on the Dutch farmlands. The sun caused perspiration and uncomfortable conditions for the men. Humidity prevented their sweaty uniforms from drying out. The wool clothes stuck to the men and felt twice as heavy.

Captain Harrison Elington left the front of the brigade and dropped back to the first battery behind the 125th North Carolina where Danny was riding and bumping along on his limbered gun.

"Danny! Danny!" Harrison yelled in joy to his son. "Are you all right?"

"It's my father!" Danny said to Peyton Caldwell.

"Mr. Elington! It's Peyton … Peyton!"

"I can't believe it! After all the ruination we've been through, you guys are still alive and well. Son, how have you been doing? Have you heard from your mother? How did you manage to get assigned to this crazy mission?" The noise and dust permeated the column's condition.

"Slow down, Father. Slow down. I can only answer one question at a time and with all of the rumbling and clatter sounding off I can't hear everything you're saying." Danny tried waving the dust from in front of his face.

"I am glad to see you, son."

"Me too, Father."

"I have been all right. The fight at Gettysburg on July 1 was really bad, even though it was counted as our victory. Company F was demolished, Danny. Lewis, Alfred, Thaddeus, Jackson; they were all killed, right in front of me. The colonel was also killed."

"Burgwyn is dead! I can't believe that. He was my age and the youngest colonel in the whole darn army. He was such an asset to our cause."

"He's gone."

"Lewis Fry is dead? It can't be."

"He was shot down on the ridge right before the town, along with Alfred and Thaddeus. Jackson was shot first. He went down in a stream, Willoughby's Run. It was west of the ridge, in front of the slope on the western side. I'll never forget that place as long as I live."

"Alfred, Thaddeus and Jackson; all dead. I can't comprehend this, Father."

The caissons and cannon continued to bump along the road toward Lancaster.

"How will Mr. and Mrs. Abshire handle the awful news? Alfred was their whole life. He was to inherit the gristmill back home in the county; back in the good old hills of North Carolina."

"I can't see how any of the parents are going to handle the news of death and loss upon their families. Lewis has three children now without a father to guide them through the decisions of life. What is Margaret to do?"

"If we make it out of this war, Father, we're going to have a lot of people to help and to counsel, including Mother and Grandfather Sumner."

"Yes, son, you're right. A lot of people are going to be damaged by these losses; human loss never to be replaced in this world."

"Peyton? How are you holding up, boy?" Harrison asked in a kind tone. "Danny told me a few weeks back that you were contemplating desertion from the army. He said some of the boys had to subdue you to keep you from execution. Is that right, Peyton?"

"Keep it quiet, Mr. Elington. Go easy on me. I can't let these ruffians from Tennessee hear this information."

"All right, Peyton. I will shut up."

"Thank you, sir. At the time I thought it was a good and admirable idea to desert. I thought at the time that all of us in the artillery fought enough and it was time to go home. I figured people back in Caldwell County would understand my plight from the army and grant me a peaceful discharge. But Danny and some other bullies convinced me otherwise."

"Good for you for staying on. Now you're on a secret mission that could get all of us killed or maimed."

"Thanks for the encouragement. You're a captain now, Mr. Elington? I noticed the men calling you captain."

"Yes. Got the promotion today from Major Fincannon. I think the major is an excellent officer and leader. I wish we had more like him in the ranks of the Army of Northern Virginia."

"You will add to the officer ranks in a grand way, Mr. Elington."

"I agree with that, Peyton," Danny added.

"Thanks, boys."

"I haven't heard from Mother since the winter," Danny said to Harrison.

"Apparently, Major Fincannon investigated my background before I was selected to be on this mission. He informed me your mother is in Philadelphia, staying with your grandfather on Pine Street. He said she left Caldwell County to try and find Jesse."

"My God, Father, she's in the North, in the Union. This is right where we're headed on the mission. If she finds out she will kill us both!"

"She's not going to kill anyone, even though she did throw a dish at me when I was on leave back in the fall."

"What did you say to her?"

"I called her a Yankee preacher and I told her of a possible invasion of the North."

"What?"

"Yes, a Yankee preacher. Boy, it seems like yesterday when I was back home."

"I hope mother stays out of the way when we make it into Philadelphia. Maybe we can get her out of there and back home to North Carolina."

"No, Danny! We can't get ourselves personally involved during this mission. We do our job on the arsenal and then leave. She won't find out we were on this mission."

"I understand, Father."

"Captain Elington, how long are we going to ride today?" Peyton asked as the caravan of Confederates progressed.

"We are going to Lancaster to forage and camp for the night. We will proceed to Philadelphia early on July 3, arriving on the 4th of July to blow that arsenal."

"I hear Lancaster is farming country where we can stock our haversacks and saddlebags with food."

"That's why we're stopping there. We know what we're doing, Peyton. Don't worry about a thing."

"Yeah, captain, until we get into the heart of Philadelphia, then what?"

"We will literally cross that bridge when we get there."

"All right."

"I have to get to the front of the brigade now, boys. I will talk to you soon."

The Titan Brigade made its way through many small Pennsylvania towns and entered the county of Lancaster. The greenery and lush landscape was like heaven to the Southern troops. Finally, they had made it to a place where the ravages and butcheries of war ceased to exist. The well-organized German farmlands, accented by rolling hills, orchards and grazing animals, made the mission turn temporarily into a saunter through paradise. Water was plentiful through the abundance of streams and creeks. Trees, willows and maples, provided shaded areas for the troops; areas unmolested by fighting and shooting.

The men camped along the Turnpike. Forage parties went out gently gathering food and buying supplies in exchange for gold requisitioned for the mission, thus enhancing the reputation of the Confederate soldier in the North as a confiscator through compensation.

To the west of Lancaster, General Lee and his three corps of troops savagely attacked the high ground south of Gettysburg, according to a courier who had caught up with the Titan Brigade in Lancaster on the night of July 2. Culp's Hill, Cemetery Hill and Little Round Top were assaulted with unheard-of valor and determination by Lee's confident troops. An unknown Union colonel saved his army's left flank by ordering a bayonet charge after his 20th Maine Regiment ran out of ammunition. General Winfield Hancock, commanding the Second Union Corps, moved troops into key locations on the fishhook-shaped battle line on Cemetery Ridge, blocking key offensive charges by the Confederates.

Along the Emmitsburg Road in Gettysburg, a wheat field and a peach orchard became places of intrepid valor and bravery. These fields changed hands several times before the second day's battle ended. General Lee, in all probability, would renew his attack on July 3 and thus produce a victory for the Confederacy upon Union soil.

The night time sky was lit by the moon and the stars seen by Confederate armies in Gettysburg and Lancaster. The next few days held a conclusion for the cause of the South one way or the other. Captain Elington dozed into a deep sleep under the pleasant summer sky in Lancaster. His last thought, before passing into his sleep, was of his wife, his home and his sons.

– Chapter 22 –
Attack upon Philadelphia

July 4, 1863

Friday, July 3, dawned and the calamities of battle brought utter pain and solemn reflection to the thousands of men sitting, standing and eating back on the field at Gettysburg. Soldiers were convinced that God Himself brought His judgment upon the armies, Union and Confederate, for the massed killings through almost three years of bloody war.

Major Fincannon led the way, riding in front of the brigade, his horse sweating and whining on the Lancaster-Philadelphia Turnpike. It was another seething hot and humid day upon the wide open lands of Pennsylvania. Again and again the men of the brigade passed wheat fields, cornfields, orchards and farms. Through the countryside, like a serpentine gray ghost, the Titan Brigade continued its advance toward Philadelphia.

The men felt the pressure building in their minds and hearts. Another battle of wills and physical strengths stood before them, unknown in details, but sure to bring on more casualties and losses for the Confederacy. Philadelphians, Captain Elington contemplated while riding his mount, will protect themselves when it comes right down to an attack on part of their city. The Democrats, with their superfluous pride and arrogance, condemned the war and its Republican leadership, but they did not speak for the majority of patriotic Philadelphians who stood as the vanguards of liberty, democratic revolution and defiance against tyrannical monarchs.

The mounted infantry columns trekked from their lush paradise of

Lancaster County, riding most of the daylight hours toward the city and then stopping west of Philadelphia to water and rest the horses. Major Fincannon ordered a halt at the village of Ardmore, along the Lancaster-Philadelphia Turnpike and about seven miles from the border of Philadelphia.

Extra pickets were posted during the night in case word of the Confederate advance reached any of the Philadelphia militia.

*****

On the morning of July 4, close to 2,200 Confederate raiders set out on their seven-mile ride to the American Paris. A few soldiers were too sick from their wounds at Harrisburg to make the attack on the Frankfort Arsenal. They stayed behind in Lancaster.

The day celebrating American emancipation from the British and their government of restraint was overspread with gray clouds and misty rain. On this day, Americans were supposed to be commemorating the cause of individual and responsible actions; citizens who plotted their own destinies through their own designs. God in His providence and wise counsel had driven the British despots from the shores of the colonies. The former British subjects were left to govern themselves. Philadelphia stood as the mother of democratic rule among men. Not since the ancient days of the Greek and Roman governments had men been free to determine their own fates.

July 4, 1863, however, brought another rebel army to the outskirts of the city where the founding fathers masterfully initiated and crafted self-government on a grand scale.

One of the last orders sent by Secretary of War Edwin Stanton to General Napoleon Dana of the Union Army in Philadelphia stated:

"It is very important that machinery for manufacturing arms should not fall into the hands of the enemy if they are to approach the city. In case of imminent danger to the arsenals of the city or to the works of Alfred Jenks and Sons, who are manufacturing arms for the government, you are authorized and impressed to use tugs, barges or any other vessel to remove the gun manufacturing machines from beyond the reach of the enemy."

Other officials in the federal government were concerned about the prospects of an invasion of Philadelphia. On June 30, President Lincoln sent a telegraph message to Governor Andrew Curtain of Pennsylvania:

"The city of Philadelphia must be protected by the great militia volunteers of the city. The Army of the Potomac is in Maryland and there is no promise from General Meade that he can quickly cover any Confederate approaches to the city. Cavalry has been dispersed to find the movements of General Lee's corps, however, they need more time. God be with your great Union state where our precious republic was formed and rooted in our hearts and minds."

Businessmen and well-to-do families loaded wagons of goods and personal belongings hoping to save the items from the gray hordes coming from the western reaches of the state. Free Africans talked of moving further north to New York or Massachusetts to escape the possibility of being sent to the South and placed in a state of slavery and misery.

Men joined the militia defending the city. General Dana maneuvered for position of artillery placements and troop movements. Negro men were part of the contingent of troops.

News that a Confederate brigade of mounted infantry had advanced into Ardmore sent the city into a startled frenzy. The pace of evacuation of property and citizens increased on the night of July 3, even though word of General George Meade's apparent victory at Gettysburg trickled into the Union stronghold. The Philadelphia Public Ledger, on the morning of July 4, reported:

"General Lewis Armistead shot and possibly killed! Many other officers killed or wounded in action as the Union men in blue held the high ground on July 3. 8,000 Confederate prisoners taken and many others wounded and killed in a grand charge by General George Pickett. Public celebrations for the 4th of July are canceled in the wake of these developments. The location of other Confederate forces in Pennsylvania cannot be substantiated at this time. Philadelphia is on alert for a possible raid or subsequent invasion from the west. Confederates have already made an attack through Harrisburg to secure a bridge for the crossing of forces to Lancaster County."

Philadelphians were confident General Meade would prevent a Confederate attack into the city. The citizens of the great revolutionary city were sure their native son could do a better job leading Union forces after Lincoln had fired General Hooker upon the defeat at Chancellorsville.

*****

Northwest of the village of Ardmore, where Fincannon's brigade had camped, was the village of Frankford. Urban in its characteristics of

261

settlement, Frankford contained many German, English and Swedish populations from the old world of European culture. Carpenters, joiners and millwrights, along with weavers, blacksmiths and silver smiths, masons, cordwainers, coachmakers, clockmakers and bookbinders occupied the village that had been incorporated into the city of Philadelphia. The tentacles of the great city continued reaching and prodding to incorporate surrounding counties and villages for its drive to expand its economy through commercial and industrial development. Various shops spread on both sides of Frankford Avenue for a mile. Sales deals, the sounds of industry, the sounds and smells of production, and the close-knit societal and cultural realm distinguished the town.

Adding to the process of industry and economy to Frankford was its United States government arsenal. Set along the Delaware River and the Frankford Creek, the complex bustled with armament activity ever since the start of the war in 1861. The arsenal was built after the War of 1812 and dedicated by the father of the United States Constitution himself, President James Madison of Virginia.

By 1863, when Frankford's population had risen to over 6,000 inhabitants, many of the citizens of the village supplied the vital work force for the arsenal and its expanded output of arms and supplies. The arsenal's unique machine shop and percussion cap factory made it an imperative resource for the Union Army. Percussion caps, used to ignite powder, were needed by thousands of soldiers to fire their muskets.

Fratricide condemned the American countryside to horrible battles where the families of America would suffer and die, heritage and history wiped out in the name of rebellion, slavery and states' rights; brother against brother to the end.

*****

They could see the smoke coiling up from the city's factories. Omnibuses weaved through the uncharacteristically quiet streets. The dome of Saints Peter and Paul Catholic Church rimmed the gray skies amidst the solemn gloom of war. Girard College, with its Greek and Roman style architecture, gave off an air of prominence and grandeur. African-Americans walked the streets in certain sections of the city as freemen and not slaves. Vendors, peddlers and hucksters made their way around the city trying to find business that wasn't materializing on this July 4th.

Major Fincannon, Captain Elington and Captain Nathan Lockert looked across the city from the area west of the Market Street Bridge. The bridge was still intact and ready for Confederate use.

The news of General Robert E. Lee's failed charge had been circulated throughout the city. Major Fincannon found out the news of Lee's repulsed charge from a courier sent by General Longstreet. The courier was able to cross the Susquehanna using old canal boats near Wrightsville and Columbia. The Philadelphians' attitudes would surely be changed and energized by the news of the victory at Gettysburg, a complete victory, by a fellow Pennsylvanian who had consummated the long-awaited triumph of glory and honor pushed aside recklessly by other Union generals in the past two years of the war.

The anticipated attack now pressed upon the immediate thoughts of Major Frederick Fincannon and his brigade of Tennesseans and North Carolinians. The firm reality of attacking Philadelphia now hit the minds of Captains Harrison Elington and Nathan Lockert. The attack would be carried out by soldiers whose main army lost a devastating battle away from their base of operations in Virginia.

The long-awaited Confederate destruction of Union forces, on Union soil, disappeared in an instant on July 3 under the command of General George Pickett.

"What are your orders, sir?" asked Captain Elington to Major Fincannon. The men continued to contemplate the grim reality of attacking the city of the first revolution; the city where Thomas Jefferson of Virginia wrote the infamous Declaration of Independence. Where fifty-five men met to rehash the Articles of Confederation that gave too much power to the state governments in the first place.

"Place the guns on the west side of that bridge in front of us. It is the Market Street Bridge. Your son, Elington, is going to have to protect our approach to the bridge and our crossing of the same. Do you understand?"

"Yes, major."

"I can see militia over the bridge, but I think we can handle them, Elington. It'll be like Harrisburg all over again."

"We will handle it, sir."

"Let's make our entrance into the city and then we will proceed to the arsenal using the devised route we all know about," Fincannon said to Elington and Captain Lockert sitting on his mount.

The massive sound of the brigade trotting toward the bridge alarmed the citizens of Philadelphia. The gray horde from the South reached a major Northern city, a hub of industrial might, a place symbolic of what the United States stood for: freedom.

Proud and dignified, the officers ordered their men to crossover into the cradle of liberty. Like talons of an eagle, the gray horde thrusted forth, confidence beamed and spirits rose. Like an army raised from the ancient phalanxes of Caesar and Alexander, an army raised from the spirits of Confederate dead, a colossus of military might and fortitude, Major Frederick Albert Fincannon led his valiant and courageous force into the city. A wave of military might was about to hit the political and economic shore of Philadelphia.

"Rein those horses in, men!" Fincannon yelled. "Stay the course to the arsenal. The day now belongs to us. We can determine the course of the war. Ride men, ride!"

Danny Elington and his fellow artillerists unlimbered their pieces and began to pour a blasting fire into the city of brotherly love. Smoke and shrapnel hissed and thundered into the skies over the city. Hot case shot and solid shot hit buildings, sending people fleeing all about. In the streets, in the market stalls, in the train stations, and in alley ways, people ducked and tried to take cover from the confusion and ruination of the fire. Ten Confederate guns kept up a relentless barrage at the city as the 2,100 man brigade made it across the Market Street Bridge and across the Schuylkill River.

Elements of the 183rd Philadelphia Regiment fired at the incoming brigade. However, the area over the east side of the bridge was shamefully defended. The 183rd soon retreated toward the Logan Square area. Musket fire rose in intensity as the Titan Brigade now entered the city, leaving behind the doubts and consternations of the anticipated mission much talked about the past few days by the men. Battery D kept firing away at the city and at the Union opposition. Fincannon ordered the guns to be turned upon the military clothing factory located just over the bridge near the river. The factory was blown apart by the highly accurate artillery. Fincannon knew secondary targets would be hit, if practicable, along the way to the arsenal. Finally, Fincannon gave the order for the guns to be limbered and to follow the mounted infantry to the destined target of operations.

With Captains Elington and Lockert leading the brigade from the front, along with Major Fincannon, the Confederates approached Center Square at the intersection of Market and Broad Streets. Terrified citizens ran down side streets and into alleys to evade capture or murder by the Confederate band of raiders, who upon this sacred day of independence rendered judgment and terror instead of celebration on their fellow Americans, a people joined forever in the defeat and humiliation of the British.

"Kill those Rebs! Kill those Rebs!" shouted citizens of the city. Some were armed with muskets and shotguns of various sorts.

"Keep a tight line, men," Fincannon ordered among the confusion and cries of invasion. The sounds of the 5th North Carolina guns, grinding along, up and down paved and unpaved streets, gave the brigade an even more ominous tone. The hooves of the horses clapped down Broad Street in the center of the city. Intermittent gunfire was heard by the men of the brigade, but the officers yelled for the soldiers to carry on their journey to the arsenal in the northeast part of the city.

Smoke stacks, puffing with black soot, coiled up into the skies above the city; massive industrial buildings lined both sides of Broad Street; hateful insults were being thrown out by ladies and gentlemen alike; and rocks and stones were hurled toward the mounted soldiers. Certain Confederates lost their tempers, halted their horses, got off their mounts and fired their carbines at the harassers, scaring them half to death. General Lee cautioned soldiers to refrain from the killing of civilians on the mission. Lee was always conscientious about the politics of war and the implications of actions by his armies.

The brigade carried on toward its target. Many residential homes made of brick and A-framed roofs rose along the way, casting shadows on the street. Churches and synagogues were numerous in the city. Shops and hotels dotted the landscape of the historic urban society. Neatly designed streets and city blocks made transportation easy and efficient for industry and citizens alike.

The cool waters of the Schuylkill and the Delaware Rivers flowed gently in the morning atmosphere. Commerce and industry went on as the Confederates rode through Broad Street and spotted the Matthews & Moore Cannon Foundry and the Baldwin & Company Locomotive factory. Both buildings were fired upon by the 5th North Carolina Artillery Battalion.

Explosions roared through the streets as the mounted infantry rode quickly away from the scene to avoid injury and destruction. Thunderous repercussions reverberated from the smaller explosions of the two factories. Workers and other civilians ran for their lives down the streets. Windows shattered into tiny pieces upon the pavements. Policemen tried their best to keep citizens calm and to appropriate escape routes for people trapped in the clutches of the Confederate talons. Smoke clouded the horizon. People coughed and shouted as they walked or jogged away from the scene. Woman and girls screamed and the fabric of urban existence unraveled. A few workers were killed in the twin explosions upon the buildings of urban industry.

Munitions and transportation facilities were destroyed by the Confederates.

"We are doing it, Lockert," Elington said, riding his reddish-brown colt. The horse was tired and worn from the hours of travel across Pennsylvania, and so was Elington. Often he glanced down at the animal to check the colt's condition. Sweat and grime smeared Elington's face. His wool uniform began to irritate his body as the heat, humidity and smoke increased along the route. He felt heat sickness cover his body, but in his will, he tried his best to force the demon from him.

"We will carry this mission out to completion," Lockert answered. We have to compensate for General Lee's loss at Gettysburg. There has to be some kind of Confederate victory upon this Union soil, or all of our planning has been in vain."

"I agree with you, Lockert."

"Keep them riding, Elington, and this mission will be over soon."

The smells of gunpowder and burning wood started to catch up with the rest of the brigade. The fire, burning back down Broad Street, was now spreading up the street. Houses and shops were set ablaze by the firing of the two factories.

I wonder what Abigail is doing right now? Harrison thought. He glanced over at the buildings and caught a glimpse of Girard College as the brigade made its way to Girard Avenue. Pine Street was located on the south side of Broad Street beyond Center Square, and Harrison knew he couldn't chance a maneuver to see what the fate of his wife and son were; not yet, anyway. He was sure his father-in-law exercised his authority as a senator to track down Jesse from the 83rd Pennsylvania. He couldn't think on that now. The arsenal was the first priority on his mind. The military power of the Union Army needed to be broken and the destruction of the arsenal was the immediate answer. *Abigail can care for herself until I can get to her,* he said to himself.

More buildings, spires of churches and black and gray factories lined the two sides of Girard Avenue. Brick and stone, concrete and mortar, tile and paint, characterized the structures of the city. *Population centers and commerce are alive and well in the city of the North,* Elington thought.

The columns of riders trotted down the avenue, reminiscent of conquers from ancient Rome, in the days of the glorious empire that ruled with an iron fist. As the soldiers clamored down the street, a loud crashing explosion was heard by Elington and the rest of the brigade.

"What was that?" asked Elington in a loud voice.

"I can't tell from here," Lockert answered.

"Maybe it was the arsenal blowing up before we get there, Captain Elington," joked one of the mounted infantry soldiers.

"That would be a jewel in our pocket, private."

"Keep riding. Keep riding! Hold steady and be prepared to take possible fire as we get close to the arsenal," Fincannon ordered.

"We're going to make it easily, major," Lockert said confidently.

"Stay confident, captain. I hope your optimism is relayed to the boys today," Fincannon said in a solemn tone, his arms folded.

*****

Philadelphia, July 4, 1863

Senator Robert Sumner and his daughter, Abigail, left their residence on Pine Street at mid-morning on the 4th of July. The senator tried to get to his office amidst the chaos of the Confederate invasion upon Philadelphia. His office temporarily moved to Broad Street, south of Center Square.

"What is going to happen, Father?" Abigail asked.

"I need to get to my staff and my office to get the latest intelligence information on the number of troops and the leaders involved in the invasion of our beloved city. Do you understand, Abby?"

"What can I do to help you?"

"Nothing, Abigail! Let's get to the office."

"I understand, Father."

"Do you think Harrison and Danny are in the city as we speak, Father?"

"I can't worry about it now. There is too much to be done in order to protect the city from the arduous task before us."

"But Father, they are family."

"You don't have to remind me of that."

People rushed by the senator and his daughter. The couple continued their conversation concerning the invasion and the fact of family possibly involved from the Confederate side.

Many citizens cared only for their material wealth and possessions. They loaded wagons and carriages heavy with their worldly goods. Other citizens cared for their children and tried their best to comfort the little ones amidst the commotion and havoc of the day. Then there were the completely self-absorbed, the self-centered who only cared for themselves and absolutely no one else. Their own safety and their own property overrode everything. You could see it on their faces. Their egocentric pride and pompous attitudes permeated the atmosphere in parts of the city.

Senator Sumner finally made it to his office, Abigail still by his side. The environment was in a state of disarray. Papers were being passed around to state senators and state assemblymen. Dispatches were being destroyed. A map of the Gettysburg area hung on the wall in the middle of two windows. The windows enabled a good view of Broad Street from the building where Senator Sumner had his temporary office. A telegraph machine dominated the sound of the room along with the voices of politicians trying to make sense out of what was happening to their Pennsylvanian city. Governor Curtain sent orders to General Napoleon Dana to defend the entrances to the city and to secure the arsenals, naval yard and imperative arms-producing factories. Dana was unable to accomplish the tasks set before him. The militia units he commanded were inexperienced and jumped at a chance to run from hardened Confederate veterans, soldiers who fought in many battles and who gained experience in killing.

"Senator Sumner!" A deep, powerful resonating voice echoed from across the office. It was Judge Jacob Bixley of the Philadelphia Trial Courts and a good friend of Senator Robert Sumner of Pennsylvania.

"Judge Bixley, I am glad you are here. Do you have any intelligence information from your sources in the Union Army? We need information pertaining to the logistics, numbers and leaders of this armed-bandit invasion!"

"As a matter of fact, senator, I do. Let's step into one of the offices so I can talk to you in private."

"Certainly, judge."

"Abby, make yourself useful while I speak to Judge Bixley. Help out with sorting those telegraph reports from Gettysburg and Ardmore."

"No, Father. I want to hear what the judge has to say to you."

"Now, Abby, you know quite well that official government business is a matter for the politicians and not their children. Come on, Abby, you know I can't invite you to a meeting concerning intelligence information. I will get fired."

"Fired by who, Father? Senators don't get fired. They just seem to fade away when they're not useful any longer, or for that matter, wealthy any longer."

"That is an unfair statement to make, especially at this time, Abby."

"Too bad, Father. It expresses how I feel about the government and this whole darn war. Now we have been invaded!"

"I will be out shortly."

Sumner entered the office where Judge Bixley was waiting with papers in hand, ready to divulge data imperative to the story of what was going to happen in the city. The judge wore a black suit with a white shirt and his customary woven and polished cotton bow tie with a turned-down shirt collar. He was an abundant man of sixty, mild-mannered and powerful in city politics. Sumner wore his favorite brown suit with his beige shirt and black cravat.

"Sit down, Robert."

"How have you been these past months?" Senator Sumner asked.

"I have been sick over this war, this Civil War that threatens to destroy the very country our founders worked to create, Robert."

"Yes, I agree. I have been agonizing over my grandson. Abby's son Jesse signed up to fight for the Union, the 83rd Pennsylvania Infantry. He was apparently wounded at Fredericksburg, but there has been no substantiated information on his whereabouts. We don't know if he died of his wounds under that incompetent General Burnside, or if he is still recovering from his wounds somewhere in a Union or Confederate hospital. Abby is haunted by the thought of Jesse being in one of the horrible Confederate prisoner of war camps."

"I did hear about Jesse and his brave display of courage and fortitude at Fredericksburg. The matter of your grandson is one I wanted to speak to you about, Robert. As hard as it will be, you can not let Abby know anything until Jesse's work is through."

"Jesse's work! I don't understand, judge."

"Jesse is alive. You need to know that information first, senator."

"What? Why couldn't I locate him with all of the connections I have in the Union armies? What is going on, Bixley?"

"All right, Robert. You need to compose yourself and calm down if I'm going to talk with you about these pressing matters. I warned you this would be hard."

"Tell me what's going on here."

"After the Battle of Fredericksburg, I secured the possession of Jesse and five other Union soldiers who performed service above and beyond their call of duty. I needed good, reliable people to work in the Intelligence Corps of the Union army. After the fiascoes of the McClellan intelligence blunders in the beginning of the war, General Winfield Hancock and President Lincoln met in Maryland after the battle of Antietam. Hancock sent a secret message to Lincoln requesting a private meeting with the president after McClellan refused to follow-up on finding the lost order. You know, 191. You know that whole story by now, right, Robert?

"Yes."

"Anyway, the president and Hancock decided to use their own intelligence force from the Union army ranks, recruiting young officers and enlisted men who were not tainted by the politics of war. Lincoln and Hancock wanted verifications of McClellan's intelligence for themselves. Hancock, especially, was distrustful of McClellan. Allen Pinckerton gathered intelligence for McClellan and the General relied heavily on those reports. This is where Jesse comes into play for his country. I know this is hard, Robert. I know your family has been split by this war. Harrison and your other grandson Daniel are fighting for the enemy. Is that still the case?"

"Yes, it is."

"Jesse was severely wounded in his left side. A piece of shrapnel tore into him pretty bad. His officers and friends testified to his valor on the field at Fredericksburg. He saved the lives of four men from the brigade his division was relieving. Anyway Robert, I got the best surgeons from Washington, D.C., to save him.

"I was contacted by President Lincoln to recruit six agents for intelligence gathering in the Secret Service of the United States government. These six agents would act independently from Allen Pinkerton, and report directly to General Hancock, President Lincoln, or to myself. Jesse recovered this past spring and he has tracked the movements of the Confederate army for the past three months. He also has specifically detailed the activities of these so-called Confederate raiders. Jesse was out in Tennessee and Missouri when General Robert E. Lee made his second attempted invasion into the North. Quantrill's raiders in Missouri, Moseby's cavalry raiders and now this guy by the name of Major Frederick Fincannon and the Titan Brigade are really causing major damage to the successful strategy of the Union cause. I needed good, loyal and intelligent men to carry out intelligence missions. Men of moral fortitude and conviction for the cause of the Union. Jesse is one good man and he knows what to do. Jesse and his partner have been given direct credit by the president for foiling at least three major raids between Kentucky and Ohio.

"Like I said before, Abby must not be informed about this right now, Robert. I know it will be hard, but we have to keep this information secret at this crucial moment in our history."

"I understand, judge. I am overwhelmed Jesse is alive and working for the cause of the Union, but what affect would there be if Abigail knew of this now? You talk like it could damage the security of the whole Union."

"One day, his mother will be proud of his service to the United States government after she learns of his intelligence work. It has to be later though, Robert."

"Will it damage the security of the Union?"

"The less people know of our executive intelligence service the better. That's all I have to say on the matter."

"I see." Senator Sumner didn't press the issue any further.

"In your capacity as a senator, Robert, and in your specialization with the army committees in Congress, you need to know about the data our intelligence sources have on the raiding force in the city, but you also need to know the information is fragmented and inconclusive. It could be of some value, though.

"First, the raiders are made up of at least 2,100 mounted infantry soldiers with an attached artillery unit. Second, Major Frederick Albert Fincannon is the officer leading the raiders. He is from the western theater of Confederate operations and Jesse's profile of his leadership qualities have been invaluable. Fincannon is not a Quantrill type personality, killing and looting for self-profit, but he is a methodical military strategist who knows how to motivate men. Third, the suspected target in Philadelphia is the Frankford Arsenal. This information cannot be substantiated. We got the data in this morning from one of our scouts riding in from the Harrisburg area who overheard Confederate mounted infantrymen talking about the arsenal when they had stopped near Lancaster yesterday. Civilians from the area were also interviewed and gave pertinent details of the Confederate operation they overheard. The brigade was able to secure a bridge to make it across the Susquehanna River after threatening Harrisburg."

"The Frankford Arsenal?"

"That's the information we have. Like I said, it can't be substantiated, but we have more militia stationed near and in the arsenal and the percussion factory is being dismantled as we sit here."

"Do you think there is enough time to secure the munitions we need from the Confederate threat, judge?"

"I don't know. We were really caught off guard by this invasion and the battle that took place at Gettysburg the last three days. Thanks to Generals Buford, Reynolds, Hancock and Philadelphia's own General Meade that we only have a raiding party in the city right now, senator, and not Lee's whole infamous Confederate army."

"He was a great man, John Reynolds," Sumner said solemnly.

"I agree, Robert; but what are we to do?"

"Thank you for the information, especially concerning my grandson," Sumner said to Bixley.

"There's one more piece of information you need to be aware of, senator. Jesse Elington is now in Philadelphia. He and three of our main scouts have been ordered to feed intelligence data to General Dana in the city, General Couch in Harrisburg and General Hancock in the Gettysburg area concerning Confederate activity in and around Philadelphia. Jesse came in from Tennessee three days ago."

As the two men got up to leave the office, gunfire ripped and crackled down the south side of Broad Street. Confederate skirmishers were caught on the southern side of Center Square and were now engaging with portions of the 183rd and 186th Philadelphia Regiments, along with the 20th Philadelphia Cavalry. The units moved south, down from north Broad Street. The popping of the guns and the cries of the wounded caused further civilian distress. The Confederates took cover in residential buildings and began firing on a smaller arsenal near Broad and Market Streets and the area of Logan Square.

"It looks like the war has finally come to our city, Judge Bixley," Senator Sumner commented.

"Yes, it has, senator. Now is our chance to prove our abilities and strengths in the midst of attack."

The roaring, thunderous sounds of explosions filled the center of the city where the Titan Brigade passed. Factories, smaller arsenals and railroad equipment were being burned up and destroyed by Confederate cannon and explosives. Civilians were killed and wounded by the show of force. Echoes of gunfire caused sounds to magnify and at times it seemed guns of all sorts fired from all directions of the city. The Day of Judgment arrived for the people of Philadelphia.

*****

July 4, 1863
High Noon

The overcast day dispersed a long, gray remnant of war upon the city. A shadow of gloom and pessimism stretched as gray as a Confederate officer's uniform. Citizens were either apathetic and stoic, or they displayed emotions of anger and displeasure over the Southern presence.

Major Fincannon, Captain Elington and Captain Lockert continued to prod and push their brigade through the historic vestiges of the city. Resistance was still relatively light, but there was a constant peppering of gunfire directed at the brigade by both militia and civilian men.

The brigade continued up Frankford Avenue after turning off of Girard Avenue. The German and northern European culture was observed by the Confederate soldiers through the names of shops and merchant stores lining both sides of the avenue. Confederates felt at home among the familiar sights and smells of the immigrant populations laboring the factories and mills in and around the city. Sausages and other aromas of meats punctuated the air on the route, spilling out of processing factories. The scent of freshly cut wood was smelled by the soldiers from the many carpenter and furniture shops. Memories of boyhood and fathers accentuated the minds of the Confederate soldiers, bringing back for a moment the safety and comfort of home, where the industry of war and the business of destruction didn't exist.

"Keep riding steady, boys," Fincannon shouted. "We are almost to the target."

In a flash, the brigade halted in the middle of Frankford Avenue. A line of unexpected Union artillery was positioned across the avenue. Wheel to wheel, caisson to caisson, the guns and crews stood there guarding the approaches to Bridge and Tacony Streets where the arsenal was located.

"Dismount! Dismount!" Fincannon ordered in a hurried fashion. "Double lines! Double lines!"

The Confederate mounted soldiers now became infantry in order to take out the guns. The mission could be completed no other way.

Captain Elington ordered the 90th Tennessee and the 125th North Carolina Regiments to double lines across the avenue. The 91st Tennessee stood in reserve.

"Load those carbines, men," Elington ordered.

"Ready and aim," Captain Lockert ordered, assisting Elington.

"Fire! Fire!" yelled Elington.

In the same moment the Confederates fired their carbines, Union cannon opened a barrage of canister fire. Loud, thunderous echoes of gunfire reverberated through the streets. Confederates from the 90th Tennessee caught the brunt of the blast from the artillery. Thirty men were down, dead, or wounded. The Confederates kept up their fire. Four artillery crews were taken out on the Union side.

"Who is manning those guns?" yelled Major Fincannon.

"I don't know, sir!" Elington answered. "I thought hardly any guns were protecting the city, sir."

"I guess we got that information wrong."

"Are those fellows militia?" Elington asked.

"I guess they are, captain," Fincannon answered.

"The militia, Elington; they are supposed to be useless to the protection of this city," Captain Lockert said. "After all, that is what we were told by General Hill and General Lee.

"Time and circumstance can heavily change the gumption and courage of men, Lockert. Believe me, I have seen it take place on fields of battle."

"Fire!" Major Fincannon yelled over the conversing captains.

Many of the Union militia ran from their positions at the guns. It seemed they were starting to break apart in organization and in courage. The carbine fire was having a physical and mental affect on the green Union militia.

Men lay on the ground. Men cried in pain. Boys longed for loved ones back home in Tennessee and North Carolina. Soldiers died on the streets of Philadelphia.

The 5th North Carolina Artillery Battalion caught up to the infantry units spread across Frankford Avenue. Battery D made its way into position seventy-five yards from the Union battle line. By this time the number of Confederate guns dwindled to eight. Two were lost since entering Philadelphia from Harrisburg and Lancaster. Two guns were lost at the bridge in Harrisburg.

Union fire raked the Confederate infantry line. Battery D's guns were unlimbered and positioned. One Confederate gun exploded near Danny. Harrison saw the incident and ran over to see if his son was all right.

"Danny!" Harrison yelled.

"I'm all right, Father. Go back to your position. They need a leader over there. Peyton and I can handle this battery of guns."

"You have to be careful, son. Your mother will not handle two Elington casualties in the same war. Do you hear me, boy?"

"Yes, sir, captain."

Reports of artillery fire surrounded the area of Frankford Avenue. The white smoke and sulfuric odor of the powder inundated the street. Citizens fled the scene. Horses were being killed and torn to pieces, whining and crying in desperate pain and agony. Sharpshooters were entering the melee of artillery and infantry. From the windows of factories and tenement buildings, Union snipers systematically took out Confederate soldiers from the Titan Brigade.

The stinging and piercing musket fire from the Union sharpshooters rang out time and again. Confederates fell in the street. Some were shot right between the eyes or in the back of the head. These shooters meant business and they weren't planning on taking prisoners.

"Keep up your fire, men!" Elington ordered from behind the fragmented line of the 125th North Carolina.

"What are we going to do next, major?" Lockert asked.

"We have to break through somehow, captain. We have to get past that artillery line, or we are doomed."

"Captain Elington, get Battery D to aim their guns at each of the Union guns and then fire simultaneously using canister. We have to put the fear of God in those boys and clear that line."

"Yes, sir, major!"

"The sharpshooters are starting to take a toll. Captain Lockert, get some of our best shooters to spot where those Union sharpshooters are located and have them blast away at their positions."

"I don't know who our best shooters are, sir."

"Well find out, captain; now!"

Blasts of shrapnel sprayed through the air. The men of both sides felt the humid conditions. The heat of the day continued to bring on exhaustion and sickness as it always did in battle. Explosions of powder and musket fire shrieked back and forth across the lines, still seventy-five yards apart. There was no relief from the fire of war. The Titan Brigade dwindled in number. The brigade was down to about 1,400 men. The present skirmish produced high casualties through sustained artillery fire upon the ranks of the Confederates. 300 were killed and 500 men wounded since entering Philadelphia five hours before. It was now one o'clock in the afternoon and the Titan Brigade had no hope of receiving reinforcements.

On this July 4th, Robert E. Lee and his three corps of infantry were on the retreat back to Virginia. The bloodstained fields of Gettysburg, Pennsylvania, were washed by driving rains. General Lee lost hope for a complete infantry victory on Union soil. He still had the welfare of the Titan Brigade on his mind. The brigade envisioned a possible victory on Union soil despite the devastating Confederate defeat at Gettysburg. Lee kept couriers traveling back and forth to monitor the situation.

"Fire! Fire! Fire!" ordered Corporal Danny Elington.

The driving, deadly impact of the 5th North Carolina's guns staggered soldiers on both sides of the battle zone. Officers in Battery D observed the deadly affects of their artillery. It was getting through to the enemy guns.

"Those militia have to break soon," Captain Elington said to Fincannon. The major dismounted his horse.

"Tell Battery D officers to sustain fire for a few more minutes," ordered Fincannon. "I haven't heard or felt Union fire for about a good ten minutes. What's happening over there? I can't see with all of the darned smoke." -

From the Confederate artillery line one more fatal salvo was hurled at the Union cannon and crew. Minutes passed and the smoke cleared. Major Fincannon, Captain Elington, Captain Lockert and the remaining men of the Titan Brigade couldn't believe what they saw. Every militia crew member on the Union line was dead. There was no movement from the stilled bodies. This engine of battle was complete in it's destruction and human carnage. Without hesitation or contemplation, Major Fincannon gave his orders:

"Charge! Charge!"

The brigade clamored forward, some not able to make the attack upon the dead enemy. Members of the brigade captured three artillery pieces still intact. Danny's battery was now up to eleven guns. The captured guns were three ten-pounder Parrott guns. At 890 pounds each and a firing range of 2,000 yards, these guns were a welcome addition to the Titan Brigade. Horses were drawn, gun carriages turned and hitched and caissons limbered to advance to the next stop, the arsenal.

Union sharpshooters continued their assault on the Titan Brigade. As one group of Confederate soldiers tried to limber the captured cannon, three of them were shot, hitting the street hard and cold.

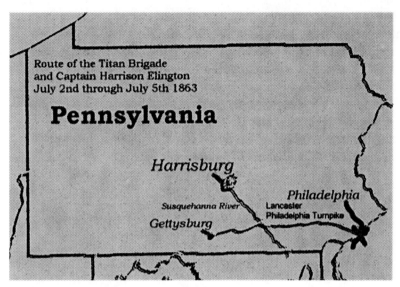

Route of the Titan Brigade
and Captain Harrison Elington
July 2nd through July 5th 1863

Pennsylvania

Harrisburg

Philadelphia

Susquehanna River Lancaster
Philadelphia Turnpike

Gettysburg

"Men! Mount and form columns," Major Fincannon ordered.

The brigade tried to reform, but it took longer than usual due to the debris and bodies on the street. Burning spokes from destroyed artillery and gunpowder scythed the air. Men desperately reached for canteens and rations from their haversacks, slowing the formations further. Confederate officers lost their patience.

"Move it, boys!"

"Columns! Columns!"

"We can't stay here all day!"

"Let's ride; columns."

The heavily burdened brigade of mounted infantry finally began to move slowly and tiredly. Run-down from hours of riding, wondering, planning and fighting, the men seemed unable to go on.

Fatigue became a brother to the soldiers.

The desperate feelings of wanting rest and vacation haunted their spirits. Home was the common goal now.

Harrison Elington longed for home since the beginning of the war. Wanting to be with his wife, sons and friends back in Caldwell County drove him to obtain an end to the war. All soldiers wanted the end to come. They were disgusted and sickened with the killing and wounding, the lack of food and rest, and the endless traveling from one place to another.

The Confederates ventured on the last phase of their mission. Thoughts of home stuck in their minds. Family, home cooked meals and children laughing filtered out the death and destruction for a few minutes, but contemporaneously motivating the soldiers to finish the mission on the arsenal. Elington could see it in their eyes. Determination was at the forefront, and now was the moment of absolute truth upon the Confederacy and its way of life.

The arsenal required destruction, a mark left upon Philadelphia by the Confederate States of America.

The hope of a nation rested in the hands of the few left from the Titan Brigade under Major Frederick Fincannon.

– Chapter 23 –
Battle is Terrible and Fearful

July 4, 1863: 2:30 p.m.

"My God in heaven. Help us to survive this mission and help us to succeed for the cause many have died for. Please, Jesus, direct our paths and follow us in your Spirit of truth."

Major Fincannon said the prayer out loud as the brigade made its way onto Tacony Street where it intersected with Bridge Street. So far in the mission to Philadelphia, Fincannon had not displayed spiritual qualities to his men. However, in this time of danger and uncertainty, the major made it known he wasn't ashamed of the gospel and of the beliefs he held from a small child, when his mother sang to him the great hymns of the Christian faith.

The incessant mental anguish of battle persisted upon the men of the Titan Brigade. Not quite 1,400, the brigade rode into position near the arsenal. The 91st Tennessee Regiment headed south down Bridge Street and halted at the front gate of the arsenal on the left. Frankford Creek flowed at the end of Bridge Street. The creek merged with the Delaware River to the North of the arsenal grounds.

It was quiet at the front gate. Signs of Union militia were absent and the grounds inside the arsenal, beyond the stone wall, were silent. A row of six cannon, probably a battery of Union defense, stood under shade-giving trees east of the officers' quarters and parade ground square. Neatly stacked decorative cannon balls were piled in front of the artillery pieces, giving the place the feel of a museum. Every Confederate knew this wasn't a museum.

Fincannon, Elington, Lockert and the 91st Tennessee entered the gate and upon the enemy's intimate resource, a United States government arsenal.

Captain Elington and Major Fincannon knew the commandant of the arsenal, Major Theodore Laidley, was an innovative engineer of arms manufacturing. Laboratories for the continued study of ballistics, chemical reactions and metallurgy were built north of the original arsenal building. The original arsenal structure stood at the north end of the parade grounds and north of the commandants quarters. Laidley constructed a machine shop to enhance the production of vital machinery needed at the arsenal in spite of the foot-dragging of private armament manufacturers. Drills, lathes, pressers and planers powered by a 150-horsepower Corliss steam engine were all housed in the T-shaped building located north of the original arsenal building. Laidley sustained the production of the percussion cap in the H-shaped building, which sat west of the machine shop. Laidley ordered the production of 250 million percussion caps a year. The destruction of this resource could damage the Union cause beyond repair.

Elington knew the intelligence information like the back of his hand, studying reports every chance he got; the shape of the buildings, the location of key targets in the arsenal and the entrance points from the streets and ports.

"Get Battery D up as quick as possible," Fincannon ordered to Captain Lockert. "I want fire placed on the primary targets of the machine shop, the percussion factory—over there to the left of the machine shop—and then we'll blow those laboratory buildings behind the original arsenal."

"Yes, sir, major!"

"Do it, Lockert! Forget the 'Yes, sirs' for today, will you."

Lockert scurried off to get the ten guns. The pernicious guns of Battery D became vital to the success of the arsenal operation.

"Bring up the guns! Bring up those guns!" yelled Lockert to Corporal Danny Elington, who happened to be leading the limbered battery. "Take Bridge Street right to the main entrance of the arsenal. The major has orders for you."

"All right, captain; we're coming, we're coming."

Danny guided his artillery pieces along with the officers from the unit. Battery D lined up their guns to get into the gate. Fincannon wanted the pieces placed in the open square of the parade grounds near the officers' quarters and houses. It was hard for the artillerists to maneuver through the columns of idle soldiers from the 90th and 125th Regiments.

From an area across the opposite side of Bridge Street and directly across from the main arsenal gate, a lunging thunderbolt of hot metal and fire belched forth and into the ranks of the Titan Brigade. The area south of the arsenal grounds was characterized by a dirt road that divided into two roads on the approach to Bridge Street. Barricades of wood and tree trunks stood in an open field. Constructed by an unknown force, the entrenchments hid artillery and infantry now firing at the Titan Brigade.

Two Confederate regiments, the 90th Tennessee and the 125th North Carolina, were still lining Bridge Street and Tacony Street when the firing began. The 91st Tennessee was inside the gate on the parade grounds, trying to guide the 5th North Carolina Artillery into firing positions. Other members of the 91st went on a search into the artillery storage buildings to confiscate the Schenkl artillery shells the Confederates planned to fire on the targeted buildings.

"Where the devil is that firing coming from?" asked Captain Elington.

"It's an ambush, captain," answered one of the lieutenants in the 91st.

The firing from the cannon and infantry continued upon the Titan Brigade. Men shot from their horses fell to the ground after the initial barrage of fire.

Peyton Caldwell looked over toward the last Confederate gun making its way into the gate of the arsenal and he saw the distinctive gray uniform of a man from his battalion lying on the ground. He saw a few of the members of the 125th North Carolina trying to care for the man who was down after the barrage of fire from across the street. Peyton looked closer and began to run back toward the gate to exit the arsenal, for he was already safely inside and sheltered from the enemy fire.

"Danny! Danny!" Peyton yelled at the top of his lungs.

He saw now that it was Danny Elington lying on the ground, shot through the chest by a piece of artillery shrapnel. Danny didn't move an inch. Blood saturated his gray uniform and his limp body was held up by two young men from the 125th. Peyton sat down on the ground by his friend's side and called for him to respond.

"Danny! Can you hear me, boy? Say something, you braggart, you show off. You think you're going to become a dead hero before me? Is that what you think, Elington?"

Another cascading round of fire smashed into the brigade at the main gate entrance, spreading all the way back west on Bridge Street. There were no alternatives except to dismount and begin firing into the hidden Union horde.

Horses dispersed from the scene, shot and felled in death and torturous wounds. Blood sprayed from all direction as tens of soldiers fell in front of the arsenal wall. Officers in the ranks ordered the Confederate soldiers to fire back with their carbines, but it seemed the soldiers were too disoriented, too tired and now too hopeless. Dead horses were now used as barricades themselves. The loyal animals that had taken the Confederate soldiers to their destination faithfully now reaped nothing but death.

"Talk to me, Danny! Say something to me. I am your friend." Peyton continued to beg his friend to respond.

"He's dead, Peyton," one of the members of the 5th North Carolina snapped.

"He can't be dead; not after all we've been through; this secret mission, journeying into Philadelphia and fighting in every major battle in this stinking war."

He began to spit out saliva from his mouth and nose, becoming upset and sickened by the death of his friend. Tears filled his eyes. Anger filled his mind.

"I hate the Confederacy! I hate the Union!" Peyton yelled out. "This whole war is a mistake. How can Americans be killing Americans? Over what? Over what? Somebody tell me. Give me a stinking answer now!"

Harrison heard the commotion coming in through the main gate area. He heard someone yelling over the sounds of the firing, fusillading back and forth across Bridge Street. Harrison got on his horse and galloped to the main gate and saw what he never wanted to see in his lifetime.

"No! No! Not Danny! My God, what has happened here?"

Men tried to restrain Harrison, but he simply fell to the ground, from his mount, and sobbed along with Peyton. Grief stabbed his heart like a saber. As a father he was supposed to protect his sons. He failed. *Jesse may be dead also,* he thought in his sorrow, *and now Danny is dead, gone forever. This conflict is from the depths of hell itself.*

"Ahh! ..."

Harrison let out a tremendous yell of agony from the ground near the gate of the arsenal. Men from all of the regiments tried to console their captain who led them well as part of Major Fincannon's staff. Since his performance at Harrisburg, many of the soldiers grew fond of Harrison and Danny for their unhesitating valor and decision making in the face of the enemy. Many of the men knew what Harrison had been through on the first day at Gettysburg, and they respected him for wanting to go the extra mile to help the Confederacy become a legitimate, sovereign state.

The annoying and constant firing kept up outside the arsenal. The thick smoke, flashes of fire, broken muskets and carbines and the faces of desperation among the waiting and fired-upon soldiers continued in the midst of the heartaches.

Major Fincannon rode up to the scene of where Danny had fallen. He said nothing. His expression showed hopelessness. He turned and left Harrison to mourn. Riding back into the arsenal, rounds of gunfire streamed past him. Fincannon ordered the rest of the 5th North Carolina Artillery to take their positions on the parade grounds.

The cannon pieces were lined up as to bypass the arsenal building to the north of the grounds. The guns were unlimbered. Schenkl shells, rounded up by the members of the 91st, were loaded. Peyton got back to his battery of guns after making sure Danny's body was securely set in an area of the arsenal where the body might be retrieved later. The original range of 250 yards had to be narrowed now that the brigade was under an ambush attack from across the street. The percussion, fused three-inch ordnance Schenkl shells, provided a good and efficient explosive.

The Union militia artillery fire coming over the wall was targeted on the Confederate cannon moving into position. Three Confederate guns were knocked out of action immediately, crew members hit by shrapnel and case shot. Major Fincannon went over to take command of the guns himself.

"Let's go, boys. You know the targets. Get ready to fire before we all get blown up ourselves."

The men rallied to load their guns. Another blast from the Union guns crashed into the parade grounds. Grass flew up and pieces of sod sprayed dirty soil into the faces of the artillerists. At the moment the Union shells hit the ground, the Confederate guns opened fire.

Two Confederate guns made direct hits on the machine shop; the T-shaped building the artillerists had studied since the mission had been detailed to them back near Gettysburg. A massive explosion riveted the arsenal grounds and the village of Frankford. For a few minutes the Union fire from across Bridge Street had stopped. Except for the sound of crackling coming from the burning machine shop, it was relatively quiet. Another blast of fire from the Confederate guns bellowed into the air and hit the percussion factory, the H-shaped building next to the machine shop. Remnants of the white-colored stucco and red brick buildings flushed toward some of the artillerists. White smoke from the cannon and white powdered cement materials coiled up into the gray sky and into the air around the village of Frankford.

"Back the guns out of the parade grounds," Fincannon ordered hastily. "Redeploy the guns over to the area of the main gate."

"Yes, sir," the major of the battery answered.

"I want the main arsenal building blown next, major."

"I know. I'm one step ahead of you, Fincannon."

"Good."

Harrison Elington was able to leave the lifeless body of his son. Peyton and two other members of the 125th North Carolina helped Harrison move Danny's body into the main officers' quarters on the south end of the parade grounds. He saw the fire burning upon the targeted buildings and watched as Fincannon ordered Danny's artillery battery over to the area of the main gate. He heard the fire continue from Bridge Street. By now, most of his brigade had made it into the arsenal and had found some safety behind the high stone wall of the structure. Bodies were piled outside the arsenal wall on Bridge Street. Not only his son, but the sons of many Southerners had died this horrible day in the city of the first revolution.

A peculiar sense of anger manifested itself over Harrison. He saw the carnage outside the gate perpetrated by a faceless enemy that still couldn't be seen or identified. Elington went over to the 125th North Carolina and ordered the colonel to form a double battle line outside of the gate and back onto Bridge Street.

"We're going to go over across the street and break apart their cowardly, faceless line. Do you hear me, colonel?"

"Yes, Captain Elington."

"I know you outrank me, colonel, but military protocol doesn't mean a darn thing on this mission, man."

"I know that, sir, and I know you are part of Fincannon's staff. That's enough rank for me, captain."

The Confederate artillery lined themselves into position to take out three more targets before a retreat was ordered from the arsenal. Major Fincannon saw Elington lining the 125th up for a double line attack. He made his way over to Elington.

"What are you doing, captain?"

"I'm going to take that stinking line out for good. They have inflicted too many casualties this day, major."

"It'll be suicide trying to take out their guns."

"I think most of their gun crews have already been taken out. They're breaking as we speak. Let's get on with it, Fincannon. We have to get out of here before more militia reinforcements come down to this arsenal and we'll really be in for it."

"I will get Captain Lockert to assist in the attack. He is over with the 91st, trying to get rations and water for the ride out of here."

"All right. He will be of good use here. Thank you, major."

Lockert came galloping up to Elington. Harrison told him to get off of his horse, or he was going to be killed in a hurry.

"The men of the 125th made their line outside of the wall covered by the 90th Tennessee and two guns from the 5th. The 5th was firing shells blindly over the walls, estimating the distance to hit their Union targets.

The hissing and whizzing of Minie balls and projectiles filled the air outside the gate. The tired, thirsty and bloodshot soldiers of the 125th did everything they could to focus their attention and aim at the enemy across the street. The colonel of the regiment took the traditional command position at the center of the regiment's line. Lockert took the left flank and Elington took command of the right flank. The regiment had about 400 soldiers left. It started the mission with 730 men.

Elington advised the colonel to first have his men kneel down to take initial cover and then send a volley of carbine fire toward the enemy.

The colonel yelled the order, "Ready! Aim! Fire!"

Battle is terrible and fearful, Elington thought as he saw the impact of the directed volley hit the barricades of the enemy. Giant splitters from the wooden entrenchments and tree trunks burst into the air. For the first time Elington saw the blue uniforms of the faceless enemy that had killed his son. Injured and dead Union militia from Philadelphia scoured upon the dirt, dust and particles on the ground. The twisted bodies of young boys from Pennsylvania were strewn across the street in high numbers. The hard-fought skirmish of the past two hours took its toll on the militia as well as the Confederate Titan Brigade.

A rumble of cannon fire came and lifted out of the arsenal walls, clobbering the Union line once again.

"Charge! Charge! Charge!" Elington shouted. "Let's get them now, men; they're breaking. Kill them all! Kill them all, for Danny's sake."

The double battle line of the 125th charged across the street, the rebel yell protruding from the gray and butternut hoard, blue and beige colors flying high. The once tired and dejected soldiers of a few minutes ago came to a new life of motivated tenacity. They fired their carbines as they charged at the double quick step. The fire was overwhelming to the Union militia and the bluebellies started to retreat further south from the arsenal.

Contemporaneously, a unit of the 6th Philadelphia Cavalry came storming from the south along Tacony Street. Sabers drawn and carbines firing at will, the 125th slammed right into the cavalry. Bodies flew, and tangled soldiers tried to cut themselves loose from moving horses. Men of the 125th were dragged for minutes.

The right side of the 125th's line fought and occupied the cavalry, trying to take cover where there was none in the open space and dirt roads across from the arsenal.

"Form your lines, boys. Dress on the colors, men of old Carolina!" Elington shouted amidst the firing and yelling of the soldiers in heated battle. The distinct blue and beige flag of the brigade snapped in the breeze. Elington's men held against the charging but inexperienced cavalry unit. Union men in blue were mowed down by the carbine fire of the 125th.

Meanwhile, the left flank of the 125th had gotten separated from the center and right portions of their line. The men on the left flank under Lockert were now heading, on their own, toward the remnants of the original Union militia line and their wooden entrenchments. This was the dreaded line that ambushed the attackers of the arsenal earlier in the day. Steadily, Captain Lockert directed his 150 men toward the remaining defenders, sitting alone in the open ground of the southern side of Bridge Street.

"Steady, boys," Lockert ordered. "Hold your fire until we are closer to the scum."

"Fire!" he then ordered.

"Charge!"

The left flank of the 125th clobbered the Union militia, who were still trying to defend themselves from the revenge of the Confederates. The beating the Confederates took for two long hours near the arsenal sparked the adrenaline needed to counterattack.

Fires raged up into the sky. Soldiers from both sides littered the grounds in and around the Frankford Arsenal. Black and white smoke coiled up into the gray skies over Philadelphia. Hell overtook part of the city. Men killed each other without hesitation or regret. The men of the North and the men of the South entered upon new carnages and desolations this 4th of July in the "Disunited States of America;" the former nation conceived in liberty four-score and seven years prior to the Southern invasion into Pennsylvania by Captain Harrison Elington and his comrades.

The 5th North Carolina and their three remaining artillery pieces fired at the old original arsenal building, sending the structure into thousands of sections. Major Theodore Laidley's house and officer's quarters were the next target of the Confederate battery. Windows shattered, pulverized upon the ground. Windows had also shattered earlier in the day in the village of Frankford, when the two massive explosions of the machine shop and the percussion cap factory occurred. Fincannon finally ordered fire placed upon the large U-shaped storage building. This monstrous unit was closest to the Delaware River.

All three of the 5th's guns let out a salvo of fire and when the shells hit the U-shaped facility, the loudest explosion of the war occurred. No one on either side had felt or seen such a destructive eruption of black smoke and yellow fire. The building must have been storing powder. The DuPont Company of Delaware, which had supplied the arsenal with quantities of powder, used the Delaware River as a convenient transportation route for delivery of the product. Writhing billows of smoke rose into the sky over Philadelphia. Men in the 91st Tennessee were killed or wounded when the backlash of debris hit them from the explosions. Minor aftershocks rumbled through the arsenal grounds and beyond.

The Confederates sparked much damage on their enemy. The machines of war were destroyed. Could this mean an abrupt end to the conflict of brutal civil war? Could this attack convince the Peace Democrats in Washington and especially in Pennsylvania to sue for peace and cessation of hostilities? Could Harrison go home for good after his service to his country? Could he at least be with Abigail and find out the fate of his son Jesse?

Could the engine of battle forever cease in its mechanical determination over the human spirit?

The 125th fought on as the afternoon of the 4th ticked away. Elington, tired and worn, hungry and thirsty, kept up the fight against the 6th Philadelphia Cavalry.

"Keep those guns on those blue devils from hell. They are all to blame for the death of Danny. None are innocent any longer."

"Captain, I think they are trying to flank our present position," a sergeant yelled from the middle of the line.

"Yes, they are, captain," a private concurred.

"Hold steady! Dress this line for the honor of the South," Elington ordered in a controlled rhythm.

The cavalry made a charge at the 125th's right flank. Horseman yelled and screamed to take the line and destroy the Rebs. The 125th held their position until the faces of the young militia were seen clearly by the Confederates.

"Fire!" Elington shouted. "Give them the hot lead!"

Horsemen fell in great numbers from the ranks of the cavalry regiment. The same scene, repeated so many times in three years of war, had now begun to harden the consciences and hearts of the Southern soldiers. It didn't matter any longer that Union soldiers died. They were the enemy and they had to be eliminated, especially on this mission, for the actions done upon the enemy on its own soil could turn the tide of the war.

A trigger was pulled from a lone horseman trying to renew the flanking maneuver toward Elington and the 125th. The billows of smoke saturated the air behind the lone rider. The carbine round plunged into Harrison Elington's right upper arm. He went down in pain for the second time in the war. Not since Malvern Hill, in old Virginia, had he felt the burning pain of metal penetrate his body. Harrison fell to the ground at the shock and dismay of his men from the left part of the 125th's line. The men were following his impeccable leadership and courage through the dark ravages of battle and death. The men started to rely on Elington. His leadership was of top quality and his character of supreme value to the soldiers of the South.

Harrison lay face up on the ground. The enemy cavalry ceased its flank attack and now all attacks stopped. The lone Union rider was shot down by men in the regiment. The pain of the wound aggravated Elington. In his hot anger, he got up from the ground, told the four private soldiers helping him to get out of his way, and he proceeded to go back to the arsenal gate. He began taking Union prisoners captured by Lockert's side of the line and he told them to line up against the cold stone wall of the arsenal. His arm bleeding, he took his Colt Navy revolver out of his holster, checked the caps on the cones and proceeded to shoot, at point blank range, three Union prisoners of war.

"You filthy scum, you will pay one at a time for the destruction of our way of life in the South, for our lost family members and for my son Danny you killed today." He yelled at the fallen men and the Union men standing by, watching the scene play out.

In a mad rage, Harrison started to fire the gun into the air until the remaining three bullets were spent. The three Union militia soldiers were dead. The men of the brigade looked at Harrison and didn't know what to make of the episode. At times they felt like doing the same thing, becoming the judge and jury of the criminals; the Northern criminals who had illegally confiscated the economy and culture of the peaceful South.

Captain Lockert ran over to Harrison, grabbed the gun and lectured him on civility in war toward prisoners. Major Fincannon harshly ordered Elington to stop his execution of the prisoners, or he would be dismissed from his command for the rest of the mission. The mission was now a matter of getting home and back to the Army of Northern Virginia. Fincannon knew he needed the aid of his captain and he wanted Elington to listen to him before anything else happened.

Elington gave up his spirit of uncontrolled anger and came back to his normal state of mind, the state of mind that had produced a decent father, a grand husband and a great officer in the army of the South. He again fell to the ground, bleeding from his right arm. He sat against the stone wall of the arsenal behind him as the buildings burned and citizens started to come over from the village of Frankford. He said nothing more and took the aid of the surgeon who attended his wounds. He had to get to Abby. She became his only hope. The only thing standing in his way for peace of mind and to see his world maintained in the South was to get out of Philadelphia with Abby.

It was six in the evening, July 4, 1863.

– Chapter 24 –
Escape from the Northern Clench

July 4, 1863

The soldiers of the Titan Brigade assembled for the ride out of the city. By seven in the evening, on the 4th of July, the brigade had been cut down to 800 men. The severely wounded were left behind. There were no ambulances attached to the brigade. Of the 600 casualties at the arsenal, about half were dead, still piled in front or inside the gates.

Peyton Caldwell and three other remaining members of the 5th North Carolina Artillery made their way back into one of the storage buildings and retrieved Corporal Danny Elington's body.

Harrison mounted his horse after the surgeon tended to his arm wound. His blood loss was placed under control and he was ready to make his way out of the city. He felt weak and faint of heart. He chewed tobacco Lockert had given him to calm his nerves.

Peyton wrapped the body of his close friend in a plaid blanket. One of the men from the 125th North Carolina supplied the blanket. The body was then placed on the caisson of one of the three remaining guns of Battery D. Danny traveled with his battalion one more time before his body left the confines of the mortal world. The three-inch ordnance gun Danny had fired so many times, and ironically his favorite piece in the battalion, now carried its owner to a final rest, a rest from the desolations of war.

I will miss you, Peyton thought. *You were my rock of strength in all we've been through.* Tears filled Peyton's eyes, his face became red and irritated from him rubbing his eyes. He was thirsty. When veteran soldiers went into battle, Danny had noticed on occasion that they became oblivious to the passage of time, their sweat had a different scent to it, their will to survive drove their thinking and food and water became unimportant. When the battle ended, though, the soldier longed for a drink of cold icy water, refreshing the body from the heat of battle.

The over-worn brigade members once again formed their two-column riding pattern. Gray uniforms were saturated with sweat, blood and tears. Matted, dirty hair, frosted in dust and grime from the hours of fighting and hours of riding, made the men look like migrant workers instead of trained soldiers.

The area of the arsenal, where the attack and the fighting had taken place, was a literal battlefield unto itself. Even though the hills and fields were missing from this fought-over terrain, the scars and blemishes of battle lingered in an intoxicating fashion. Here, there stood no rocky hills like Little Round Top, or bloody cornfields like at Antietam Creek. However, a stone wall, an open field stacked with wooden entrenchments and a street in a city stood as monuments to an urban battle fought as hard and with as many casualties as other battles fought in the past three years of civil war.

Philadelphia would be forever blistered by the invasion of the Confederate brigade. Not since 1777, when a British Army of 3,000 under General William Howe attacked Philadelphia, had the city been invaded by an enemy army.

*****

Major Fincannon, his arms folded and standing next to his black mount, turned back to look down Tacony Street. The brigade proceeded out from Bridge Street to even out its columns. Captain Harrison Elington and Captain Nathan Lockert sat on their horses, bloodied and exhausted. Elington's arm throbbed in pain and all he could think about now was the fate of the rest of his family.

Fincannon looked north and saw the billows of black smoke coiling up from the rear of the Frankford Arsenal. He looked upon the bodies wearing blue, gray and butternut, twisted and mangled on the ground. He turned and saw Danny's body set upon the caisson of his favorite artillery piece. More citizens continued to converge on the arsenal from the northern ends of Tacony Street. The quagmire portrayed on this day seemed hopeless and full of portentous apathy. *The destruction in human and property costs of the past four days has been frightening,* the major thought. He stared at the arsenal one last time before mounting his faithful black horse.

"Forward, brigade," he ordered.

*****

The columns rode through the streets of Philadelphia, tracking the route they took earlier in the day.

Elington bounced up and down in his saddle holding his arm in pain and holding back tears for his son. He couldn't hold back. As the men of the South trotted toward their exit of the city, Harrison cried in silent mourning for his youngest son. Tears welled up, his eyes became bloodshot and his breathing became uneven. He silently asked God to forgive him for not caring properly for his sons in time of war. The old agitations of loyalty swelled his mind once again. Harrison asked himself the main question of his life: *How will I explain this invasion and the death of Danny to Abigail? How will she ever forgive me for invading the north and getting my son killed? If this war does not end after these battles in Pennsylvania, what shall my loyalties be to, if anything?*

His tapping hand slapped against his leg. Elington was nervous over the fate of Abby. He knew she was probably still in the city with her father. He wanted to get to her desperately. The brigade made its way back onto Broad Street and was getting ready to turn right onto Market Street to cross the bridge over the Schuylkill River and then out of Pennsylvania for good.

Captain Elington rode beside Major Fincannon. Elington looked as though he had been through hell. Mentally and physically he was ready to break down. He needed sleep and he needed to know his wife was all right.

"Major, let me divert down South Broad Street when we get to Centre Square. I need to stop by my father-in-law's house to see if my wife is all right and to tell her I am still alive."

"No, Harrison. I can't slow our progress. We have to get out of this city before we get trapped by other militia units who are most likely tracking our movements. Besides, you are in no condition to make house calls right now."

"Sir! I have to make an attempt to contact Abigail. Through this whole bloody conflict she has shown patience and a willingness to put up with the dreaded horror of her family divided and her thoughts haunted by the possibility of death upon her sons and her husband."

"All of our families have had to endure that, captain."

"When we get to the intersection, I can ride down Broad Street to Pine Street; it isn't far. If you can give me two or three companion riders I know I can get in and out of there in a hurry."

"I have to refuse your request. I can't spare the lives of any more men in this brigade. You know the casualties we have incurred. No, captain!"

"All right, sir. I guess I can see your point."

"You'll surely get some furlough time for that wound if we make it out of here. You can then be reunited with your wife and hopefully your other son."

He heard the firing of the muskets ahead of the brigade on Broad Street, approaching Centre Square. There was a contingent of mixed militia regiments trying to block the route of the Titan Brigade. Fincannon ordered sabers drawn and the Confederates charged their harassers. As the front part of the brigade charged, screaming the old rebel yell, Elington halted his horse and dropped back in the column. He dashed down a side street, trying desperately to avoid being fired on from the militia. He yelled at his horse to ride on faster.

Elington made his way onto South Broad Street and rode furiously down the main artery of the city until arriving at Pine Street. Citizens yelled at him, seeing his dirtied gray uniform and identifying him as the enemy. Others went about their business, thinking the man was part of the city defenses who was carrying out his duty.

Captain Lockert and Major Fincannon saw Elington race away on his mount.

"Stop him! Stop him!" Fincannon yelled down the line to his officers.

"What is he doing?" Lockert asked.

"He wants to go and see if his wife is all right. She is here in the city with her father, the Honorable Robert Sumner, United States senator from the state of Pennsylvania."

"He's going to get himself shot and killed, major."

"I told him he couldn't go, but he decided to anyhow."

"You said a United States senator is down that street?"

"Yes, I did."

"He can be used as collateral."

"And what do you mean by that?"

"We can use him as a hostage for us. He can guarantee our safe and secure passage out of the city, major. That's what I mean."

"In time of war, captain, there is always the unpredictable. As much as I admire Captain Harrison Elington, our safe passage out of here is most important to us. We have acquired too many losses on this mission. We have to be able to leave this city without taking more."

"I agree, sir."

"Take five men with you and go see if the Senator is at home. He lives on 20th and Pine Streets. I'm sure you will see Harrison's horse in the vicinity of the house. Bring him to me and inform Harrison of our plan. Tell him his father-in-law will only be used as our security to get out of the city safely and then the senator will be released when we can rejoin our army and get back to Virginia."

"I am on it, major."

The charge quickly pushed the weak militia out of the way of the Confederate brigade. The serpentine columns made their way up Market Street toward the bridge. Citizens kept harassing the remnants of the Titan Brigade. Rocks and bottles were thrown maliciously at the men. Fincannon ordered his brigade to hold steady and continue riding amidst the torment.

Gunfire rang out again along Market Street. It seemed a volley of fire came from a multi-storied factory building on the left side of the street. Ten Confederate soldiers were knocked off of their horses by the gunfire. Cheers were heard from three of the windows on the upper floors of the building.

"Halt, brigade," Fincannon ordered. "Load your weapons, men, and form a defensive position here until we can proceed."

The men dismounted. Some served as holders for the horses and others took their defensive stance on Market Street. As the men waited for further direction, the brigade fired on the upper floors of the factory building and blew out the windows and some of the bricks where the last volley of shots was fired at them. Other soldiers walked up and down Market Street, confiscating fruits and juices, raw meats and vegetables, and taking wagon loads of breads. After all, Market Street in Philadelphia was a place where many food products were sold. It was where many Philadelphians made their livings and prospered economically.

Elington raced through the city blocks, making his way closer to 20th Street. He hoped Abigail would be at her father's house and not somewhere else. He desperately needed to know she was all right in the midst of the invasion.

*****

Elington gently knocked on the door of the house. No one came to the door. He knocked again. He thought he heard people conversing inside the house, but he wasn't sure. The commotions coming from the people on the streets outside muffled his ability to hear.

The door opened and Senator Robert Sumner appeared. A Union guard was behind him in the foyer of the house. The federal government provided most high-ranking government officials with protective guards since the invasion of Pennsylvania.

At first the senator didn't recognize the visitor in gray. Sumner squinted and then a look of confusion masked his face. The guard behind him asked the caller to identify himself. Harrison said nothing.

"Senator?" Harrison asked quietly.

"Harrison? Harrison, is it you, son?"

"Yes, it is, Robert."

"I can't believe my eyes. You mean you've been part of all this? This devilish invasion of our city."

The Union guard came forward to take hold of Elington. He held his right arm in pain. His uniform was bloodied and stained from the day's fight at the arsenal. Elington wore his black slouch hat and his Colt Navy revolver was in his left hand, hidden behind his thigh. He lifted the gun and fired at the Union guard, killing him instantly.

A woman screamed from the parlor of the house and she came running to the foyer, standing behind her father's safe presence. She peeked over his shoulder and glanced down at the body of the Union soldier on the front steps. She then looked up and saw the Confederate officer standing over the body. She could recognize Confederate officer's uniforms right away.

"My God! Harrison! Is it you?"

"Yes, it is."

"Father, let him into the house."

"Come in, son."

Abigail flung her arms around her husband. She couldn't believe it was him. They held each other for a couple of minutes, neither of them saying anything.

"What has happened?" Abigail asked.

He stood there in the parlor of the house he last saw when the United States was one country, when the innocence of youth and first love dominated everything in his life. He placed both of his hands over his face and rubbed his forehead and cheeks and then slowly dropped his hands to his side. He knew he had to break the news of the death of Danny, somehow, to Abigail. He seemed to forget about the wound in his arm until Abigail saw the blood and he felt the cutting pain.

"Have you been wounded again?" Abigail asked.

"Yes. My arm was hit when we were attacking the arsenal."

"It was you who attacked the Frankford Arsenal?"

"Not just me. I am part of a brigade of mounted infantry dispatched from Gettysburg. I was asked to be part of the mission by the high command of our army. Like I told you before, Abby, I had a feeling General Lee wanted to invade the North again after Sharpsburg. Well, we did it and paid a high price for it. Don't be upset with me."

"I am not upset with anyone. I can't fight any longer. The war has torn my ability to feel one way or the other. My sons are divided in their loyalty. I love them equally, so I will leave it in God's hands now. He knows what the outcome will be in this dirty conflict. He will guide us through. This is how I have decided to think, Harrison."

"They're all dead, Abby."

"Who? Who do you mean?"

"Alfred, Jackson, Thaddeus and even Lewis, that crazy hothead who always gave me a challenge as an officer."

"My God! My God, Harrison!"

Abigail fell on the couch of the parlor and began to weep, especially for Alfred Abshire, who she thought the world of and who she thought of as a third son. Mr. and Mrs. Abshire, back in Caldwell County, would be absolutely devastated for their only son.

"What a waste of lives," she sobbed. "What a waste of lives and young dreams, of marriages never consummated and children never born. Generations of Southerners will be forever lost over the stubborn ambitions of both the Confederate and Union leaders. Who do these people think they are to wash away the country's most promising people? Oh, I just can't get started on these bitter political feelings any longer." Her tears flowed down her smooth-skinned face.

"It's all right," Harrison said gently as he held his wife.

"It will never be all right again."

"Abby, there is one more thing I need to tell you."

"Not now, I can't think right. Later!"

At that moment a loud knock came at the front door. People were hollering and yelling outside on the street. Senator Sumner looked out his front window to see another Confederate officer on his front steps and five others on horses. The men on the horses were trying to calm the residents of the street inquiring about the safety of Senator Sumner and his daughter.

"Harrison, what should I do?" asked the Senator. "There is another one of your officers out there with five cavalrymen."

"Let me see what is going on. I left my brigade without permission from Major Fincannon."

As Harrison went to open the door, Captain Lockert pushed the unlocked door open and the two captains came face to face.

"Elington! We found you."

"What's going on here, Lockert?

"Major Fincannon told me to come and get you before you got yourself killed."

"Why do you have five riders with you?"

"Well, Harrison, we are taking another person with us. I have been ordered to take your father-in-law hostage to ensure our safe exit from the city."

"What?"

"You know the casualties we have taken; Danny being among them."

"Be quiet, Lockert! They don't know."

"What did you say about Danny, captain?" Abby asked Lockert.

"He was killed at the arsenal, ma'am."

"Lockert! You stupid idiot. I didn't even get a chance to tell them he had been killed."

"I am awful sorry. Please accept my sympathies, ma'am. I am truly sorry, Elington."

Abigail couldn't believe what she had heard. She slumped down on the couch and fainted from the shock. Her light brown hair gently brushed the back of the couch as she dropped down into the pillows. Harrison went over to see if she was all right.

"Let her rest," Senator Sumner said, "she will be all right. Abigail has fainted before and there has never been any permanent damage to her, but I don't know how she will get over this."

"I am sorry, Robert, for all of this pain. I am sorry for disgracing you as a senator."

"You have nothing to be sorry for, Elington," Lockert said. "You have fought with bravery, honor and courage for the cause of the South and states' rights, which I am sure this senator doesn't know anything about."

"Stay out of this! You are not part of our family and you have no right to give your opinions on any matters relating to the senator. He has his convictions like all of us."

"Elington, we have to go. I am under orders to take the senator. Our brigade is under fire again on Market Street and we have to get past that bridge."

"We will not take the senator. No one else in my family is going to be a pawn in this Civil War chess match any longer. Do you hear me, captain?"

"I am under orders."

"Too bad for your orders this time."

"Gentlemen!" Sumner said. "I will go. There will not be any fighting in this household today over this issue. Harrison, I will come of my own free will so casualties on both sides can possibly be spared."

"But, Robert, you will assist in a Confederate unit escaping in time of war? Won't you be censured for such actions, possibly brought up on charges of treason?"

"Not if I am considered a hostage. Now let's go!"

"What about Abigail?" Harrison asked.

"She will be taken care of by Judge Jacob Bixley. You remember him, don't you?"

"Yes, I do."

"Also, you need to know something right now, son," Sumner said. "Jacob Bixley informed me today that Jesse is alive. I was finally able to find out what happened to your son."

"He's alive? Thank God in heaven."

"Yes. He is working for Union intelligence. I was not to tell Abigail, but she knows. How could I have kept such joyous information from her? We'll talk more about it later."

*****

The senator and the Confederate soldiers made their way back to Market Street. Major Fincannon saw the group of riders approach the area near the factory where the defensive position had been formed. As soon as he saw the senator riding on the back of a private soldier's horse, he announced to the crowd and to the shooters in the factory that a Pennsylvanian senator had been taken hostage. He informed the crowds of the senator's name and told the people to pass the word onto the military officials who were ordering the attacks on the Confederate brigade. Fincannon said the senator would not be harmed if the brigade was able to exit the city peaceably.

Fincannon also noticed a woman riding on the back of Harrison's reddish brown mount. It was Abigail, awake now, and ready to ride home with her husband. Fincannon was not angry. This time he understood the radical circumstances of the war. He knew the situation of Harrison, his wife and his relationship to a United States senator. He saw no cause to question or to harass Captain Elington on the issue.

"How are you, Senator Sumner?" Fincannon asked.

"I am devastated by the attack on our city and the destruction of the arsenal. I am sickened by the loss of life here today."

"This mission was deemed necessary by General Lee and General Hill of our army."

"You know, major, the arsenal will be repaired before you even make it back to Virginia. There is talk that some Union spies got the percussion cap machine onto a barge and sent it to the navy yard across the city."

"I can't think on those speculations. I was assigned to a mission and I executed it to the best of my ability as an officer in the Confederate army. I cannot control what happens after an attack like this one, senator."

"Whatever happens to me doesn't matter," Sumner said. "In the end we will win the war. Our industry will win it. The very thing your mission tried to destroy will overcome your Confederate army."

"Enough," Fincannon answered.

"Gettysburg, major. What about that victory? Our own General George Meade beat up bad on your General Robert E. Lee. I think the victory there and at Vicksburg has set the tone for the remaining part of the war."

"Vicksburg? Vicksburg, Mississippi, has fallen to Grant?

"Yes. It happened today. It was wired to my office a few hours ago. Your country has been split in two, major."

"I said enough! I don't want to hear anymore."

"Brigade! Move out!" ordered Captain Lockert.

The Market Street bridge was cleared. The Titan Brigade crossed the Schuylkill again. The battered gray columns of soldiers, their major dejected over the news of Vicksburg, galloped from the sight of the mission. Abigail and Senator Sumner rode on their own horse, a dappled beige mare, confiscated from the markets of Philadelphia.

Captain Harrison Elington didn't tell Abigail or Senator Sumner the body on the caisson was Danny's. He would wait for later, when the time and place was right for burial of his son.

Fincannon had ordered the other two remaining artillery pieces to be left in Philadelphia before the brigade had crossed the bridge over the Schuylkill. He didn't think there was use for the guns now. The immediate order of business was to get the brigade to a safe spot, to rest and then to rejoin General Lee's corps somewhere in Maryland. It seemed, for now, the fighting was left behind. The remaining 800 soldiers of the Titan Brigade, Fincannon thought, had to have some sense of pride and honor in the execution of their mission to the Frankford Arsenal. The only Southern troops to ever make it into a major Northern industrial city were under his command. In the midst of all of the loss and darkness there remained a ray of hope and light this 4th of July, 1863. For the repercussions of the attack on the arsenal would have to be fully evaluated by additional scouts, spies and intelligence information.

The brigade connected onto the Philadelphia-Lancaster Turnpike and proceeded to ride back to the Ardmore area to rest. The horses were watered and rested. Again, the Confederates bivouacked about seven miles outside of the city.

Abigail rested that night with her husband by her side and her father still being used as a hostage by Major Fincannon. The men didn't all get food rations. The villagers in Ardmore didn't respond to the requests of supplying food for the remaining brigade troopers. Some foraging went on, but many of the Confederates were too tired to hunt for food. They wanted sleep and silence from battle.

– Chapter 25 –
Lightning and Death from the West

July 5, 1863

The brigade made it to the outskirts of Lancaster County on the evening of July 5. The men experienced tranquil conditions there a few days before. The remaining 800 or so soldiers rode slowly. The consequences of hardened battles had put too much of a strain on man and beast alike. It was going to be an uneasy journey back to General Lee and the remnants of the Army of Northern Virginia.

Major Fincannon, his blue eyes dim from the weariness of battle and of decision making, noticed a flash of light in the darkening western skies. He thought a good rain shower would cool everyone off in the brigade and bring relief. He thought of his remaining soldiers and their skills in military prowess and their common commitment to the Confederate States of America.

"Lightning from the west," Fincannon whispered as he continued his ride toward Lancaster. "A sure sign from God we shall be safe now. His infinite providence directs our fate. I long to go home and see my family once again."

In an instant, without warning or any hint of danger, the barrels of thirty-five Union cannon opened fire across the turnpike. An arc of guns rammed an ungodly and volcanic eruption upon the Titan Brigade, a brigade no longer the target of inexperienced militia, but now the target of experienced artillerists. Hot iron and flaming lead balls from canister rounds, flashes of fire and a massed wind of death drilled the living souls left in Fincannon's mounted infantry. Five more times, salvoes of man-made lightning and thunder crashed and mangled the Confederate columns along the pike before silence spread through the area.

Seething multitudes of metal demons did their duty in the darkening skies. Federal cannon were dispatched along the Philadelphia-Lancaster Turnpike in order to intercept the Southern brigade leaving Philadelphia. General George Gordon Meade, of Philadelphia, would not tolerate a Confederate attack on his native city without the invaders paying a mighty price for their deeds of destruction. Meade ordered the artillery from Gettysburg; General Henry Hunt's guns from Cemetery Hill. Those same men and guns had completed much havoc on Pickett's led charge of July 3.

Major Frederick Albert Fincannon was dead, shot to pieces by the artillery. Captain Nathan Lockert, the boyish, tea-drinking officer, also lay dead under his twisted and mangled horse. Fincannon and Lockert were unrecognizable. The metal barrages and salvoes fired at the two men simply tore them to pieces. 785 other members of the brigade were killed in the assault, along with Fincannon and Lockert. Fifteen men, including Harrison Elington, escaped the cannon fire. Abigail was still with her husband. Senator Robert Sumner was let go back in the village of Ardmore.

Somehow, Elington diverted his horse away from the fire. After he saw the first flashes of light from the west and heard the deep, subtle rumbles of fired shell, his instincts told him the flashes weren't strikes of lightning and the rumble wasn't thunder. Riding in the rear of the brigade as it neared Lancaster County, he had managed to race his horse, with Abigail against his back, down a sunken lane off of the turnpike. Fifteen of the mounted infantry followed the captain in fear of the artillery fire blasting away at the front of the brigade.

Did General Meade ever get the word that the Titan Brigade was carrying a hostage with them? Harrison thought galloping on his horse. *One of their own United States senators had been placed in a dangerous situation and it seemed the Union command didn't care.*

*****

Elington, his wife and the remaining fifteen mounted infantry troopers rode the rest of the night. Into the morning of July 6, they made their way south into Maryland and to safe conditions. Prodding, hiding out and foraging for food, the small remnant of the Titan Brigade hurried its way to rendezvous with Lee's army.

On July 13, Captain Harrison Elington reported back to his chief commanding officer, General Robert E. Lee, and briefed him on the attack upon the Frankford Arsenal and the aftermath of the invasion of Philadelphia. General Lee directed his army to Williamsport, Maryland, from Chambersburg, Pennsylvania. His wounded army crossed the swollen Potomac River and made it safely back to Virginia.

In time, the Confederacy found that all of their efforts in the North in June and July 1863 had minimal effects on the Union army, for the industrial power of the North was too overwhelming for the weakening Confederate armies in the eastern and western theatres of operation.

– Chapter 26 –
God's Grace and Mercy

Christmas 1863,
Caldwell County, North Carolina

The snow cascaded in white sheets upon the mountains. The house on Sunset Street showed signs of life under its roof once again. A small gathering of friends and families, crushed and scarred by three years of civil war, sat in the living room of the Elington residence. The smell of freshly cooked ham and turkey resonated through the home. Conversation filled the house that up to a few months ago was deserted, with only the ghosts of a family teetering in its rooms.

Mr. and Mrs. Abshire reminisced about the happy times when Alfred was a student and when he was safe and secure at home. Krista Morris of Maine, Alfred's fiancée, sent the Abshires a letter of remorse. She was devastated by the death of Alfred on the fields of Gettysburg. The mothers of Jackson Coffey and Thaddeus Curtis sipped tea and paid homage to their sons who gave their lives for a cause of independence. The Coffeys and the Curtises lost other sons beside Jackson and Thaddeus. Their families truly became a consecration for the Confederacy. The wife of Lewis Fry sat with her three children, silent and without hope for her future. Her husband embodied the light of life and the strength of her heart. The Elingtons spoke of Danny and remembered how he always got in trouble through his adventurous boyhood pranks. They also remembered his unhesitating service to the Confederate States of America in almost every major battle of the war.

Peyton Caldwell wasn't home this Christmas either. He was killed in the lightning fusillade of fire east of Lancaster County when his brigade tried to make it home. His body was sent back to Caldwell County to be buried on the grounds of his ancestors.

Attention shifted focus to the center of the living room, where a young man in a blue Union officer's uniform sat. He smiled at Abigail and at Harrison. He conversed with the parents of the lost Confederate soldiers. He drank apple cider and ate home-baked cookies from the warm kitchen. He talked of his wounds and spending cold nights upon the fields of battle. He spoke of the charity and sympathy of the Confederate soldiers who had helped Union wounded. He tried his best to console the families he had grown up with even though they knew his allegiance and that he fought for the Union. He felt personal and real loss over the deaths of many of his friends. He thanked God for his life this Christmas, for he knew it was a miracle from God he was alive. His wounds were described as fatal, but the providence of God intervened into his mind and body.

Major Jesse Elington turned and hugged his mother. He was the only son left among many mourning Confederate parents. A Union son.

Brother against brother, father against son and friend against friend, the war between the states truly cast a ghastly disease over the United States. Fratricide consumed generations of citizens, from President Lincoln himself to General Robert E. Lee, and unto every enlisted man in the Confederate and Union armies.

Captain Harrison Elington achieved survival in the war thus far. His wish for returning home was temporarily granted, but at a horrible price in human loss. The war raged on in Virginia, Tennessee and in many other parts of the Confederacy. Elington was sure of what his future held now. He retired from the army and would spend his remaining days with his wife, even though the remnants of the 26th North Carolina Infantry beckoned to him to return one more time. Jesse returned to his intelligence operations for the Union effort and in the service of the president of the United States.

The time came for peace. Without peace, the great experiment of Democracy and of the United States of America itself would expire and its posterity might be, again, subject to the bygone days of blind, autocratic rule.

The End

Printed in the United States
92306LV00006B/189/A